LITERATURE FROM CRESCENT MOON PUBLISHING

I0656279

German Romantic Poetry: Goethe, Novalis, Heine, Hölderlin
by Carol Appleby

Stepping Forward: Essays, Lectures and Interviews
by Wolfgang Iser

Friedrich Hölderlin: *Selected Poems*
translated by Michael Hamburger

Rainer Maria Rilke: *Selected Poems*
translated by Michael Hamburger

Hymns To the Night and Spiritual Songs
by Novalis

Beauties, Beasts and Enchantment: Classic French Fairy Tales
edited and translated by Jack Zipes

Rilke: Space, Essence and Angels in the Poetry of Rainer Maria Rilke
by B.D. Barnacle

The Ghost Dance: Origins of Religion
by Weston La Barre

Julia Kristeva: Art, Love, Melancholy, Philosophy, Semiotics
by Kelly Ives

Luce Irigaray: Lips, Kissing, and the Politics of Sexual Difference
by Kelly Ives

Hélène Cixous I Love You: The Jouissance of Writing
by Kelly Ives

Thomas Hardy's Jude the Obscure: A Critical Study
by Margaret Elvy

Thomas Hardy's Tess of the d'Urbervilles: A Critical Study
by Margaret Elvy

Samuel Beckett Goes Into the Silence
by Jeremy Mark Robinson

In the Dim Void: Samuel Beckett's Late Trilogy:
Company, Ill Seen, Ill Said and Worstward Ho
by Gregory Johns

Thomas Hardy: The Tragic Novels
by Tom Spenser

Thomas Hardy and John Cowper Powys: Wessex Revisited
by Jeremy Mark Robinson

Sexing Hardy: Thomas Hardy and Feminism
by Margaret Elvy

Lawrence Durrell: Between Love and Death, Between East and West
by Jeremy Mark Robinson

Andrea Dworkin
by Jeremy Mark Robinson

Shakespeare: Love, Poetry and Magic in Shakespeare's Sonnets and Plays
by B.D. Barnacle

Cavafy: Anatomy of a Soul
by Matt Crispin

D.H. Lawrence: Infinite Sensual Violence
by M.K. Pace

D.H. Lawrence: Symbolic Landscapes
by Jane Foster

'Cosmo Woman': The World of Women's Magazines
by Oliver Whitehorne

The Ecstasies of John Cowper Powys
by A.P. Seabright

Postmodern Powys: New Essays on John Cowper Powys
by Joe Boulter

Rimbaud: Arthur Rimbaud and the Magic of Poetry
by Jeremy Mark Robinson

J.R.R. Tolkien
by Jeremy Mark Robinson

Emily Dickinson: *Selected Poems*
selected and introduced by Miriam Chalk

Petrarch, Dante and the Troubadours: The Religion of Love and Poetry
by Cassidy Hughes

Dante: *Selections From the Vita Nuova*
translated by Thomas Okey

Walking In Cornwall
by Ursula Le Guin

Brothers Grimm

German Popular Stories

German Popular Stories

Brothers Grimm

ADAPTED *by* EDGAR TAYLOR

EDITED *by* JACK ZIPES

CRESCENT MOON

CRESCENT MOON PUBLISHING
P.O. Box 1312, Maidstone
Kent, ME14 5XU
Great Britain, wwwcrmoon.com

This edition 2013. Introduction © Jack Zipes 2012, 2013.

Printed and bound in the U.S.A.
Set in Book Antiqua 10 on 12pt.

The right of Jack Zipes to be identified as the editor of this book has been asserted generally in accordance with sections 77 and 78 of the Copyright, Designs and Patents Act 1988.

British Library Cataloguing in Publication data available for this title.

ISBN-13 9781861714572 (Pbk)
ISBN-13 9781861713513 (Hbk)

Contents

---

1 The English titles are the ones selected by Taylor and do not always correspond to the German titles, which I have listed below Taylor's titles followed by literal English translations in parentheses. JZ.

APPENDICES

A Note On the Text

The present edition of *German Popular Stories* is based on the 1868 book, authorized by Edgar Taylor's widow and published by John Camden Hotten in London. This volume is particularly significant because it was the first time that Taylor was acknowledged as the translator on the title page, and it does not cite the Brothers Grimm. It does highlight George Cruikshank as illustrator and John Ruskin as the writer of the introduction and included part of a letter by Sir Walter Scott. Most important, the 1868 book contained reprints of the first two editions of 1823 and 1826 in one volume along with the original notes.

We have reorganized the book by placing Ruskin's introduction as an appendix at the end of the book and have also published Scott's full letter as an appendix. In addition, we have added Taylor's correspondence with the Brothers Grimm; the beginning of *Gammer Grethel* (1838), another one of Taylor's adaptations of the Grimms' tales; and R. Meek's introduction to *Grimm's Goblins* (1876). By including all these documents, we hope that readers will have a full picture of Taylor's significance and how he changed the destiny of the Grimms' tales in English-speaking worlds.

The spelling, in the stories and in the notes, follows that of the original edition.

I should very much like to express my gratitude to Jeremy Robinson and his entire editorial staff for taking such great care in preparing this book for publication. It is thanks to their assistance that Edgar Taylor's unusual book has come to life again.

J.Z.

The Brothers Grimm, by Elisabeth Jerichau-Baumann, 1855,
Staatliche Museen zu Berlin

George Cruikshank, *Self-Portrait*,
from *Omnibus*, 1842 (above).

Edgar Taylor, by Charles Turner,
after Eden Upton Eddis, 1841 (right).

German Popular Stories
as Revolutionary Book

JACK ZIPES

We have recently been translated into English, that is, part of the
children's tales. Everything neatly printed, and it seems to me, very
readable (except the selection is not remarkable). Yes, except for the
rhymes, more readable and smoother at times than the German text.
The succinct nice English in itself suits the storytelling children's tone
much more than the somewhat stiff high German. We had not taken
necessary care of the style for reasons that I would now abandon or
modify.

Jacob Grimm, letter to Karl Lachmann, May 12, 1823[1]

With all its faults, Taylor's translation has achieved a sort of classic
status of its own. If modern readers were aware that it is a period
piece, that would not much matter, but most do not realize how
skewed a picture of the Grimms' collection they get through reading
Taylor. Not that Taylor attempted to camouflage what he was doing
in adapting, combining and expurgating his originals – on the
contrary, he signalled his changes very frankly in the notes he
appended to the tales. But what he presents is not what a modern
reader would be entitled to expect.

David Blamires, "The Early Reception of the Grimms' *Kinder- und
Hausmärchen* in England"[2]

Cruikshank's etchings here have long been recognized as one of his
greatest achievements; what is less frequently noticed is the aptness of
their setting. The coherence of Taylor's text, the typography, the mis-
en-page all combine with the illustrations to make *German Popular
Stories* one of the most attractive books of its time, and one entirely
suited to its humble but revolutionary contents.

Brian Alderson, "The Spoken and the Read: *German Popular Stories*
and English Popular Diction"

It may seem strange if not startling to refer to Edgar Taylor's (1793-1839) translation of the Grimms' *Kinder- und Hausmärchen* (literally, *Children's and Household Tales*) as a revolutionary book, but his *German Popular Stories*, including the two volumes of 1823 and 1826 and George Cruikshank's (1792-1878) unusual and delightful illustrations, radically changed the destiny of what we today call the fairy tales of the Brothers Grimm.

First of all, Taylor did not translate the tales. Rather, he *adapted* them, initially with the help of his friend David Jardine in 1823, and later, alone in 1826 and in 1839. He re-wrote and re-conceived them in such a careful and innovative way that they were transformed into amusing stories which emphasized the importance of freeing the imagination of children while catering at the same time to the puritanical tastes and expectations of young middle-class readers and their families. Not only did Taylor sanitize a small amount of tales selected from the Grimms' collection of 1819, deleting anything that smacked of obscenity, irreverence, and violence, but he also rearranged the plots, combined stories, and changed the tone of the language, often making the tales illogical and unrecognizable from their original German stories. In short, he appropriated the tales, turning them upside down, and this anglicized transformation laid the basis for a misunderstanding of the German tales in Great Britain and America for the next sixty odd years or more until Margaret Hunt's more faithful rendition of the stories appeared in 1884. And even later, Taylor's adaptations continued to be disseminated throughout the twentieth century and mistaken as "genuine" translations of the Grimms' tales.[3]

Second, as pioneer, that is, the first English translator of the Grimms' tales, Taylor benefited from the numerous illustrations that spruced up his book. Charles Baldwyn, his publisher, recruited George Cruikshank to provide etchings, and Taylor welcomed this decision. As a consequence, the tales were enriched by images long before the Grimms thought of doing something like this. Indeed, Baldwyn and Taylor were fortunate to have hired the gifted and well-known caricaturist. His comic illustrations were in keeping with Taylor's adaptations which he depicted with levity and made Taylor's texts appear even more humorous than they actually were. (Cruikshank could not read German and based his illustrations on Taylor's adaptations.) In this regard, the diverse and serious implications of the German texts were discarded in favor of droll satire to foster amusement. The tales were visually homogenized to emphasize quaintness and community.4 Cruikshank's illustrations provoke laughter, not reflection and moral education, two goals that the Grimms had sought to achieve, something that the sentimental illustrations of their brother Ludwig were to show later in the German editions.

Finally, *German Popular Stories* is revolutionary and extra-ordinary because the book prompted the Brothers Grimm to revise their publishing strategy and seek a broader readership for their collected stories in Germany. Initially, when they published their first edition in two volumes with scholarly notes in 1812 and 1815, they did not have children in mind as their primary audience. It is also the case with their second edition of 1819, two volumes containing 170 tales (along with a third volume filled with comprehensive notes, published separately in 1822). It is true that, in the second edition, the Grimms modified many of the tales to please potential young readers or auditors and their parents. New tales were added; some that were overly violent were eliminated. However, the Grimms were still more inclined to favor the philological and historical qualities of the tales, and it was this scholarly 1819 edition on which Taylor, along with Jardine, based his so-called translation of 31 tales in 1823, and 24 in 1826. Ironically, thanks to the success of Taylor's work *more directed at children* in England, the Grimms decided in 1825 to create a smaller edition of 50 tales taken from their large collection of 1819, and they intended this Small Edition to appeal more to family audiences. Referred to as the *Kleine Ausgabe*, it was issued periodically along with the large edition (*Grosse Ausgabe*) until 1858.5 So, it was under Taylor's influence that Wilhelm, who was fully in charge of both the small and large editions after 1819, began editing the German tales for the benefit of children, keenly aware that parents of solid bourgeois families might object to scatological topics, irreverent language, and provocative infer-ences. The Grimms did not believe this kind of editing com-promised their goal of recovering "pure" folk tales. Therefore, Wilhelm shaped the tales in all editions according to an idealistic concept of the Protestant ethic and folk poetry. He reinforced what the Grimms considered to be the natural virtues of the stories that were to serve as exemplary lessons without didactic morals. Together, the Brothers, who had already begun to "revolutionize" the study of ancient and medieval literature and to lay the groundwork for the study of folklore in Europe and North America, were stimulated by Taylor to make changes that resulted in the transformation of their collection into one of the great classics of *children's literature* worldwide.[6]

To understand the revolutionary and extraordinary qualities of Edgar Taylor's *German Popular Tales*, its broad international and intercultural impact, and the ironies and coincidences of history that contributed to the success of his book as well as the reputation of the Grimms' original collection in German, I want to recount and analyze the Grimms' intentions in collecting and publishing the two volumes of the first edition of their tales in 1812 and 1815 as well as the second edition of 1819. Then I want to review the history of how Taylor came upon their tales in the early 1820s and why he decided to "translate" them into English. Finally, I want to conclude this introduction by discussing how Taylor partici- pated in the Romantic antiquarian movement, what we would today call folklore, to recapture neglected relics of the past and to defend the imagination against rationalism. Taylor belonged to a group of British writers and intellectuals, who confronted a general trend among English educators, religious groups, writers, and publishers who questioned fairy tales and popular literature as appropriate literature for children. In some respects, it was through Taylor that the Grimms made the fairy tale more respectable and paved the way for Hans Christian Andersen's fairy tales and the remarkable rise of experimental literary fairy and folk tales in Victorian England.

The Daring Quest of the Brothers Grimm

Interestingly, Jacob (1785-1863) and Wilhelm Grimm (1786-1859) did not demonstrate a particular interest in folk tales during their youth in the small town of Hanau. Both of them were precocious students, and when they were sent to study at the Lyzeum in Kassel after their father had died in 1897, they made every effort to succeed in a classical curriculum at school, to prepare them- selves to study law at the University of Marburg, and to find employment as civil servants to help support their family.

Folklore was not on their minds. Their father, Philip Wilhelm Grimm, a prominent district magistrate in Hanau, had died suddenly and had left the large family in pecuniary circumstances. Jacob and Wilhelm had three younger brothers and a sister, and their mother had to depend on financial support from her father and relatives to keep the family together. Socially disadvantaged, the Grimms sought to compensate by achieving recognition in their studies at school and at the university. They wanted to follow diligently in their father's footsteps. However, neither became a lawyer or magistrate.

While studying at the University of Marburg from 1802 to 1806, the Grimms were inspired and mentored by Friedrich Carl von Savigny, a young professor of jurisprudence, who opened their eyes to the historical and philosophical aspects of law as well as literature. It was Savigny's historical approach to jurisprudence, his belief in the organic connection of all cultural creations of the *Volk* (understood as an entire ethnic group) to the historical development of this *Volk*, that drew the attention of the Grimms. Furthermore, Savigny stressed that the present could only be fully grasped and appreciated by studying the past. He insisted that the legal system had to be studied through an inter-disciplinary method to explore and grasp the mediations between the customs, beliefs, values, and laws of a people. For Savigny – and also for the Grimms – culture was originally the common property of all members of a *Volk*. The Germanic culture had become divided over the years into different realms such as religion, law, literature, and so on, and its cohesion could only be restored through historical investigation. The Brothers felt that language rather than law was the ultimate bond that united the German people and were thus drawn to the study of old German literature – though they were in agreement with Savigny's methods and desire to create a stronger sense of community among the German people.

The Grimms, who had always been voracious readers and had digested popular courtly romances during their teenage years, turned more and more to a serious study of medieval and ancient literature during their university years. Since literature and philology were not recognized fields at German universities, however, they set their sight on becoming librarians and independent scholars of German literature. They began collecting old books, tracts, calendars, newspapers, and manuscripts, wrote about medieval literature, and even debated with formidable professors and researchers of old Germanic and Nordic texts. They had concluded a pact to remain and work together for the rest of their lives, and together they cultivated a passion for recovering the true essence of the German people. Yet, these were difficult times, and their plans were not easily realized.

By 1805 the entire family had moved to Kassel, and the Brothers were constantly plagued by money problems and concerns about their siblings. Their situation was further aggravated by the rampant Napoleonic Wars. Jacob interrupted his studies to serve the Hessian War Commission in 1806. Meanwhile, Wilhelm passed his law exams enabling him to become a civil servant and to find work as a librarian in the royal library with a meager salary. In 1807 Jacob lost his position with the War Commission, when the French occupied Kassel, but he was then hired as a librarian for the new King Jérome, Napoleon's brother, who now ruled Westphalia. Amidst all the upheavals, their mother died in 1808, and Jacob and Wilhelm became fully responsible for their brothers and sister. Despite the loss of their mother and difficult personal and financial circumstances from 1805 to 1812, the Brothers managed to prove themselves to be innovative scholars in the new field of German philology and literature – and it should be noted that Jacob and Wilhelm were still in their early twenties.

Thanks to Savigny, who remained a good friend and mentor for the rest of their lives, the Grimms made the acquaintance of Clemens Brentano, one of the most gifted German Romantic poets, in 1803, and three years later, Achim von Arnim, one of the foremost German Romantic novelists. These encounters had a profound impact on their lives, for Brentano and Arnim had already begun collecting old songs, tales, and manuscripts and shared the Grimms' interest in reviving ancient and medieval German literature. In the fall of 1805 Arnim and Brentano published the first volume of *Des Knaben Wunderhorn* (*The Boy's Wonder Horn*), a collection of old German folk songs, and they wanted to continue publishing more songs and folk tales in additional volumes. Since they were aware of the Grimms' remarkable talents as scholars of old German literature, they requested help from them in 1807, and the Brothers made a major contribution to the final two volumes of *The Boy's Wonder Horn*, published in 1808. At the same time, Brentano enlisted them to help collect folk tales, fables, and other stories for a new project. The Grimms responded by gathering tales from old books and recruiting friends and acquaintances in and around Kassel to tell them tales or to gather them from friends. In this initial phase, the Grimms were unable to devote all their energies to their research and did not have a clear idea about the significance of collecting folk tales. However, they were totally devoted to uncovering the "natural poetry" (*Naturpoesie*) of the German people, and all of their research was geared toward exploring the epics, sagas, and tales that contained what they thought were essential truths about the German cultural heritage. Underlying their work was a pronounced patriotic urge to excavate and preserve German cultural contributions made by the common people before they became extinct. In this respect their collecting "Germanic" tales was a gesture of protest against French occupation and a gesture of solidarity with those people who wanted to forge a unified German nation.

What fascinated or compelled the Grimms to concentrate on old German literature was a belief that the most natural and pure forms of culture – those which held the community together – were linguistic and were to be located in the past. Moreover, modern literature, even though it might be remarkably rich, was artificial and thus could not express the genuine essence of *Volk* culture that emanated naturally from people's experiences and bound the people together. In their letters between 1807 and 1812 and in such early essays as Jacob's "Von Übereinstimmung der alten Sagen" ("About the Correspondences between the Old Legends," 1807) and "Gedanken wie sich die Sagen zur Poesie und Geschichte verhalten" ("Thoughts about the Relationship between the Legends and Poetry," 1808) and Wilhelm's "Über die Entstehung der deutschen Poesie und ihr Verhältnis zu der nordeutschen" ("About the Origins of German Poetry and its Relationship to Nordic Poetry,"1809), they began to formulate similar views about the origins of literature based on tales and legends or what was once oral art. The purpose of their collecting folk songs, tales, proverbs, legends, and documents was to write a history of old German *Poesie* and to demonstrate how *Kunstpoesie* (cultivated literature) evolved out of traditional folk material and how *Kunstpoesie* had gradually forced *Naturpoesie* (natural literature such as tales, legends, etc.) to recede during the Renaissance and take refuge among the folk in an oral tradition.

Very early in their careers, the Brothers saw their task as literary historians whose task was to preserve the pure sources of modern German literature and to reveal the debt or connection of literate culture to the oral tradition.

By 1809 the Grimms had amassed a large amount of tales, legends, and other documents, and they sent Brentano 54 texts because he had told them that he would probably adapt them freely, and therefore they could make use of the tales as they wished. Before they sent him these tales, they copied them. Brentano never did make use of them and left them fortunately in a monastery in the Ölenberg Monastery in Alsace. I say fortunately because the Grimms destroyed the texts after using them in their first edition of *Children's and Household Tales* in 1812. The handwritten texts that the Grimms had sent to Brentano, now referred to as the Ölenberg manuscript, were only discovered in 1925 and have provided researchers with important information about the Grimms' editing process.[7] All the 54 tales of the Ölenberg manuscript, most of them collected by Jacob, were transformed in their first edition of 1812 by the Brothers into carefully formed stories that corresponded to the Grimms' philological and poetical concept of a folk tale.

In 1812, Arnim, perhaps Brentano's closest friend at that time, visited the Grimms in Kassel, and he was aware that Brentano might not do anything with their texts. Moreover, he knew the Grimms had spent an enormous amount of time collecting all sorts of tales, legends, and animal stories, even more than they had sent to Brentano. So, he encouraged the Grimms to publish their own collection, which would represent their ideal of "natural poetry," and he provided them with the contact to the publisher Georg Andreas Reimer in Berlin. Thanks to Arnim's advice and intervention, the Brothers spent the rest of the year organizing and preparing 86 tales for publication that formed volume one of the first edition of 1812.

In one of the most recent significant studies of the Grimms' poetics, Jens Sennewald stresses that the Grimms intended from the very beginning to recover folk tales so that they could breathe new life into the German cultural heritage. According to Sennewald the frame of the *Children's and Household Tales* is the complete body of their philological and poetlogical works, including frontispieces, prefaces, tales, illustrations, and notes from 1810 until the last large edition of 1857. The frame/ body provides the space in which they felt they could "heal" people's lives and salvage the essence of the tales. It is through the frame that the Grimms wanted to provide "authentic transmission" of original stories.[8] For Sennewald, it is a given that the Grimms believed folk tales stemmed from a profound, if not divine tradition of storytelling. The goal and purpose of the Grimms' collecting was to discover "true" and original tales that emanated from the common folk and did not lie. They did not make a distinction between wonder tales, animal stories, legends, and other simple genres. Sennewald demonstrates that the Grimms dealt with their collected and selected tales according to two premises: 1) the collected fragments of the relics (stories) had to be part of a meaningful whole; 2) the entire collection of written words had to be grouped around an internal middle, which was *not* script. This internal essence, which is not present in script, was to provide the words with a voice.[9] Sennewald maintains that that the motivation of the Grimms' philology consisted in showing that the internal voice can be heard in each individual "relic" and that the relics were dynamic. To do this they continued to edit and enlarge one collection of tales after another because it is only through the collection that the relics received their voice. It is because the wholeness of an original language had been lost that the collecting of relics becomes necessary, for such collecting, according to the Grimms, is what first makes the origins of language thinkable.

Although the Grimms had not entirely formalized their concept while they worked on the publication of the first edition, the principles outlined by Sennewald could already be seen in their previous works. Unfortunately, the first volume of *Children's and Household Tales* of 1812 was not well-received by friends and critics, who thought that the stories were too crude, were not shaped enough to appeal to children, and were weighed down by the scholarly notes. Nevertheless, the Brothers were not deterred from following their original philological and poetical concept. Even though there were some differences between Jacob and Wilhelm, who later was to favor more drastic poetical editing of the collected tales, they basically held to their original principles to salvage relics from the past. Just how important these principles were can be seen in their correspondence with Arnim between 1812 and 1815, when the second volume of the first edition appeared. In a very long letter of October 29, 1810, Jacob wrote to

Arnim:

> Contrary to your viewpoint, I am completely convinced that all the
> tales in our collection without exception had already been told with
> all their particulars centuries ago. Many beautiful things were only
> gradually left out. In this sense all the tales have long since been fixed,
> while they continue to move around in endless variations. That is,
> they do not fix themselves. Such variations are similar to the mani-
> fold dialects that should not suffer any violation either.[10]

And in another letter, written on January 28, 1813, Jacob
wrote in support of Wilhelm's views:

> The difference between children's and household tales and the crit-
> ique of this combination in our title is more hairsplitting than true.
> Otherwise one would literally have to bring the children out of the
> house where they have belonged forever and confine them in a room.
> Have children's tales really been conceived and invented for child-
> ren? I don't believe this at all just as I don't affirm the general quest-
> ion. What we possess in publicized and traditional teachings and
> precepts is accepted by old and young, and what they do not grasp
> about them, all that glides away from their minds until they are
> ready to learn it. This is the case with all true teachings that ignite
> and illuminate everything that was already present and known, not
> teaching that brings both wood and fire with it.[11]

In the same letter Jacob also wrote:

> My old saying, which I have already defended earlier, is still valid:
> one should write according to one's ability and desires and not
> adapt to outside forces and comply with them. Therefore, I don't
> consider the book of tales (*Märchenbuch*) as being written for child-
> ren, but it does suit them very well, and I am very happy about that.
> However, I would not have worked on it with pleasure if I hadn't
> believed in its importance for the most serious and adult people as
> well as for poesy, mythology, and history. These tales only live for
> children and adults 1) because children are receptive to the epic; thus,
> we are thankful for their minds that have retained these records. 2)
> Because the badly educated people disdain them.[12]

Though the Grimms made it clear in the second volume of the
first edition of *Children's and Household Tales*, published in 1815,
that they would follow the agenda of their first volume, they also
explained the important difference they made between a book for
children and educational manual (*Erziehungsbuch*) in their preface:

> In creating our collection we wanted to do more than just perform a
> service for the history of poesy. It was our intention at the same time

to enable poesy itself, which is alive in the collection, to have an effect: it was to give pleasure to anyone who could take pleasure in it, and therefore, our collection was also to become an intrinsic educational manual. There have been some complaints about this latter intention because there are things here and there [in our collection] that cause embarrassment and complaints that the collection is unsuitable for children or indecent (such as the references to certain incidents and conditions, also children should not hear about the devil and anything evil). Accordingly, parents should not offer the collection to children. In individual cases this concern may be correct, and thus one can easily choose which tales are to be read. On the whole it is certainly not necessary. Nothing can better defend us than nature itself, which has let certain flowers and leaves grow in a particular color and shape. Whoever does not find them wholesome, suitable for their special needs, which nobody knows, can easily walk right by them. But he cannot demand that they should be colored and cut in another way… Everything that is natural can become beneficial, and we should try to strive to grasp this. Incidentally we know of no other healthy and powerful book that has edified the folk other than the Bible, which we place above all, and here, too, people would have some misgivings. The right usage, however, will not draw out evil things, rather, as some beautiful words say: [they draw out] testimonies from our heart. Children point to the stars without fear, while, according to the folk belief, others insult angels.[13]

Though mindful of the educational value of their collection, the Grimms shied away from making their tales moralistic. They viewed the morality in the tales as organic, and readers, young and old, could intuit lessons from them spontaneously because of their essential poetry. The readers' interpretations are natural because of the profound if not divine nature of the tales, and in this sense, the Grimms envisioned themselves as cultivators and their collection as an educational manual that would grow on readers who would grow by reading these living relics of the past.

After the publication of the second volume in 1815, however, the Grimms were once again disappointed by the critical reception. They were convinced that reviewers and readers were misunderstanding them. Although they did not abandon their basic notions about the origins and significance of folk tales in the second edition of 1819, there are definitely significant indications that they had been influenced by their critics to make the tales more accessible to a general public and more considerate of children as readers and listeners of the stories. There had been 156 tales published in the first edition, and the number now grew to 170 without the extensive scholarly notes. As I have mentioned above, they appeared later in a separate volume in 1822. Wilhelm did most of the editing and often made changes to avoid indecent scenes such as Rapunzel's pregnancy, eliminated tales that might be offensive, and stylized them to evoke their folk poetry and original virtues. Yet, despite these changes, it was clear that the Grimms continued to place great emphasis on the philological significance of the collection that was to make a major contribution to understanding the origins and evolution of language and storytelling. The layout and contents of the two volumes of 1819 make it abundantly clear that the Grimms were still dedicating the tales to the perusal of adults. The preface in the first volume is long and academic and is followed by another long introduction "About the Essence of Tales" ("Über das Wesen der Märchen"); the second volume begins with Ludwig Grimm's portrait of Dorothea Viehmann, as the exemplary genuine peasant story-teller, and is followed by a very scholarly essay "The Essence of Children and their Customs" ("Kinderwesen und Kindersitten"). The 1822 third volume of notes, which completes the second edition, is only for scholars. In short, although many changes were made in the second edition, including the addition of relig-ious legends, and although the Grimms now wanted to include children more directly as part of their audience, they remained philologically true to their principles. Their book, *Children's and Household Stories* was not a book for children. Not yet.

It was only after the Grimms received a letter and a copy of *German Popular Stories* in 1823 from the young Englishman, Edgar Taylor, that they clearly began to alter the tendency of future editions of *Children's and Household Tales* by creating the Small Edition and taking greater pains to address a bourgeois reading public. [See Appendix C] In this respect, Taylor's sudden appear-ance in their lives – his letter and book came out of the blue – represented a momentous occasion that caused the Grimms to rethink their "marketing" strategy and how they might better guarantee the reception of the tales.

Just who was this Edgar Taylor, and how did he come to translate the *Children's and Household Tales*? More precisely, why did a young successful lawyer – ironically, a man who joined the very profession that the Grimms had abandoned during their studies – take an interest in German literature and take the time to translate German folk tales primarily for English children?

Taylor was born 1793 into a wealthy, prominent family in Norfolk.₁₄ There were ministers, merchants, and industrialists among his forefathers. His own father was a landlord interested in new modes of agriculture; his mother died when Taylor was two. As a young boy he was sent to Palgrave in Suffolk to attend a private boarding school, where he studied the classics and also learned Italian, Spanish, German, and French. By 1809, when he was only sixteen, he left school to enter an apprenticeship as law clerk in his uncle Meadow Taylor's firm in Diss, a small city close to Norwich, the county town of Norfolk. At that time Norwich was one of the leading cultural cities in England, and Taylor had numerous opportunities to mix with the intelligentsia of the region where there was a strong interest in German literature. Some of Taylor's acquaintances had translated important German authors and had personal ties to them. Given Taylor's knowledge of European languages and literature, the groundwork for his future scholarly work was laid in Norwich, which was experiencing a cultural boom. But first came law.

In 1814, after he finished his apprenticeship, he moved to London to practice law, and there he met Robert Roscoe, the son of a famous historian; together they founded their own law firm in 1817. Both young men had similar interests in literature and used their spare time to develop them. They also cultivated friendships among intellectuals and writers interested in English Romantic literature as well as German culture. One of Taylor's acquaintances was Sir Francis Cohen (1788-1861), also a lawyer and scholar, who had already been corresponding with the Grimms and wrote some complimentary remarks about *Children's and Household Tales* in the May 1819 issue of *The Quarterly Review*. It was Cohen who first referred to the Grimms' book as "German Popular Stories," which he considered the most important addition to nursery literature; he did not use the term fairy tales or tales for children. What is striking about this article by an early British folklorist is his great erudition and scholarly perspective on popular tales that was very similar to that of the Grimms. For instance, he argued:

> The man of letters should not disdain the chap book, or the nursery story. Humble as these efforts of the human intellect may appear, they shew its secret workings, its mode and progress, and human nature be studied in all its productions... Hence, we may yet trace no small proportion of mystic and romantic lore in the tales which gladden the cottage fireside, or, century after century, sooth the infant to its slumbers.15

More than likely, it was Cohen who first stirred Taylor's interest in the Grimms' tales.16 In addition, during 1819 and 1821, the time that Taylor may have made Cohen's acquaintance, he began publishing a series of articles titled "German Popular and Traditionary Literature," in the *New Monthly Magazine and Literary Journal*17 that cited Cohen and corresponded to Cohen's thinking about the importance of preserving folk culture. For example, Taylor, who also demonstrated a comprehensive knowledge of folklore and ancient literature, wrote:

> Our scholars busy themselves in tracing out the genealogy and mythological connexions of Tom Thumb and Jack the Giant Killer; and surely if the grave and learned embark in these speculations, we are justified in expecting to be able to welcome the æra when our children shall be allowed once more to regale themselves with that mild food which will enliven their imaginations, and tempt them on through the thorny paths of education; – when the gay dreams of fairy innocence shall again hover around them, and scientific compendiums, lisping botanies, and leading-string mechanics, shall be postponed to the Delights of Valentine and Orson, the beautiful Magalona, or Fair Rosamond.18

Clearly Cohen and Taylor were on the same page in their writings about the Grimms' tales. But it was not only Cohen who may have influenced Taylor to adapt *Children's and Household Tales*. It may have also been David Jardine, who led him to translate them. Jardine, a friend, had been a student of theology at the University of Göttingen. Taylor acknowledged that Jardine assisted him in translating the Grimms' tales in the 1823 volume of *German Popular Tales,* which contained 31 stories, but Jardine evidently had nothing to do with Taylor's second new 1826 volume of *German Popular Tales,* which contained 24 additional stories. Not all the tales in the second volume were selected from the Grimms' collection. Taylor, who had a vast knowledge of German literature, chose two from Johann Gustav Büsching's *Volks-Sagen, Märchen und Legenden* (1812), one from Otmar's *Volks-Sagen* (1800), and one called "Die Elfen" from Ludwig Tieck's *Phantasus* (1812-16). Altogether, Taylor's two volumes of *German Popular Stories* (1823/ 1826) contain 55 titles. With the exception of the four taken from other books mentioned above, Taylor actually created amalgamations of other stories and used 61 of the Grimms' tales taken from their 1819 edition, and one from the 1812 edition. Taylor's first volume contained two tales in Pomeranian and Hamburg dialect, "The Fisherman and his Wife," and "The Juniper Tree," and since Taylor had not spent any time in Germany to become familiar with dialects, he would have needed the assistance of someone like Jardine, who was more fluent in German, to have translated those tales. Aside from Jardine, Taylor had the help of George Cruikshank, who contributed a total of 22 illustrations to the editions of 1823 and 1826.

As Robert Patten points in his informative essay, "George Cruikshank's Grimm Humor," the motives of Baldwyn, Taylor, and Cruikshank in producing *German Popular Tales* in 1823 and 1826 were very different. Baldwyn was trying to avoid bankruptcy and needed a "bestseller" to stabilize the financial basis of his publishing house. Taylor sought to transform unusual folk tales from Germany and make them accessible to the scholarly interests of antiquarians and to provide amusement for middle-class families and their children. In doing this he emphasized the moral qualities of the tales without being didactic. Cruikshank had no great expectations in accepting the commission but used the occasion to demonstrate his great imaginative capacity to capture the playful and humorous aspects of the tales as they had been adapted by Taylor and Jardine. He wanted to breathe life and movement into the pictures to help tell the stories. Somehow his motives jelled with those of Baldwyn and Taylor, and as Patten comments,

> the resulting publication, *German Popular Stories* (Volume I, 1823; Volume II, 1826), was one of the most influential of the nineteenth century. It established precedents in the literature and visualization of fairy tales that profoundly affected Hans Christian Andersen, John Ruskin, and legions of artists from Richard Doyle to Walt Disney.[19]

The first volume was an immediate success and led to a

second printing that very same year and two other printings in 1824 and 1825 before the second volume appeared in 1826. Taylor was also gratified by a letter in 1823 from Sir Walter Scott, who wrote,

> I have to return my best thanks for the very acceptable present your goodness has made me in your interesting volume of German tales and traditions. I have often wished to see such a work undertaken by a gentleman of taste sufficient to adapt the simplicity of the German narrative to our own, which you have done so successfully. [See Appendix B][20]

And it was this success that evidently prompted Taylor to expand the first volume, just as the Grimms continued to do so with their edition. But it was not just success that motivated Taylor. He had always had a serious scholarly interest in medieval literature and the history of law, as his essays and correspondence with the Grimms reveal. While working on his second volume of *German Popular Stories*, he published *Lays of the Minnesingers* in 1825. Unfortunately, he was struck by an incurable disease in 1827, which was to plague him until his death in 1839. Though the illness hampered his legal work, Taylor continued to publish important scholarly books such as *The Book of Rights: or Constitutional Acts and Parliamentary Proceedings Affecting Civil and Religious Liberty in England from Magna Charter to the Present Time* (1833) and *Master Wace's Chronicle of the Norman Conquest, from the Roman de Rou* (1837).[21] In the year of his death he produced a revised edition of *German Popular Stories* under a new title, *Gammer Grethel or German Fairy Tales, and Popular Stories*, which included 42 revised Grimms' tales, Cruikshank's engravings converted into woodcuts by John Byfield, and Ludwig Emil Grimm's wood-engraved portrait of the so-called peasant storyteller, Dorothea Viehmann, at the beginning of the book. This was a gesture of thanks to the Grimms, who had extolled Viehmann as the ideal peasant storyteller, and she is pictured as a type of Mother Goose or Mother Bunch, who tells tales to sooth children and to impart the verities of life. [See Appendix D]

Curiously, from this point on, two different editions of Taylor's adaptations were published throughout the nineteenth century and competed with one another: *German Popular Stories*, which combined the 1823 and 1826 editions into one volume, and *Gammer Grethel*, which provided a totally different framework for a smaller selection of tales once again heavily revised by Taylor.

The numerous publications were due to the lack of copyright and the popularity of the tales. Publishers could easily obtain rights or publish pirated editions. Some of the titles were vastly changed. For instance, Taylor's translations were often labeled *German Popular Tales and Household Stories* or *Grimms' Fairy Tales*. One of the more exotic titles is: *Grimm's Goblins. Grimm's Household Stories, Translated from the Kinder und Haus Marchen by E. Taylor* in 1876. Robert Meek, the enthusiastic publisher of this latter edition, wrote an introduction that reflects the popular reception of the Grimms' tales as children's literature that was largely brought about by Taylor during the Victorian period:

> The Brothers Grimm, with an imagination as rich and fanciful as any writers of Fairy Tales, leave most kindred writers far behind in the especial adaptability of their tales to the tastes of children. In many, animals represent the leading characters and with inimitable drollery retain their animal traits with a fidelity that teaches as much natural History as a study of Buffon would to some minds. In the finer ideal embodiments of men and things, birds and butterflies, beasts and fishes, they rival Hans Andersen, that prince of fairy writers; wonderful word pictures have they revealed to the fresh pure minds of millions of little ones, in the magic mirror of Fairyland – creations in words, that all artists in colour falls short of their intrinsic merit to be called the princes of Fairy Tale writers, is pre-eminent in the bewitchery of the style and grace of these stories... the Brothers Grimm are entitled to the augmented blessings of every fresh reader, who, we trust, will be added to the innumerable company that have gone before the publication of this Edition. May this present Edition increase their number by fresh thousands; and may every reader (big or little) swell the paean of praise and blessing we now raise to the immortal Brothers Grimm for this work of theirs, which is the paradise of our nurseries and the heaven of our infancy. [See Appendix E][22]

Though there was some competition from Hans Christian Andersen's stories, as Meek notes, the Grimms' tales were considered classical fairy tales by the end of the nineteenth century and set a model for what a fairy tale should be in Great Britain and North America as well, even though there are hardly any fairies in their tales. Indeed, it was Taylor, who re-introduced several, but his major accomplishment was to *adapt* the tales so they would be acceptable for a rising bourgeois class and a general population that was becoming more and more literate. His English renditions also appealed to adults and were reinforced by the general positive reception of Perrault's tales. Yet, from the beginning there was a certain ambivalence on the part of Taylor, who also regarded the tales as unusual folk tales that could liberate the imagination of children and adults, not restrain them with didactic and moralistic stories. In this regard he was attune to the German and English Romantic movement that sought to break with the stringent rationalist and religious ideologies of the late eighteenth and early nineteenth centuries.

Ironies of Taylor's Revolutionary Work

Taylor's adaptations of the Grimms' tales are extraordinary and significant because his ideological and poetical premises were based on ideals and myths about the origins and dissemination of the folk tales that the Grimms perpetuated. Indeed, he fulfilled them to such an extreme that he subverted the Grimms' intentions, even though he thought he was following them. In no way, despite the Grimms' creation of the Small Edition in 1826, did they want their German tales to be treated as tales for children. In no way did they want, nor Taylor for that matter, the philological and historical attributes of *Children's and Household Tales* to be neglected. Yet, this was exactly what happened throughout the nineteenth century: the Grimms' different kinds of folk tales, derived allegedly from ancient German sources, became English "fairy tales" for the entertainment of children. And it was not until the latter part of the twentieth century that the mis-reception and misunderstanding of the Grimms' tales were rectified in English-speaking countries. Of course, the "rectification" has been limited due to the Disneyfication and infantilization of the tales, processes that became dominant in the twentieth century and continue into the twenty-first.

Taylor's adaptation of the tales is, of course, partially to blame for the "degeneration" of the tales from the highest kind of the Grimms' models of *Naturpoesie* to amusing popular reading matter for children. But some of the blame for this ironic turn in history must be placed on the Grimms themselves, who created certain exaggerated "myths" about the sanctity of the tales that led Taylor to adapt them the way he did. And, of course, the tales in Taylor's hands did not lose their historical and intrinsically cultural value, for they have always provided more than mere entertainment. As Jacob Grimm commented, Taylor's appropriated tales read well. In fact, they are out-of-the-ordinary nursery tales because he favored the oral tradition and cleverly shaped the tales to be read to children while endeavoring to maintain their "antiquarian" quality. In reaching out to a family reading audience, both the Grimms and Taylor ironically created the conditions for a mixed reception of the tales favoring bourgeois households that has become their legacy in Europe and North America.

In Martin Sutton's superb book, *The Sin-Complex: A Critical Study of English Versions of the Grimms' Kinder- und Hausmärchen in the Nineteenth Century*, he quotes an important passage from F.J. Harvey Darton's *Children's Books in England* to explain what he means by "sin-complex," and Darton's remarks are worth repeating here:

> The fear or dislike of fairy-tales, in fact, was not and is not dependent to a marked extent on the feeling of any one period. It is a habit of the mind which has often been dominant in the history of children's books without much aid from contemporary circumstances. It is a manifestation, in England, of a deep-rooted sin-complex. It involves the belief that anything fantastic on the one hand, or anything primitive on the other, is inherently noxious, or at least so void of good as to be actively dangerous.[23]

During Taylor's youth in England, the general attitude toward fairy tales among literate people was more disparaging than positive, and he was well aware of this. This does not mean that fairy tales and folk tales did not circulate and were not accepted by readers. The times were changing. As Sutton, Alderson, Jennifer Schacker, and more recently Matthew Grenby have pointed out from different perspectives,[24] books of fairy and folk tales for middle-class children and adults remained popular from the seventeenth century up through the nineteenth century. Their reception was more ambivalent than black and white because these tales of fantasy and magic were questioned by conservative religious groups but not totally rejected. The debates always centered around their moral qualities and how they might be used and printed to elevate the behavior of young readers. They were somehow tainted by the sin-complex. What was somewhat different during Taylor's formative years is that that the tales were gradually treated by intellectuals and antiquarians as historical and cultural relics that revealed cultural and national values and international commonalities. By emphasizing how historically significant the tales were and how pure and refreshing they were for children, Taylor, following the Grimms, wanted to appeal to the scholarly interests of adults and the curious, "innocent" minds of young readers. He could point to the uniqueness of the Grimms tales because they were much different from the French fairy tales of Mme d'Aulnoy and Charles Perrault and *The Arabian Nights* that had been prevalent in England up through the 1820s. Not all of the Grimms' stories were *fairy* tales but comic anecdotes, animal stories, fables, wonder tales, and religious legends – closer to the soil of the common people.

It is interesting to note that Taylor changed the order of the Grimms' tales in the 1819 edition and began with "Hans in Luck" (an anecdote), followed by "The Travelling Musicians" (animal story), "The Golden Bird" (wonder tale), and "The Fisherman and his Wife" (a dialect tall tale). Three of these four tales are comical. In contrast, the Grimms always began with more serious and somewhat horrific tales: "The Frog King, or Iron Heinrich," "The Companionship of the Cat and Mouse," "The Virgin Mary's Child," and "A Tale about the Boy Who Went Forth to Learn What Fear Was." In these tales a princess lies to a helpful frog and throws him against the wall; a cat eats a mouse; a woman is almost burned at the stake; and a young boy learns what fear means. In the seven Large Editions published by the Grimms, they always ended their collections with a short tale, "The Golden Key," which was intended to keep the dynamic flow of folk tales alive and keep readers curious. It is about a poor boy who discovers a golden key and iron casket in the snow. He searches for a keyhole to see if the casket contains a treasure. However, the tale is neverending as we learn: "He tried the key, and fortunately it fit. So, he began turning it, and now we must wait until he unlocks the casket completely and lifts the cover. That's when we'll learn what wonderful things he found."[25] In contrast, Taylor ended his combined two volumes with "The Juniper Tree," a ghastly tale about a woman who murders her stepson and feeds him in a stew to his father. Yet, all's well that ends well when the stepson returns in the form of a bird to kill the woman and is re-transformed into a human to live happily ever after with his stepsister and father. Taylor's framework for the tales contains the storytelling that begins with a comic tale and concludes with a happy end to a gruesome tale, whereas the Grimms' framework allows for an open end and more tales to be told.

But it was not simply the order and choice of tales that made Taylor's *German Popular Tales* different from the Grimms' collection and more suitable for children, it was an editing process that was geared to propriety, something to which the Grimms also paid attention, but Taylor was much more the consummate censor: he artfully made the tales more succinct, changed titles, characters, and incidents, mis-translated rhymes, deleted references to God and Christianity, downplayed brutality, and eliminated sexual innuendoes. For example in the first two tales, the titles "Hans in Luck" and "The Travelling Musicians" depart from the German and should be designated "Lucky Hans" and "The Bremen Town Musicians." Throughout these tales there are all sorts of errors. Hans carries gold not silver; two references to God are changed; the rhymed verse that the scissor-grinder sings makes no sense; the word *Sonntagskind* should be fortune's child; horsepond should be a dark hole. In "The Travelling Musicians," the dog's master does not want to knock him on the head, he wants to kill him; the cat is not a "good lady"; the role of the captain of the robbers is changed; a judge is turned into a devil; and there are numerous other misleading translations.

Two of the most egregious adaptations are "Hansel and Grethel" and "The Frog King."

Taylor's tale, "Hansel and Grettel" is actually the Grimms' "Brother and Sister," and his "Roland and May-Bird" is an amalgamation of "Foundling," "Sweetheart Roland," and "Hansel and Grethel." In the Grimms' original "Brother and Sister," a stepmother, who is a witch, beats a brother and sister, who run away. In the woods, the brother drinks from a brook, contaminated by the stepmother, and is turned into a fawn. His sister takes care of him in a cottage in the woods until a king discovers the fawn while out hunting. He follows the fawn to a hut and is so taken by the sister's beauty that he weds her and takes her and the fawn/brother to his castle. Later, after the young queen gives birth, her stepmother the witch learns about her happiness and seeks to destroy her. The stepmother goes to the castle, kills the young queen, and replaces her with her own nasty daughter. However, thanks to God, the queen had not really died and visits her infant son at midnight. A nanny informs the king what has been transpiring, and on the third night, he interrupts her visitation. The "true" queen tells him what has happened, and the king has his false bride and the witch mother executed. The fawn is then transformed into a human, and they all live happily ever after.

In Taylor's "Hansel and Grettel," the stepmother is an evil fairy. All references to God are deleted. The tale is cut in half and ends with the king taking Grettel and the fawn Hansel to his castle where they inform the king about the wicked fairy. Instead of having the fairy killed, the king compels the fairy to change Hansel back into his human form. Once she does that, she is mildly punished and disappears, while the king lives happily ever after with Hansel and Grettel.

Whereas Taylor's "Hansel and Grettel' is a sweet and simple version of the Grimms' "Brother and Sister," devoid of any tension and sadism, his "Roland and May-Bird" is a convoluted tale that borders on being a nonsensical version of the Grimms' "Hansel and Grethel." In this tale, the baby May-Bird is kidnapped and carried off to a tree by a vulture. A poor wood-cutter finds her and raises her with his son Roland. They are like brother and sister and happy to be together. However, the wood-cutter is so poor that his wife convinces him to abandon the children in a forest. Lost, the youngsters find the sweetmeat house of a spiteful fairy, who wants to eat Roland. However, May-Bird steals the fairy's wand, and she runs off with Roland, pursued by the fairy, who wears seven-league boots. Yet, they manage to trick the fairy with her own wand until she becomes entangled in thorns. Freed of the fairy, Roland wants to rush home for help, but May-Bird is too tired to accompany him. So, he leaves her in the woods and promises that he will return and marry her. However, he meets another maiden and falls in love. May-Bird is desolate and wants to commit suicide. Instead, she changes herself into a flower. A shepherd picks her off a field and wants to wed her, but she wants to remain true to Roland. Therefore, she tells the shepherd about her plight, and he lets her stay and clean house for him. In the meantime, she discovers that Roland is going to marry the maiden he found. Compelled to attend the wedding, May-Bird sings before Roland marries the maiden, and her singing makes him realize who his true love is, and he marries May-Bird.

It is clear that Taylor let his imagination run away with him in this tale. The patchwork does not work. The motives of the characters and the fairy-tale motifs do not blend. None of the original German tales are done justice in this weird adaptation, and the invented story's only saving grace is in the amusing hodge-podge conflation of the three tales. Taylor was less adventurous in his adaptation of the Grimms' "Frog King." However, he did change the title, did not allow the frog to sleep with the princess, introduced yet another wicked fairy who had turned the prince into a frog, and reduced the role played by faithful Heinrich the prince's servant. In Taylor's chaste version the spell cast on the prince is broken because the princess allows the frog to sleep on her pillow for three nights. There is no slamming the frog against a wall. In the end the prince takes the princess to his father's castle where they will be married.

In almost all the tales that Taylor adapted, he made key changes that basically "cleansed" the tales of dubious allusions to religion and sex and minimized horror and brutality. Sutton does a thorough line by line comparison of the Grimms' "Snow White" and Taylor's "Snow-drop" to demonstrate how radically Taylor changed the tone and tenor of the original German.[26] His notion of harmony and happiness was much different from that of the Grimms, and he takes pains not to offend any potential ethically minded reader. Very rarely does Taylor allow anyone to be tortured or punished severely. So, instead of having the wicked queen dance to her death in red-hot shoes, he has her simply choke with passion, fall ill, and die.

There are other notable changes that Taylor made. For instance, Rumpelstiltskin is not allowed to stamp his foot into the ground and tear himself in half when the queen announces his name in the German text. Instead, he pulls out his leg from the ground and runs off. A devil is turned into a giant in "The Devil with the Three Golden Hairs." "Chanticleer and Partlet" is another fascinating amalgamation of "Riffraff," "Herr Korbes," and "The Death of the Hen." Ludwig Tieck's powerful tale, "The Elves," is bowdlerized. One can find numerous errors of translation in almost every tale, but these errors do not necessarily diminish the quality of Taylor's stories, and we must remember that there were different standards of translation in the early part of the nineteenth century. The emphasis was not placed on literal translation or exact fidelity to the original text. Taylor explained how and why he changed the stories, and he even felt impelled to change his own adaptations.

His final revolutionary contribution to transforming the Grimms' folk tales into a classic of children's literature was

Gammer Grethel, or German Fairy Tales, and Popular Stories, published in 1839, the year of his death. What is significant about the
title is the addition of the character "Gammer Grethel" and the
term fairy tales to give the impression that the tales were ancient
and taken straight from the mouths of peasants. In fact, the entire
book is shaped around the figure of a storyteller, based on a
fictitious representation of Dorothea Viehmann by the Brothers
Grimm, as an authentic peasant storyteller, which she wasn't. [See
Appendix D] In addition, emphasis is now placed on *fairy tales*
thanks in part to Taylor's introducing fairies into the Grimms'
tales. Altogether there were 42 tales selected for this edition
organized in a different sequence from *German Popular Stories.*
There are twelve evenings with three or four tales told each
evening. The anonymous collector and translator of the tales
informs readers that he had gathered the tales in Germany from
Gammer Grethel, an honest farmer's wife, and asked her
permission to write them down for the benefit of young friends in
England. The very first tale is *not* a comic anecdote as in *German
Popular Stories,* but rather a moralistic fairy tale, "The Golden
Goose," which Taylor greatly revised. For instance, in *German
Popular Stories,* his adaptation of the Grimms' tale begins as
follows:

> There was a man who had three sons. The youngest was called
> Dummling, and was on all occasions despised and ill-treated by the
> whole family.

In *Gammer Grethel,* we read:

> There was a man who had three sons. The youngest was called
> Dummling – which is much the same as Dunderhead, for all thought
> he was more than half a fool – and he was at all times mocked and
> ill-treated by the whole household.

In the end of both versions it is the virtuous Dummling, not
his selfish brothers, who triumphs. After he helps an old man
neglected by his brothers, he is given a golden goose, and people
who want to steal its feathers become attached to it. As Dummling
drags the people with him, he arrives in a city where the king
has promised to reward anyone with his daughter if he can make
the solemn princess laugh. Dummling easily accomplishes this
with the goose and the helpless people attached to it. (Cruikshank's illustration is delightful.) Then he is rewarded by a king

who allows him to marry his daughter and become his heir.

Of course, both adaptations are very different from the 1819 German text, which is much longer and complicated, for the haughty king of the German tale refuses to give his daughter to Dummling after he makes her laugh, and the young man must complete three tasks, helped by the mysterious old man, before the king relents and they all live happily ever after. Taylor's "new" book, *Gammer Grethel*, did not want to offer complication but simplicity. It is the simple small hero, the "Tom Thumbs" of the world, who are to be rewarded for their virtuous childlike behavior.

In *Gammer Grethel*, Taylor made his ideological approach to folk tales much more explicit than in any of his previous adaptations. Aside from shortening and stylizing the tales from *German Popular Stories* and focusing on children, he changed the titles of some of the tales and added names to the characters. For instance "Peter the Goatherd" became "Karl Katz," and animals were given names in "The Grateful Beasts," which was now called "Fritz and his Friends." There was only one new German tale, "Das Schrätel und der Wasserbär," translated under the title "The Bear and the Skrattel." In the note to this tale, Taylor stated that he took it from the Grimms' preface to Thomas Crofton Croker's *Fairy Legends and Traditions of the South of Island*, which they had translated into German as *Irische Elfenmärchen* in 1826. It was a medieval German text in verse which Taylor translated because of its "authentic antiquity." By including it in *Gammer Grethel* in 1839, the connection to the Grimm Brothers was completed.

However, the Taylor revolutionary touch continued to make itself felt throughout the rest of the nineteenth century in England and America in numerous reprints and new editions. For instance, in 1843 the publisher James Burns included some of Taylor's texts, slightly changed, in *Popular Tales and Legends* and followed this publication in 1845 with *Household Tales and Traditions of England, Germany, France, Scotland, etc. etc.*, in which he stole and adapted more of Taylor's translations without giving credit. Gradually, Taylor's adaptations were regarded as fairy tales not popular stories. Indeed, his cousin John Edward Taylor, a London printer, published another selection of the Grimms' tales in 1846 under the title *The Fairy Ring: A New Collection of Popular Tales, collected from the German of Jacob and Wilhelm Grimm*. This volume, which contained 36 Grimms' tales never translated before, was illustrated by Richard Doyle, one of the great Victorian illustrators, and it added to the popularity of the Grimms' collection as a children's book. But the fact is that Edgar Taylor's revolution had already been successful by the time this new adaptation had appeared and had set the tone for what was to be considered "authentic" fairy tales from Germany. Interestingly, the very first so-called "genuine" translation of the Grimms' German tales in France, *Vieux Contes pour l'Amusement des Grands et des Petits enfans* (1824), published by Antoine Boulland, was actually based totally on Taylor's English adaptations with Cruikshank's illustrations. However, the greatest irony in the history of the Grimms' tales in England is that Taylor had already turned the Grimms' stories into *classical* folk and fairy tales for children with a British flavor while the Brothers were still alive and struggling to preserve the role of authentic folk tales in the German cultural heritage.

Notes

1. Albert, Leitzmann, ed., *Briefwechsel der Brüder Jacob und Wilhelm Grimm mit Karl Lachmann.* Vol. 1. (Jena: Verlag der Frommannschen Buchhandlung, 1927): 390. Lachmann was one of the foremost German philologists of the nineteenth century and became a professor at the Humboldt University in Berlin.

2. David Blamires, "The Early Reception of the *Grimms' Kinder- und Hausmärchen* in England," *Bulletin of the John Rylands University Library of Manchester,* 71.3 (1989): 69.

3. In 1948, Puffin Classics (Penguin) published an edition with the title *Grimms' Fairy Tales,* which does not indicate who the translator is, but it does highlight Cruikshank's illustrations. The cover is a colored rendition of "Hans in Luck."

4. For information about Cruikshank's work see Robert Patten, "George Cruikshank's Grimm Humor," in Joachim Müller, ed., *Imagination on a Long Rein: English Literature Illustrated* (Marburg: Jonas, 1988): 3-28 and *George Cruikshank: Life, Times, and Art,* 2 vols. (New Brunswick, NJ: Rutgers University Press, 1992).

5. The dates of the Large Edition are: 1812/ 1815, 1819, 1837, 1840, 1843, 1850, 1857. The last edition contained 210 tales. The dates of the Small Edition are: 1825, 1833, 1836, 1839, 1841, 1844, 1847, 1850, 1853, 1858. They always contained 50 tales that were generally revised in accordance with the same tales in the Large Edition, though there were some small differences. The Small Edition began with "The Frog King" and ended with the "The Star Coins," two tales clearly adapted for young readers. The illustrations by Ludwig Pietsch tend to be realistic and somewhat sanctimonious. See Heinz Rölleke's "Nachwort" in *Kinder- und Hausmärchen gesammelt durch die Brüder Grimm: Kleine Ausgabe von 1858* (Frankfurt am Main: Insel, 1985): 291-95.

6. Most of the recent scholarship on Taylor's "revolutionary" transformation of the Grimms' tales are in agreement on this point with slight differences of emphasis. See David Blamires, "The Early Reception of the *Grimms' Kinder- und Hausmärchen* in England," *Bulletin of the John Rylands University Library of Manchester,* 71.3 (1989): 63-77; Martin Sutton, *The Sin-Complex: A Critical Study of English Versions of the Grimms' Kinder- und Hausmärchen in the Nineteenth Century* (Kassel: Schriften der Brüder Grimm-Gesellschaft, 1996); Jennifer Schacker, *National Dreams: The Remaking of Fairy Tales in Nineteenth Century England* (Philadelphia: University of Pennsylvania Press, 2003); Gillian Lathey, *The Role of Translators*

in *Children's Literature: Invisible Storyteller* (New York: Routledge, 2010).

7. See Heinz Rölleke, ed., *Die älteste Märchensammlung der Brüder Grimm. Synopse der handschriftlichen Urfassung von 1810 und der Erstdrucke von 1812* (Cologny-Geneva: Fondation Martin Bodmer, 1975).

8. Jens Sennewald, *Das Buch, das Wir sind: Zur Poetik der "Kinder- und Hausmärchen, gesammelt durch die Brüder Grimm"* (Würzbrug: Königshausen & Neumann, 2004): 14-18.

9. *Ibid.*, 42-7.

10. Reinhold Steig and Herman Grimm, eds., *Achim von Arnim und die ihm nahe standen.* Vol. 3 (Stuttgart: J. G. Cotta'schen Buchhandlung, 1904): 237.

11. *Ibid.*, 270.

12. *Ibid.*, 271.

13. *Kinder- und Hausmärchen gesammelt durch die Brüder Grimm* [1812/1815, Erstausgabe]. Ed. Ulrike Marquardt and Heinz Rölleke. vol. 2. (Göttingen: Vandenhoeck & Ruprecht, 1986): vii-x.

14. Some more biographical information about Taylor can be found in: Ruth Michaelis-Jena, "Edgar and John Edward Taylor, die ersten englischen Übersetzer der Kinder- und Hausmärchen," in *Brüder Grimm Gedenken*, ed. Ludwig Denecke. Vol. 2. (Marburg: N. G. Elwert, 1975): 183-202; Sutton, *The Sin-Complex: A Critical Study of English Versions of the Grimms' Kinder- und Hausmärchen in the Nineteenth Century*; and Schacker, *National Dreams: The Remaking of Fairy Tales in Nineteenth Century England*.

15. Francis Cohen, "Antiquities of Nursery Literature: Review of *Fairy Tales, or the Lilliputian Cabinet, Containing Twenty-four Choice Pieces of Fancy and Fiction, collected by Benjamin Tabart*," *Quarterly Review* 21.41 (January 1819): 92-3.

16. For the most thorough account of Cohen's life and his correspondence with the Grimms, see Lothar Bluhm, "Sir Francis Cohen/ Palgrave. Zur frühen Rezeption der *Kinder- und Hausmärchen* in England," in Ludwig Denecke, ed., *Brüder Grimm Gedenken*, Vol. 7 (Marburg: N. G. Elwert, 1987): 224-42.

17. See Edgar Taylor, "German Popular and Traditionary Literature," *New Monthly Magazine and Literary Journal*, 2 (1821): 146-52, 329-36, 537-44, and 4 (1822): 289-96.

18. *Ibid.*, 2: 146-47.

19. Robert Patten, "George Cruikshank's Grimm Humor" in Joachim Müller, ed., *Imagination on a Long Rein: English Literature Illustrated* (Marburg: Jonas, 1988): 14.

20. Sir Walter Scott, "Letter to Edgar Taylor, January 16 1823," in *The Letters of Sir Walter Scott*, ed. Herbert Grierson, vol. 7 (London: Constable, 1934): 310.

21. Cohen also has an interest in this work.

22. *Grimm's Goblins. Grimm's Household Stories, Translated from the Kinder und Haus Marchen.* Illustr. George Cruikshank (London: R. Meek, 1876): viii.

23. F. J. Harvey Darton, *Children's Books in England: Five Centuries of Social Life*, 3rd Rev. Ed. by Brian Alderson (Cambridge: Cambridge University Press, 1982): 99.

24. See Sutton, *The Sin-Complex: A Critical Study of English Versions of the Grimms' Kinder- und Hausmärchen in the Nineteenth Century;* Schacker, *National Dreams: The Remaking of Fairy Tales in Nineteenth Century England*: and Matthew Grenby, "Tame Fairies Make Good Teachers: The Popularity of Early British Fairy Tales," *The Lion and the Unicorn,* 30 (2006): 1-24.
25. Jacob and Wilhelm Grimm, *The Complete Tales of the Brothers Grimm,* trans. Jack Zipes, 3rd Expanded Ed. (New York: Bantam, 2003): 582.
26. See Sutton, 22-47.

A Note On the Illustrator
George Cruikshank (1792-1878)

One of the foremost graphic artists and satirists of the nineteenth century, Cruikshank came to illustrate Edgar Taylor's *German Popular Stories* via caricature. Born in London into a Scottish family of artists, he served as apprentice to his father Isaac Cruikshank, regarded at that time as one of the finest engravers and caricaturists in England. During his adolescence, Cruikshank quickly established his own reputation as a talented artist by drawing sketches of well-known actors and social caricatures of English life for popular publications such as *The Scourge* and *Blackwood's*. Cruikshank did not have a particular ideological axe to grind and mercilessly attacked anyone and everyone with his droll drawings – Tories, Whigs, Radicals, and even members of the royal family. Since much of his early work was done during the Napoleonic Wars, he also addressed the conflicts in Europe and exhibited patriotic zeal for England, particularly when his sketches dealt with France. Once England achieved victory in 1816, Cruikshank focused mainly on social and political themes within England. His most controversial accomplishment was *The Political House That Jack Built* (1819), a collaboration with William Hone, a reformist, who candidly criticized the government and leading political figures. It was partly due to Hone, who inspired Cruikshank's satirical drawings, that Cruikshank established him as the most gifted political caricaturist in England.

However, Cruikshank's interest in politics and caricature began to wane in the 1820s, while book publishing and illustration, which were on the rise, began to have more of an appeal to him. In 1821 he provided stunning illustrations for Pierce Egan's *Life in London*, in which he depicted unusual scenes from English high and low life. At the same time, Cruikshank had already taken an interest in folklore and fairy tales. He illustrated William Gardiner's *The Magic Spell* (1819) and *Original Tales from My Landlord* (1821). He followed this work with illustrations for a series of such classical tales as "Tom Thumb," "Sleeping Beauty," "Puss in Boots," and others for the publishers Dean and Munday in 1821 and 1823. He also contributed drawings with his brother Robert to two collections, *Daddy Gander's Entertaining Fairy Tales* and *Mother Bunch's Entertaining Fairy Tales*.

In 1823, he made the most important contact for his career as an illustrator by agreeing with the publisher Charles Morris Baldwyn to do the engravings for two very popular books, *Points of Humour* (1823) and *Italian Points of Humour, Gallantry and Romance* (1824), which contained humorous poems, stories, anecdotes, and fables. Baldwyn was one of the more enterprising publishers in London, and he was approached some time in early 1823 by his printer, Richard Taylor, a relative of Edgar, to see if he would be interested in publishing a translation of German tales. Once Baldwyn met and signed a contract with Edgar Taylor to produce two volumes of tales, *German Popular* Stories, which appeared in 1823 and 1826, he commissioned Cruikshank to provide illustrations for both volumes. Neither had the slightest inkling that Taylor's unusual adaptations of the Grimms' tales, partially translated by David Jardine and Marriott Martineau in the first volume, and Cruikshank's pungent illustrations, would become very successful and remain extremely popular for the rest of the century, not only in England but also in America.

Cruikshank's drawings appealed to young and old readers and emphasized the hilarity and exuberance of the tales. The frontispieces of the two volumes reveal a common thread that runs throughout the books: the warmth of storytelling. People of all ages are portrayed in a communal gathering around elderly storytellers, who are sitting next to a fireplace to share tales. The listeners are seemingly entranced by the unusual tales, and the illustrations throughout the books, 18 in all, punctuate the joy of reading at crucial moments in the stories. Cruikshank had an eye for capturing the most compelling incident in each of the tales that he illustrated. Just as Taylor changed the Grimms' tales into amusing odd stories for young readers and their families, Cruikshank set a new frolic tone with his explosive and optimistic illustrations. Gone are the satiric barbs of his caricatures, and yet, his humor is still untamed. Moreover, his understanding of the subtle and somewhat dark aspects of fairy tales were developed in this stage of his career as can be seen in his engravings for Adelbert von Chamisso's extraordinary fairy tale, *Peter Schlemihl* (1824), produced for the publishers G. and W. B. Whittaker.

The work that Cruikshank did for these publishers and Baldwyn, who tragically died in 1824, was given a great reception, and he was recognized as a unique illustrator. From this point onward, Cruikshank had no difficulty obtaining commissions to illustrate books, and he even endeavored to found his own publishing company in 1826 with the book, *Phrenological Illustrations*. However, Cruikshank was not a very good businessman and stopped self-publishing in 1836. At the same time, he continued work with a variety of publishing houses and journals. His most notable artwork in the 1830s was for Charles Dickens' books: *Sketches by Boz* (1836), *The Mudfog Papers* (1837–38) and *Oliver Twist* (1838). Cruikshank became close friends with Dickens and even acted in Dickens' amateur theatrical company. However, their friendship dwindled when Cruikshank became a leader in the temperance and anti-smoking movement during the 1840s.

His radical transformation did not prevent him from accepting the usual commissions from publishers. Throughout his career Cruikshank continued creating political caricatures for magazines and journals, and he illustrated important novels by William Ainsworth, *The Miser's Daughter* (1841) and *Windsor Castle* (1843), and books such as *The Bachelor's Own Book* (1844) and *The Table Book* (1845). However, he became a fanatical teetotaler by 1847 and began devoting a good deal of his time to producing engravings for the Total Abstinence Society and the National Temperance Society. Some of his highly didactic drawings appeared in *The Bottle* (1847) and *The Drunkard's Children* (1848). Cruikshank also turned to adapting fairy tales to support the temperance movement in 1853, when he began a series called *The Fairy Library*. Not only did Cruikshank seek to re-write the tales as tracts demonstrating how one should lead a virtuous life, but he also drew all the illustrations that were unintentionally comical. The series consisted of *Hop' o' my Thumb and the Seven League Boots* (1853), *Jack and the Beanstalk* (1854), *Cinderella and the Glass Slipper* (1854), and *Puss in Boots* (1864). This series signaled a decline in Cruikshank's artistry and originality. Though he started a magazine called *George Cruikshank's Magazine* in 1854, did illustrations for other books such as Giambattista Basile's *The Pentamerone* (1854) and Robert Barnabas Brough's *Life of Sir John Falstaff* (1857), provided woodcuts for children's books such as Juliana Ewing's, *The Brownies and Other Tales* (1871) and three tales collected in *Lob Lie-by-the-Fire*, or the *Luck of Lingborough* (1874), and turned to oil painting, often with temperance themes such as *The Worship of Bacchus* (1862), Cruikshank's works received little attention toward the end of his life.

Praised by such great writers as Sir Walter Scott, William Makepeace Thackeray, Charles Dickens, and John Ruskin, Cruik-shank held to his beliefs like a stubborn child, even when he lost their praise. He felt his work would redeem itself and did not seem to care what the world thought of him. His art had become a mission. After his death, the obituary in *Punch* provided an apt picture of the remarkable illustrator, who stamped the reception of the Grimms' tales in England and America with childlike, merry abandonment and almost ruined fairy tales with his sobriety late in his life:

> His nature had something childlike in its transparency. You saw through him completely. There was neither wish nor effort to disguise his self-complacency, his high appreciation of himself, his delight in the appreciation of others, any more than there was to make himself out better, or cleverer, or more unselfish than his neighbours. In him England has lost one who was, in every sense, as true a man as he was a rare and original genius, and a pioneer in the arts of illustration.

GERMAN
POPULAR STORIES

With Illustrations

AFTER THE ORIGINAL DESIGNS OF GEORGE CRUIKSHANK.

G. Cruikshank fec.

EDITED BY EDGAR TAYLOR,

WITH INTRODUCTION BY JOHN RUSKIN, M.A.

LONDON:
JOHN CAMDEN HOTTEN, PICCADILLY.

"Now you must imagine me to sit by a good fire, amongst a company of good fellows, over a well spiced wassel bowle of Christmas ale, telling of these merrie tales which hereafter followe."

– Pref. to Hist. of "Tomb Thumbe the Little" – 1621

"And so, Gentle Reader, craving thy kind acceptance, I wish thee as much willingness to the reading as I have forward in the printing, and so I end – Farewell"

– Pref. to Valentine and Orson... with new pictures lively expressing the history." – 1677

G Cruikshank fecit

Advertisement By the Publisher

MORE than forty years ago (in 1823), Mr. Edgar Taylor presented to English readers the first selection which had been made from the famous "Hausmarchen," or *German Popular Stories of the Brothers Grimm*. The first volume, which had been selected and translated by Mr. Taylor and a circle of relatives, appeared with twelve wonderful etchings by George Cruikshank, and was received with so much favour that, three years after, a *second* series was prepared by Mr. Taylor alone, to which the same artist contributed ten more illustrations. Both series passed through two or three editions soon after publication; and when Messrs. Robins the publishers retired from business, the work became very scarce. At the present day, when the collectors of the works of Cruikshank are greatly increasing in number, the two volumes, originally sold for 12*s.*, are worth at least £5 or £6! They are the most prized of all the fine works of the great master. On the continent, too, these etchings quickly attracted attention. Copies were made in Germany, and one Ambrose Tardieu, a Frenchman, took such a special fancy to them that he copied the first series to the best of his ability, and then issued them in a small volume *as his own production.*[1]

The present volume is a faithful reprint of *both series*. The etchings, most carefully following the originals, are considered masterpieces of reproduction. What is thought of these designs by artists in this country Mr. John Ruskin very eloquently told us many years ago in his "Elements of Drawing;" and, only recently, Mr. Hamerton, in his new work, "Etching and Etchers," speaks of the favourite of all these etchings, the well-known "Two Elves and the Shoemaker," in these words: – "This pleasant tale was so well adapted to the genius of Cruikshank, that it has suggested one of the very best of all his etchings. The two Elves,

1 The title of the book was "VIEUX CONTES *pour l' Amusement des Grands et des Pétits enfants, ornés de 12 gravures comiques, Paris, A. Boulland*, 1830." I had never seen the impudent little volume until M. Octave Delepierre obligingly showed it to me.

especially the nearer one, who is putting on his breeches, are drawn with a point at once so precise and vivacious, so full of keen fun and inimitably happy invention, that I have not found their equal in comic etching anywhere. * * * It is said that these elves are regarded with peculiar affection by the great master who created them, which is only natural, for he has a right to be proud of them. The picturesque details of the room are etched with the same felicitous intelligence, but the marvel of the work is in the expression of the strange little faces, and the energy of the comical wee limbs."

I have to express my obligations to the Widow of Mr. Edgar Taylor for obligingly giving her consent to my reprinting the original translation, the labour of reproducing which has been very carefully performed by Messrs. Taylor and Francis, who printed the first editions nearly half a century ago. I had at first thought of reproducing it in two volumes the same size as the originals, but it was Mr. Ruskin's wish that the new edition should appeal to young readers rather than to adults, and the present convenient form was decided upon.

The notes, reprinted from the original editions, are by Mr. Edgar Taylor; and to his Widow I am indebted for the loan of the interesting letter from Sir Walter Scott, printed at p. 334.

J.C.H.

Piccadilly.

Hans In Luck

HANS had served his master seven years, and at last said to him, "Master, my time is up, I should like to go home and see my mother; so give me my wages." And the master said, "You have been a faithful and good servant, so your pay shall be handsome." Then he gave him a piece of silver that was as big as his head.

Hans took out his pocket-handkerchief, put the piece of silver into it, threw it over his shoulder, and jogged off homewards. As he went lazily on, dragging one foot after another, a man came in sight, trotting along gaily on a capital horse. "Ah!" said Hans aloud, "what a fine thing it is to ride on horseback! there he sits as if he was at home in his chair, he trips against no stones, spares his shoes, and yet gets on he hardly knows how." The horseman, heard this, and said, "Well, Hans, why do you go on foot then?" "Ah!" said he, "I have this load to carry; to be sure it is silver, but it is so heavy that I can't hold up my head, and it hurts my shoulder sadly." "What do you say to changing?" said the horseman; "I will give you my horse, and you shall give me the silver." "With all my heart," said Hans: "but I tell you one thing, – you'll have a weary task to drag it along." The horseman got off, took the silver, helped Hans up, gave him the bridle into his hand, and said, "When you want to go very fast, you must smack your lips loud, and cry 'Jip.'"

Hans was delighted as he sat on the horse, and rode merrily on. After a time he thought he should like to go a little faster, so he smacked his lips and cried "Jip." Away went the horse full gallop; and before Hans knew what he was about, he was thrown off, and lay in a ditch by the roadside; and his horse would have run off, if a shepherd who was coming by, driving a cow, had not stopt it. Hans soon came to himself, and got upon his legs again. He was sadly vexed, and said to the shepherd, "This riding is no joke when a man gets on a beast like this, that stumbles and flings him off as if he would break his neck. However, I am off now once for all: I like your cow a great deal better; one can walk along at one's leisure behind her, and have milk, butter, and cheese every day into the bargain. What would I give to have such a cow!" "Well," said the shepherd, "if you are so fond of her, I will change my cow for your horse." "Done!" said Hans merrily. The shepherd jumped upon the horse and away he rode.

Hans drove off his cow quietly, and thought his bargain a very lucky one. "If I have only a piece of bread (and I certainly shall be able to get that), I can, whenever I like, eat my butter and cheese with it; and when I am thirsty I can milk my cow and drink the milk: what can I wish for more?" When he came to an inn, he halted, ate up all his bread, and gave away his last penny for a glass of beer: then he drove his cow towards his mother's village; and the heat grew greater as noon came on, till at last he found himself on a wide heath that would take him more than an hour to cross, and he began to be so hot and parched that his tongue clave to the roof of his mouth. "I can find a cure for this," thought he, "now will I milk my cow and quench my thirst;" so he tied her to the stump of a tree, and held his leathern cap to milk into; but not a drop was to be had.

While he was trying his luck and managing the matter very clumsily, the uneasy beast gave him a kick on the head that knocked him down, and there he lay a long while senseless. Luckily a butcher soon came by driving a pig in a wheel-barrow, "What is the matter with you?" said the butcher as he helped him up. Hans told him what had happened, and the butcher gave him a flask, saying "There, drink and refresh yourself; your cow will give you no milk, she is an old beast good for nothing but the slaughter-house." "Alas, alas!" said Hans, "who would have thought it? If I kill her, what would she be good for? I hate cow-beef, it is not tender enough for me. If it were a pig now, one could do something with it, it would at any rate make some sausages." "Well," said the butcher, "to please you I'll change, and give you the pig for the cow." "Heaven reward you for your kindness!" said Hans as he gave the butcher the cow, and took the pig off the wheel-barrow, and drove it off, holding it by the string that was tied to its leg.

So on he jogged, and all seemed now to go right with him; he had met with some misfortunes, to be sure; but he was now well repaid for all. The next person he met was a countryman carrying a fine white goose under his arm. The countryman stopped to ask what was o'clock; and Hans told him all his luck, and how he had made so many good bargains. The countryman said he was going to take the goose to a christening; "Feel," said he, "how heavy it is, and yet it is only eight weeks old. Whoever roasts and eats it may cut plenty of fat off it, it has lived so well!" "You're right," said Hans as he weighed it in his hand; "but my pig is no trifle." Meantime the countryman began to look grave, and shook his head. "Hark ye," said he, "my good friend; your pig may get you into a scrape; in the village I just come from, the squire has had a pig stolen out of his stye. I was dreadfully afraid, when I saw you, that you had got the squire's pig; it will be a bad job if they catch you; the least they'll do, will be to throw you into the horsepond."

Poor Hans was sadly frightened. "Good man," cried he, "pray get me out of this scrape; you know this country better than I, take my pig and give me the goose." "I ought to have something into the bargain," said the countryman; "however, I will not bear hard upon you, as you are in trouble." Then he took the string in his hand, and drove off the pig by a side path; while Hans went on the way homewards free from care. "After all," thought he, "I have the best of the bargain: first there will be a capital roast; then the fat will find me in goose-grease for six months; and then there are all the beautiful white feathers; I will put them into my pillow, and then I am sure I shall sleep soundly without rocking. How happy my mother will be!"

As he came to the last village, he saw a scissor-grinder, with his wheel, working away, and singing

O'er hill and o'er dale so happy I roam,
Work light and live well, all this world is my home;
Who so blythe, so merry as I?

Hans stood looking for a while, and at last said, "You must be well off, master grinder, you seem so happy at your work." "Yes," said the other, "mine is a golden trade; a good grinder never puts his hand in his pocket without finding money in it: – but where did you get that beautiful goose?" "I did not buy it, but changed a pig for it." "And where did you get the pig?" "I gave a cow for it." "And the cow?" "I gave a horse for it." "And the horse?" "I gave a piece of silver as big as my head for that." "And the silver?" "Oh! I worked hard for that seven long years." "You have thriven well in the world hitherto," said the grinder, "now if you could find money in your pocket whenever you put your hand into it, your fortune would be made." "Very true: but how is that to be managed?" "You must turn grinder like me," said the other, "you only want a grindstone; the rest will come of itself. Here is one that is a little the worse for wear: I would not ask more than the value of your goose for it; – will you buy?" "How can you ask such a question?" replied Hans; "I should be the happiest man in the world if I could have money whenever I put my hand in my pocket; what could I want more? there's the goose!" "Now," said the grinder, as he gave him a common rough stone that lay by his side, "this is a most capital stone; do but manage it cleverly, and you can make an old nail cut with it."

Hans took the stone and went off with a light heart: his eyes sparkled for joy, and he said to himself, "I must have been born in a lucky hour; every thing that I want or wish for comes to me of itself."

Meantime he began to be tired, for he had been travelling ever since daybreak; he was hungry, too, for he had given away his last penny in his joy at getting the cow. At last he could go no further, and the stone tired him terribly; he dragged himself to the side of a pond, that he might drink some water and rest awhile; so he laid the stone carefully by his side on the bank: but as he stooped down to drink, he forgot it, pushed it a little, and down it went plump into the pond. For awhile he watched it sinking in the deep clear water, then sprang up for joy, and again fell upon his knees, and thanked heaven with tears in his eyes for its kindness in taking away his only plague, the ugly heavy stone. "How happy am I!" cried he: "no mortal was ever so lucky as I am." Then up he got with a light and merry heart, and walked on free from all his troubles, till he reached his mother's house.

The Travelling Musicians

AN honest farmer had once an ass that had been a faithful servant to him a great many years, but was now growing old and every day more and more unfit for work. His master therefore was tired of keeping him and began to think of putting an end to him; but the ass who saw that some mischief was in the wind, took himself slyly off, and began his journey towards the great city, "for there," thought he, "I may turn musician."

After he had travelled a little way he spied a dog lying by the roadside and panting as if he were very tired. "What makes you pant so, my friend?" said the ass. "Alas!" said the dog, "my master was going to knock me on the head, because I am old and weak, and can no longer make myself useful to him in hunting; so I ran away: but what can I do to earn my livelihood?" "Hark ye!" said the ass, "I am going to the great city to turn musician: suppose you go with me, and try what you can do in the same way?" The dog said he was willing, and they jogged on together.

They had not gone far before they saw a cat sitting in the middle of the road and making a most rueful face. "Pray, my good lady," said the ass, "what's the matter with you? you look quite out of spirits!" "Ah me!" said the cat, "how can one be in good spirits when one's life is in danger? Because I am beginning to grow old, and had rather lie at my ease by the fire than run about the house after the mice, my mistress laid hold of me, and was going to drown me; and though I have been lucky enough to get away from her, I do not know what I am to live upon." "O!" said the ass, "by all means go with us to the great city; you are a good night singer, and may make your fortune as a musician." The cat was pleased with the thought, and joined the party.

Soon afterwards, as they were passing by a farmyard, they

saw a cock perched upon a gate, and screaming out with all his might and main. "Bravo!" said the ass; "upon my word you make a famous noise; pray what is all this about?" "Why," said the cock, "I was just now saying that we should have fine weather for our washing-day, and yet my mistress and the cook don't thank me for my pains, but threaten to cut off my head tomorrow, and make broth of me for the guests that are coming on Sunday!" "Heaven forbid!" said the ass, "come with us Master Chanticleer; it will be better, at any rate, than staying here to have your head cut off! Besides, who knows? If we take care to sing in tune, we may get up some kind of a concert: so come along with us." "With all my heart," said the cock: so they all four went on jollily together.

They could not, however, reach the great city the first day; so when night came on they went into the wood to sleep. The ass and the dog laid themselves down under a great tree, and the cat climbed up into the branches; while the cock, thinking that the higher he sat the safer he should be, flew up to the very top of the tree, and then according to his custom, before he went to sleep, looked out on all sides of him to see that everything was well. In doing this he saw afar off something bright and shining; and calling to his companions said, "There must be a house no great way off, for I see a light." "If that be the case," said the ass, "we had better change our quarters, for our lodging is not the best in the world!" "Besides," added the dog, "I should not be the worse for a bone or two, or a bit of meat." So they walked off together towards the spot where Chanticleer had seen the light; and as they drew near, it became larger and brighter, till they at last came close to a house in which a gang of robbers lived.

The ass, being the tallest of the company, marched up to the window and peeped in. "Well, Donkey," said Chanticleer, "what do you see?" "What do I see?" replied the ass, "why I see a table spread with all kinds of good things, and robbers sitting round it making merry." "That would be a noble lodging for us," said the cock. "Yes," said the ass, "if we could only get in:" so they consulted together how they should contrive to get the robbers out; and at last they hit upon a plan. The ass placed himself upright on his hind-legs, with his fore feet resting against the window; the dog got upon his back; the cat scrambled up to the dog's shoulders, and the cock flew up and sat upon the cat's head. When all was ready, a signal was given, and they began their

music. The ass brayed, the dog barked, the cat mewed, and the cock screamed; and then they all broke through the window at once, and came tumbling into the room, amongst the broken glass, with a most hideous clatter! The robbers, who had been not a little frightened by the opening concert, had now no doubt that some frightful hobgoblin had broken in upon them, and scampered away as fast as they could.

The coast once clear, our travellers soon sat down, and dispatched what the robbers had left, with as much eagerness as if they had not expected to eat again for a month. As soon as they had satisfied themselves, they put out the lights, and each once more sought out a resting-place to his own liking. The donkey laid himself down upon a heap of straw in the yard; the dog stretched himself upon a mat behind the door; the cat rolled herself up on the hearth before the warm ashes; and the cock perched upon a beam on the top of the house; and, as they were all rather tired with their journey, they soon fell asleep.

But about midnight, when the robbers saw from afar that the lights were out and that all seemed quiet, they began to think that they had been in too great a hurry to run away; and one of them, who was bolder than the rest, went to see what was going on. Finding every thing still, he marched into the kitchen, and groped about till he found a match in order to light a candle; and then, espying the glittering fiery eyes of the cat, he mistook them for live coals, and held the match to them to light it. But the cat, not understanding this joke, sprung at his face, and spit, and scratched at him. This frightened him dreadfully, and away he ran to the back door; but there the dog jumped up and bit him in the leg; and as he was crossing over the yard the ass kicked him; and the cock, who had been awakened by the noise, crowed with all his might. At this the robber ran back as fast as he could to his comrades, and told the captain "how a horrid witch had got into the house, and had spit at him and scratched his face with her long bony fingers; how a man with a knife in his hand had hidden himself behind the door, and stabbed him in the leg; how a black monster stood in the yard and struck him with a club, and how the devil sat upon the top of the house and cried out, 'Throw the rascal up here!'" After this the robbers never dared to go back to the house; but the musicians were so pleased with their quarters, that they took up their abode there; and there they are, I dare say, at this very day.

The Golden Bird

A CERTAIN king had a beautiful garden, and in the garden stood a tree which bore golden apples. These apples were always counted, and about the time when they began to grow ripe it was found that every night one of them was gone. The king became very angry at this, and ordered the gardener to keep watch all night under the tree. The gardener set his eldest son to watch; but about twelve o'clock he fell asleep, and in the morning another of the apples was missing. Then the second son was ordered to watch; and at midnight he too fell asleep, and in the morning another apple was gone. Then the third son offered to keep watch; but the gardener at first would not let him, for fear some harm should come to him: however, at last he consented, and the young man laid himself under the tree to watch. As the clock struck twelve he heard a rustling noise in the air, and a bird came flying that was of pure gold; and as it was snapping at one of the apples with its beak, the gardener's son jumped up and shot an arrow at it. But the arrow did the bird no harm; only it dropped a golden feather from its tail, and then flew away. The golden feather was brought to the king in the morning, and all the council was called together. Every one agreed that it was worth more than all the wealth of the kingdom; but the king said, "One feather is of no use to me, I must have the whole bird."

Then the gardener's eldest son set out and thought to find the golden bird very easily; and when he had gone but a little way, he came to a wood, and by the side of the wood he saw a fox sitting; so he took his bow and made ready to shoot at it. Then the fox said, "Do not shoot me, for I will give you good counsel; I know what your business is, and that you want to find the golden bird. You will reach a village in the evening; and when you get there, you will see two inns opposite to each other, one of which is very pleasant and beautiful to look at: go not in there, but rest for the night in the other, though it may appear to you to be very poor and mean." But the son thought to himself, "What can such a beast as this know about the matter?" So he shot his arrow at the fox; but he missed it, and it set up its tail above its back and ran into the wood. Then he went his way, and in the evening came to the village where the two inns were; and in one of these were people singing, and dancing, and feasting; but the other looked very dirty and poor. "I should be very silly," said he, "if I went to that shabby house, and left this charming place;" so he went into the smart house, and ate and drank at his ease, and forgot the bird and his country too.

Time passed on; and as the eldest son did not come back, and no tidings were heard of him, the second son set out, and the same thing happened to him. He met the fox, who gave him the same good advice: but when he came to the two inns, his eldest brother was standing at the window where the merrymaking was, and called to him to come in; and he could not withstand the temptation, but went in, and forgot the golden bird and his country in the same manner.

Time passed on again, and the youngest son too wished to set out into the wide world to seek for the golden bird; but his father would not listen to it for a long while, for he was very fond of his son, and was afraid that some ill luck might happen to him also, and prevent his coming back. However, at last it was agreed he should go, for he would not rest at home; and as he came to the wood, he met the fox, and heard the same good counsel. But he was thankful to the fox, and did not attempt his life as his brothers had done; so the fox said, "Sit upon my tail, and you will travel faster." So he sat down, and the fox began to run, and away they went over stock and stone so quick that their hair whistled in the wind.

When they came to the village, the son followed the fox's counsel, and without looking about him went to the shabby inn and rested there all night at his ease. In the morning came the fox again and met him as he was beginning his journey, and said, "Go straight forward, till you come to a castle, before which lie a whole troop of soldiers fast asleep and snoring: take no notice of them, but go into the castle and pass on and on till you come to a room, where the golden bird sits in a wooden cage; close by it stands a beautiful golden cage; but do not try to take the bird out of the shabby cage and put it into the handsome one, otherwise you will repent it." Then the fox stretched out his tail again, and the young man sat himself down, and away they went over stock and stone till their hair whistled in the wind.

Before the castle gate all was as the fox had said: so the son went in and found the chamber where the golden bird hung in a wooden cage, and below stood a golden cage, and the three golden apples that had been lost were lying close by it. Then thought he to himself, "It will be a very droll thing to bring away such a fine bird in this shabby cage;" so he opened the door and took hold of it and put it into the golden cage. But the bird set up such a loud scream that all the soldiers awoke, and they took him prisoner and carried him before the king. The next morning the court sat to judge him; and when all was heard, it sentenced him to die, unless he should bring the king the golden horse which could run as swiftly as the wind; and if he did this, he was to have the golden bird given him for his own.

So he set out once more on his journey, sighing, and in great despair, when on a sudden his good friend the fox met him, and said, "You see now what has happened on account of your not listening to my counsel. I will still, however, tell you how to find the golden horse, if you will do as I bid you. You must go straight on till you come to the castle where the horse stands in his stall: by his side will lie the groom fast asleep and, snoring: take away the horse quietly, but be sure to put the old leathern saddle upon him, and not the golden one that is close by it." Then the son sat down on the fox's tail, and away they went over stock and stone till their hair whistled in the wind.

All went right, and the groom lay snoring with his hand upon the golden saddle. But when the son looked at the horse, he thought it a great pity to put the leathern saddle upon it. "I will give him the good one," said he; "I am sure he deserves it." As he took up the golden saddle the groom awoke and cried out so loud, that all the guards ran in and took him prisoner, and in the morning he was again brought before the court to be judged, and was sentenced to die. But it was agreed, that, if he could bring thither the beautiful princess, he should live, and have the bird and the horse given him for his own.

Then he went his way again very sorrowful; but the old fox came and said, "Why did not you listen to me? If you had, you would have carried away both the bird and the horse; yet will I once more give you counsel. Go straight on, and in the evening you will arrive at a castle. At twelve o'clock at night the princess goes to the bathing-house: go up to her and give her a kiss, and she will let you lead her away; but take care you do not suffer her to go and take leave of her father and mother." Then the fox stretched out his tail, and so away they went over stock and stone till their hair whistled again.

As they came to the castle, all was as the fox had said, and at twelve o'clock the young man met the princess going to the, bath and gave her a kiss, and she agreed to run away with him, but begged with many tears that he would let her take leave of her father. At first he refused, but she wept still more and more, and fell at his feet, till at last he consented; but the moment she came to her father's house, the guards awoke and he was taken prisoner again.

Then he was brought before the king, and the king said, "You shall never have my daughter unless in eight days you dig away the hill that stops the view from my window." Now this hill was so big that the whole world could not take it away: and when he had worked for seven days, and had done very little, the fox came and said, "Lie down and go to sleep; I will work for you." And in the morning he awoke and the hill was gone; so he went merrily to the king, and told him that now that it was removed he must give him the princess.

Then the king was obliged to keep his word, and away went the young man and the princess; and the fox came and said to him, "We will have all three, the princess, the horse, and the bird." "Ah!" said the young man, "that would be a great thing, but how can you contrive it?"

"If you will only listen," said the fox, "it can soon be done. When you come to the king, and he asks for the beautiful princess, you must say, 'Here she is!' Then he will be very joyful; and you will mount the golden horse that they are to give you, and put out your hand to take leave of them; but shake hands with the princess last. Then lift her quickly on to the horse behind you; clap your spurs to his side, and gallop away as fast as you can."

All went right: then the fox said, "When you come to the castle where the bird is, I will stay with the princess at the door, and you will ride in and speak to the king; and when he sees that

it is the right horse, he will bring out the bird; but you must sit still, and say that you want to look at it, to see whether it is the true golden bird; and when you get it into your hand, ride away."

This, too, happened as the fox said; they carried off the bird, the princess mounted again, and they rode on to a great wood. Then the fox came, and said, "Pray kill me, and cut off my head and my feet." But the young man refused to do it: so the fox said, "I will at any rate give you good counsel: beware of two things; ransom no one from the gallows, and sit down by the side of no river." Then away he went. "Well," thought the young man, "it is no hard matter to keep that advice."

He rode on with the princess, till at last he came to the village where he had left his two brothers. And there he heard a great noise and uproar; and when he asked what was the matter, the people said, "Two men are going to be hanged." As he came nearer, he saw that the two men were his brothers, who had turned robbers; so he said, "Cannot they in any way be saved?" But the people said "No," unless he would bestow all his money upon the rascals and buy their liberty. Then he did not stay to think about the matter, but paid what was asked, and his brothers were given up, and went on with him towards their home.

And as they came to the wood where the fox first met them, it was so cool and pleasant that the two brothers said, "Let us sit down by the side of the river, and rest awhile, to eat and drink." So he said, "Yes," and forgot the fox's counsel, and sat down on the side of the river; and while he suspected nothing, they came behind, and threw him down the bank, and took the princess, the horse, and the bird, and went home to the king their master, and said, "All this have we won by our labour." Then there was great rejoicing made; but the horse would not eat, the bird would not sing, and the princess wept.

The youngest son fell to the bottom of the river's bed: luckily it was nearly dry, but his bones were almost broken, and the bank was so steep that he could find no way to get out. Then the old fox came once more, and scolded him for not following his advice; otherwise no evil would have befallen him: "Yet," said he, "I cannot leave you here, so lay hold of my tail and hold fast." Then he pulled him out of the river, and said to him, as he got upon the bank, "Your brothers have set watch to kill you, if they find you in the kingdom." So he dressed himself as a poor man, and came secretly to the king's court, and was scarcely within the doors when the horse began to eat, and the bird to sing, and the princess left off weeping. Then he went to the king, and told him all his brothers' roguery; and they were seized and punished, and he had the princess given to him again; and after the king's death he was heir to his kingdom.

A long while after, he went to walk one day in the wood, and the old fox met him, and besought him with tears in his eyes to kill him, and cut off his head and feet. And at last he did so, and in a moment the fox was changed into a man, and turned out to be the brother of the princess, who had been lost a great many many years.

The Fisherman and His Wife

THERE was once a fisherman who lived with his wife in a ditch, close by the sea-side. The fisherman used to go out all day long a-fishing; and one day, as he sat on the shore with his rod, looking at the shining water and watching his line, all on a sudden his float was dragged away deep under the sea: and in drawing it up he pulled a great fish out of the water. The fish said to him, "Pray let me live: I am not a real fish, I am an enchanted prince, put me in the water again, and let me go." "Oh!" said the man, "you need not make so many words about the matter; I wish to have nothing to do with a fish that can talk; so swim away as soon as you please." Then he put him back into the water, and the fish darted straight down to the bottom, and left a long streak of blood behind him.

When the fisherman went home to his wife in the ditch, he told her how he had caught a great fish, and how it had told him it was an enchanted prince, and that on hearing it speak he had let it go again. "Did you not ask it for anything?" said the wife. "No," said the man, "what should I ask for?" "Ah!" said the wife, "we live very wretchedly here in this nasty stinking ditch; do go back, and tell the fish we want a little cottage."

The fisherman did not much like the business: however, he went to the sea, and when he came there the water looked all yellow and green. And he stood at the water's edge, and said,

"O man of the sea!
Come listen to me,
For Alice my wife,
The plague of my life,
Hath sent me to beg a boon of thee!"

Then the fish came swimming to him, and said, "Well, what does she want?" "Ah!" answered the fisherman, "my wife says that when I had caught you, I ought to have asked you for something before I let you go again; she does not like living any longer in the ditch, and wants a little cottage." "Go home, then," said the fish, "she is in the cottage already." So the man went home, and saw his wife standing at the door of a cottage. "Come in, come in," said she; "is not this much better than the ditch?" And there was a parlour, and a bed-chamber, and a kitchen; and behind the cottage there was a little garden with all sorts of flowers and fruits, and a courtyard full of ducks and chickens. "Ah!" said the fisherman, "how happily we shall live!" "We will try to do so at least," said his wife.

Everything went right for a week or two, and then Dame Alice said, "Husband, there is not room enough in this cottage, the courtyard and garden are a great deal too small; I should like to have a large stone castle to live in; so go to the fish again, and tell him to give us a castle." "Wife," said the fisherman, "I don't like to go to him again, for perhaps he will be angry; we ought to be content with the cottage." "Nonsense!" said the wife; "he will do it very willingly; go along and try."

The fisherman went; but his heart was very heavy; and when he came to the sea it looked blue and gloomy, though it was quite calm, and he went close to it, and said,

"O man of the sea!
Come listen to me,
For Alice my wife,
The plague of my life,
Hath sent me to beg a boon of thee!"

"Well, what does she want now?" said the fish. "Ah!" said the man very sorrowfully, "my wife wants to live in a stone castle." "Go home then," said the fish, "she is standing at the door of it already." So away went the fisherman, and found his wife standing before a great castle. "See," said she, "is not this grand?" With that they went into the castle together, and found a great many servants there, and the rooms all richly furnished and full of golden chairs and tables; and behind the castle was a garden, and a wood half a mile long, full of sheep, and goats, and hares, and deer; and in the courtyard were stables and cow-houses. "Well!" said the man, "now will we live contented and happy in this beautiful castle for the rest of our lives." "Perhaps we may," said the wife; "but let us consider and sleep upon it before we make up our minds:" so they went to bed.

The next morning, when Dame Alice awoke, it was broad daylight, and she jogged the fisherman with her elbow, and said, "Get up, husband, and bestir yourself, for we must be king of all the land." "Wife, wife," said the man, "why should we wish to be king? I will not be king." "Then I will," said Alice. "But, wife," answered the fisherman, "how can you be king? the fish cannot make you a king." "Husband," said she, "say no more about it, but go and try; I will be king!" So the man went away, quite sorrowful to think that his wife should want to be king. The sea looked a dark-grey colour, and was covered with foam as he cried out,

"O man of the sea!
Come listen to me,
For Alice my wife,
The plague of my life,
Hath sent me to beg a boon of thee!"

"Well, what would she have now?" said the fish. "Alas!" said the man, "my wife wants to be king." "Go home," said the fish; "she is king already."

Then the fisherman went home; and as he came close to the palace, he saw a troop of soldiers, and heard the sound of drums and trumpets; and when he entered in, he saw his wife sitting on a high throne of gold and diamonds, with a golden crown upon her head; and on each side of her stood six beautiful maidens, each a head taller than the other. "Well, wife," said the fisher-man, "are you king?" "Yes," said she, "I am king." And when he had looked at her for a long time, he said, "Ah, wife! what a fine thing it is to be king! now we shall never have anything more to wish for." "I don't know how that may be," said she; "never is a long time. I am king, 'tis true, but I begin to be tired of it, and I think I should like to be emperor." "Alas, wife! why should you wish to be emperor?" said the fisherman. "Husband," said she, "go to the fish; I say I will be emperor." "Ah, wife!" replied the fisherman, "the fish cannot make an emperor, and I should not like to ask for such a thing." "I am king," said Alice, "and you are my slave, so go directly!" So the fisherman was obliged to go; and he muttered as he went along, "This will come to no good, it is too much to ask, the fish will be tired at last, and then we shall repent of what we have done." He soon arrived at the sea, and the water was quite black and muddy, and a mighty whirlwind, blew over it; but he went to the shore, and said,

> "O man of the sea!
> Come listen to me,
> For Alice my wife,
> The plague of my life,
> Hath sent me to beg a boon of thee!"

"What would she have now?" said the fish. "Ah!" said the fisherman, "she wants to be emperor." "Go home," said the fish; "she is emperor already."

So he went home again; and as he came near he saw his wife sitting on a very lofty throne made of solid gold, with a great crown on her head full two yards high, and on each side of her stood her guards and attendants in a row, each one smaller than the other, from the tallest giant down to a little dwarf no bigger than my finger. And before her stood princes and dukes, and earls: and the fisherman went up to her and said, "Wife, are you emperor?" "Yes," said she, "I am emperor." "Ah!" said the man as he gazed upon her, "what a fine thing it is to be emperor!" "Husband," said she, "why should we stay at being emperor? I will be pope next." "O wife, wife!" said he, "how can you be pope? there is but one pope at a time in Christendom." "Husband," said she, "I will be pope this very day." "But," replied the husband, "the fish cannot make you pope." "What nonsense!" said she, "if he can make an emperor, he can make a pope, go and try him." So the fisherman went. But when he came to the shore the wind was raging, and the sea was tossed up and down like boiling water, and the ships were in the greatest distress and danced upon the waves most fearfully; in the middle of the sky there was a little blue, but towards the south it was all red as if a dreadful storm was rising. At this the fisherman was terribly frightened, and trembled, so that his knees knocked together: but he went to the shore and said,

> "O man of the sea!
> Come listen to me,
> For Alice my wife,
> The plague of my life,
> Hath sent me to beg a boon of thee!"

"What does she want now?" said the fish. "Ah!" said the fisherman, "my wife wants to be pope." "Go home," said the fish, "she is pope already."

Then the fisherman went home, and found his wife sitting on a throne that was two miles high; and she had three great crowns on her head, and around stood all the pomp and power of the Church; and on each side were two rows of burning lights, of all sizes, the greatest as large as the highest and biggest tower in the world, and the least no larger than a small rushlight. "Wife," said the fisherman as he looked at all this grandeur, "are you pope?" "Yes," said she, "I am pope." "Well, wife," replied he, "it is a grand thing to be pope; and now you must be content, for you can be nothing greater." "I will consider of that," said the wife. Then they went to bed: but Dame Alice could not sleep all night for thinking what she should be next. At last morning cane, and the sun rose. "Ha!" thought she as she looked at it through the window, "cannot I prevent the sun rising?" At this she was very angry, and she wakened her husband, and said, "Husband, go to the fish and tell him I want to be lord of the sun and moon." The fisherman was half asleep, but the thought frightened him so much, that he started and fell out of bed. "Alas, wife!" said he, "cannot you be content to be pope?" "No," said she, "I am very uneasy, and cannot bear to see the sun and moon rise without my leave. Go to the fish directly."

Then the man went trembling for fear; and as he was going down to the shore a dreadful storm arose, so that the trees and the rocks shook; and the heavens became black, and the lightning played, and the thunder rolled; and you might have seen in the sea great black waves like mountains with a white crown of foam upon them, and the fisherman said,

"O man of the sea!
Come listen to me,
For Alice my wife,
The plague of my life,
Hath sent me to beg a boon of thee!"

"What does she want now?" said the fish. "Ah!" said he, "she wants to be lord of the sun and moon." "Go home," said the fish, "to your ditch again!" And there they live to this very day.

The Tom-tit and the Bear

ONE summer day, as the wolf and the bear were walking together in a wood, they heard a bird singing most delightfully. "Brother," said the bear, "what can that bird be that is singing so sweetly?" "O!" said the wolf, "that is his majesty the king of the birds, we must take care to show him all possible respect." (Now I should tell you that this bird was after all no other than the tom-tit.) "If that is the case," said the bear, "I should like to see the royal palace; so pray come along and show it to me." "Gently, my friend," said the wolf, "we cannot see it just yet, we must wait till the queen comes home."

Soon afterwards the queen came with food in her beak, and she and the king began to feed their young ones. "Now for it!" said the bear; and was about to follow them, to see what was to be seen. "Stop a little, master Bruin," said the wolf, "we must wait now till their majesties are gone again." So they marked the hole where they had seen the nest, and went away. But the bear, being very eager to see the royal palace, soon came back again, and peeping into the nest, saw five or six young birds lying at the bottom of it. "What nonsense!" said Bruin, "this is not a royal palace: I never saw such a filthy place in my life; and you are no royal children, you little base-born brats!" As soon as the young tom-tits heard this they were very angry, and screamed out "We are not base-born, you stupid bear! our father and mother are honest good sort of people: and depend upon it you shall suffer for your insolence!" At this the wolf and the bear grew frightened, and ran away to their dens. But the young tom-tits kept crying and screaming; and when their father and mother came home and offered them food, they all said, "We will not touch a bit; no, not the leg of a fly, though we should die of hunger, till that rascal Bruin has been punished for calling us base-born brats." "Make yourselves easy, my darlings," said the old king, "you may be sure he shall meet with his deserts."

So he went out and stood before the bear's den, and cried out with a loud voice, "Bruin the bear! thou hast shamefully insulted our lawful children: we therefore hereby declare bloody and cruel war against thee and thine, which shall never cease until thou hast been punished as thou so richly deservest." Now when the bear heard this, he called together the ox, the ass, the stag, and all the beasts of the earth, in order to consult about the means of his defence. And the tom-tit also enlisted on his side all the birds of the air, both great and small, and a very large army of hornets, gnats, bees, and flies, and other insects.

As the time approached when the war was to begin, the tom-tit sent out spies to see who was the commander-in-chief of the enemy's forces; and the gnat, who was by far the cleverest spy of them all, flew backwards and forwards in the wood where the enemy's troops were, and at last hid himself under a leaf on a tree, close by which the orders of the day were given out. And the bear, who was standing so near the tree that the gnat could hear all he said, called to the fox and said, "Reynard, you are the cleverest of all the beasts; therefore you shall be our general and lead us to battle: but we must first agree upon some signal, by which we may know what you want us to do." "Behold," said the fox, "I have a fine, long, bushy tail, which is very like a plume of red feathers, and gives me a very warlike air: now remember, when you see me raise up my tail, you may be sure that the battle is won, and you have then nothing to do but to rush down upon the enemy with all your force. On the other hand, if I drop my tail, the day is lost, and you must run away as fast as you can." Now when the gnat had heard all this, she flew back to the tom-tit and told him everything that had passed.

At length the day came when the battle was to be fought; and as soon as it was light, behold! the army of beasts came rushing forward with such a fearful sound that the earth shook. And his majesty the tom-tit, with his troops, came flying along in warlike array, flapping and fluttering, and beating the air, so that it was quite frightful to hear; and both armies set themselves in order of battle upon the field. Now the tom-tit gave orders to a troop of hornets that at the first onset they should march straight towards Captain Reynard, and fixing themselves about his tail, should sting him with all their might and main. The hornets did as they were told: and when Reynard felt the first sting, he started aside and shook one of his legs, but still held up his tail with wonderful bravery; at the second sting he was forced to drop his tail for a moment; but when the third hornet had fixed itself, he could bear it no longer, but clapped his tail between his legs and scampered away as fast as he could. As soon as the beasts saw this, they thought of course all was lost, and scoured across the country in the greatest dismay, leaving the birds masters of the field.

And now the king and queen flew back in triumph to their children, and said, "Now, children, eat, drink, and be merry, for the victory is ours!" But the young birds said, "No: not till Bruin has humbly begged our pardon for calling us base-born." So the king flew back to the bear's den, and cried out, "Thou villain bear! come forthwith to my abode, and humbly beseech my children to forgive thee the insult thou hast offered them; for, if thou wilt not do this, every bone in thy wretched body shall be broken to pieces." So the bear was forced to crawl out of his den very sulkily, and do what the king bade him: and after that the young birds sat down together, and ate and drank and made merry till midnight.

The Twelve Dancing Princesses

THERE was a king who had twelve beautiful daughters. They slept in twelve beds all in one room; and when they went to bed, the doors were shut and locked up; but every morning their shoes were found to be quite worn through, as if they had been danced in all night; and yet nobody could find out how it happened, or where they had been.

Then the king made it known to all the land, that if any person could discover the secret, and find out where it was that the princesses danced in the night, he should have the one he liked best for his wife, and should be king after his death; but whoever tried and did not succeed, after three days and nights, should be put to death.

A king's son soon came. He was well entertained, and in the evening was taken to the chamber next to the one where the princesses lay in their twelve beds. There he was to sit and watch where they went to dance; and, in order that nothing might pass without his hearing it, the door of his chamber was left open. But the king's son soon fell asleep; and when he awoke in the morning he found that the princesses had all been dancing, for the soles of their shoes were full of holes. The same thing happened the second and third night: so the king ordered his head to be cut off. After him came several others; but they had all the same luck, and all lost their lives in the same manner.

Now it chanced that an old soldier, who had been wounded in battle, and could fight no longer, passed through the country where this king reigned: and as he was travelling through a wood, he met an old woman, who asked him where he was going. "I hardly know where I am going, or what I had better do," said the soldier; "but I think I should like very well to find out where it is that the princesses dance, and then in time I might be a king." "Well," said the old dame, "that is no very hard task: only take care not to drink any of the wine which one of the princesses will bring to you in the evening; and as soon as she leaves you pretend to be fast asleep."

Then she gave him a cloak, and said, "As soon as you put that on you will become invisible, and you will then be able to follow the princesses wherever they go." When the soldier heard all this good counsel, he determined to try his luck: so he went to the king, and said he was willing to undertake the task.

He was as well received as the others had been, and the king ordered fine royal robes to be given him; and when the evening came he was led to the outer chamber. Just as he was going to lie down, the eldest of the princesses brought him a cup of wine; but the soldier threw it all away secretly, taking care not to drink a drop. Then he laid himself down on his bed, and in a little while began to snore very loud as if he was fast asleep. When the twelve princesses heard this they laughed heartily; and the eldest said, "This fellow too might have done a wiser thing than lose his life in this way!" Then they rose up and opened their drawers and boxes, and took out all their fine clothes, and dressed themselves at the glass, and skipped about as if they were eager to begin dancing.

But the youngest said, "I don't know how it is, while you are so happy I feel very uneasy; I am sure some mischance will befall us." "You simpleton," said the eldest, "you are always afraid; have you forgotten how many kings' sons have already watched us in vain? And as for this soldier, even if I had not given him his sleeping draught, he would have slept soundly enough."

When they were all ready, they went and looked at the soldier; but he snored on, and did not stir hand or foot: so they thought they were quite safe; and the eldest went up to her own bed and clapped her hands, and the bed sunk into the floor and a trap-door flew open. The soldier saw them going down through the trap-door one after another, the eldest leading the way; and thinking he had no time to lose, he jumped up, put on the cloak which the old woman had given him, and followed them; but in the middle of the stairs he trod on the gown of the youngest princess, and she cried out to her sisters, "All is not right; someone took hold of my gown." "You silly creature!" said the eldest, "it is nothing but a nail in the wall." Then down they all went, and at the bottom they found themselves in a most delightful grove of trees; and the leaves were all of silver, and glittered and sparkled beautifully. The soldier wished to take away some token of the place; so he broke off a little branch, and there came a loud noise from the tree. Then the youngest daughter said again, "I am sure all is not right – did not you hear that noise? That never happened before." But the eldest said, "It is only our princes, who are shouting for joy at our approach."

Then they came to another grove of trees, where all the leaves were of gold; and afterwards to a third, where the leaves were all glittering diamonds. And the soldier broke a branch from each; and every time there was a loud noise, which made the youngest sister tremble with fear; but the eldest still said, It was only the princes, who were crying for joy. So they went on till they came to a great lake; and at the side of the lake there lay twelve little boats with twelve handsome princes in them, who seemed to be waiting there for the princesses.

One of the princesses went into each boat, and the soldier stepped into the same boat with the youngest. As they were rowing over the lake, the prince who was in the boat with the youngest princess and the soldier said, "I do not know why it, is, but though I am rowing with all my might we do not get on so fast as usual, and I am quite tired: the boat seems very heavy today." "It is only the heat of the weather," said the princess; "I feel it very warm too."

On the other side of the lake stood a fine illuminated castle, from which came the merry music of horns and trumpets. There they all landed, and went into the castle, and each prince danced with his princess; and the soldier, who was all the time invisible, danced with them too; and when any of the princesses had a cup of wine set by her, he drank it all up, so that when she put the cup to her mouth it was empty, At this, too, the youngest sister was terribly frightened, but the eldest always silenced her. They danced on till three o'clock in the morning, and then all their shoes were worn out, so that they were obliged to leave off. The princes rowed them back again over the lake (but this time the soldier placed himself in the boat with the eldest princess); and on the opposite shore they took leave of each other, the princesses promising to come again the next night.

When they came to the stairs, the soldier ran on before the

princesses, and laid himself down; and as the twelve sisters slowly came up very much tired, they heard him snoring in his bed; so they said, "Now all is quite safe;" then they undressed themselves, put away their fine clothes, pulled off their shoes, and went to bed. In the morning the soldier said nothing about what had happened, but determined to see more of this strange adventure, and went again the second and third night; and every thing happened just as before; the princesses danced each time till their shoes were worn to pieces, and then returned home. However, on the third night the soldier carried away one of the golden cups as a token of where he had been.

As soon as the time came when he was to declare the secret, he was taken before the king with the three branches and the golden cup; and the twelve princesses stood listening behind the door to hear what he would say. And when the king asked him "Where do my twelve daughters dance at night?" he answered, "With twelve princes in a castle under ground." And then he told the king all that had happened, and showed him the three branches and the golden cup which he had brought with him. Then the king called for the princesses, and asked them whether what the soldier said was true: and when they saw that they were discovered, and that it was of no use to deny what had happened, they confessed it all. And the king asked the soldier which of them be would choose for his wife; and he answered, "I am not very young, so I will have the eldest." – And they were married that very day, and the soldier was chosen to be the king's heir.

Rose-bud

ONCE upon a time there lived a king and queen, who had no children; and this they lamented very much. But one day as the queen was walking by the side of the river, a little fish lifted its head out of the water, and said, "Your wish shall be fulfilled, and you shall soon have a daughter." What the little fish had foretold soon came to pass; and the queen had a little girl that was so very beautiful that the king could not cease looking on it for joy, and determined to hold a great feast. So he invited not only his relations, friends, and neighbours, but also all the fairies, that they might be kind and good to his little daughter. Now there were thirteen fairies in his kingdom, and he had only twelve golden dishes for them to eat out of, so that he was obliged to leave one of the fairies without an invitation. The rest came, and after the feast was over they gave all their best gifts to the little princess: one gave her virtue, another beauty, another riches, and so on till she had all that was excellent in the world. When eleven had done blessing her, the thirteenth, who had not been invited, and was very angry on that account, came in, and determined to take her revenge. So she cried out, "The king's daughter shall in her fifteenth year be wounded by a spindle, and fall down dead." Then the twelfth, who had not yet given her gift, came forward and said, that the bad wish must be fulfilled, but that she could soften it, and that the king's daughter should not die, but fall asleep for a hundred years.

But the king hoped to save his dear child from the threatened evil, and ordered that all the spindles in the kingdom should be bought up and destroyed. All the fairies' gifts were in the mean time fulfilled; for the princess was so beautiful, and well-behaved, and amiable, and wise, that every one who knew her loved her. Now it happened that on the very day she was fifteen years old the king and queen were not at home, and she was left alone in the palace. So she roved about by herself, and looked at all the rooms and chambers, till at last she came to an old tower, to which there was a narrow staircase ending with a little door. In the door there was a golden key, and when she turned it the door sprang open, and there sat an old lady spinning away very busily. "Why, how now, good mother," said the princess, "what are you doing there?" "Spinning," said the old lady, and nodded her head. "How prettily that little thing turns round!" said the princess, and took the spindle and began to spin. But scarcely had she touched it before the prophecy was fulfilled, and she fell down lifeless on the ground.

However, she was not dead, but had only fallen into a deep sleep; and the king and the queen, who just then came home, and all their court, fell asleep too; and the horses slept in the stables, and the dogs in the court, the pigeons on the housetop, and the flies on the walls. Even the fire on the hearth left off blazing, and went to sleep; and the meat that was roasting stood still; and the cook, who was at that moment pulling the kitchen-boy by the hair to give him a box on the ear for something he had done amiss, let him go, and both fell asleep; and so every thing stood still, and slept soundly.

A large hedge of thorns soon grew round the palace, and every year it became higher and thicker, till at last the whole palace was surrounded and hid, so that not even the roof or the chimneys could be seen. But there went a report through all the land of the beautiful sleeping Rose-Bud (for so was the king's daughter called); so that from time to time several kings' sons came, and tried to break through the thicket into the palace. This they could never do; for the thorns and bushes laid hold of them as it were with hands, and there they stuck fast and died miserably.

After many many years there came a king's son into that land, and an old man told him the story of the thicket of thorns, and how a beautiful palace stood behind it, in which was a wondrous princess, called Rose-Bud, asleep with all her court. He told too, how he had heard from his grandfather that many many princes had come, and had tried to break through the thicket, but had stuck fast and died. Then the young prince said, "All this shall not frighten me, I will go and see Rose-Bud." The old man tried to dissuade him, but he persisted in going.

Now that very day were the hundred years completed; and as the prince came to the thicket he saw nothing but beautiful flowering shrubs, through which he passed with ease, and they closed after him as firm as ever. Then he came at last to the palace, and there in the court lay the dogs asleep, and the horses in the stables, and on the roof sat the pigeons fast asleep with their heads under their wings; and when he came into the palace, the flies slept on the walls, and the cook in the kitchen was still holding up her hand as if she would beat the boy, and the maid sat with a black fowl in her hand ready to be plucked.

Then he went on still further, and all was so still that he could hear every breath he drew; till at last he came to the old tower and opened the door of the little room in which Rose-Bud was, and there she lay fast asleep, and looked so beautiful that he could not take his eyes off, and he stooped down and gave her a kiss. But the moment he kissed her she opened her eyes and awoke, and smiled upon him. Then they went out together, and presently the king and queen also awoke, and all the court, and they gazed on each other with great wonder. And the horses got up and shook themselves, and the dogs jumped about and barked; the pigeons took their heads from under their wings, and looked about and flew into the fields; the flies on the walls buzzed away; the fire in the kitchen blazed up and cooked the dinner, and the roast meat turned round again; the cook gave the boy the box on his ear so that he cried out, and the maid went on plucking the fowl. And then was the wedding of the prince and Rose-Bud celebrated, and they lived happily together all their lives long.

Tom Thumb

THERE was once a poor woodman sitting by the fire in his cottage, and his wife sat by his side spinning. "How lonely it is," said he, "for you and me to sit here by ourselves without any children to play about and amuse us, while other people seem so happy and merry with their children!" "What you say is very true," said the wife, sighing and turning round her wheel; "how happy should I be if I had but one child! and if it were ever so small, nay, if it were no bigger than my thumb, I should be very happy, and love it dearly." Now it came to pass that this good woman's wish was fulfilled just as she desired; for, some time afterwards, she had a little boy who was quite healthy and strong, but not much bigger than my thumb. So they said, "Well, we cannot say we have not got what we wished for, and, little as he is, we will love him dearly," and they called him Tom Thumb.

They gave him plenty of food, yet he never grew bigger, but remained just the same size as when he was born; still his eyes were sharp and sparkling, and he soon showed himself to be a clever little fellow, who always knew well what he was about. One day, as the woodman was getting ready to go into the wood to cut fuel, he said, "I wish I had someone to bring the cart after me, for I want to make haste." "O father!" cried Tom, "I will take care of that; the cart shall lie in the wood by the time you want it." Then the woodman laughed, and said, "How can that be? you cannot reach up to the horse's bridle." "Never mind that, father," said Tom: "if my mother will only harness the horse, I will get into his ear, and tell him which way to go." "Well," said the father, "we will try for once."

When the time came, the mother harnessed the horse to the cart, and put Tom into his ear; and as he sat there, the little man told the beast how to go, crying out, "Go on," and "Stop," as he wanted; so the horse went on just as if the woodman had driven it himself into the wood. It happened that, as the horse was going a little too fast, and Tom was calling out "Gently! gently!" two strangers came up. "What an odd thing that is!" said one, "there is a cart going along, and I hear a carter talking to the horse, but can see no one." "That is strange," said the other; "let us follow the cart and see where it goes." So they went on into the wood, till at last they came to the place where the woodman was. Then Tom Thumb, seeing his father, cried out, "See, here, here I am, with the cart, all right and safe; now take me down." So his father took hold of the horse with one hand, and with the other took his son out of the ear; then he put him down upon a straw, where he sat as merry as you please. The two strangers were all this time looking on, and did not know what to say for wonder. At last one took the other aside and said, "That little urchin will make our fortune if we can get him, and carry him about from town to town as a show: we must buy him." So they went to the woodman and asked him what he would take for the little man: "He will be better off," said they, "with us than with you." "I won't sell him at all," said the father, "my own flesh and blood is dearer to me than all the silver and gold in the world." But Tom, hearing of the bargain they wanted to make, crept up his father's coat to his shoulder, and whispered in his ear, "Take the money, father, and let them have me, I'll soon come back to you."

So the woodman at last agreed to sell Tom to the strangers for a large piece of gold. "Where do you like to sit?" said one of them. "Oh! put me on the rim of your hat, that will be a nice gallery for me; I can walk about there, and see the country as we go along." So they did as he wished; and when Tom had taken leave of his father, they took him away with them. They journeyed on till it began to be dusky, and then the little man said, "Let me get down, I'm tired." So the man took off his hat and set him down on a clod of earth in a ploughed field by the side of the road. But Tom ran about amongst the furrows, and at last slipt into an old mouse-hole. "Good night, masters," said he, "I'm off! mind and look sharp after me the next time." They ran directly to the place, and poked the ends of the sticks into the mouse-hole, but all in vain; Tom only crawled further and further in, and at last it became quite dark, so that they were obliged to go their way without their prize, as sulky as you please.

When Tom found they were gone, he came out of his hiding-place. "What dangerous walking it is," said he, "in this ploughed field! If I were to fall from one of these great clods, I should certainly break my neck." At last, by good luck, he found a large empty snail-shell. "This is lucky," said he, "I can sleep here very well," and in he crept. Just as he was falling asleep he heard two men passing, and one said to the other, "How shall we manage to steal that rich parson's silver and gold?" "I'll tell you," cried Tom.

"What noise was that?" said the thief, frightened, "I am sure I heard someone speak." They stood still listening, and Tom said, "Take me with you, and I'll soon show you how to get the parson's money." "But where are you?" said they. "Look about on the ground," answered he, "and listen where the sound comes from." At last the thieves found him out, and lifted him up in their hands. "You little urchin!" said they, "what can you do for us?" "Why I can get between the iron window-bars of the parson's house, and throw you out whatever you want." "That's a good thought," said the thieves, "come along, we shall see what you can do."

When they came to the parson's house, Tom slipt through the window-bars into the room, and then called out as loud as he could bawl, "Will you have all that is here?" At this the thieves were frightened, and said, "Softly, softly! Speak low, that you may not awaken anybody." But Tom pretended not to understand them, and bawled out again, "How much will you have? Shall I throw it all out?" Now the cook lay in the next room, and hearing a noise she raised herself in her bed and listened. Meantime the thieves were frightened, and ran off to a little distance; but at last they plucked up courage, and said, "The little urchin is only trying to make fools of us." So they came back and whispered softly to him, saying, "Now let us have no more of your jokes, but throw out some of the money." Then Tom called out as loud as he could, "Very well: hold your hands, here it comes." The cook heard this quite plain, so she sprang out of bed and ran to open the door. The thieves ran off as if a wolf was at their tails; and the maid, having groped about and found nothing, went away for a light. By the time she returned, Tom had slipt off into the barn; and when the cook had looked about and searched every hole and corner, and found nobody, she went to bed, thinking she must have been dreaming with her eyes open. The little man crawled about in the hay-loft, and at last found a glorious place to finish his night's rest in; so he laid himself down, meaning to sleep till daylight, and then find his way home to his father and mother. But, alas! how cruelly was he disappointed! what crosses and sorrows happen in this world! The cook got up early before day-break to feed the cows: she went straight to the hay-loft, and carried away a large bundle of hay with the little man in the middle of it fast asleep. He still, however, slept on, and did not awake till he found himself in the mouth of the cow, who had taken him up with a mouthful of hay: "Good lack-a-day!" said he, "how did I manage to tumble into the mill?" But he soon found out where he really was, and was obliged to have all his wits about him in order that he might not get between the cow's teeth, and so be crushed to death. At last down he went into her stomach. "It is rather dark here," said he; "they forgot to build windows in this room to let the sun in: a candle would be no bad thing."

Though he made the best of his bad luck, he did not like his quarters at all; and the worst of it was, that more and more hay was always coming down, and the space in which he was became smaller and smaller. At last he cried out as loud as he could, "Don't bring me any more hay! Don't bring me any more hay!" The maid happened to be just then milking the cow, and hearing someone speak and seeing nobody, and yet being quite sure it was the same voice that she had heard in the night, she was so frightened that she fell off her stool and overset the milk-pail. She ran off as fast as she could to her master the parson, and said, "Sir, sir, the cow is talking!"

But the parson, said, "Woman, thou art surely mad!" However, he went with her into the cow-house to see what was the matter. Scarcely had they set their foot on the threshold when Tom called out, "Don't bring me anymore hay!" Then the parson himself was frightened; and thinking the cow was surely bewitched, ordered that she should be killed directly. So the cow was killed, and the stomach, in which Tom lay, was thrown out upon a dunghill.

Tom soon set himself to work to get out, which was not a very easy task; but at last, just as he had made room to get his head out, a new misfortune befell him: a hungry wolf sprung out, and swallowed the whole stomach, with Tom in it, at a single gulp, and ran away. Tom, however, was not disheartened; and thinking the wolf would not dislike having some chat with him as he was going along, he called out, "My good friend, I can show you a famous treat." "Where's that?" said the wolf. "In such and such a house," said Tom, describing his father's house, "you can crawl through the drain into the kitchen, and there you will find cakes, ham, beef, and every thing your heart can desire." The wolf did not want to be asked twice; so that very night he went to the house and crawled through the drain into the kitchen, and ate and drank there to his heart's content. As soon as he was satisfied, he wanted to get away; but he had eaten so much that he could not get out the same way that he came in. This was just what Tom had reckoned upon; and he now began to get up a great shout, making all the noise he could. "Will you be quiet?" said the wolf: "you'll awaken everybody in the house." "What's that to me?" said the little man: "you have had your frolic, now I've a mind to be merry myself;" and he began again singing and shouting as loud as he could.

The woodman and his wife, being awakened by the noise, peeped through a crack in the door; but when they saw that the wolf was there, you may well suppose that they were terribly frightened; and the woodman ran for his axe, and gave his wife a scythe. – "Now do you stay behind," said the woodman; "and when I have knocked him on the head, do you rip up his belly for him with the scythe." Tom heard all this, and said, "Father, father! I am here, the wolf has swallowed me:" and his father said, "Heaven be praised! we have found our dear child again;" and he told his wife not to use the scythe, for fear she should hurt him. Then he aimed a great blow, and struck the wolf on the head, and killed him on the spot; and when he was dead they cut open his body and set Tommy free. "Ah!" said the father, "what fears we have had for you!" "Yes, father," answered he, "I have travelled all over the world, since we parted, one way or other; and now I am very glad to get fresh air again." "Why, where have you been?" said his father. "I have been in a mouse-hole, in a snail-shell, down a cow's throat, and in the wolf's belly; and yet here I am again safe and sound." "Well," said they, "we will not sell you again for all the riches in the world." So they hugged and kissed their dear little son, and gave him plenty to eat and drink, and fetched new clothes for him, for his old ones were quite spoiled on his journey.

The Grateful Beasts

A CERTAIN man, who had lost almost all his money, resolved to set off with the little that was left him, and travel into the wide world. Then the first place he came to was a village, where the young people were running about arguing and shouting. "What is the matter?" asked he. "See here," answered they, "we have got a mouse that we make dance to please us. Do look at him: what a droll sight it is! how he jumps about!" But the man pitied the poor little thing, and said, "Let the mouse go, and I will give you money." So he gave them some, and took the mouse and let him run; and he soon jumped into a hole that was close by, and was out of their reach.

Then he travelled on and came to another village, and there the children had got an ass that they made stand on its hind legs and tumble, at which they laughed and shouted, and gave the poor beast no rest. So the good man gave them also some money to let the poor ass alone.

At the next village he came to, the young people had got a bear that had been taught to dance, and they were plaguing the poor thing sadly. Then he gave them too some money to let the beast go, and the bear was very glad to get on his four feet, and seemed quite happy.

But the man had now given away all the money he had in the world, and had not a shilling in his pocket. Then said he to himself, "The king has heaps of gold in his treasury that he never uses; I cannot die of hunger, I hope I shall be forgiven if I borrow a little, and when I get rich again. I will repay it all."

Then he managed to get into the treasury, and took a very little money; but as he came out the king's guards saw him, so they said he was a thief, and took him to the judge, and he was sentenced to be thrown into the water in a box. The lid of the box was full of holes to let in air, and a jug of water and a loaf of bread were given him.

Whilst he was swimming along in the water very sorrowfully, he heard something nibbling and biting at the lock; and all of a sudden it fell off, the lid flew open, and there stood his old friend the little mouse, who had done him this service. And then came the ass and the bear, and pulled the box ashore; and all helped him, because he had been kind to them.

But now they did not know what to do next, and began to consult together; when on a sudden a wave threw on the shore a beautiful white stone that looked like an egg. Then the bear said, "That's a lucky thing: this is the wonderful stone, and whoever has it may have every thing else that he wishes." So the man went and picked up the stone, and wished for a palace and a garden, and a stud of horses; and his wish was fulfilled as soon as he had made it. And there he lived in his castle and garden, with fine stables and horses; and all was so grand and beautiful, that he never could wonder and gaze at it enough.

After some time, some merchants passed by that way. "See," said they, "what a princely palace! The last time we were here, it was nothing but a desert waste." They were very curious to know how all this had happened; so they went in and asked the master of the palace how it had been so quickly raised. "I have done nothing myself," answered he, "it is the wonderful stone that did all." – "What a strange stone that must be!" said they: then he invited them in and showed it to them. They asked him whether he would sell it, and offered him all their goods for it; and the goods seemed so fine and costly, that he quite forgot that the stone would bring him in a moment a thousand better and richer things, and he agreed to make the bargain.

Scarcely was the stone, however, out of his hands before all his riches were gone, and he found himself sitting in his box in the water, with his jug of water and loaf of bread by his side. The grateful beasts, the mouse, the ass, and the bear, came directly to help him; but the mouse found she could not nibble off the lock this time, for it was a great deal stronger than before. Then the bear said, "We must find the wonderful stone again, or all our endeavours will be fruitless."

The merchants, meantime, had taken up their abode in the palace; so away went the three friends, and when they came near, the bear said, "Mouse, go in and look through the keyhole and see where the stone is kept: you are small, nobody will see you." The mouse did as she was told, but soon came back and said, "Bad news! I have looked in, and the stone hangs under the looking-glass by a red silk string, and on each side of it sits a great cat with fiery eyes to watch it."

Then the others took council together and said, "Go back again, and wait till the master of the palace is in bed asleep, then nip his nose and pull his hair." Away went the mouse, and did as they directed her; and the master jumped up very angry, and rubbed his nose, and cried, "Those rascally cats are good for nothing at all, they let the mice eat my very nose and pull the hair off my head." Then he hunted them out of the room; and so the mouse had the best of the game.

Next night as soon as the master was asleep, the mouse crept in again, and nibbled at the red silken string to which the stone hung, till down it dropped, and she rolled it along to the door; but when it got there, the poor little mouse was quite tired; so she said to the ass, "Put in your foot, and lift it over the threshold." This was soon done: and they took up the stone, and set off for the water-side. Then the ass said, "How shall we reach the box?" But the bear answered, "That is easily managed; I can swim very well, and do you, donkey, put your fore feet over my shoulders; – mind and hold fast, and take the stone in your mouth: as for you, mouse, you can sit in my ear."

It was all settled thus, and away they swam. After a time, the bear began to brag and boast: "We are brave fellows, are not we, ass?" said he; "what do you think?" But the ass held his tongue, and said not a word. "Why don't you answer me?" said the bear, "you must be an ill-mannered brute not to speak when you're spoken to." When the ass heard this, he could hold no longer; so he opened his mouth, and dropped the wonderful stone. "I could not speak," said he; "did not you know I had the stone in my mouth? now 'tis lost, and that's your fault." "Do but hold your tongue and be quiet," said the bear; "and let us think what's to be done."

Then a council was held: and at last they called together all the frogs, their wives and families, relations and friends, and said: "A great enemy is coming to eat you all up; but never mind, bring us up plenty of stones, and we'll build a strong wall to guard you." The frogs hearing this were dreadfully frightened, and set to work, bringing up all the stones they could find. At last came a large fat frog pulling along the wonderful stone by the silken string: and when the bear saw it, he jumped for joy, and said, "Now we have found what we wanted." So he released the old frog from his load, and told him to tell his friends they might go about their business as soon as they pleased.

Then the three friends swam off again for the box; and the lid flew open, and they found that they were but just in time, for the bread was all eaten, and the jug almost empty. But as soon as the good man had the stone in his hand, he wished himself safe and sound in his palace again; and in a moment there he was, with his garden and his stables and his horses; and his three faithful friends dwelt with him, and they all spent their time happily and merrily as long as they lived.

Jorinda and Jorindel

THERE was once an old castle that stood in the middle of a large thick wood, and in the castle lived an old fairy. All the day long she flew about in the form of an owl, or crept about the country like a cat; but at night she always became an old woman again. When any youth came within a hundred paces of her castle, he became quite fixed, and could not move a step till she came and set him free: but when any pretty maiden came within that distance, she was changed into a bird; and the fairy put her into a cage and hung her up in a chamber in the castle. There were seven hundred of these cages hanging in the castle, and all with beautiful birds in them.

Now there was once a maiden whose name was Jorinda: she was prettier than all the pretty girls that ever was seen; and a shepherd whose name was Jorindel was very fond of her, and they were soon to be married. One day they went to walk in the wood, that they might be alone: and Jorindel said, "We must take care that we don't go too near to the castle." It was a beautiful evening; the last rays of the setting sun shone bright through the long stems of the trees upon the green underwood beneath, and the turtledoves sang plaintively from the tall birches.

Jorinda sat down to gaze upon the sun; Jorindel sat by her side; and both felt sad, they knew not why; but it seemed as if they were to be parted from one another for ever. They had wandered a long way; and when they looked to see which way they should go home, they found themselves at a loss to know what path to take.

The sun was setting fast, and already half of his circle had disappeared behind the hill: Jorindel on a sudden looked behind him, and as he saw through the bushes that they had, without knowing it, sat down close under the old walls of the castle, he shrank for fear, turned pale, and trembled. Jorinda was singing,

> The ring-dove sang from the willow spray,
>> Well-a-day! well-a-day!
> He mourn'd for the fate
> Of his lovely mate,
>> Well-a-day!

The song ceased suddenly. Jorindel turned to see the reason, and beheld his Jorinda changed into a nightingale; so that her song ended with a mournful jug, jug. An owl with fiery eyes flew three times round them, and three times screamed Tu whu! Tu whu! Tu whu! Jorindel could not move: he stood fixed as a stone, and could neither weep, nor speak, nor stir hand or foot. And now the sun went quite down; the gloomy night came, the owl flew into a bush; and a moment after the old fairy came forth pale and meagre, with staring eyes, and a nose and chin that almost met one another.

She mumbled something to herself, seized the nightingale, and went away with it in her hand. Poor Jorindel saw the nightingale was gone, – but what could he do? he could not speak, he could not move from the spot where he stood. At last the fairy came back, and sang with a hoarse voice,

> Till the prisoner's fast,
> And her doom is cast,
>> There stay! Oh, stay!
> When the charm is around her,
> And the spell, has bound her,
>> Hie away! away!

On a sudden Jorindel found himself free. Then he fell on his knees before the fairy, and prayed her to give him back his dear Jorinda: but she said he should never see her again, and went her way.

He prayed, he wept, he sorrowed, but all in vain. "Alas!" he said, "what will become of me?"

He could not return to his own home, so he went to a strange village, and employed himself in keeping sheep. Many a time did he walk round and round as near to the hated castle as he dared go. At last he dreamt one night that he found a beautiful purple flower, and in the middle of it lay a costly pearl; and he

dreamt that he plucked the flower, and went with it in his hand into the castle, and that every thing he touched with it was disenchanted, and that there he found his dear Jorinda again.

In the morning when he awoke, he began to search over hill and dale for this pretty flower; and eight long days he sought for it in vain: but on the ninth day, early in the morning, he found the beautiful purple flower; and in the middle of it was a large dew-drop as big as a costly pearl.

Then he plucked the flower, and set out and travelled day and night till he came again to the castle. He walked nearer than a hundred paces to it, and yet he did not become fixed as before, but found that he could go close up to the door.

Jorindel was very glad to see this: he touched the door with the flower, and it sprang open, so that he went in through the court, and listened when he heard so many birds singing. At last he came to the chamber where the fairy sat, with the seven hundred birds singing in the seven hundred cages. And when she saw Jorindel she was very angry, and screamed with rage; but she could not come within two yards of him; for the flower he held in his hand protected him. He looked, around at the birds, but alas! there were many many nightingales, and how then should he find his Jorinda? While he was thinking what to do, he observed that the fairy had taken down one of the cages, and was making her escape through the door. He ran or flew to her, touched the cage with the flower, – and his Jorinda stood before him. She threw her arms round his neck and looked as beautiful as ever, as beautiful as when they walked together in the wood.

Then he touched all the other birds with the flower, so that they resumed their old forms; and took his dear Jorinda home, where they lived happily together many years.

The Wonderful Musician

THERE was once a capital musician who played delightfully on the fiddle, and he went rambling in a forest in a merry mood. Then he said to himself, "Time goes rather heavily on, I must find a companion." So he took up his fiddle, and fiddled away till the wood resounded with his music.

Presently up came a wolf. "Dear me! there's a wolf coming to see me," said the musician. But the wolf came up to him, and said, "How very prettily you play! I wish you would teach me." "That is easily done," said the musician, "if you, will only do what I bid you." "Yes," replied the wolf, "I shall be a very apt scholar." So they went on a little way together, and came at last to an old oak tree that was hollow within, and had a large crack in the middle of the trunk. "Look there," said the musician, "if you wish to learn to fiddle, put your fore feet into that crack." The wolf did as he was bid: but the musician picked up a large stone and wedged both his fore feet fast into the crack, so as to make him a prisoner. "Now be so good as to wait there till I come back," said he, and jogged on.

After a while, he said again to himself, "Time goes very heavily, I must find another companion." So he took his fiddle, and fiddled away again in the wood. Presently up came a fox that was wandering close by. "Ah! there is a fox," said he. The fox came up and said, "You delightful musician, how prettily you play! I must and will learn to play as you do." "That you may soon do," said the musician, "if you do as I tell you." "That I will," said the fox. So they travelled on together till they came to a narrow footpath with high bushes on each side. Then the musician bent a stout hazel stem down to the ground from one side of the path, and set his foot on the top, and held it fast; and bent another from the other side, and said to the fox, "Now, pretty fox, if you want to fiddle, give me hold of your left paw." So the fox gave him his paw; and he tied it fast to the top of one of the hazel stems. "Now give me your right," said he; and the fox did as he was told: then the musician tied that paw to the other hazel; and took off his foot, and away up flew the bushes, and the fox too, and hung sprawling and swinging in the air. "Now be so kind as to stay there till I come back," said the musician, and jogged on.

But he soon said to himself, "Time begins to hang heavy, I must find a companion." So he took up his fiddle, and fiddled away divinely. Then up came a hare running along. "Ah! there is a hare," said the musician. And the hare said to him, "You fine fiddler, how beautifully you play! will you teach me?" "Yes," said the musician, I will soon do that, if you will follow my orders." "Yes," said the hare, "I shall make a good scholar." Then they went on together very well for a long while, till they came to an open space in the wood. The musician tied a string round the hare's neck, and fastened the other end to the tree. "Now," said he, "pretty hare, quick, jump about, run round the tree twenty times." So the silly hare did as she was bid: and when she had run twenty times round the tree, she had twisted the string twenty times round the trunk, and was fast prisoner; and she might pull and pull away as long as she pleased, and only pulled the string faster about her neck. "Now wait there till I come back," said the musician.

But the wolf had pulled and bitten and scratched at the stone a long while, till at last he had got his feet out and was at liberty. Then he said in a great passion, "I will run after that rascally musician and tear him in pieces." As the fox saw him run by, he said, "Ah, brother wolf, pray let me down, the musician has played tricks with me." So the wolf set to work at the bottom of the hazel stem, and bit it in two; and away went both together to find the musician; and as they came to the hare, she cried out too for help. So they went and set her free, and all followed the enemy together.

Meantime the musician had been fiddling away, and found another companion; for a poor woodcutter had been pleased with the music; and could not help following him with his axe under his arm. The musician was pleased to get a man for his companion, and behaved very civilly to him, and played him no

tricks, but stopped and played his prettiest tunes till his heart overflowed for joy. While the woodcutter was standing listening, he saw the wolf, the fox, and the hare coming, and knew by their faces that they were in a great rage, and coming to do some mischief. So he stood before the musician with his great axe, as much as to say, No one shall hurt him as long as I have this axe. And when the beasts saw this, they were so frightened that they ran back into the wood. Then the musician played the woodcutter one of his best tunes for his pains, and went on with his journey.

The Queen Bee

TWO king's sons once upon a time went out into the world to seek their fortunes; but they soon fell into a wasteful foolish way of living, so that they could not return home again. Then their young brother, who was a little insignificant dwarf, went out to seek for his brothers: but when he had found them they only laughed at him, to think that he, who was so young and simple, should try to travel through the world, when they, who were so much wiser, had been unable to get on. However, they all set out on their journey together, and came at last to an ant-hill. The two elder brothers would have pulled it down, in order to see how the poor ants in their fright would run about and carry off their eggs. But the little dwarf said, "Let the poor things enjoy themselves, I will not suffer you to trouble them."

So on they went, and came to a lake where many many ducks were swimming about. The two brothers wanted to catch two, and roast them. But the dwarf said, "Let the poor things enjoy themselves, you shall not kill them." Next they came to a bees'-nest in a hollow tree, and there was so much honey that it ran down the trunk; and the two brothers wanted to light a fire under the tree and kill the bees, so as to get their honey. But the dwarf held them back, and said, "Let the pretty insects enjoy themselves, I cannot let you burn them."

At length the three brothers came to a castle: and as they passed by the stables they saw fine horses standing there, but all were of marble, and no man was to be seen. Then they went through all the rooms, till they came to a door on which were three locks: but in the middle of the door was a wicket, so that they could look into the next room. There they saw a little grey old man sitting at a table; and they called to him once or twice, but he did not hear; however, they called a third time, and then he rose and came out to them.

He said nothing, but took hold of them and led them to a beautiful table covered with all sorts of good things: and when they had eaten and drunk, he showed each of them to a bedchamber.

The next morning he came to the eldest and took him to a marble table, where were three tablets, containing an account of the means by which the castle might be disenchanted. The first tablet said – "In the wood, under the moss, lie the thousand pearls belonging to the king's daughter; they must all be found: and if one be missing by set of sun, he who seeks them will be turned into marble."

The eldest brother set out, and sought for the pearls the whole day; but the evening came, and he had not found the first hundred: so he was turned into stone as the tablet had foretold.

The next day the second brother undertook the task; but he succeeded no better than the first; for he could only find the second hundred of the pearls; and therefore he too was turned into stone.

At last came the little dwarf's turn; and he looked in the moss; but it was so hard to find the pearls, and the job was so tiresome! – so he sat down upon a stone and cried. And as he sat there, the king of the ants (whose life he had saved) came to help him, with five thousand ants; and it was not long before they had found all the pearls and laid them in a heap.

The second tablet said – "The key of the princess's bed-chamber must be fished up out of the lake." And as the dwarf came to the brink of it, he saw the two ducks whose lives he had saved swimming about; and they dived down and soon brought up the key from the bottom.

The third task was the hardest. It was to choose out the youngest and the best of the king's three daughters. Now they were all beautiful, and all exactly alike: but he was told that the eldest had eaten a piece of sugar, the next some sweet syrup, and the youngest a spoonful of honey; so he was to guess which it was that had eaten the honey.

Then came the queen of the bees, who had been saved by the little dwarf from the fire, and she tried the lips of all three; but at last she sat upon the lips of the one that had eaten the honey: and so the dwarf knew which was the youngest. Thus the spell was broken, and all who had been turned into stones awoke, and took their proper forms. And the dwarf married the youngest and the best of the princesses, and was king after her father's death, but his two brothers married the other two sisters.

The Dog and the Sparrow

A SHEPHERD'S dog had a master who took no care of him, but often let him suffer the greatest hunger. At last he could bear it no longer; so he took to his heels, and off he ran in a very sad and sorrowful mood. On the road he met a sparrow, that said to him, "Why are you so sad, my friend?" "Because," said the dog, "I am very very hungry, and have nothing to eat." "If that be all," answered the sparrow, "come with me into the next town, and I will soon find you plenty of food." So on they went together into the town: and as they passed by a butcher's shop, the sparrow said to the dog, "Stand there a little while, till I peck you down a piece of meat." So the sparrow perched upon the shelf: and having first looked carefully about her to see if any one was watching her, she peeked and scratched at a steak that lay upon the edge of the shelf, till at last down it fell. Then the dog snapped it up, and scrambled away with it into a corner, where he soon ate it all up. "Well," said the sparrow, "you shall have some more if you will; so come with me to the next shop, and I will peck you down another steak." When the dog had eaten this too, the sparrow said to him, "Well, my good friend, have you had enough now?" "I have had plenty of meat," answered he, "but I should like to have a piece of bread to eat after it." "Come with me then," said the sparrow, "and you shall soon have that too." So she took him to a baker's shop, and pecked at two rolls that lay in the window, till they fell down: and as the dog still wished for more, she took him to another shop and pecked down some more for him. When that was eaten, the sparrow asked him whether he had had enough now. "Yes," said he; "and now let us take a walk a little way out of the town." So they both went out upon the high road: but as the weather was warm, they had not gone far before the dog said, "I am very much tired, – I should like to take a nap." "Very well," answered the sparrow, "do so, and in the mean time I will perch upon that bush." So the dog stretched himself out on the road, and fell fast asleep. "Whilst he slept, there came by a carter with a cart drawn by three horses, and loaded with two casks of wine. The sparrow, seeing that the carter did not turn out of the way, but would go on in the track in which the dog lay, so as to drive over him, called out, "Stop! stop! Mr. Carter, or it shall be the worse for you." But the carter, grumbling to himself, "You make it the worse for me, indeed! what can you do" He cracked his whip, and drove his cart over the poor dog, so that the wheels crushed him to death. "There," cried the sparrow, "thou cruel villain, thou hast killed my friend the dog. Now mind what I say. This deed of thine shall cost thee all thou art worth." "Do your worst, and welcome," said the brute, "what harm can you do me?" and passed on. But the sparrow crept under the tilt of the cart, and pecked at the bung of one of the casks till she loosened it; and then all the wine ran out, without the carter seeing it. At last he looked round, and saw that the cart was dripping, and the cask quite empty. "What an unlucky wretch I am!" cried he. "Not wretch enough yet!" said the sparrow, as she alighted upon the head of one of the horses, and pecked at him till he reared up and kicked. When the carter saw this, he drew out his hatchet and aimed a blow at the sparrow, meaning to kill her; but she flew away, and the blow fell upon the poor horse's head with such force, that he fell down dead. "Unlucky wretch that I am!" cried he. "Not wretch enough yet!" said the sparrow. And as the carter went on with the other two horses, she again crept under the tilt of the cart, and pecked out the bung of the second cask, so that all the wine ran out. When the carter saw this, he again cried out, "Miserable wretch that I am!" But the sparrow answered, "Not wretch enough yet!" and perched on the head of the second horse, and pecked at him too. The carter ran up and struck at her again with his hatchet; but away she flew, and the blow fell upon the second horse and killed him on the spot. "Unlucky wretch that I am!" said he. "Not wretch enough yet!" said the sparrow; and perching upon the third horse, she began to peck him too. The carrier was mad with fury; and without looking about him, or caring what he was about, struck again at the sparrow; but killed his third horse as he had done the other two. "Alas! miserable wretch that I am!" cried he. "Not wretch enough yet!" answered the sparrow as she flew away; "now will I plague and punish thee at thy own house." The carter was forced at last to leave his cart behind him, and to go home overflowing with rage and vexation. "Alas!" said he to his wife, "what ill luck has befallen me! – my wine is all spilt, and my horses all three dead." "Alas! husband," replied she, "and a wicked bird has come into the house, and has brought with her all the birds of the world, I am sure, and they have fallen upon our corn in the loft, and are eating it up at such a rate!" Away ran the husband upstairs, and saw thousands of birds sitting upon the floor eating up his corn, with the sparrow in the midst of them, "Unlucky wretch that I am!" cried the carter; for he saw that the corn was almost all gone. "Not wretch enough yet!" said the sparrow; "thy cruelty shall cost thee thy life yet!" and away she flew.

The carter seeing that he had thus lost all that he had, went down into his kitchen; and was still not sorry for what he had done, but sat himself angrily and sulkily in the chimney corner. But the sparrow sat on the outside of the window, and cried "Carter! thy cruelty shall cost thee thy life!" With that he jumped up in a rage, seized his hatchet, and threw it at the sparrow; but it missed her, and only broke the window. The sparrow now hopped in, perched upon the window-seat, and cried, "Carter! it shall cost thee thy life!" Then he became mad and blind with rage, and struck the window-seat with such force that he cleft it in two: and as the sparrow flew from place to place, the carter and his wife were so furious, that they broke all their furniture, glasses, chains, benches, the table, and at last the walls, without touching the bird at all. In the end, however, they caught her; and the wife said, "Shall I kill her at once?" "No," cried he, "that is letting her off too easily: she shall die a much more cruel death; I will eat her." But the sparrow began to flutter about, and stretched out her neck and cried, "Carter! it shall cost thee thy life yet!" With that he could wait no longer: so he gave his wife the hatchet, and cried, "Wife, strike at the bird and kill her in my hand." And the wife struck; but she missed her aim, and hit her husband on the head so that he fell down dead, and the sparrow flew quietly home to her nest.

Frederick and Catherine

THERE was once a man called Frederick: he had a wife whose name was Catherine, and they had not long been married. One day Frederick said, "Kate! I am going to work in the fields; when I come back I shall be hungry, so let me have something nice cooked, and a good draught of ale." "Very well," said she, "it shall all be ready." When dinner-time drew nigh, Catherine took a nice steak, which was all the meat she had, and put it on the fire to fry. The steak soon began to look brown, and to crackle in the pan; and Catherine stood by with a fork and turned it: then she said to herself, "The steak is almost ready, I may as well go to the cellar for the ale." So she left the pan on the fire, and took a large jug and went into the cellar and tapped the ale cask. The beer ran into the jug, and Catherine stood looking on. At last it popped into her head, "The dog is not shut up – he may be running away with the steak; that's well thought of." So up she ran from the cellar; and sure enough the rascally cur had got the steak in his mouth, and was making off with it.

Away ran Catherine, and away ran the dog across the field: but he ran faster than she, and stuck close to the steak. "It's all gone, and what can't be cured must be endured," said Catherine. So she turned round; and as she had run a good way and was tired, she walked home leisurely to cool herself. Now all this time the ale was running too, for Catherine had not turned the cock; and when the jug was full the liquor ran upon the floor till the cask was empty. When she got to the cellar stairs she saw what had happened. "My stars!" said she, "what shall I do to keep Frederick from seeing all this slopping about?" So she thought a while; and at last remembered that there was a sack of fine meal bought at the last fair, and that if she sprinkled this over the floor it would suck up the ale nicely, "What a lucky thing," said she, "that we kept that meal! we have now a good use for it." So away she went for it: but she managed to set it down just upon the great jug full of beer, and upset it; and thus all the ale that had been saved was set swimming on the floor also. "Ah! well," said she, "when one goes, another may as well follow." Then she strewed the meal all about the cellar, and was quite pleased with her cleverness, and said, "How very neat and clean it looks!"

At noon Frederick came home. "Now, wife," cried he, "what have you for dinner?" "O Frederick!" answered she, "I was cooking you a steak; but while I went down to draw the ale, the dog ran away with it; and while I ran after him, the ale all ran out; and when I went to dry up the ale with the sack of meal that we got at the fair, I upset the jug; but the cellar is now quite dry, and looks so clean!" "Kate, Kate," said he, "how could you do all this? Why did you leave the steak to fry and the ale to run, and then spoil all the meal?" "Why, Frederick," said she, "I did not know I was doing wrong, you should have told me before."

The husband thought to himself, If my wife manages matters thus, I must look sharp myself. Now he had a good deal of gold in the house: so he said to Catherine, "What pretty yellow buttons these are! I shall put them into a box and bury them in the garden; but take care that you never go near or meddle with them." "No, Frederick," said she, "that I never will." As soon as he was gone, there came by some pedlars with earthenware plates and dishes, and they asked her whether she would buy. "Oh dear me, I should like to buy very much, but I have no money: if you had any use for yellow buttons, I might deal with you." "Yellow buttons!" said they: "let us have a look at them." "Go into the garden and dig where I tell you, and you will find the yellow buttons: I dare not go myself." So the rogues went: and when they found what these yellow buttons were, they took them all away, and left her plenty of plates and dishes. Then she set them all about the house for a show: and when Frederick came back, he cried out, "Kate, what have you been doing?" "See," said she, "I have bought all these with your yellow buttons: but I did not touch them myself; the pedlars went themselves and dug them up." "Wife, wife," said Frederick, "what a pretty piece of work you have made! those yellow buttons were all my money: How came you to do such a thing?" "Why," answered she, "I did not know there was any harm it; you should have told me."

Catherine stood musing for a while, and at last said to her husband, "Hark ye, Frederick, we will soon get the gold back: let us run after the thieves." "Well, we will try," answered he; "but take some butter and cheese with you, that we may have something to eat by the way." "Very well," said she; and they set out: and as Frederick walked the fastest, he left his wife some way behind. "It does not matter," thought she: "when we turn back, I shall be so much nearer home than he."

Presently she came to the top of a hill; down the side of which there was a road so narrow that the cart-wheels always chafed the trees on each side as they passed. "Ah, see now," said she, "how they have bruised and wounded those poor trees; they will never get well." So she took pity on them, and made use of the butter to grease them all, so that the wheels might not hurt them so much. While she was doing this kind office, one of her cheeses fell out of the basket, and rolled down the hill. Catherine looked, but could not see where it had gone; so she said, "Well, I suppose the other will go the same way and find you; he has younger legs than I have." Then she rolled the other cheese after it; and away it went, nobody knows where, down the hill. But she said she supposed that they knew the road, and would follow her, and she could not stay there all day waiting for them.

At last she overtook Frederick, who desired her to give him something to eat. Then she gave him the dry bread. "Where are the butter and cheese?" said he. "Oh!" answered she, "I used the butter to grease those poor trees that the wheels chafed so: and one of the cheeses ran away, so I sent the other after it to find it, and I suppose they are both on the road together somewhere." "What a goose you are to do such silly things!" said the husband. "How can you say so?" said she; "I am sure you never told me not."

They ate the dry bread together; and Frederick said, "Kate, I hope you locked the door safe when you came away." "No," answered she, "you did not tell me." "Then go home, and do it now before we go any further," said Frederick, "and bring with you something to eat."

Catherine did as he told her, and thought to herself by the way, "Frederick wants something to eat; but I don't think he is very fond of butter and cheese: I'll bring him a bag of fine nuts, and the vinegar, for I have often seen him take some."

When she reached home, she bolted the back door, but the

front door she took off the hinges, and said, "Frederick told me to lock the door, but surely it can no where be so safe as if I take it with me." So she took her time by the way; and when she overtook her husband she cried out, "There, Frederick, there is the door itself, now you may watch it as carefully as you please." "Alas! alas!" said he, "what a clever wife I have! I sent you to make the house fast, and you take the door away, so that every body may go in and out as they please: – however, as you have brought the door, you shall carry it about with you for your pains." "Very well," answered she, "I'll carry the door; but I'll not carry the nuts and vinegar bottle also, – that would be too much of a load; so, if you please, I'll fasten them to the door."

Frederick of course made no objection to that plan, and they set off into the wood to look for the thieves; but they could not find them: and when it grew dark, they climbed up into a tree to spend the night there. Scarcely were they up, than who should come by but the very rogues they were looking for. They were in truth great rascals, and belonged to that class of people who find things before they are lost; they were tired; so they sat down and made a fire under the very tree where Frederick and Catherine were. Frederick slipped down on the other side, and picked up some stones. Then he climbed up again, and tried to hit the thieves on the head with them: but they only said, "It must be near morning, for the wind shakes the fir-apples down."

Catherine, who had the door on her shoulder, began to be very tired; but she thought it was the nuts upon it that were so heavy: so she said softly, "Frederick, I must let the nuts go." "No," answered he, "not now, they will discover us." "I can't help that, they must go." "Well then, make haste and throw them down, if you will." Then away rattled the nuts down among the boughs; and one of the thieves cried, "Bless me, it is hailing."

A little while after, Catherine thought the door was still very heavy: so she whispered to Frederick, "I must throw the vinegar down." "Pray don't," answered he, "it will discover us." "I can't help that," said she, "go it must." So she poured all the vinegar down; and the thieves said, "What a heavy dew there is!"

At last it popped into Catherine's head that it was the door itself that was so heavy all the time: so she whispered, "Frederick, I must throw the door down soon." But he begged and prayed her not to do so, for he was sure it would betray them. "Here goes, however," said she: and down went the door with such a clatter upon the thieves, that they cried out "Murder!" and not knowing what was coming, ran away as fast as they could, and left all the gold. So when Frederick and Catherine came down, there they found all their money safe and sound.

The Three Children of Fortune

ONCE upon a time a father sent for his three sons, and gave to the eldest a cock, to the second a scythe, and to the third a cat. "I am now old," said he, "my end is approaching, and I would fain provide for you before I die. Money I have none, and what I now give you seems of but little worth; yet it rests with yourselves alone to turn my gifts to good account. Only seek out for a land where what you have is as yet unknown, and your fortune is made."

After the death of the father, the eldest set out with his cock: but wherever he went, in every town he saw from afar off a cock sitting upon the church steeple, and turning round with the wind. In the villages he always heard plenty of them crowing, and his bird was therefore nothing new; so there did not seem much chance of his making his fortune. At length it happened that he came to an island where the people who lived there had never heard of a cock, and knew not even how to reckon the time. They knew, indeed, if it were morning or evening; but at night, if they lay awake, they had no means of knowing how time went. "Behold," said he to them, "what a noble animal this is! how like a knight he is! he carries a bright red crest upon his head, and spurs upon his heels; he crows three times every night, at stated hours, and at the third time the sun is about to rise. But this is not all; sometimes he screams in broad daylight, and then you must take warning for the weather is surely about to change." This pleased the natives mightily; they kept awake one whole night, and heard, to their great joy, how gloriously the cock called the hour, at two, four, and six o'clock. Then they asked him whether the bird was to be sold, and how much he would sell it for. "About as much gold as an ass can carry," said he. "A very fair price for such an animal," cried they with one voice, and agreed to give him what he asked.

When he returned home with his wealth, his brothers wondered greatly; and the second said, "I will now set forth likewise, and see if I can turn my scythe to as good an account." There did not seem, however, much likelihood of this; for go where he would, he was met by peasants who had as good a scythe on their shoulders as he had. But at last, as good luck would have it, he came to an island where the people had never heard of a scythe; there, as soon as the corn was ripe, they went into the fields and pulled it up; but this was very hard work, and a great deal of it was lost. The man then set to work with his scythe; and mowed down their whole crop so quickly, that the people stood staring open-mouthed with wonder. They were willing to give him what he asked for such a marvellous thing: but he only took a horse laden with as much gold as it could carry.

Now the third brother had a great longing to go and see what he could make of his cat. So he set out: and at first it happened to him as it had to the others, so long as he kept upon the main land, he met with no success; there were plenty of cats everywhere, indeed too many, so that the young ones were for the most part, as soon as they came into the world, drowned in the water. At last he passed over to an island, where, as it chanced most luckily for him, nobody had ever seen a cat; and they were overrun with mice to such a degree, that the little wretches danced upon the tables and chairs, whether the master of the house were at home or not. The people complained loudly of this grievance; the king himself knew not how to rid himself of them in his palace; in every corner mice were squeaking, and they gnawed everything that their teeth could lay hold of. Here was a fine field for Puss – she soon began her chase, and had cleared two rooms in the twinkling of an eye; when the people besought their king to buy the wonderful animal, for the good of the public, at any price. The king willingly gave what was asked, – a mule laden with gold and jewels; and thus the third brother returned home with a richer prize than either of the others.

Meantime the cat feasted away upon the mice in the royal palace, and devoured so many that they were no longer in any great numbers. At length, quite spent and tired with her work, she became extremely thirsty; so she stood still, drew up her head, and cried, "Miau, Miau!" The king gathered together all his subjects when they heard this strange cry, and many ran shrieking in a great fright out of the palace. But the king held a council below as to what was best to be done, and it was at length fixed to send a herald to the cat, to warn her to leave the castle forthwith, or that force would be used to remove her. "For," said the counsellors, "we would far more willingly put up with the mice (since we are used to that evil), than get rid of them at the risk of our lives." A page accordingly went, and asked the cat, "whether she were willing to quit the castle?" But Puss, whose thirst became every moment more and more pressing, answered nothing but "Miau! Miau!" which the page interpreted to mean "No! No!" and therefore carried this answer to the king. "Well," said the counsellors, "then we must try what force will do." So the guns were planted, and the palace was fired upon from all sides. When the fire reached the room where the cat was, she sprang out of the window and ran away; but the besiegers did not see her, and went on firing until the whole palace was burnt to the ground.

King Grisly-Beard

A GREAT king had a daughter who was very beautiful, but so proud and haughty and conceited, that none of the princes who came to ask her in marriage were good enough for her, and she only made sport of them.

Once upon a time the king held a great feast, and invited all her suitors; and they sat in a row according to their rank, kings and princes and dukes and earls. Then the princess came in and passed by them all, but she had something spiteful to say to every one. The first was too fat: "He's as round as a tub," said she. The next was too tall: "What a maypole!" said she. The next was too short: "What a dumpling!" said she. The fourth was too pale, and she called him "Wan-face." The fifth was too red, so she called him "Cockscomb." The sixth was not straight enough, so she said he was like a green stick that had been laid to dry over a baker's oven. And thus she had some joke to crack upon every one; but she laughed more than all at a good king who was there. "Look at him," said she, "his beard is like an old mop, he shall be called Grisly-beard." So the king got the nickname of Grisly-beard.

But the old king was very angry when he saw how his daughter behaved, and how she ill-treated all his guests; and he vowed that, willing or unwilling, she should marry the first beggar that came to the door.

Two days after there came by a travelling musician, who began to sing under the window, and beg alms: and when the king heard him, he said, "Let him come in." So they brought in a dirty-looking fellow; and when he had sung before the king and the princess, he begged a boon. Then the king said, "You have sung so well, that I will give you my daughter for your wife."

The princess begged and prayed; but the king said, "I have sworn to give you to the first beggar, and I will keep my word." So words and tears were of no avail; the parson was sent for, and she was married to the musician. When this was over, the king said, "Now get ready to go; you must not stay here; you must travel on with your husband."

Then the beggar departed, and took her with him; and they soon came to a great wood. "Pray," said she, "whose is this wood?" "It belongs to king Grisly-beard," answered he; "hadst thou taken him, all had been thine." "Ah! unlucky wretch that I am!" sighed she, "would that I had married king Grisly-beard!" Next they came to some fine meadows. "Whose are these beautiful green meadows?" said she. "They belong to king Grisly-beard; hadst thou taken him, they had all been thine." "Ah! unlucky wretch that I am!" said she, "would that I had married king Grisly-beard!"

They then came to a great city. "Whose is this noble city?" said she. "It belongs to king Grisly-beard; hadst thou taken him, it had all been thine." "Ah! miserable wretch that I am!" sighed she, "why did I not marry king Grisly-beard?" "That is no business of mine," said the musician; "why should you wish for another husband? am not I good enough for you?"

At last they came to a small cottage. "What a paltry place!" said she; "to whom does that little dirty hole belong?" The musician answered, "That is your and my house, where we are to live." "Where are your servants?" cried she. "What do we want with servants?" said he, "you must do for yourself whatever is to be done. Now make the fire, and put on water and cook my supper, for I am very tired." But the princess knew nothing of making fires and cooking, and the beggar was forced to help her. When they had eaten a very scanty meal they went to bed; but the musician called her up very early in the morning to clean the house. Thus they lived for two days: and when they had eaten up all there was in the cottage, the man said, "Wife, we can't go on thus, spending money and earning nothing. You must learn to weave baskets." Then he went out and cut willows and brought them home, and she began to weave; but it made her fingers very sore. "I see this work won't do," said he, "try and spin; perhaps you will do that better." So she sat down and tried to spin; but the threads cut her tender fingers till the blood ran. "See now," said the musician, "you are good for nothing, you can do no work; – what a bargain I have got! However, I'll try and set up a trade in pots and pans, and you shall stand in the market and sell them." "Alas!" sighed she, "when I stand in the market and any of my father's court pass by and see me there, how they will laugh at me!"

But the beggar did not care for that; and said she must work, if she did not wish to die of hunger. At first the trade went well; for many people, seeing such a beautiful woman, went to buy her wares, and paid their money without thinking of taking away the goods. They lived on this as long as it lasted, and then her husband bought a fresh lot of ware, and she sat herself down with it in the corner of the market; but a drunken soldier soon came by, and rode his horse against her stall and broke all her goods into a thousand pieces. Then she began to weep, and knew not what to do. "Ah! what will become of me!" said she; "what will my husband say?" So she ran home and told him all. "Who would have thought you would have been so silly," said he, "as to put an earthenware stall in the comer of the market, where every body passes? – But let us have no more crying; I see you are not fit for this sort of work: so I have been to the king's palace, and asked if they did not want a kitchen-maid, and they have promised to take you, and there you will have plenty to eat."

Thus the princess became a kitchen-maid, and helped the cook to do all the dirtiest work: she was allowed to carry home some of the meat that was left, and on this she and her husband lived.

She had not been there long, before she heard that the king's eldest son was passing by, going to be married; and she went to one of the windows and looked out. Every thing was ready, and all the pomp and splendour of the court was there. Then she thought with an aching heart on her own sad fate, and bitterly grieved for the pride and folly which had brought her so low. And the servants gave her some of the rich meats, which she put into her basket to take home.

All on a sudden, as she was going out, in came the king's son in golden clothes: and when he saw a beautiful woman at the door, he took her by the hand, and said she should be his partner in the dance: but she trembled for fear, for she saw that it was king Grisly-beard, who was making sport of her. However, he kept fast hold and led her in; and the cover of the basket came off, so that the meats in it fell all about.

Then every body laughed and jeered at her; and she was so abashed that she wished herself a thousand feet deep in the earth. She sprang to the door to run away; but on the steps king Grisly-beard overtook and brought her back, and said, "Fear me not! I am the musician who has lived with you in the hut: I brought you there because I loved you. I am also the soldier who overset your stall. I have done all this only to cure you of pride, and to punish you for the ill-treatment you bestowed on me. Now all is over; you have learnt wisdom, your faults are gone, and it is time to celebrate our marriage feast!"

Then the chamberlains came and brought her the most beautiful robes: and her father and his whole court were there already, and congratulated her on her marriage. Joy was in every face. The feast was grand, and all were merry, and I wish you and I had been of the party.

The Adventures of Chanticleer and Partlet

1. How they went to the Mountains to eat Nuts.

"THE nuts are quite ripe now," said Chanticleer to his wife Partlet, "suppose we go together to the mountains, and eat as many as we can, before the squirrel takes them all away." "With all my heart," said Partlet, "let us go and make a holiday of it together."

So they went to the mountains, and as it was a lovely day, they stayed there till the evening. Now, whether it was that they had eaten so many nuts that they could not walk, or whether they were lazy and would not, I do not know: however, they took it into their heads that it did not become them to go home on foot. So Chanticleer began to build a little carriage of nut-shells: and when it was finished, Partlet jumped into it and sat down, and bid Chanticleer harness himself to it and draw her home. "That's a good joke!" said Chanticleer; "no, that will never do; I had rather by half walk home; I'll sit on the box and be coachman, if you like, but I'll not draw." While this was passing, a duck came quacking up and cried out, "You thieving vagabonds, what business have you in my grounds? I'll give it you well for your insolence!" and upon that she fell upon Chanticleer most lustily. But Chanticleer was no coward, and returned the duck's blows with his sharp spurs so fiercely that she soon began to cry out for mercy; which was only granted her upon condition that she would draw the carriage home for them. This she agreed to do; and Chanticleer got upon the box, and drove, crying, "Now, duck, get on as fast as you can." And away they went at a pretty good pace.

After they had travelled along a little way, they met a

needle and a pin walking together along the road: and the needle cried out, "Stop! stop!" and said it was so dark that they could hardly find their way, and such dirty walking they could not get on at all: he told him that he and his friend, the pin, had been at a public house a few miles off, and had sat drinking till they had forgotten how late it was; he begged therefore that the travellers would be so kind as to give them a lift in their carriage. Chanticleer observing that they were but thin fellows, and not likely to take up much room, told them they might ride, but made them promise not to dirty the wheels of the carriage in getting in, nor to tread on Partlet's toes.

Late at night they arrived at an inn; and as it was bad travelling in the dark, and the duck seemed much tired, and waddled about a good deal from one side to the other, they made up their minds to fix their quarters there: but the landlord at first was unwilling, and said his house was full, thinking they might not be very respectable company: however, they spoke civilly to him, and gave him the egg which Partlet had laid by the way, and said they would give him the duck, who was in the habit of laying one every day: so at last he let them come in, and they bespoke a handsome supper, and spent the evening very jollily.

Early in the morning, before it was quite light, and when nobody was stirring in the inn, Chanticleer awakened his wife and, fetching the egg, they pecked a hole in it, ate it up, and threw the shells into the fire-place: they then went to the pin and needle, who were fast asleep, and, seizing them by their heads, stuck one into the landlord's easy chair, and the other into his handkerchief; and having done this, they crept away as softly as possible. However, the duck, who slept in the open air in the yard, heard them coming, and jumping into the brook which ran close by the inn, soon swam out of their reach.

An hour or two afterwards the landlord got up, and took his handkerchief to wipe his face, but the pin ran into him and pricked him: then he walked into the kitchen to light his pipe at the fire, but when he stirred it up the egg-shells flew into his eyes, and almost blinded him. "Bless me!" said he, "all the world seems to have a design against my head this morning:" and so saying, he threw himself sulkily into his easy chair; but, oh dear! the needle ran into him; and this time the pain was not in his head. He now flew into a very great passion, and, suspecting the company who had come in the night before, he went to look after them, but they were all off; so he swore that he never again would take in such a troop of vagabonds, who ate a great deal, paid no reckoning, and gave him nothing for his trouble but their apish tricks.

2. How Chanticleer and Partlet went to visit Mr. Korbes.

Another day, Chanticleer and Partlet wished to ride out together; so Chanticleer built a handsome carriage with four red wheels, and harnessed six mice to it; and then he and Partlet got into the carriage, and away they drove. Soon afterwards a cat met them, and said, "Where are you going?" And Chanticleer replied,

"All on our way
A visit to pay
To Mr. Korbes, the fox, to-day."

Then the cat said, "Take me with you." Chanticleer said, "With all my heart: get up behind, and be sure you, do not fall off."

"Take care of this handsome coach of mine,
Nor dirty my pretty red wheels so fine!
Now, mice, be ready,
And, wheels, run steady!
For we are going a visit to pay
To Mr. Korbes, the fox, to-day."

Soon after came up a mill-stone, an egg, a duck, and a pin; and Chanticleer gave them all leave to get into the carriage and go with them.

When they arrived at Mr. Korbes's house, he was not at home; so the mice drew the carriage into the coach-house, Chanticleer and Partlet flew upon a beam, the cat sat down in the fire-place, the duck got into the washing cistern, the pin stuck himself into the bed pillow, the mill-stone laid himself over the house door, and the egg rolled herself up in the towel.

When Mr. Korbes came home, he went to the fire-place to make a fire; but the cat threw all the ashes in his eyes: so he ran to the kitchen to wash himself; but there the duck splashed all the water in his face; and when he tried to wipe himself, the egg broke to pieces in the towel all over his face and eyes. Then he was very angry, and went without his supper to bed; but when he laid his head on the pillow, the pin ran into his cheek: at this he became quite furious, and, jumping up, would have run out of the house; but when he came to the door, the mill-stone fell down on his head, and killed him on the spot.

3. How Partlet died and was buried, and how Chanticleer died of grief.

Another day Chanticleer and Partlet agreed to go again to the mountains to eat nuts; and it was settled that all the nuts which they found should be shared equally between them. Now Partlet found a very large nut; but she said nothing about it to Chanticleer, and kept it all to herself: however, it was so big that she could not swallow it, and it stuck in her throat. Then she was in a great fright, and cried out to Chanticleer, "Pray run as fast as you can, and fetch me some water, or I shall be choked." Chanticleer ran as fast as he could to the river, and said, "River, give me some water, for Partlet lies on the mountain, and will be choked by a great nut." The river said, "Run first to the bride, and ask her for a silken cord to draw up the water." Chanticleer ran to the bride, and said, "Bride, you must give me a silken cord, for then the river will give me water, and the water I will carry to Partlet, who lies on the mountain, and will be choked by a great nut." But the bride said, "Run first, and bring me my garland that is hanging on a willow in the garden." Then Chanticleer ran to the garden, and took the garland from the bough where it hung, and brought it to the bride; and then the bride gave him the silken cord, and he took the silken cord to the river, and the river gave him water, and he carried the water to Partlet; but in the meantime she was choked by the great nut, and lay quite dead, and never moved any more.

Then Chanticleer was very sorry, and cried bitterly; and all the beasts came and wept with him over poor Partlet. And six mice built a little hearse to carry her to her grave; and when it was ready they harnessed themselves before it, and Chanticleer drove them. On the way they met the fox. "Where are you going, Chanticleer?" said he. "To bury my Partlet," said the other. "May

I go with you?" said the fox. "Yes; but you must get up behind, or my horses will not be able to draw you." Then the fox got up behind; and presently the wolf, the bear, the goat, and all the beasts of the wood, came and climbed upon the hearse.

So on they went till they came to a rapid stream. "How shall we get over?" said Chanticleer. Then said a straw, "I will lay myself across, and you may pass over upon me." But as the mice were going over, the straw slipped away and fell into the water, and the six mice all fell in and were drowned. What was to be done? Then a large log of wood came and said, "I am big enough; I will lay myself across the stream, and you shall pass over upon me." So he laid himself down; but they managed so clumsily, that the log of wood fell in and was carried away by the stream. Then a stone, who saw what had happened, came up and kindly offered to help poor Chanticleer by laying himself across the stream; and this time he got safely to the other side with the hearse, and managed to get Partlet out of it; but the fox and the other mourners, who were sitting behind, were too heavy, and fell back into the water and were all carried away by the stream and drowned.

Thus Chanticleer was left alone with his dead Partlet; and having dug a grave for her, he laid her in it, and made a little hillock over her. Then he sat down by the grave, and wept and mourned, till at last he died too: and so all were dead.

Snow-Drop

IT was in the middle of winter, when the broad flakes of snow were falling around, that a certain queen sat working at a window, the frame of which was made of fine black ebony; and as she was looking out upon the snow, she pricked her finger, and three drops of blood fell upon it. Then she gazed thoughtfully upon the red drops which sprinkled the white snow, and said, "Would that my little daughter may be as white as that snow, as red as the blood, and as black as the ebony window-frame!" And so the little girl grew up: her skin was as white as snow, her cheeks as rosy as the blood, and her hair as black as ebony; and she was called Snowdrop.

But this queen died; and the king soon married another wife, who was very beautiful, but so proud that she could not bear to think that any one could surpass her. She had a magical looking-glass, to which she used to go and gaze upon herself in it, and say,

> "Tell me, glass, tell me true!
> Of all the ladies in the land,
> Who is the fairest? tell me who?"

And the glass answered,

"Thou, queen, art fairest in the land."

But Snow-drop grew more and more beautiful; and when she was seven years old, she was as bright as the day, and fairer than the queen herself. Then the glass one day answered the queen, when she went to consult it as usual,

"Thou, queen, may'st fair and beauteous be,
But Snow-drop is lovelier far than thee!"

When she heard this she turned pale with rage and envy; and called to one of her servants and said, "Take Snow-drop away into the wide wood, that I may never see her more." Then the servant led her away; but his heart melted when she begged him to spare her life, and he said, "I will not hurt thee, thou pretty child." So he left her by herself; and though he thought it most likely that the wild beasts would tear her in pieces, he felt as if a great weight were taken off his heart when he had made up his mind not to kill her, but leave her to her fate.

Then poor Snow-drop wandered along through the wood in great fear; and the wild beasts roared about her, but none did her any harm. In the evening she came to a little cottage, and went in there to rest herself, for her little feet would carry her no further. Every thing was spruce and neat in the cottage: on the table was spread a white cloth, and there were seven little plates with seven little loaves, and seven little glasses with wine in them; and knives and forks laid in order; and by the wall stood seven little beds. Then as she was very hungry, she picked a little piece off each loaf, and drank a very little wine out of each glass; and after that she thought she would lie down and rest. So she tried all the little beds; and one was too long, and another was too short, till at last the seventh suited her; and there she laid herself down and went to sleep. Presently in came the masters of the cottage, who were seven little dwarfs that lived among the mountains, and dug and searched about for gold. They lighted up their seven lamps, and saw directly that all was not right. The first said, "Who has been sitting on my stool?" The second, "Who has been eating off my plate?" The third, "Who has been picking my bread?" The fourth, "Who has been meddling with my spoon?" The fifth, "Who has been handling my fork?" The sixth, "Who has been cutting with my knife?" The seventh, "Who has been drinking my wine?" Then the first looked round and said, "Who has been lying on my bed?" And the rest came running to him, and every one cried out that somebody had been upon his bed. But the seventh saw Snow-drop, and called all his brethren to come and see her; and they cried out with wonder and astonishment, and brought their lamps to look at her, and said, "Good heavens! what a lovely child she is!" And they were delighted to see her, and took care not to wake her; and the seventh dwarf slept an hour with each of the other dwarfs in turn, till the night was gone.

In the morning Snow-drop told them all her story; and they pitied her, and said if she would keep all things in order, and cook and wash, and knit and spin for them, she might stay where she was, and they would take good care of her. Then they went out all day long to their work, seeking for gold and silver in the mountains; and Snow-drop remained at home: and they warned her, and said, "The queen will soon find out where you are, so take care and let no one in."

But the queen, now that she thought Snow-drop was dead, believed that she was certainly the handsomest lady in the land; and she went to her glass and said,

> "Tell me, glass, tell me true!
> Of all the ladies in the land,
> Who is fairest? tell me who?"

And the glass answered,

> "Thou queen, art the fairest in all this land;
> But over the hills, in the greenwood shade,
> Where the seven dwarfs their dwelling have made,
> There Snow-drop is hiding her head, and she
> Is lovelier far, O queen, than thee."

Then the queen was very much alarmed; for she knew that the glass always spoke the truth, and was sure that the servant had betrayed her. And she could not bear to think that any one lived who was more beautiful than she was; so she disguised herself as an old pedlar and went her way over the hills to the place where the dwarfs dwelt. Then she knocked at the door, and cried, "Fine wares to sell!" Snow-drop looked out at the window, and said, "Good-day, good-woman; what have you to sell?" "Good wares, fine wares," said she; "laces and bobbins of all colours." "I will let the old lady in; she seems to be a very good sort of body," thought Snow-drop; so she ran down, and unbolted the door, "Bless me!" said the old woman, "how badly your stays are laced! Let me lace them, up with one of my nice new laces." Snow-drop did not dream of any mischief; so she stood up before the old woman; but she set to work so nimbly, and pulled the lace so tight, that Snow-drop lost her breath, and fell down as if she were dead. "There's an end of all thy beauty," said the spiteful queen, and went away home.

In the evening the seven dwarfs returned; and I need not say how grieved they were to see their faithful Snow-drop stretched upon the ground motionless, as if she were quite dead. However, they lifted her up, and when they found what was the matter, they cut the lace; and in a little time she began to breathe, and soon came to life again. Then they said, "The old woman was the queen herself; take care another time, and let no one in when we are away."

When the queen got home, she went straight to her glass, and spoke to it as usual; but to her great surprise it still said,

"Thou, queen, art the fairest in all this land;
But over the hills, in the greenwood, shade,
Where the seven dwarfs their dwelling have made,
There Snow-drop is hiding her head; and she
Is lovelier far, O queen! than thee."

Then the blood ran cold in her heart with spite and malice to see that Snow-drop still lived; and she dressed herself up again in a disguise, but very different from the one she wore before, and took with her a poisoned comb. When she reached the dwarfs' cottage, she knocked at the door, and cried, "fine wares to sell!" but Snow-drop said, "I dare not let any one in." Then the queen said, "Only look at my beautiful combs;" and gave her the poisoned one. And it looked so pretty that she took it up and put it into her hair to try it; but the moment it touched her head the poison was so powerful that she fell down senseless. "There you may lie," said the queen, and went her way. But by good luck the dwarfs returned very early that evening; and when they saw Snow-drop lying on the ground, they thought what had happened, and soon found the poisoned comb. And when they took it away, she recovered, and told them all that had passed; and they warned her once more not to open the door to any one.

Meantime the queen went home to her glass, and trembled with rage when she received exactly the same answer as before; and she said, "Snow-drop shall die, if it costs me my life." So she went secretly into a chamber, and prepared a poisoned apple: the outside looked very rosy and tempting, but whoever tasted it was sure to die. Then she dressed herself up as a peasant's wife, and travelled over the hills to the dwarfs' cottage, and knocked at the door; but Snow-drop put her head out of the window, and said, "I dare not let any one in, for the dwarfs have told me not." Do as you please," said the old woman, "but at any rate take this pretty apple; I will make you a present of it." "No," said Snow-drop, "I dare not take it." "You silly girl!" answered the other, "what are you afraid of? do you think it is poisoned? Come! do you eat one part, and I will eat the other." Now the apple was so prepared that one side was good, though the other side was poisoned. Then Snow-drop was very much tempted to taste, for the apple looked exceedingly nice; and when she saw the old woman eat, she could refrain no longer. But she had scarcely put the piece into her mouth, when she fell down dead upon the ground. "This time nothing will save thee," said the queen; and she went home to her glass, and at last it said

"Thou queen art the fairest of all the fair."

And then her envious heart was glad, and as happy as such a heart could be.

When evening came, and the dwarfs returned home, they found Snow-drop lying on the ground: no breath passed her lips, and they were afraid that she was quite dead. They lifted her up, and combed her hair, and washed her face with wine and water; but all was in vain, for the little girl seemed quite dead. So they laid her down upon a bier, and all seven watched and bewailed her three whole days; and then they proposed to bury her: but her cheeks were still rosy, and her face looked just as it did while she was alive; so they said, "We will never bury her in the cold ground." And they made a coffin of glass so that they might still look at her, and wrote her name upon it, in golden letters, and that she was a king's daughter. And the coffin was placed upon the hill, and one of the dwarfs always sat by it and watched. And the birds of the air came too, and bemoaned Snow-drop: first of all came an owl, and then a raven, but at last came a dove.

And thus Snow-drop lay for a long long time, and still only looked as though she were asleep; for she was even now as white as snow, and as red as blood, and as black as ebony. At last a prince came and called at the dwarfs' house; and he saw Snow-drop, and read what was written in golden letters. Then he offered the dwarfs money, and earnestly prayed them to let him take her away; but they said, "We will not part with her for all the gold in the world." At last however they had pity on him, and gave him the coffin: but the moment he lifted it up to carry it home with him, the piece of apple fell from between her lips, and Snow-drop awoke, and said "Where am I?" And the prince answered, "Thou art safe with me." Then he told her all that had happened, and said, "I love you better than all the world: come with me to my father's palace, and you shall be my wife." And Snow-drop consented, and went home with the prince; and every thing was prepared with great pomp and splendour for their wedding.

To the feast was invited, among the rest, Snow-drop's old enemy the queen; and as she was dressing herself in fine rich clothes, she looked in the glass and said,

"Tell me, glass, tell me true!
Of all the ladies in the land,
Who is fairest? tell me who?"

And the glass answered,

"Thou, lady, art loveliest here, I ween;
But lovelier far is the new-made queen."

When she heard this, she started with rage; but her envy and curiosity were so great, that she could not help setting out to see the bride. And when she arrived, and saw that it was no other than Snow-drop, who, as she thought, had been dead a long while, she choked with passion, and fell ill and died; but Snow-drop and the prince lived and reigned happily over that land many many years.

The Elves and the Shoemaker

THERE was once a shoemaker who worked very hard and was very honest; but still he could not earn enough to live upon, and at last all he had in the world was gone, except just leather enough to make one pair of shoes. Then he cut them already to make up the next day, meaning to get up early in the morning to work. His conscience was clear and his heart light amidst all his troubles; so he went peaceably to bed, left all his cares to heaven, and fell asleep. In the morning, after he had said his prayers, he set himself down to his work, when, to his great wonder, there stood the shoes, all ready made, upon the table. The good man knew not what to say or think of this strange event. He looked at the workmanship; there was not one false stitch in the whole job; and all was so neat and true, that it was a complete masterpiece.

That same day a customer came in, and the shoes pleased him so well that he willingly paid a price higher than usual for them; and the poor shoemaker with the money bought leather enough to make two pairs more. In the evening he cut out the work, and went to bed early that he might get up and begin betimes next day: but he was saved all the trouble, for when he got up in the morning the work was finished ready to his hand. Presently in came buyers, who paid him handsomely for his goods, so that he bought leather enough for four pairs more. He cut out the work again over night, and found it finished in the morning as before; and so it went on for some time: what was got ready in the evening was always done by daybreak, and the good man soon became thriving and prosperous again.

One evening about Christmas time, as he and his wife were sitting over the fire chatting together, he said to her, "I should like to sit up and watch to-night, that we may see who it is that comes and does my work for me." The wife liked the thought; so they left a light burning, and hid themselves in the corner of the room behind a curtain that was hung up there, and watched what should happen.

As soon as it was midnight, there came two little naked dwarfs; and they sat themselves upon the shoemaker's bench, took up all the work that was cut out, and began to ply with their little fingers, stitching and rapping and tapping away at such a rate, that the shoemaker was all amazement, and could not take his eyes off for a moment. And on they went till the job was quite finished, and the shoes stood ready for use upon the table. This was long before day-break; and then they bustled away as quick as lightning.

The next day the wife said to the shoemaker, "These little wights have made us rich, and we ought to be thankful to them, and do them a good office in return. I am quite vexed to see them run about as they do; they have nothing upon their backs to keep off the cold. I'll tell you what, I will make each of them a shirt, and a coat and waistcoat, and a pair of pantaloons into the bargain; do you make each of them a little pair of shoes."

The thought pleased the good shoemaker very much; and one evening, when all the things were ready, they laid them on the table instead of the work that they used to cut out, and then went and hid themselves to watch what the little elves would do. About midnight they came in, and were going to sit down to their work as usual; but when they saw the clothes lying for them, they laughed and were greatly delighted. Then they dressed them-selves in the twinkling of an eye, and danced and capered and sprang about as merry as could be, till at last they danced out of the door over the green; and the shoemaker saw them no more: but every thing went well with him from that time forward, as long as he lived.

The Turnip

THERE were two brothers who were both soldiers; the one was rich and the other poor. The poor man thought he would try to better himself; so, pulling off his red coat, he became a gardener, and dug his ground well, and sowed turnips.

When the seed came up, there was one plant bigger than all the rest; and it kept getting larger and larger, and seemed as if it would never cease growing; so that it might have been called the prince of turnips, for there never was such a one seen before, and never will again. At last it was so big that it filled a cart, and two oxen could hardly draw it; and the gardener knew not what in the world to do with it, nor whether it would be a blessing or a curse to him. One day he said to himself, "What shall I do with it? if I sell it, it will bring no more than another; and for eating, the little turnips are better than this; the best thing perhaps is to carry it and give it to the king as a mark of respect."

Then he yoked his oxen, and drew the turnip to the Court, and gave it to the king. "What a wonderful thing!" said the king; "I have seen many strange things, but such a monster as this I never saw. Where did you get the seed? or is it only your good luck? If so, you are a true child of fortune." "Ah, no!" answered the gardener, "I am no child of fortune; I am a poor soldier, who never could get enough to live upon; so I laid aside my red coat, and set to work, tilling the ground. I have a brother, who is rich, and your majesty knows him well, and all the world knows him; but because I am poor, everybody forgets me."

The king then took pity on him, and said, "You shall be poor no longer, I will give you so much that you shall be even richer than your brother." Then he gave him gold and lands and flocks, and made him so rich that his brother's fortune could not at all be compared with his.

When the brother heard of all this, and how a turnip had made the gardener so rich, he envied him sorely, and bethought himself how he could contrive to get the same good fortune for himself. However, he determined to manage more cleverly than his brother, and got together a rich present of gold and fine horses for the king; and thought he must have a much larger gift in return: for if his brother had received so much for only a turnip, what must his present be worth?

The king took the gift very graciously, and said he knew not what to give in return more valuable and wonderful than the great turnip; so the soldier was forced to put it into a cart, and drag it home with him. When he reached home, he knew not upon whom to vent his rage and spite; and at length wicked thoughts came into his head, and he resolved to kill his brother.

So he hired some villains to murder him; and having shown them where to lie in ambush, he went to his brother and said, "Dear brother, I have found a hidden treasure; let us go and dig it up, and share it between us." The other had no suspicions of his roguery: so they went out together, and as they were travelling along, the murderers rushed out upon him, bound him, and were going to hang him on a tree.

But whilst they were getting all ready, they heard the trampling of a horse at a distance, which so frightened them that they pushed their prisoner neck and shoulders together into a sack, and swung him up by a cord to the tree, where they left him dangling, and ran away. Meantime he worked and worked away, till he made; a hole large enough to put out his head.

When the horseman came up, he proved to be a student, a merry fellow, who was journeying along on his nag, and singing as he went. As soon as the man in the sack saw him passing under the tree, he cried out, "Good morning! good morning to thee, my friend!" The student looked about every where; and seeing no one, and not knowing where the voice came from, cried out, "Who calls me?"

Then the man in the tree answered, "Lift up thine eyes, for behold here I sit in the sack of wisdom; here have I, in a short time, learned great and wondrous things. Compared to this seat, all the learning of the schools is as empty air. A little longer, and I shall know all that man can know, and shall come forth wiser than the wisest of mankind. Here I discern: the signs and motions

of the heavens and the stars; the laws that control the winds; the number of the sands on the sea-shore; the healing of the sick; the virtues of all simples, of birds, and of precious stones. Wert thou but once here, my friend, thou wouldst feel and own the power of knowledge."

The student listened to all this and wondered much; at last he said, "Blessed be the day and hour when I found you; cannot you contrive to let me into the sack for a little while?" Then the other answered, as if very unwillingly, "A little space I may allow thee to sit here, if thou wilt reward me well and entreat me kindly; but thou must tarry yet an hour below, till I have learnt some little matters that are yet unknown to me."

So the student sat himself down and waited, a while; but the time hung heavy upon him, and he begged earnestly that he might ascend forthwith, for his thirst of knowledge was great. Then the other pretended to give way, and said, "Thou must let the sack of wisdom descend, by untying yonder cord, and then thou shalt enter." So the student let him down, opened the sack, and set him free. "Now then," cried he, "let me ascend quickly." As he began to put himself into the sack heels first, "Wait a while," said the gardener, "that is not the way." Then he pushed him in head first, tied up the sack, and soon swung up the searcher after wisdom dangling in the air. "How is it with thee, friend?" said he, "dost thou not feel that wisdom comes unto thee? Rest there in peace, till thou art a wiser man than thou wert."

So saying, he trotted off on the student's nag, and left the poor fellow to gather wisdom till somebody should come and let him down.

Old Sultan

A SHEPHERD had a faithful dog, called Sultan, who was grown very old, and had lost all his teeth. And one day when the shepherd and his wife were standing together before the house the shepherd said, "I will shoot old Sultan to-morrow morning, for he is of no use now." But his wife said, "Pray let the poor faithful creature live; he has served us well a great many years, and we ought to give him a livelihood for the rest of his days." "But what can we do with him?" said the shepherd, "he has not a tooth in his head, and the thieves don't care for him at all; to be sure he has served us, but then he did it to earn his livelihood; to-morrow shall be his last day, depend upon it."

Poor Sultan, who was lying close by them, heard all that the shepherd and his wife said to one another, and was very much frightened to think to-morrow would be his last day; so in the evening he went to his good friend the wolf, who lived in the wood, and told him all his sorrows, and how his master meant to kill him in the morning. "Make yourself easy," said the wolf, "I will give you some good advice. Your master, you know, goes out every morning very early with his wife into the field; and they take their little child with them, and lay it down behind the hedge in the shade while they are at work. Now do you lie down close by the child, and pretend to be watching it, and I will come out of the wood and run away with it: you must run after me as fast as you can, and I will let it drop; then you may carry it back, and they will think you have saved their child, and will be so thankful to you that they will take care of you as long as you live." The dog liked this plan very well; and accordingly so it was managed. The wolf ran with the child a little way; the shepherd and his wife screamed out; but Sultan soon overtook him, and carried the poor little thing back to his master and mistress. Then the shepherd patted him on the head, and said, "Old Sultan has saved our child from the wolf, and therefore he shall live and be well taken care of, and have plenty to eat. Wife, go home, and give him a good dinner, and let him have my old cushion to sleep on as long as he lives." So from this time forward Sultan had all that he could wish for.

Soon afterwards the wolf came and wished him joy, and said, "Now, my good fellow, you must tell no tales, but turn your head the other way when I want to taste one of the old shepherd's fine fat sheep." "No," said Sultan; "I will be true to my master." However, the wolf thought he was in joke, and came one night to get a dainty morsel. But Sultan had told his master what the wolf meant to do; so he laid wait for him behind the barn-door, and when the wolf was busy looking out for a good fat sheep, he had a stout cudgel laid about his back, that combed his locks for him finely.

Then the wolf was very angry, and called Sultan "an old rogue," and swore he would have his revenge. So the next morning the wolf sent the boar to challenge Sultan to come into the wood to fight the matter out. Now Sultan had nobody he could ask to be his second but the shepherd's old three-legged cat; so he took her with him, and as the poor thing limped along with some trouble, she stuck up her tail straight in the air.

The wolf and the wild boar were first on the ground; and when they espied their enemies coming, and saw the cat's long tail standing straight in the air, they thought she was carrying a sword for Sultan to fight with; and every time she limped, they thought she was picking up a stone to throw at them; so they said they should not like this way of fighting, and the boar lay down behind a bush, and the wolf jumped up into a tree. Sultan and the cat soon came up, and looked about, and wondered that no one was there. The boar, however, had not quite hidden himself, for his ears stuck out of the bush; and when he shook one of them a little, the cat, seeing something move, and thinking it was a mouse, sprang upon it, and bit and scratched it, so that the boar jumped up and grunted, and ran away, roaring out, "Look up in the tree, there sits the one who is to blame." So they looked up, and espied the wolf sitting amongst the branches; and they called him a cowardly rascal, and would not suffer him to come down till he was heartily ashamed of himself, and had promised to be good friends again with old Sultan.

The Lady and the Lion

A MERCHANT, who had three daughters, was once setting out upon a journey; but before he went he asked each daughter what gift he should bring back for her. The eldest wished for pearls; the second for jewels; but the third said, "Dear father, bring me a rose." Now it was no easy task to find a rose, for it was the middle of winter; yet, as she was the fairest daughter, and was very fond of flowers, her father said he would try what he could do. So he kissed all three, and bid them good bye. And when the time came for his return, he had bought pearls and jewels for the two eldest, but he had sought everywhere in vain for the rose; and when he went into any garden and inquired for such a thing, the people laughed at him, and asked him whether he thought roses grew in snow. This grieved him very much, for his third daughter was his dearest child; and as he was journeying home, thinking what he should, bring her, he came to a fine castle; and around the castle was a garden, in half of which it appeared to be summer time, and in the other half winter. On one side the finest flowers were in full bloom, and on the other everything looked desolate and buried in snow. "A lucky hit!" said he as he called to his servant, and told him to go to a beautiful bed of roses that was there, and bring him away one of the flowers. This done, they were riding away well pleased, when a fierce lion sprung up, and roared out, "Whoever dares to steal my roses shall be eaten up alive." Then the man said, "I knew not that the garden belonged to you; can nothing save my life?" "So!" said the lion, "nothing, unless you promise to give me whatever meets you first on your return home; if you agree to this, I will give you your life, and the rose too for your daughter." But the man was unwilling to do so, and said, "It may be my youngest daughter, who loves me most, and always runs to meet me when I go home." Then the servant was greatly frightened, and said, "It may perhaps be only a cat or a dog." And at last the man yielded with a heavy heart, and took the rose; and promised the lion whatever should meet him first on his return.

And as he came near home, it was his youngest and dearest daughter that met him; she came running and kissed him, and welcomed him home; and when she saw that he had brought her the rose, she rejoiced still more. But her father began to be very melancholy, and to weep, saying, "Alas! my dearest child! I have bought this flower dear, for I have promised to give you to a wild lion, and when he has you, he will tear you in pieces, and eat you." And he told her all that had happened; and said she should not go, let what would happen.

But she comforted him, and said, "Dear father, what you have promised must be fulfilled; I will go to the lion, and soothe him, that he may let me return again safe home."

The next morning she asked the way she was to go, and took leave of her father, and went forth with a bold heart into the wood. But the lion was an enchanted prince, and by day he and all his court were lions, but in the evening they took their proper forms again. And when the lady came to the castle, he welcomed her so courteously that she consented, to marry him. The wedding-feast was held, and they lived happily together a long time. The prince was only to be seen as soon as evening came, and then he held his court; but every morning he left his bride, and went away by himself, she knew not whither, till night came again.

After some time he said to her, "Tomorrow there will be a great feast in your father's house, for your eldest sister is to be married; and, if you wish to go to visit her, my lions shall lead you thither." Then she rejoiced much at the thoughts of seeing her father once more, and set out with the lions; and every one was overjoyed to see her, for they had thought her dead long since. But she told them how happy she was; and stayed till the feast was over, and then went back to the wood.

Her second sister was soon after married; and when she was invited to the wedding, she said to the prince, "I will not go alone this time; you must go with me." But he would not, and said that would be a very hazardous thing, for if the least ray of the torch light should fall upon him, his enchantment would become still worse, for he should be changed into a dove, and be obliged to wander about the world for seven long years. However, she gave him no rest, and said she would take care no light should fall upon him. So at last they set out together, and took with them their little child too; and she chose a large hall with thick walls, for him to sit in while the wedding torches were lighted; but unluckily no one observed that there was a crack in the door. Then the wedding was held with great pomp; but as the train came from the church, and passed with the torches before the hall, a very small ray of light fell upon the prince. In a moment he disappeared; and when his wife came in, and sought him, she found only a white dove. Then he said to her, "Seven years must I fly up and down over the face of the earth; but every now and then I will let fall a white feather, that shall show you the way I am going; follow it, and at last you may overtake and set me free."

This said, he flew out at the door, and she followed; and every now and then a white feather fell, and showed her the way she was to journey. Thus she went roving on through the wide world, and looked neither to the right hand nor to the left, nor took any rest for seven years. Then she began to rejoice, and thought to herself that the time was fast coming when all her troubles should cease; yet repose was still far off: for one day as she was travelling on, she missed the white feather, and when she lifted up her eyes she could no where see the dove. "Now," thought she to herself, "no human aid can be of use to me;" so she went to the sun, and said, "Thou shinest everywhere, on the mountain's top, and the valley's depth; hast thou anywhere seen a white dove?" "No," said the sun, "I have not seen it; but I will give thee a casket – open it when thy hour of need comes." So she thanked the sun, and went on her way till eventide; and when the moon arose, she cried unto it, and said, "Thou shinest through all the night, over field and grove: hast thou nowhere seen a white dove?" "No," said the moon, "I cannot help thee; but I will give thee an egg – break it when need comes." Then she thanked the moon, and went on till the night-wind blew; and she raised up her voice to it, and said, "Thou blowest through every tree and under every leaf: hast thou not seen the white dove?" "No," said the night-wind; "but I will ask three other winds; perhaps they have seen it." Then the east wind and the west wind came, and said they too had not seen it; but the south wind said, "I have seen the white dove; he has fled to the Red Sea, and is changed once more into a lion, for the seven years are passed away; and there he is fighting with a dragon, and the dragon is an enchanted princess, who seeks to separate him from you." Then the night-wind said, "I will give thee counsel: go to the Red Sea; on the right shore stand many rods; number them, and when thou comest to the eleventh, break it off and smite the dragon with it; and so the lion will have the victory, and both of them will appear to you in their human forms. Then instantly set out with thy beloved prince, and journey home over sea and land."

So our poor wanderer went forth, and found all as the night-wind had said; and she plucked the eleventh rod, and smote the dragon, and immediately the lion became a prince and the dragon a princess again. But she forgot the counsel which the night-wind had given; and the false princess watched her opportunity, and took the prince by the arm, and carried him away.

Thus the unfortunate traveller was again forsaken and forlorn; but she took courage and said, "As far as the wind blows, and so long as the cock crows, I will journey on till I find him once again." She went on for a long long way, till at length she came to the castle whither the princess had carried the prince; and there was a feast prepared, and she heard that the wedding was about to be held. "Heaven aid me now!" said she; and she took the casket that the sun had given her, and found that within it lay a dress as dazzling as the sun itself. So she put it on, and went into the palace; and all the people gazed upon her, and the dress pleased the bride so much that she asked whether it was to be sold: "Not for gold and silver," answered she; "but for flesh and blood." The princess asked what she meant; and she said, "Let me speak with the bridegroom this night in his chamber, and I will give thee the dress." At last the princess agreed; but she told her chamberlain to give the prince a sleeping-draught, that he might not hear or see her. When evening came, and the prince had fallen asleep, she was led into his chamber, and she sat herself down at his feet and said, "I have followed thee seven years; I have been to the sun, the moon, and the night-wind, to seek thee; and at last I have helped thee to overcome the dragon. Wilt thou then forget me quite?" But the prince slept so soundly that her voice only passed over him, and seemed like the murmuring of the wind among the fir-trees.

Then she was led away, and forced to give up the golden dress; and when she saw that there was no help for her, she went out into a meadow and sat herself down and wept. But as she sat she bethought herself of the egg that the moon had given her; and when she broke it, there ran out a hen and twelve chickens of pure gold, that played about, and then nestled under the old one's wings, so as to form the most beautiful sight in the world. And she rose up, and drove them before her till the bride saw them from her window, and was so pleased that she came forth, and asked her if she would sell the brood. "Not for gold or silver; but for flesh and blood: let me again this evening speak with the bridegroom in his chamber."

Then the princess thought to betray her as before, and agreed to what she asked; but when the prince went to his chamber, he asked the chamberlain why the wind had murmured so in the night. And the chamberlain told him all; how he had given him a sleeping-draught, and a poor maiden had come and spoken to him in his chamber, and was to come again that night. Then the prince took care to throw away the sleeping-draught; and when she came and began again to to tell him what woes had befallen her, and how faithful and true to him she had been, he knew his beloved wife's voice, and sprung up, and said, "You have awakened me as from a dream; for the strange princess had thrown a spell around me, so that I had altogether forgotten you: but heaven hath sent you to me in a lucky hour."

And they stole away out of the palace by night secretly (for they feared the princess), and journeyed home; and there they found their child, now grown comely and fair, and lived happily together to the end of their days.

The Jew In the Bush

A FARMER had a faithful and diligent servant, who had worked hard for him three years, without having been paid any wages. At last it came into the man's head that he would not go on thus without pay any longer; so he went to his master, and said "I have worked hard for you a long time, I will trust to you to give me what I deserve to have for my trouble." The farmer was a sad miser, and knew that his man was very simple-hearted; so he took out threepence, and gave him for every year's service a penny. The poor fellow thought it was a great deal of money to have, and said to himself, "Why should I work hard, and live here on bad fare any longer? I can now travel into the wide world, and make myself merry." With that he put his money into his purse, and set out roaming over hill and valley.

As he jogged along over the fields, singing and dancing, a little dwarf met him, and asked him what made him so merry. "Why, what should make me down-hearted?" said he; "I am sound in health and rich in purse, what should I care for? I have saved up my three years' earnings, and have it all safe in my pocket." "How much may it come to?" said the little man. "Full threepence," replied the countryman. "I wish you would give them to me," said the other; "I am very poor." Then the man pitied him, and gave him all he had; and the little dwarf said in return, "As you have such a kind honest heart, I will grant you three wishes – one for each penny; so choose whatever you like." Then the countryman rejoiced at his good luck, and said, "I like many things better than money: first I will have a bow that will bring down every thing I shoot at; secondly, a fiddle that will set every one dancing that hears me play upon it; and thirdly, I should like that every one should grant what I ask." The dwarf said he should have his three wishes; so he gave him the bow and fiddle, and went his way.

Our honest friend journeyed on his way too; and if he was merry before, he was now ten times more so. He had not gone far before he met an old Jew: close by them stood a tree, and on the topmost twig sat a thrush singing away most joyfully. "Oh, what a pretty bird!" said the Jew; "I would give a great deal of money to have such a one." "If that's all," said the countryman, "I will soon bring it down." Then he took up his bow, and down fell the thrush into the bushes at the foot of the tree. The Jew crept into the bush to find it; but directly he had got into the middle, his companion took up his fiddle and played away, and the Jew began to dance and spring about, capering higher and higher in the air. The thorns soon began to tear his clothes till they all hung in rags about him, and he himself was all scratched and wounded, so that the blood ran down. "Oh, for heaven's sake!" cried the Jew, "master! master! pray let the fiddle alone. What have I done to deserve this?" "Thou hast shaved many a poor soul close enough," said the other; "thou art only meeting thy reward:" so he played up another tune. Then the Jew began to beg and promise, and offered money for his liberty; but he did not come up to the musician's price for some time, and he danced him along brisker and brisker, and the Jew bid higher and higher, till at last he offered a round hundred of florins that he had in his purse, and had just gained by cheating some poor fellow. When the countryman saw so much money, he said, "I will agree to your proposal." So he took the purse, put up his fiddle, and travelled on very well pleased with his bargain.

Meanwhile the Jew crept out of the hush half naked and in a piteous plight, and began to ponder how he should take his revenge, and serve his late companion some trick. At last he went to the judge, and complained that a rascal had robbed him of his money, and beaten him into the bargain; and that the fellow who did it carried a bow at his hack and a fiddle hung round his neck. Then the judge sent out his officers to bring up the accused wherever they should find him; and he was soon caught and brought up to be tried.

The Jew began to tell his tale, and said he had been robbed of his money. "No, you gave it me for playing a tune to you," said the countryman; but the judge told him that was not likely, and cut the matter short by ordering him off to the gallows.

So away he was taken; but as he stood on the steps he said, "My Lord Judge, grant me one last request." "Any thing but thy life," replied the other. "No," said he, "I do not ask my life; only let me play upon my fiddle for the last time." The Jew cried out, "Oh, no! no! for heaven's sake don't listen to him! don't listen to him!" But the judge said, "It is only for this once, he will soon have done." The fact was, he could not refuse the request, on account of the dwarf's third gift.

Then the Jew said, "Bind me fast, bind me fast, for pity's sake." But the countryman seized his fiddle, and struck up a tune, and at the first note, judge, clerks, and jailer, were in motion; all began capering, and no one could hold the Jew. At the second note the hangman let his prisoner go, and danced also, and by the time he had played the first bar of the tune, all were dancing together – judge, court, and Jew, and all the people who had followed to look on. At first the thing was merry and pleasant enough; but when it had gone on a while, and there seemed to be no end of playing or dancing, they began to cry out, and beg him to leave off; but he stopt not a whit the more for their entreaties, till the judge not only gave him his life, but promised to return him the hundred florins.

Then he called to the Jew, and said, "Tell us now, you vagabond, where you got that gold, or I shall play on for your amusement only." "I stole it," said the Jew in the presence of all the people: "I acknowledge that I stole it, and that you earned it fairly." Then the countryman stopt his fiddle, and left the Jew to take his place at the gallows.

The King of the Golden Mountain

A CERTAIN merchant had two children, a son and daughter, both very young, and scarcely able to run alone. He had two richly laden ships then making a voyage upon the seas, in which he had embarked all his property, in the hope of making great gains, when the news came that they were lost. Thus from being a rich man he became very poor, so that nothing was left him but one small plot of land; and, to relieve his mind a little of his trouble, he often went out to walk there.

One day, as he was roving along, a little rough-looking dwarf stood before him, and asked him why he was so sorrowful, and what it was that he took so deeply to heart. But the merchant replied, "If you could do me any good, I would tell you." "Who knows but I may?" said the little man; "tell me what is the matter, and perhaps I can be of some service." Then the merchant told him how all his wealth was gone to the bottom of the sea, and how he had nothing left except that little plot of land. "Oh! trouble not yourself about that," said the dwarf; "only promise to bring me here, twelve years hence, whatever meets you first on your return home, and I will give you as much gold as you please." The merchant thought this was no great request; that it would most likely be his dog, or something of that sort, but forgot his little child: so he agreed to the bargain, and signed and sealed the engagement to do what was required.

But as he drew near home, his little boy was so pleased to see him, that he crept behind him and laid fast hold of his legs. Then the father started with fear, and saw what it was that he had bound himself to do; but as no gold was come, he consoled himself by thinking that it was only a joke that the dwarf was playing him.

About a month afterwards he went up stairs into an old lumber room to look for some old iron, that he might sell it and raise a little money; and there he saw a large pile of gold lying on the floor. At the sight of this he was greatly delighted, went into trade again, and became a greater merchant than before.

Meantime his son grew up, and as the end of the twelve years drew near, the merchant became very anxious and thoughtful; so that care and sorrow were written upon his face. The son one day asked what was the matter: but his father refused to tell for some time; at last however he said that he had, without knowing it, sold him to a little ugly-looking dwarf for a great quantity of gold; and that the twelve years were coming round when he must perform his agreement. Then the son said, "Father, give yourself very little trouble about that; depend upon it I shall be too much for the little man."

When the time came, they went out together to the appointed place; and the son drew a circle on the ground, and set himself and his father in the middle. The little dwarf soon came, and said to the merchant, "Have you brought me what you promised?" The old man was silent, but his son answered, "What do you want here?" The dwarf said, "I come to talk with your father, not with you." "You have deceived and betrayed my father," said the son; "give him up his bond." "No," replied the other, "I will not yield up my rights."

Upon this a long dispute arose; and at last it was agreed that the son should be put into an open boat, that lay on the side of a piece of water hard by, and that the father should push him off with his own hand; so that he should be turned adrift. Then he took leave of his father, and set himself in the boat; and as it was pushed off it heaved, and fell on one side into the water: so the merchant thought that his son was lost, and went home very sorrowful.

But the boat went safely on, and did not sink; and the young man sat securely within, till at length it ran ashore upon an unknown land. As he jumped upon the shore, he saw before him a beautiful castle, but empty and desolate within, for it was enchanted. At last, however, he found a white snake in one of the chambers.

Now the white snake was an enchanted princess; and she rejoiced greatly to see him, and said, "Art thou at last come to be my deliverer? Twelve long years have I waited for thee, for thou alone canst save me. This night twelve men will come: their faces will be black, and they will be hung round with chains. They will ask what thou dost here; but be silent, give no answer, and let them do what they will – beat and torment thee. Suffer all, only speak not a word; and at twelve o'clock they must depart. The second night twelve others will come; and the third night twenty-four, who will even cut off thy head; but at the twelfth hour of that night their power is gone, and I shall be free, and will come and bring thee the water of life, and will wash thee with it, and restore thee to life and health." And all came to pass as she had said; the merchant's son spoke not a word, and the third night the princess appeared, and fell on his neck and kissed him; joy and gladness burst forth throughout the castle; the wedding was celebrated, and he was king of the Golden Mountain.

They lived together very happily, and the queen had a son. Eight years had passed over their heads when the king thought of his father: and his heart was moved, and he longed to see him once again. But the queen opposed his going, and said, "I know well that misfortunes will come." However, he gave her no rest till she consented. At his departure she presented him with a wishing-ring, and said, "Take this ring, and put it on your finger; whatever you wish it will bring you: only promise that you will not make use of it to bring me hence to your father's." Then he promised what she asked, and put the ring on his finger, and wished himself near the town where his father lived. He found himself at the gates in a moment; but the guards would not let him enter because he was so strangely clad. So he went up to a neighbouring mountain where a shepherd dwelt, and borrowed his old frock, and thus passed unobserved into the town. When he came to his father's house, he said he was his son; but the merchant would not believe him, and said he had had but one son, who he knew was long since dead: and as he was only dressed like a poor shepherd, he would not even offer him any thing to eat. The king however persisted that he was his son, and said, "Is there no mark by which you would know if I am really your son?" "Yes," observed his mother, "our son has a mark like a raspberry under the right arm." Then he showed them the mark, and they were satisfied that what he had said was true. He next told them how he was king of the Golden Mountain, and was married to a princess, and had a son seven years old. But the merchant said, "That can never be true; he must be a fine king truly who travels about in a shepherd's frock." At this the son was very angry; and, forgetting his promise, turned his ring, and wished for his queen and son. In an instant they stood before him; but the queen wept, and said he had broken his word, and misfortune would follow. He did all he could to soothe her, and she at last appeared to be appeased; but she was not so in reality, and only meditated how she should take her revenge.

One day he took her to walk with him out of the town, and showed her the spot where the boat was turned adrift upon the wide waters. Then he sat himself down, and said, "I am very much tired; sit by me, I will rest my head in your lap, and sleep a while." As soon as he had fallen asleep, however, she drew the ring from his finger, and crept softly away, and wished herself and her son at home in their kingdom. And when the king awoke, he found himself alone, and saw that the ring was gone from his finger. "I can never return to my father's house," said he; "they would say I am a sorcerer: I will journey forth into the world till I come again to my kingdom."

So saying, he set out and travelled till he came to a mountain, where three giants were sharing their inheritance; and as they saw him pass, they cried out and said "Little men have sharp wits; he shall divide the inheritance between us." Now it consisted of a sword that cut off an enemy's head whenever the wearer gave the words "Heads off!" – a cloak that made the owner invisible, or gave him any form he pleased; and a pair of boots that transported the person who put them on wherever he wished. The king said they must first let him try these wonderful things, that he might know how to set a value upon them. Then they gave him the cloak, and he wished himself a fly, and in a moment he was a fly. "The cloak is very well," said he; "now give me the sword." "So," said they, "not unless you promise not to say 'Heads off!' for if you do, we are all dead men." So they gave it him on condition that he tried its virtue only on a tree. He next asked for the boots also; and the moment he had all three in his possession he wished himself at the Golden Mountain; and there he was in an instant. So the giants were left behind with no inheritance to divide or quarrel about.

As he came near to the castle he heard the sound of merry music; and the people around told him that his queen was about to celebrate her marriage with another prince. Then he threw his cloak around him, and passed through the castle, and placed

himself by the side of his queen, where no one saw him. But when any thing to eat was put upon her plate, he took it away and eat it himself; and when a glass of wine was handed to her, he took and drank it: and thus, though they kept on serving her with meat and drink, her plate continued always empty.

Upon this, fear and remorse came over her, and she went into her chamber and wept; and he followed her there. "Alas!" said she to herself, "did not my deliverer come? why then doth enchantment still surround me?"

"Thou traitress!" said he, "thy deliverer indeed came, and now is near thee: has he deserved this of thee?" And he went out and dismissed the company, and said the wedding was at an end, for that he was returned to his kingdom: but the princes and nobles and counsellors mocked at him. However, he would enter into no parley with them, but only demanded whether they would depart in peace, or not. Then they turned and tried to seize him; but he drew his sword, and, with a word, the traitors' heads fell before him; and he was once more king of the Golden Mountain.

The Golden Goose

THERE was a man who had three sons. The youngest was called Dummling, and was on all occasions despised and ill-treated by the whole family. It happened that the eldest took it into his head one day to go into the wood to cut fuel; and his mother gave him a delicious pasty and a bottle of wine to take with him, that he might refresh himself at his work. As he went into the wood, a little old man bid him good day, and said, "Give me a little piece of meat from your plate, and a little wine out of your bottle; I am very hungry and thirsty." But this clever young man said, "Give you my meat and wine! No, I thank you; I should not have enough left for myself:" and away he went. He soon began to cut down a tree; but he had not worked long before he missed his stroke, and cut himself, and was obliged to go home to have the wound dressed. Now it was the little old man that caused him this mischief.

Next went out the second son to work; and his mother gave him too a pasty and a bottle-of wine. And the same little old man met him also, and asked him for something to eat and drink. But he too thought himself vastly clever, and said, "Whatever you get, I shall lose; so go your way!" The little man took care that he should have his reward; and the second stroke that he aimed against a tree, hit him on the leg; so that he too was forced to go home.

Then Dummling said, "Father, I should, like to go and cut wood too." But his father answered, "Your brothers have both lamed themselves; you had better stay at home, for you know nothing of the business." But Dummling was very pressing; and at last his father said, "Go your way; you will be wiser when you have suffered for your folly." And his mother gave him only

163

some dry bread, and a bottle of sour beer; but when he went into the wood, he met the little old man, who said, "Give me some meat and drink, for I am very hungry and thirsty." Dummling said, "I have only dry bread and sour beer; if that will suit you, we will sit down and eat it together." So they sat down, and when the lad pulled out his bread behold it was turned into a capital pasty, and his sour beer became delightful wine. They ate and drank heartily; and when they had done, the little man said, "As you have a kind heart, and have been willing to share every thing with me, I will send a blessing upon you. There stands an old tree, cut it down and you will find something at the root." Then he took his leave, and went his way.

Dummling set to work, and cut down the tree; and when it fell, he found in a hollow under the roots a goose with feathers of pure gold. He took it up, and went on to an inn, where he proposed to sleep for the night. The landlord had three daughters; and when they saw the goose, they were very curious to examine what this wonderful bird could be, and wished very much to pluck one of the feathers out of its tail. At last the eldest said, "I must and will have a feather." So she waited till his back was turned, and then seized the goose by the wing; but to her great surprise there she stuck, for neither hand nor finger could she get away again. Presently in came the second sister, and thought to have a feather too; but the moment she touched her sister, there she too hung fast. At last came the third, and wanted a feather; but the other two cried out, "Keep away! for heaven's sake, keep away!" However, she did not understand what they meant. "If they are there," thought she, "I may as well be there too." So she went up to them; but the moment she touched her sisters she stuck fast, and hung to the goose as they did. And so they kept company with the goose all night.

The next morning Dummling carried off the goose under his arm, and took no notice of the three girls, but went out with them sticking fast behind; and wherever he travelled, they too were obliged to follow, whether they would or no, as fast as their legs could carry them.

In the middle of a field the parson met them; and when he saw the train, he said, "Are you not ashamed of yourselves, you bold girls, to run after the young man in that way over the fields? is that proper behaviour?" Then he took the youngest by the hand to lead her away; but the moment he touched her he too

hung fast, and followed in the train. Presently up came the clerk; and when he saw his master the parson running after the three girls, he wondered greatly, and said, "Hollo! hollo! your reverence! whither so fast? there is a christening to-day." Then he ran up, and took him by the gown, and in a moment he was fast too. As the five were thus trudging along, one behind another, they met two labourers with their mattocks coming from work; and the parson cried out to them to set him free. But scarcely had they touched him, when they too fell into the ranks, and so made seven, all running after Dummling and his goose.

At last they arrived at a city, where reigned a king who had an only daughter. The princess was of so thoughtful and serious a turn of mind that no one could make her laugh; and the king had proclaimed to all the world, that whoever could make her laugh should have her for his wife. When the young man heard this, he went to her with his goose and all its train; and as soon as she saw the seven all hanging together, and running about, treading on each other's heels, she could not help bursting into a long and loud laugh. Then Dummling claimed her for his wife; the wedding was celebrated, and he was heir to the kingdom, and lived long and happily with his wife.

Mrs Fox

THERE was once a sly old fox with nine tails, who was very curious to know whether his wife was true to him: so he stretched himself out under a bench, and pretended to be as dead as a mouse.

Then Mrs Fox went up into her own room and locked the door: but her maid, the cat, sat at the kitchen fire cooking; and soon after it became known that the old fox was dead, someone knocked at the door, saying,

> "Miss Pussy! Miss Pussy! how fare you to-day?
> Are you sleeping or watching the time away?"

Then the cat went and opened the door, and there stood a young fox; so she said to him,

> "No, no, Master Fox, I don't sleep in the day,
> I'm making some capital white wine whey.
> Will your honour be pleased, to dinner to stay?"

"No, I thank you," said the fox; "but how is poor Mrs Fox?" Then the cat answered,

> "She sits all alone in her chamber up stairs,
> And bewails her misfortune with floods of tears:
> She weeps till her beautiful eyes are red;
> For, alas! alas! Mr Fox is dead."

"Go to her," said the other, "and say that there is a young fox come, who wishes to marry her."

> Then up went the cat, – trippety trap,
> And knocked at the door, – tippety tap;

"Is good Mrs Fox within?" said she.
"Alas! my dear, what want you with me?"
"There waits a suitor below at the gate."

Then said Mrs Fox,

"How looks he, my dear! is he tall and straight?
Has he nine good tails? There must be nine,
Or he never shall be a suitor of mine."

"Ah!" said the cat, "he has but one." "Then I will never have him," answered Mrs Fox.

So the cat went down, and sent this suitor about his business. Soon after, someone else knocked at the door; it was another fox that had two tails, but he was not better welcomed than the first. After this came several others, till at last one came that had really nine tails just like the old fox.

When the widow heard this, she jumped up and said,

"Now, Pussy, my dear, open windows and doors,
And bid all our friends at our wedding to meet;
And as for that nasty old master of ours,
Throw him out of the window, Puss, into the street."

But when the wedding feast was all ready, up sprung the old gentleman on a sudden, and taking a club drove the whole company, together with Mrs Fox, out of doors.

After some time, however, the old fox really died; and soon afterwards a wolf came to pay his respects, and knocked at the door.

Wolf. Good day, Mrs Cat, with your whiskers so trim;
       How comes it you're sitting alone so prim?
       What's that you are cooking so nicely, I pray?
Cat.   O, that's bread and milk for my dinner to-day.
       Will your worship be pleased to stay and dine,
       Or shall I fetch you a glass of wine?

"No, I thank you: Mrs Fox is not at home, I suppose?"

Cat.   She sits all alone,
       Her griefs to bemoan;
       For, alas! alas! Mr Fox is gone.
Wolf. Ah! dear Mrs Puss, that's a loss indeed;
       D'ye think she'd take me for a husband instead?
Cat.   "Indeed, Mr Wolf, I don't know but she may,

If you'll sit down a moment, I'll step up and see."
So she gave him a chair, and shaking her ears,
She very obligingly tripped it up stairs.
She knocked at the door with the rings on her toes,
And said, "Mrs Fox, you're within, I suppose?"
"O yes," said the widow, "pray come in, my dear,
And tell me whose voice in the kitchen I hear."
"It's a wolf," said the cat, "with a nice smooth skin,
Who was passing this way, and just stepped in
To see (as old Mr Fox is dead)
If you like to take him for a husband instead."

"But," said Mrs Fox, "has he red feet and a sharp snout?" "No," said the cat. "Then he won't do for me." Soon after the wolf was sent about his business, there came a dog, then a goat, and after that a bear, a lion, and all the beasts, one after another. But they all wanted something that old Mr Fox had, and the cat was ordered to send them all away. At last came a young Fox, and Mrs Fox said. "Has he four red feet and a sharp snout? "Yes," said the cat.

"Then, Puss, make the parlour look clean and neat,
And throw the old gentleman into the street;
A stupid old rascal! I'm glad that he's dead,
Now I've got such a charming young fox instead."
So the wedding was held, and the merry bells rung,
And the friends and relations they danced and they sung,
And feasted, and drank, I can't tell how long.

Hansel and Gretel

HANSEL one day took his sister Gretel by the hand, and said, "Since our poor mother died we have had no happy days; for our new mother beats us all day long, and when we go near her, she pushes us away. We have nothing but hard crusts to eat; and the little dog that lies by the fire is better off than we; for he sometimes has a nice piece of meat thrown to him. Heaven have mercy upon us! O if our poor mother knew how we are used! Come, we will go and travel over the wide world." They went the whole day walking over the fields, till in the evening they came to a great wood; and then they were so tired and hungry that they sat down in a hollow tree and went to sleep.

In the morning when they awoke, the sun had risen high above the trees, and shone warm upon the hollow tree. Then Hansel said, "Sister, I am very thirsty; if I could find a brook, I would go and drink, and fetch you some water too. Listen, I think I hear the sound of one." Then Hansel rose up and took Gretel by the hand and went in search of the brook. But their cruel step-mother was a fairy, and had followed them into the wood to work them mischief: and when they had found a brook that ran sparkling over the pebbles, Hansel wanted to drink; but Gretel thought she heard the brook, as it babbled along, say, "Whoever drinks here will be turned in to a tiger." Then she cried out, "Ah, brother! do not drink, or you will be turned into a wild beast and tear me to pieces." Then Hansel yielded, although he was parched with thirst. "I will wait," said he, "for the next brook." But when they came to the next, Gretel listened again, and thought she heard, "Whoever drinks here will become a wolf." Then she cried out "Brother, brother, do not drink, or you will become a wolf and eat me." So he did not drink, but said, "I will wait for the next brook; there I must drink, say what you will, I am so thirsty."

As they came to the third brook, Gretel listened, and heard "Whoever drinks here will become a fawn." "Ah brother!" said she, "do not drink, or you will be turned into a fawn and run away from me." But Hansel had already stooped down upon his knees, and the moment he put his lips into the water he was turned into a fawn.

Gretel wept bitterly over the poor creature, and the tears too rolled down his eyes as be laid himself beside her. Then she said, "Rest in peace, dear fawn, I will never never leave thee." So she took off her golden necklace and put it round his neck, and plucked some rushes and plaited them into a soft string to fasten to it; and led the poor little thing by her side further into the wood.

After they had travelled a long way, they came at last to a little cottage; and Gretel, having looked in and seen that it was quite empty, thought to herself, "We can stay and live here." Then she went and gathered leaves and moss to make a soft bed for the fawn: and every morning she went out and plucked nuts, roots, and berries for herself, and sweet shrubs and tender grass for her companion; and it ate out of her hand, and was pleased, and played and frisked about her. In the evening, when Gretel was tired, and had said her prayers, she laid her head upon the fawn for her pillow, and slept: and if poor Hansel could but have his right form again, they thought they should lead a very happy life.

They lived thus a long while in the wood by themselves, till it chanced that the king of that country came to hold a great hunt there. And when the fawn heard all around the echoing of the horns, and the baying of the dogs, and the merry shouts of the huntsmen, he wished very much to go and see what was going on. "Ah sister, sister!" said he, "let me go out into the wood, I can stay no longer." And he begged so long, that she at last agreed to let him go. "But," said she, "be sure to come to me in the evening; I shall shut up the door to keep out those wild huntsmen; and if you tap at it, and say 'Sister, let me in,' I shall know you; but if you don't speak, I shall keep the door fast." Then away sprang the fawn, and frisked and bounded along in the open air. The king and his huntsmen saw the beautiful creature, and followed but could not overtake him; for when they thought they were sure of their prize, he sprang over the bushes and was out of sight in a moment.

As it grew dark he came running home to the hut, and tapped, and said "Sister, sister, let me in." Then she opened the little door, and in he jumped and slept soundly all night on his soft bed.

Next morning the hunt began again; and when he heard the huntsmens' horns, he said "Sister, open the door for me, I must go again." Then she let him out, and said "Come back in the evening, and remember what you are to say." When the king and the huntsmen saw the fawn with the golden collar again, they gave him chase; but he was too quick for them. The chase lasted the whole day; but at last the huntsmen nearly surrounded him, and one of them wounded him in the foot, so that he became sadly lame and could hardly crawl home. The man who had wounded him followed close behind, and hid himself, and heard the little fawn say, "Sister, sister, let me in:" upon which the door opened and soon shut again. The huntsman marked all well, and went to the king and told him what he had seen and heard; then the king said, "To-morrow we will have another chase."

Gretel was very much frightened when she saw that her dear little fawn was wounded; but she washed the blood away and put some healing herbs on it, and said, "Now go to bed, dear fawn, and you will soon be well again." The wound was so small, that in the morning there was nothing to be seen of it; and when the horn blew, the little creature said "I can't stay here, I must go and look on; I will take care that none of them shall catch me." But Gretel said, "I am sure they will kill you this time, I will not let you go." "I shall die of vexation," answered he, "if you keep me here: when I hear the horns, I feel as if I could fly." Then Gretel was forced to let him go; so she opened the door with a heavy heart, and he bounded out gaily into the wood.

When the king saw him he said to his huntsman, "Now chase him all day long till you catch him; but let none of you do him any harm." The sun set, however, without their being able to overtake him, and the king called away the huntsmen, and said to the one who had watched, "Now come and show me the little hut," So they went to the door and tapped, and said, "Sister, sister, let me in." Then the door opened and the king went in, and there stood a maiden more lovely than any he had ever seen. Gretel was frightened to see that it was not her fawn, but a king with a golden crown that was come into her hut: however, he spoke kindly to her, and took her hand, and said, "Will you come with me to my castle and be my wife?" "Yes," said the maiden; "but my fawn must go with me, I cannot part with that." "Well," said the king, "he shall come and live with you all your life, and want for nothing." Just at that moment in sprung the little fawn; and his sister tied the string to his neck, and they left the hut in the wood together.

Then the king took Gretel to his palace, and celebrated the marriage in great state. And she told the king all her story; and he sent for the fairy and punished her: and the fawn was changed into Hansel again, and he and his sister loved one another, and lived happily together all their days.

The Giant With
the Three Golden Hairs

THERE was once a poor man who had an only son born to him. The child was born under a lucky star; and those who told his fortune said that in his fourteenth year he would marry the king's daughter. It so happened that the king of that land soon after the child's birth passed through the village in disguise, and asked whether there was any news. "Yes," said the people, "a child has just been born, that they say is to be a lucky one, and when he is fourteen years old, he is fated to marry the king's daughter." This did not please the king; so he went to the poor child's parents and asked them whether they would sell him their son? "No," said they; but the stranger begged very hard and offered a great deal of money, and they had scarcely bread to eat, so at last they consented, thinking to themselves, he is a luck's child, he can come to no harm.

The king took the child, put it into a box, and rode away, but when he came to a deep stream, he threw it into the current, and said to himself, "That young gentleman will never be my daughter's husband." The box however floated down the stream; some kind spirit watched over it so that no water reached the child, and at last about two miles from the king's capital it stopt at the dam of a mill. The miller soon saw it, and took a long pole, and drew it towards the shore, and finding it heavy, thought there was gold inside; but when he opened it, he found a pretty little boy, that smiled upon him merrily. Now the miller and his wife had no children, and therefore rejoiced to see the prize, saying, "Heaven has sent it to us," so they treated it very kindly, and brought it up with such care that every one admired and loved it.

About thirteen years passed over their heads, when the king came by accident to the mill, and asked the miller if that was his son. "No," said he, "I found him when a babe in a box in the mill-dam." "How long ago?" asked the king. "Some thirteen years," replied the miller. "He is a fine fellow," said the king, "can you spare him to carry a letter to the queen? it will please me very much, and I will give him two pieces of gold for his trouble." "As your majesty pleases," answered the miller.

Now the king had soon guessed that this was the child whom he had tried to drown; and he wrote a letter by him to the queen, saying, "As soon as the bearer of this arrives, let him be killed and immediately buried, so that all may be over before I return."

The young man set out with this letter, but missed his way, and came in the evening to a dark wood. Through the gloom he perceived a light at a distance, towards which he directed his course, and found that it proceeded from a little cottage. There was no one within except an old woman, who was frightened at seeing him, and said, "Why do you come hither, and whither are you going?" "I am going to the queen, to whom I was to have delivered a letter; but I have lost my way, and shall be glad if you will give me a night's rest." "You are very unlucky," said she, "for this is a robbers' hut, and if the band returns while you are here it may be worse for you." "I am so tired, however," replied he, "that I must take my chance, for I can go no further;" so he laid the letter on the table, stretched himself out upon a bench, and fell asleep.

When the robbers came home and saw him, they asked, the old woman who the strange lad was. "I have given him shelter for charity," said she; "he had a letter to carry to the queen, and lost his way." The robbers took up the letter, broke it open and read the directions which it contained to murder the bearer. Then their leader tore it, and wrote a fresh one desiring the queen, as soon as the young man arrived, to marry him to the king's daughter. Meantime they let him sleep on till morning broke, and then showed him the right way to the queen's palace; where, as soon as she had read the letter, she had all possible preparations made for the wedding; and as the young man was very beautiful, the princess took him willingly for her husband.

After a while the king returned; and when he saw the prediction fulfilled, and that this child of fortune was, notwithstanding all his cunning, married to his daughter, he inquired eagerly how this had happened, and what were the orders which he had given. "Dear husband," said the queen, "here is your letter, read it for yourself." The king took it, and seeing that an exchange had been made, asked his son-in-law what he had done with the letter which he had given him to carry. "I know nothing of it," answered he; "it must have been taken away in the night while I slept." Then the king was very wroth, and said, "No man shall have my daughter who does not descend into the wonderful cave and bring me three golden hairs from the head of the giant king who reigns there; do this and you shall have my consent." "I will soon manage that," said the youth; – so he took leave of his wife and set out on his journey.

At the first city that he came to, the guard of the gate stopt him, and asked what trade he followed and what he knew. "I know everything," said he. "If that be so," replied they, "you are just the man we want; be so good as to tell us why our fountain in the market-place is dry and will give no water; find out the cause of that, and we will give you two asses loaded with gold." "With all my heart," said he, "when I come back."

Then he journeyed on and came to another city, and there the guard also asked him what trade he followed, and what he understood. "I know everything," answered he. "Then pray do us a piece of service," said they, "tell us why a tree which used to bear us golden apples, now does not even produce a leaf." "Most willingly," answered he, "as I come back."

At last his way led him to the side of a great lake of water over which he must pass. The ferryman soon began to ask, as the others had done, what was his trade, and what he knew. "Everything," said he. "Then," said the other, "pray inform me why I am bound for ever to ferry over this water, and have never been able to get my liberty; I will reward you handsomely." "I will tell you all about it," said the young man, "as I come home."

When he had passed the water, he came to the wonderful cave, which looked terribly black and gloomy. But the wizard king was not at home, and his grandmother sat at the door in her easy chair. "What do you seek?" said she. "Three golden hairs from the giant's head," answered he. "You run a great risk," said she, "when he returns home; yet I will try what I can do for you." Then she changed him into an ant, and told him to hide himself in the folds of her cloak. "Very well," said he: "but I want also to know why the city fountain is dry, why the tree that bore golden apples is now leafless, and what it is that binds the ferryman to his post." "Those are three puzzling questions," said the old dame; "but lie quiet and listen to what the giant says when I pull the golden hairs."

Presently night set in and the old gentleman returned home. As soon as he entered he began to snuff up the air, and cried, "All is not right here: I smell man's flesh." Then he searched all round in vain, and the old dame scolded, and said, "Why should you turn everything topsy-turvy? I have just set all in order." Upon this he laid his head in her lap and soon fell asleep. As soon as he began to snore, she seized one of the golden hairs and pulled it out. "Mercy!" cried he, starting up, "what are you about?" "I had a dream that disturbed me," said she, "and in my trouble I seized your hair: I dreamt that the fountain in the market-place of the city was become dry and would give no water; what can be the cause?" "Ah! if they could find that out, they would be glad," said the giant: "under a stone in the fountain sits a toad; when they kill him, it will flow again."

This said, he fell asleep, and the old lady pulled out another hair. "What would you be at?" cried he in a rage. "Don't be angry," said she, "I did it in my sleep; I dreamt that in a great kingdom there was a beautiful tree that used to bear golden apples, and now has not even a leaf upon it; what is the reason of that?" "Aha!" said the giant, "they would like very well to know that secret: at the root of the tree a mouse is gnawing; if they were to kill him, the tree would bear golden apples again; if not, it will soon die. Now let me sleep in peace; if you wake me again, you shall rue it."

Then he fell once more asleep; and when she heard him snore she pulled out the third golden hair, and the giant jumped up and threatened her sorely; but she soothed him, and said, "It was a strange dream: methought I saw a ferryman who was fated to ply backwards and forwards over a lake, and could never be set at liberty; what is the charm that binds him?" "A silly fool!" said the giant; "if he were to give the rudder into the hand of any passenger, he would find himself at liberty, and the other would be obliged to take his place. Now let me sleep."

In the morning the giant arose and went out; and the old woman gave the young man the three golden hairs, reminded him of the answers to his three questions, and sent him on his way.

He soon came to the ferryman, who knew him again, and asked for the answer which he had promised him. "Ferry me over first," said he, "and then I will tell you." When the boat arrived on the other side, he told him to give the rudder to any of his passengers, and then he might run away as soon as he pleased. The next place he came to was the city where the barren tree stood: "Kill the mouse," said he, "that gnaws the root, and you will have golden apples again." They gave him a rich present, and he journeyed on to the city where the fountain had dried up, and the guard demanded his answer to their question. So he told them how to cure the mischief, and they thanked him and gave him the two asses laden with gold.

And now at last this child of fortune reached home, and his wife rejoiced greatly to see him, and to hear how well every thing had gone with him. He gave the three golden hairs to the king, who could no longer raise any objection to him, and when he saw all the treasure, cried out in a transport of joy, "Dear son, where did you find all this gold?" "By the side of a lake," said the youth, "where there is plenty more to be had." "Pray, tell me," said the king, "that I may go and get some too." "As much as you please," replied the other; "you will see the ferryman, on the lake, let him carry you across, and there you will see gold as plentiful as sand upon the shore."

Away went the greedy king; and when he came to the lake, he beckoned to the ferryman, who took him into his boat, and as soon as he was there gave the rudder into his hand, and sprung ashore, leaving the old king to ferry away as a reward for his sins.

"And is his majesty plying there to this day?" You may be sure of that, for nobody will trouble himself to take the rudder out of his hands.

The Frog-Prince

ONE fine evening a young princess went into a wood, and sat down by the side of a cool spring of water. She had a golden ball in her hand, which was her favourite play-thing, and she amused herself with tossing it into the air and catching it again as it fell. After a time she threw it up so high that when she stretched out her hand to catch it, the ball bounded away and rolled along upon the ground, till at last it fell into the spring. The princess looked into the spring after her ball; but it was very deep, so deep that she could not see the bottom of it. Then she began to lament her loss, and said, "Alas! if I could only get my ball again, I would give all my fine clothes and jewels, and every thing that I have in the world." Whilst she was speaking a frog put its head out of the water and said "Princess, why do you weep so bitterly?" "Alas!" said she, "what can you do for me, you nasty frog? My golden ball has fallen into the spring." The frog said, "I want not your pearls and jewels and fine clothes; but if you will love me and let me live with you, and eat from your little golden plate, and sleep upon your little bed, I will bring you your ball again." "What nonsense," thought the princess, "this silly frog is talking! He can never get out of the well: however, he may be able to get my ball for me; and therefore I will promise him what he asks." So she said to the frog, "Well, if you will bring me my ball, I promise to do all you require." Then the frog put his head down, and dived deep under the water; and after a little while he came up again with the ball in his mouth, and threw it on the ground. As soon as the young princess saw her ball, she ran to pick it up, and was so overjoyed to have it in her hand again, that she never thought of the frog, but ran home with it as fast as she could. The frog called after her, "Stay, princess, and take me with you as you promised," but she did not stop to hear a word.

The next day, just as the princess had sat down to dinner, she heard a strange noise, tap-tap, as if somebody was coming up the marble staircase; and soon afterwards something knocked gently at the door, and said,

"Open the door, my princess dear,
Open the door to thy true love here!
And mind the words that thou and I said
By the fountain cool in the greenwood shade."

Then the princess ran to the door and opened it, and there she saw the frog, whom she had quite forgotten; she was terribly frightened, and shutting the door as fast as she could, came back to her seat. The king her father asked her what had frightened her. "There is a nasty frog," said she, "at the door, who lifted my ball out of the spring this morning: I promised him that he should live with me here, thinking that he could never get out of the spring; but there he is at the door and wants to come in!" While she was speaking the frog knocked again at the door, and said,

"Open the door, my princess dear,
Open the door to thy true love here!
And mind the words that thou and I said
By the fountain cool in the greenwood shade."

The king said to the young princess, "As you have made a promise, you must keep it; so go and let him in." She did so, and the frog hopped into the room, and came up close to the table. "Pray lift me upon a chair," said he to the princess, "and let me sit next to you." As soon as she had done this, the frog said "Put your plate closer to me that I may eat out of it." This she did, and when he had eaten as much as he could, he said "Now I am tired; carry me up stairs and put me into your little bed." And the princess took him up in her hand and put him upon the pillow of her own little bed, where he slept all night long. As soon as it was light he jumped up, hopped down stairs, and went out of the house. "Now," thought the princess, "he is gone, and I shall be troubled with him no more."

But she was mistaken; for when night came again, she heard the same tapping at the door, and when she opened it, the frog came in and slept upon her pillow as before till the morning broke: and the third night he did the same; but when the princess awoke on the following morning, she was astonished to see, instead of the frog, a handsome prince gazing on her with the most beautiful eyes that ever were seen, and standing at the head of her bed.

He told her that he had been enchanted by a malicious fairy, who had changed him into the form of a frog, in which he was fated to remain till some princess should take him out of the spring and let him sleep upon her bed for three nights. "You," said the prince, "have broken this cruel charm, and now I have nothing to wish for but that you should go with me into my father's kingdom, where I will marry you, and love you as long as you live."

The young princess, you may be sure, was not long in giving her consent; and as they spoke a splendid, carriage drove up with eight beautiful horses decked with plumes of feathers and golden harness, and behind rode the prince's servant, the faithful Henry, who had bewailed the misfortune of his dear master so long and bitterly that his heart had well nigh burst. Then all set out full of joy for the Prince's kingdom; where they arrived safely, and lived happily a great many years.

The Fox and the Horse

A FARMER had a horse that had been an excellent faithful servant to him: but he was now grown too old to work; so the farmer would give him nothing more to eat, and said "I want you no longer, so take yourself off out of my stable; I shall not take you back again until you are stronger than a lion." Then he opened the door and turned him adrift.

The poor horse was very melancholy, and wandered up and down in the wood, seeking some little shelter from the cold, wind and rain. Presently a fox met him: "What's the matter, my friend?" said he, "why do you hang down your head and look so lonely and woe-begone?" "Ah!" replied the horse, "justice and avarice never dwell in one house; my master has forgotten all that I have done for him so many years, and because I can no longer work he has turned me adrift, and says unless I become stronger than a lion he will not take me back again; what chance can I have of that? he knows I have none, or he would not talk so."

However, the fox bid him be of good cheer, and said, "I will help you; lie down there, stretch yourself out quite stiff, and pretend to be dead." The horse did as he was told, and the fox went straight to the lion who lived in a cave close by, and said to him, "A little way off lies a dead horse; come with me and you may make an excellent meal of his carcass." The lion was greatly pleased, and set off immediately, and when they came to the horse, the fox said "You will not he able to eat him comfortably here; I'll tell you what – I will tie you fast to his tail, and then you can draw him to your den, and eat him at your leisure."

This advice pleased the lion, so he laid himself down quietly for the fox to make him fast to the horse. But the fox managed to tie his legs together and bound all so hard and fast that with all his strength he could not set himself free. When the work was done, the fox clapped the horse on the shoulder, and said "Jip! Dobbin! Jip!" Then up he sprang, and moved off, dragging the lion behind him. The beast began to roar and bellow, till all the birds of the wood flew away for fright; but the horse let him sing on, and made his way quietly over the fields to his master's house.

"Here he is, master," said he, "I have got the better of him:" and when the farmer saw his old servant, his heart relented, and he said, "Thou shall stay in thy stable and be well taken care of." And so the poor old horse had plenty to eat, and lived – till he died.

Rumpel-Stilts-Kin

IN a certain kingdom once lived a poor miller who had a very beautiful daughter. She was moreover exceedingly shrewd and clever; and the miller was so vain and proud of her, that he one day told the king of the land that his daughter could spin gold out of straw. Now this king was very fond of money, and when he heard the miller's boast, his avarice was excited, and he ordered the girl to be brought before him. Then he led her to a chamber where there was a great quantity of straw, gave her a spinning-wheel, and said, "All this must be spun into gold before morning, as you value your life." It was in vain that the poor maiden declared that she could do no such thing, the chamber was locked and she remained alone.

She sat down in one corner of the room and began to lament over her hard fate, when on a sudden the door opened, and a droll-looking little man hobbled in, and said "Good morrow to you, my good lass, what are you weeping for?" "Alas! "answered she, "I must spin this straw into gold, and I know not how." "What will you give me," said the little man, "to do it for you?" "My necklace," replied the maiden. He took her at her word, and set himself down to the wheel; round about it went merrily, and presently the work was done and the gold all spun.

When the king came and saw this, he was greatly aston-ished and pleased; but his heart grew still more greedy of gain, and he shut up the poor miller's daughter again, with a fresh task. Then she knew not what to do, and sat down once more to weep; but the little man presently opened the door, and said "What will you give me to do your task?" "The ring on my finger," replied she. So her little friend took the ring, and began to work at the wheel, till by the morning all was finished again.

The king was vastly delighted to see all this glittering treasure; but still he was not satisfied, and took the miller's daughter into a yet larger room, and said, "All this must be spun to-night; and if you succeed, you shall be my queen." As soon as she was alone the dwarf came in, and said "What will you give me to spin gold for you this third time?" "I have nothing left," said she. "Then promise me," said the little man, "your first little child when you are queen." "That may never be," thought the miller's daughter; and as she knew no other way to get her task done, she promised him what he asked, and he spun once more the whole heap of gold. The king came in the morning, and finding all he wanted, married her, and so the miller's daughter really became queen.

At the birth of her first little child the queen rejoiced very much, and forgot the little man and her promise; but one day he came into her chamber and reminded her of it. Then she grieved sorely at her misfortune, and offered him all the treasures of the kingdom in exchange; but in vain, till at last her tears softened him, and he said "I will give you three days' grace, and if during that time you tell me my name, you shall keep your child."

Now the queen lay awake all night, thinking of all the odd names that she had ever heard, and dispatched messengers all over the land to inquire after new ones. The next day the little man came, and she began with Timothy, Benjamin, Jeremiah, and all the names she could remember; but to all of them he said, "That's not my name."

The second day she began with all the comical names she could hear of, Bandy-legs, Hunch-back, Crook-shanks, and so on, but the little gentleman still said to every one of them, "That's not my name."

The third day came back one of the messengers, and said "I can hear of no one other name; but yesterday, as I was climbing a high hill among the trees of the forest where the fox and the hare bid each other good night, I saw a little hut, and before the hut burnt a fire, and round about the fire danced a funny little man upon one leg, and sung,

"Merrily the feast I'll make,
To-day I'll brew, to-morrow bake;
Merrily I'll dance and sing,
For next day will a stranger bring;
Little does my lady dream;

Rumpel-Stilts-Kin is my name!"

When the queen heard this, she jumped for joy, and as soon as her little visitor came, and said, "Now, lady, what is my name?" "Is it John?" asked she. "No!" "Is it Tom?" "No!"

"Can your name be Rumpel-stilts-Kin?"

"Some witch told you that! Some witch told you that!" cried the little man, and dashed his right foot in a rage so deep into the floor, that he was forced to lay hold of it with both hands to pull it out. Then he made the best of his way off, while everybody laughed at him for having had all his trouble for nothing.

The Goose-Girl

AN old queen, whose husband had been dead some years, had a beautiful daughter. When she grew up, she was betrothed to a prince who lived a great way off; and as the time drew near for her to be married, she got ready to set off on her journey to his country. Then the queen her mother packed up a great many costly things; jewels, and gold, and silver; trinkets, fine dresses, and in short everything that became a royal bride; for she loved her child very dearly: and she gave her a waiting-maid to ride with her, and give her into the bridegroom's hands; and each had a horse for the journey. Now the princess's horse was called Falada, and could speak.

When the time came for them to set out, the old queen went into her bed-chamber, and took a little knife, and cut off a lock of her hair, and gave it to her daughter, and said, "Take care of it, dear child; for it is a charm that may be of use to you on the road." Then they took a sorrowful leave of each other, and the princess put the lock of her mother's hair into her bosom, got upon her horse, and set off on her journey to her bridegroom's kingdom. One day as they were riding along by the side of a brook, the princess began to feel very thirsty, and said to her maid, "Pray get down and fetch me some water in my golden cup out of yonder brook, for I want to drink." "Nay," said the maid, "if you are thirsty, get down yourself, and lie down by the water and drink; I shall not be your waiting-maid any longer." Then she was so thirsty that she got down, and knelt over the little brook and drank, for she was frightened, and dared not bring out her golden, cup; and then she wept, and said, "Alas! what will become of me?" And the lock of hair answered her, and said,

> "Alas! alas! if thy mother knew it;
> Sadly, sadly her heart would rue it."

But the princess was very humble and meek, so she said nothing to her maid's ill behaviour, but got upon her horse again.

Then all rode further on their journey, till the day grew so warm, and the sun so scorching, that the bride began to feel very thirsty again; and at last when they came to a river she forgot her maid's rude speech, and said, "Pray get down and fetch me some water to drink in my golden cup." But the maid answered her, and even spoke more haughtily than before, "Drink if you will, but I shall not be your waiting-maid." Then the princess was so thirsty that she got off her horse and lay down, and held her head over the running stream, and cried, and said, "What will become of me?" And the lock of hair answered her again,

> "Alas! alas! if thy mother knew it,
> Sadly, sadly her heart would rue it."

And as she leaned down to drink, the lock of hair fell from her bosom and floated away with the water, without her seeing it, she was so frightened. But her maid saw it, and was very glad, for she knew the charm, and saw that the poor bride would be in her power, now that she had lost the hair. So when the bride had done, and would have got upon Falada again, the maid said, "I shall ride upon Falada, and you may have my horse instead:" so she was forced to give up her horse, and soon afterwards to take off her royal clothes, and put on her maid's shabby ones.

At last as they drew near the end of their journey, this treacherous servant threatened to kill her mistress if she ever told any one what had happened. But Falada saw it all, and marked it well. Then the waiting-maid got upon Falada, and the real bride was set upon the other horse, and they went on in this way till at last they came to the royal court. There was great joy at their coming, and the prince flew to meet them, and lifted the maid from her horse, thinking she was the one who was to be his wife; and she was led up stairs to the royal chamber, but the true princess was told to stay in the court below.

But the old king happened to be looking out of the window, and saw her in the yard below; and as she looked very pretty, and too delicate for a waiting-maid, he went into the royal chamber to ask the bride who it was she had brought with her,

G.Cruikshank fec^t

that was thus left standing in the court below. "I brought her with me for the sake of her company on the road," said she; "pray give the girl some work to do, that she may not be idle." The old king could not for some time think of any work for her to do; but at last he said, "I have a lad who takes care of my geese; she may go and help him." Now the name of this lad, that the real bride was to help in watching the king's geese, was Curdken.

Soon after, the false bride said to the prince, "Dear husband, pray do me one piece of kindness." "That I will," said the prince. "Then tell one of your slaughterers to cut off the head of the horse I rode upon, for it was very unruly, and plagued me sadly on the road:" but the truth was, she was very much afraid lest Falada should speak, and tell all she had done to the princess. She carried her point, and the faithful Falada was killed: but when the true princess heard of it, she wept, and begged the man to nail up Falada's head against a large dark gate in the city through which she had to pass every morning and evening, that there she might still see him sometimes. Then the slaughterer said he would do as she wished; cut off the head, and nailed it fast under the dark gate.

Early the next morning, as she and Curdken went out through the gate, she said sorrowfully,

"Falada, Falada, there thou art hanging!"

and the head answered,

"Bride, bride, there thou art ganging!
Alas! alas! if thy mother knew it,
Sadly, sadly her heart would rue it."

Then they went out of the city, and drove the geese on. And when she came to the meadow, she sat down upon a bank there, and let down her waving locks of hair, which were all of pure silver; and when Curdken saw it glitter in the sun, he ran up, and would have pulled some of the locks out; but she cried,

"Blow, breezes, blow!
Let Curdken's hat go!
Blow, breezes, blow,
Let him after it go!
O'er hills, dales, and rocks,
Away be it whirl'd,

Till the silvery locks
Are all comb'd and curl'd!"

Then there came a wind, so strong that it blew off Curdken's hat, and away it flew over the hills, and he after it; till, by the time he came back, she had done combing and curling her hair, and put it up again safe. Then he was very angry and sulky, and would not speak to her at all; but they watched the geese until it grew dark in the evening, and then drove them homewards.

The next morning, as they were going through the dark gate, the poor girl looked up at Falada's head, and cried,

"Falada, Falada, there thou art hanging!"

and it answered,

"Bride, bride, there thou art ganging!
Alas! alas! if thy mother knew it,
Sadly, sadly her heart would rue it."

Then she drove on the geese and sat down again in the meadow, and began to comb out her hair as before; and Curdken ran up to her, and wanted to take hold of it; but she cried out quickly,

"Blow, breezes, blow!
Let Curdken's hat go!
Blow, breezes, blow!
Let him after it go!
O'er hills, dales, and rocks,
Away be it whirl'd,
Till the silvery locks
Are all comb'd and curl'd!"

Then the wind came and blew his hat, and off it flew a great way, over the hills and far away, so that he had to run after it; and when he came back, she had done up her hair again, and all was safe. So they watched the geese till it grew dark.

In the evening, after they came home, Curdken went to the old king, and said, "I cannot have that strange girl to help me to keep the geese any longer." "Why?" said the king. "Because she does nothing but tease me all day long." Then the king made him tell all that had passed. And Curdken said, "When we go in

G. Cruikshank fec.

the morning through the dark gate with our flock of geese, she weeps, and talks with the head of a horse that hangs upon the wall, and says,

"Falada, Falada, there thou art hanging!"

and the head answers,

"Bride, bride, there thou art ganging!
Alas! alas! if thy mother knew it,
Sadly, sadly her heart would rue it."

And Curdken went on telling the king what had happened upon the meadow where the geese fed; and how his hat was blown away, and he was forced to run after it, and leave his flock. But the old king told him to go out again as usual the next day: and when morning came, he placed himself behind the dark gate, and heard how she spoke to Falada, and how Falada answered; and then he went into the field and hid himself in a bush by the meadow's side, and soon saw with his own eyes how they drove the flock of geese, and how, after a little time, she let down her hair that glittered in the sun; and then he heard her say,

"Blow, breezes, blow!
Let Curdken's hat go!
Blow, breezes, blow!
Let him after it go!
O'er hills, dales, and rocks,
Away be it whirl'd,
Till the silvery locks
Are all comb'd and curl'd!"

And soon came a gale of wind, and carried away Curdken's hat, while the girl went on combing and curling her hair. All this the old king saw: so he went home without being seen; and when the little goose-girl came back in the evening, he called her aside, and asked her why she did so: but she burst into tears, and said, "That I must not tell you or any man, or I shall lose my life."

But the old king begged so hard, that she had no peace till she had told him all, word for word: and it was very lucky for her that she did so, for the king ordered royal clothes to be put upon her, and gazed on her with wonder, she was so beautiful. Then he called his son, and told him that he had only the false bride, for that she was merely a waiting-maid, while the true one stood by. And the young king rejoiced when he saw her beauty, and heard how meek and patient she had been; and without saying any thing, ordered a great feast to be got ready for all his court. The bridegroom sat at the top, with the false princess on one side, and the true one on the other; but nobody knew her, for she was quite dazzling to their eyes, and was not at all like the little goose-girl, now that she had her brilliant dress.

When they had eaten and drank, and were very merry, the old king told all the story, as one that he had once heard of, and asked the true waiting-maid what she thought ought be done to any one who would behave thus. "Nothing better," said this false bride, "than that she should be thrown into a cask stuck round with sharp nails, and that two white horses should be put to it, and should drag it from street to street till she is dead." "Thou art she!" said the old king, "and since thou hast judged thyself, it shall be so done to thee." And the young king was married to his true wife, and they reigned over the kingdom in peace and happiness all their lives.

Faithful John

AN OLD king fell sick; and when he found his end drawing near, he said, "Let Faithful John come to me." Now Faithful John was the servant that he was fondest of, and was so called because he had been true to his master all his life long. Then when he came to the bed-side, the king said, "My faithful John, I feel that my end draws nigh, and I have now no cares save for my son, who is still young, and stands in need of good counsel. I have no friend to leave him but you; if you do not pledge yourself to teach him all he should know, and to be a father to him, I shall not shut my eyes in peace." Then John said, "I will never leave him, but will serve him faithfully, even though it should cost me my life." And the king said, "I shall now die in peace: after my death, show him the whole palace; all the rooms and vaults, and all the treasures and stores which lie there: but take care how you show him one room, – I mean the one where hangs the picture of the daughter of the king of the golden roof. If he sees it, he will fall deeply in love with her, and will then be plunged into great dangers on her account: guard him in this peril." And when Faithful John had once more pledged his word to the old king, he laid his head on his pillow, and died in peace.

Now when the old king had been carried to his grave, Faithful John told the young king what had passed upon his death-bed, and said, "I will keep my word truly, and be faithful to you as I was always to your father, though it should cost me my life." And the young king wept, and said, "Neither will I ever forget your faithfulness."

The days of mourning passed away, and then Faithful John said to his master, "It is now time that you should see your heritage; I will show you your father's palace." Then he led him about everywhere, up and down, and let him see all the riches and all the costly rooms; only one room, where the picture stood, he did not open. Now the picture was so placed, that the moment the door opened, you could see it; and it was so beautifully done, that one would think it breathed and had life, and that there was nothing more lovely in the whole world. When the young king saw that Faithful John always went by this door, he said, "Why do you not open that room?" "There is something inside," he answered, "which would frighten you." But the king said, "I have seen the whole palace, and I must also know what is in there;" and he went and began to force open the door: but Faithful John held him back, and said, "I gave my word to your father before his death, that I would take heed how I showed you what stands in that room, lest it should lead you and me into great trouble." "The greatest trouble to me," said the young king, "will be not to go in and see the room; I shall have no peace by day or by night until I do; so I shall not go hence until you open it."

Then Faithful John saw that with all he could do or say the young king would have his way; so, with a heavy heart and many foreboding sighs, he sought for the key out of his great bunch; and he opened the door of the room, and entered in first, so as to stand between the king and the picture, hoping he might not see it: but he raised himself upon tiptoes, and looked over John's shoulders; and as soon as he saw the likeness of the lady, so beautiful and shining with gold, he fell down upon the floor senseless. Then Faithful John lifted him up in his arms, and carried him to his bed, and was full of care, and thought to himself, "This trouble has come upon us; O Heaven! what will come of it?"

At last the king came to himself again; but the first thing that he said was, "Whose is that beautiful picture?" "It is the picture of the daughter of the king of the golden roof," said Faithful John. But the king went on, saying, "My love towards her is so great, that if all the leaves on the trees were tongues, they could not speak it; I care not to risk my life to win her; you are my faithful friend, you must aid me."

Then John thought for a long time what was now to be done; and at length said to the king, "All that she has about her is of gold: the tables, stools, cups, dishes, and all the things in her house are of gold; and she is always seeking new treasures. Now in your stores there is much gold; let it be worked up into every kind of vessel, and into all sorts of birds, wild beasts, and wonderful animals; then we will take it and try our fortune." So the king ordered all the goldsmiths to be sought for; and they worked day and night, until at last the most beautiful things were made: and Faithful John had a ship loaded with them, and put on a merchant's dress, and the king did the same, that they might not be known.

When all was ready they put out to sea, and sailed till they came to the coast of the land where the king of the golden roof reigned. Faithful John told the king to stay in the ship, and wait for him; "for perhaps," said he, "I may be able to bring away the king's daughter with me: therefore take care that every thing be in order; let the golden vessels and ornaments be brought forth, and the whole ship be decked out with them." And he chose out something of each of the golden things to put into his basket, and got ashore, and went towards the king's palace. And when he came to the castle yard, there stood by the well side a beautiful maiden, who had two golden pails in her hand, drawing water. And as she drew up the water, which was glittering with gold, she turned herself round, and saw the stranger, and asked him who he was. Then he drew near, and said, "I am a merchant," and opened his basket, and let her look into it; and she cried out, "Oh! what beautiful things!" and set down her pails, and looked at one after the other. Then she said, "The king's daughter must see all these; she is so fond of such things, that she will buy all of you." So she took him by the hand, and led him in; for she was one of the waiting-maids of the daughter of the king.

When the princess saw the wares, she was greatly pleased, and said, "They are so beautiful that I will buy them all." But Faithful John said, "I am only the servant of a rich merchant; what I have here is nothing to what he has lying in yonder ship: there he has the finest and most costly things that ever were made in gold." The princess wanted to have them all brought ashore; but he said, "That would take up many days, there are such a number; and more rooms would be wanted to place them in than there are in the greatest house." But her wish to see them grew still greater, and at last she said, "Take me to the ship, I will go myself, and look at your master's wares."

Then Faithful John led her joyfully to the ship, and the king, when he saw her, thought that his heart would leap out of his breast; and it was with the greatest trouble that he kept himself still. So she got into the ship, and the king led her down; but Faithful John stayed behind with the steersman, and ordered the ship to put off: "Spread all your sail," cried he, "that she may fly over the waves like a bird through the air."

And the king showed the princess the golden wares, each one singly: the dishes, cups, basins, and the wild and wonderful beasts; so that many hours flew away, and she looked at every thing with delight, and was not aware that the ship was sailing away. And after she had looked at the last, she thanked the merchant, and said she would go home; but when she came upon the deck, she saw that the ship was sailing far away from land upon the deep sea, and that it flew along at full sail. "Alas!" she cried out in her fright, "I am betrayed; I am carried off, and have fallen into the power of a roving trader; I would sooner have died." But then the king took her by the hand, and said, "I am not a merchant, I am a king, and of as noble birth as you. I have taken you away by stealth, but I did so because of the very great love I have for you; for the first time that I saw your face, I fell on the ground in a swoon." When the daughter of the king of the golden roof heard all, she was comforted, and her heart soon turned towards him, and she was willing to become his wife.

But it so happened, that whilst they were sailing on the deep sea, Faithful John, as he sat on the prow of the ship playing on his flute, saw three ravens flying in the air towards him. Then he left off playing, and listened to what they said to each other, for he understood their tongue. The first said, "There he goes! he is bearing away the daughter of the king of the golden roof; let him go!" "Nay," said the second, "there he goes, but he has not got her yet." And the third said, "There he goes; he surely has her, for she is sitting by his side in the ship." Then the first began again, and cried out, "What boots it to him? See you not that when they come to land, a horse of a foxy-red colour will spring towards him; and then he will try to get upon it, and if he does, it will spring away with him into the air, so that he will never gee his love again." "True! true!" said the second, "but is there no help?" "Oh! yes, yes!" said the first; "if he who sits upon the horse takes the dagger which is stuck in the saddle and strikes him dead, the young king is saved: but who knows that? and who will tell him, that he who thus saves the king's life will turn to stone from the toes of his feet to his knee?" Then the second said, "True! true! but I know more still; though the horse be dead, the king loses his bride: when they go together into the palace, there lies the bridal dress on the couch, and looks as if it were woven of gold and silver, but it is all brimstone and pitch; and if he puts it on, it will burn him, marrow and bones." "Alas! alas! is there no help?" said the third. "Oh! yes, yes!" said the second, "if someone draws near and throws it into the fire, the young king will be saved. But what boots that? who knows and will tell him, that, if he does, his body from the knee to the heart will be turned to stone?" "More! more! I know more," said the third: "were the dregs burnt, still the king loses his bride. After the wedding, when the dance begins, and the young queen dances on, she will turn pale, and fall as though she were dead; and if someone does not draw near and lift her up, and take from her right breast three drops of blood, she will surely die. But if any one knew this, he would tell him, that if he does do so, his body will turn to stone, from the crown of his head to the tip of his toe."

Then the ravens flapped their wings, and flew on; but Faithful John, who had understood it all, from that time was sorrowful, and did not tell his master what he had heard; for he saw that if he told him, he must himself lay down his life to save him: at last he said to himself, "I will be faithful to my word, and save my master, if it costs me my life."

Now when they came to land, it happened just as the ravens had foretold, for there sprung out a fine foxy-red horse. "See," said the king, "he shall bear me to my palace:" and he tried to mount, but Faithful John leaped before him, and swung himself quickly upon it, drew the dagger, and smote the horse dead. Then the other servants of the king, who were jealous of Faithful John, cried out, "What a shame to kill the fine beast that was to take the king to his palace!" But the king said, "Let him alone, it is my Faithful John; who knows but he did it for some good end?"

Then they went on to the castle, and there stood a couch in one room, and a fine dress lay upon it, that shone with gold and silver; and the young king went up to it to take hold of it, but Faithful John cast it on the fire, and burnt it. And the other servants began again to grumble, and said, "See, now he is burning the wedding dress." But the king said, "Who knows what he does it for? let him alone! he is my faithful servant John."

Then the wedding feast was held, and the dance began, and the bride also came in; but Faithful John took good heed, and looked in her face; and on a sudden she turned pale, and fell as though she were dead upon the ground. But he sprung towards her quickly, lifted her up, and took her and laid her upon a couch, and drew three drops of blood from her right breast. And she breathed again, and came to herself. But the young king had seen all, and did not know why Faithful John had done it; so he was angry at his boldness, and said, "Throw him into prison."

The next morning Faithful John was led forth, and stood upon the gallows, and said, "May I speak out before I die?" and when the king answered "It shall be granted thee," he said, "I am wrongly judged, for I have always been faithful and true:" and then he told what he had heard the ravens say upon the sea, and how he meant to save his master, and had therefore done all these things.

When he had told all, the king called out, "O my most faithful John! pardon! pardon! take him down!" But Faithful John had fallen down lifeless at the last word he spoke, and lay as a stone: and the king and the queen mourned over him; and the king said, "Oh, how ill have I rewarded thy truth!" And he ordered the stone figure to be taken up, and placed in his own room near to his bed; and as often as he looked at it he wept, and said, "O that I could bring thee back to life again, my Faithful John!"

After a time, the queen had two little sons, who grew up, and were her great joy. One day, when she was at church, the two children stayed with her father; and as they played about, he looked at the stone figure, and sighed, and cried out, "O that I could bring thee back to life my Faithful John!" Then the stone began to speak, and said, "O king! thou canst bring me back to life if thou wilt give up for my sake what is dearest to thee." But the king said, "All that I have in the world would I give up for thee." "Then," said the stone, "cut off the heads of thy children, sprinkle their blood over me, and I shall live again." Then the king was greatly shocked: but he thought how Faithful John had died for his sake, and because of his great truth towards him; and rose up and drew his sword to cut off his children's heads and sprinkle the stone with their blood; but the moment he drew his sword Faithful John was alive again, and stood before his face, and said, "Your truth is rewarded." And the children sprang about and played as if nothing had happened.

Then the king was full of joy: and when he saw the queen

coming, to try her, he put Faithful John and the two children in a large closet; and when she came in he said to her, "Have you been at church?" "Yes," said she, "but I could not help thinking of Faithful John, who was so true to us." "Dear wife," said the king, "we can bring him back to life again, but it will cost us both our little sons, and we must give them up for his sake." When the queen heard this, she turned pale and was frightened in her heart; but she said, "Let it be so; we owe him all, for his great faith and truth." Then he rejoiced because she thought as he had thought, and went in and opened the closet, and brought out the children and Faithful John, and said, "Heaven be praised! he is ours again, and we have our sons safe too." So he told her the whole story; and all lived happily together the rest of their lives.

The Blue Light

A SOLDIER had served a king his master many years, till at last he was turned off without pay or reward. How he should get his living he did not know: so he set out and journeyed homeward all day in a very downcast mood, until in the evening he came to the edge of a deep wood. The road leading that way, he pushed forward, but had not gone far before he saw a light glimmering through the trees, towards which he bent his weary steps; and soon came to a hut where no one lived but an old witch. The poor fellow begged for a night's lodging and something to eat and drink; but she would listen to nothing: however, he was not easily got rid of; and at last she said, "I think I will take pity on you this once: but if I do you must dig over all my garden for me in the morning." The soldier agreed very willingly to any thing she asked, and he became her guest.

The next day he kept his word and dug the garden very neatly. The job lasted all day; and in the evening, when his mistress would have sent him away, he said," I am so tired of my work that I must beg you to let me stay over the night." The old lady vowed at first she would not do any such thing; but after a great deal of talk he carried his point, agreeing to chop up a whole cart-load of wood for her the next day.

This task too was duly ended; but not till towards night; and then he found himself so tired, that he begged a third night's rest; and this too was given, but only on his pledging his word that he next day would fetch the witch the blue light that burnt at the bottom of the well.

When morning came she led him to the well's mouth, tied him to a long rope, and let him down. At the bottom sure enough he found the blue light as the witch had said, and at once made the signal for her to draw him up again. But when she had pulled him up so near to the top that she could reach him with her hands, she said "Give me the light, I will take care of it," – meaning to play him a trick, by taking it for herself and letting him fall again to the bottom of the well. But the soldier saw through her wicked thoughts, and said, "No, I shall not give you the light till I find myself safe and sound out of the well." At this she became very angry, and dashed him, with the light she had longed for many a year, down to the bottom. And there lay the poor soldier for a while in despair, on the damp mud below, and feared that his end was nigh. But his pipe happened to be in his pocket still half full, and he thought to himself, "I may as well make an end of smoking you out; it is the last pleasure I shall have in this world." So he lit it at the blue light, and began to smoke.

Up rose a cloud of smoke, and on a sudden a little black dwarf was seen making his way through the midst of it. "What do you want with me, soldier?" said he. "I have no business with you," answered he. But the dwarf said, "I am bound to serve you in every thing, as lord and master of the blue light." "Then first of all be so good as to help me out of this well." No sooner said than done: the dwarf took him by the hand and drew him up, and the blue light of course with him. "Now do me another piece of kindness," said the soldier: "Pray let that old lady take my place in the well." When the dwarf had done this, and lodged the witch safely at the bottom, they began to ransack her treasures; and the soldier made bold to carry off as much of her gold and silver as he well could. Then the dwarf said, "If you should chance at any time to want me, you have nothing to do but to light your pipe at the blue light, and I will soon be with you."

The soldier was not a little pleased at his good luck, and went into the best inn in the first town he came to, and ordered some fine clothes to be made and a handsome room to be got ready for him. When all was ready, he called his little man to him, and said, "The king sent me away pennyless, and left me to hunger and want: I have a mind to show him that it is my turn to be master now; so bring me his daughter here this evening, that she may wait upon me, and do what I bid her." "That is rather a dangerous task," said the dwarf. But away he went, took the princess out of her bed, fast asleep as she was, and brought her to the soldier.

G Cruikshank fec.

Very early in the morning he carried her back: and as soon as she saw her father, she said, "I had a strange dream last night: I thought I was carried away through the air to a soldier's house, and there I waited upon him as his servant." Then the king wondered greatly at such a story; but told her to make a hole in her pocket and fill it with peas, so that if it were really as she said, and the whole was not a dream, the peas might fall out in the streets as she passed through, and leave a clue to tell whither she had been taken. She did so; but the dwarf had heard the king's plot; and when evening came, and the soldier said he must bring him the princess again, he strewed peas over several of the streets, so that the few that fell from her pocket were not known from the others; and the people amused themselves all the next day picking up peas, and wondering where so many came from.

When the princess told her father what had happened to her the second time, he said, "Take one of your shoes with you, and hide it in the room you are taken to." The dwarf heard this also; and when the soldier told him to bring the king's daughter again he said, "I cannot save you this time; it will be an unlucky thing for you if you are found out – as I think you will." But the soldier would have his own way. "Then you must take care and make the best of your way out of the city gate very early in the morning," said the dwarf. The princess kept one shoe on as her father bid her, and hid it in the soldier's room: and when she got back to her father, he ordered it to be sought for all over the town; and at last it was found where she had hid it. The soldier had run away, it is true! but he had been too slow, and was soon caught and thrown into a strong prison, and loaded with chains: – what was worse, in the hurry of his flight, he had left behind him his great treasure the blue light and all his gold, and had nothing left in his pocket but one poor ducat.

As he was standing very sorrowful at the prison grating, he saw one of his comrades, and calling out to him said, "If you will bring me a little bundle I left in the inn, I will give you a ducat." His comrade thought this very good pay for such a job: so he went away, and soon came back bringing the blue light and the gold. Then the soldier soon lit his pipe: up rose the smoke, and with it came his old friend the little dwarf. "Do not fear, master," said he: "keep up your heart at your trial and leave every thing to take its course; – only mind to take the blue light with you." The trial soon came on; the matter was sifted to the bottom; the prisoner found guilty, and his doom passed: he was ordered to be hung forthwith on the gallows tree.

But as he was let out, he said he had one favour to beg of the king. "What is it?" said his majesty. "That you will deign to let me smoke one pipe on the road." "Two, if you like," said the king. Then he lit his pipe at the blue light, and the black dwarf was before him in a moment. "Be so good as to kill, slay, or put to flight all these people," said the soldier: "and as for the king, you may cut him into three pieces." Then the dwarf began to lay about him, and soon got rid of the crowd around: but the king begged hard for mercy; and to save his life, agreed to let the soldier have the princess for his wife, and to leave the kingdom to him when he died.

Ashputtel

THE wife of a rich man fell sick: and when she felt that her end drew nigh, she called her only daughter to her bed-side, and said, "Always be a good girl, and I will look down from heaven and watch over you." Soon afterwards she shut her eyes and died, and was buried in the garden; and the little girl went every day to her grave and wept, and was always good and kind to all about her. And the snow spread a beautiful white covering over the grave; but by the time the sun had melted it away again, her father had married another wife. This new wife had two daughters of her own, that she brought home with her: they were fair in face but foul at heart, and it was now a sorry time for the poor little girl. "What does the good-for-nothing thing want in the parlour?" said they; "they who would eat bread should first earn it; away with the kitchen maid!" Then they took away her fine clothes, and gave her an old gray frock to put on, and laughed at her and turned her into the kitchen.

There she was forced to do hard work; to rise early before day-light, to bring the water, to make the fire, to cook and to wash. Besides that, the sisters plagued her in all sorts of ways and laughed at her. In the evening when she was tired she had no bed to lie down on, but was made to lie by the hearth among the ashes; and then, as she was of course always dusty and dirty, they called her Ashputtel.

It happened once that the father was going to the fair, and asked his wife's daughters what he should bring them, "Fine clothes," said the first: "Pearls and diamonds," cried the second. "Now, child," said he to his own daughter, "what will you have?" "The first sprig, dear father, that rubs against your hat on your way home," said she. Then he bought for the two first the fine clothes and pearls and diamonds they had asked for: and on his way home as he rode through a green copse, a sprig of hazel brushed against him, and almost pushed off his hat: so he broke it off and brought it away; and when he got home he gave it to his daughter. Then she took it and went to her mother's grave and planted it there, and cried so much that it was watered with her tears; and there it grew and became a fine tree. Three times every day she went to it and wept; and soon a little bird came and built its nest upon the tree, and talked with her, and watched over her, and brought her whatever she wished for.

Now it happened that the king of the land held a feast which was to last three days, and out of those who came to it his son was to choose a bride for himself: and Ashputtel's two sisters were asked to come. So they called her up, and said, "Now, comb our hair, brush our shoes, and tie our sashes for us, for we are going to dance at the king's feast." Then she did as she was told, but when all was done she could not help crying, for she thought to herself, she should have liked to go to the dance too; and at last she begged her mother very hard to let her go. "You! Ashputtel?" said she; "you who have nothing to wear, no clothes at all, and who cannot even dance – you want to go to the ball?" And when she kept on begging, – to get rid of her, she said at last, "I will throw this basin-full of peas into the ash heap, and if you have picked them all out in two hours time you shall go to the feast too." Then she threw the peas into the ashes: but the little maiden ran out at the back door into the garden, and cried out –

> "Hither, hither, through the sky,
> Turtle-doves and linnets fly.
> Blackbird, thrush, and chaffinch gay,
> Hither, hither, haste away!
> One and all, come help me quick,
> Haste ye, haste ye, – pick, pick, pick!"

Then first came two white doves flying in at the kitchen window; and next came two turtle-doves; and after them all the little birds under heaven came chirping and fluttering in, and flew down into the ashes: and the little doves stooped their heads down and set to work, pick, pick, pick; and then the others began to pick, pick, pick; and picked out all the good grain and put it in a dish, and left the ashes. At the end of one hour the work was done, and all flew out again at the windows. Then she brought the dish to her mother, overjoyed at the thought that now she should go to the wedding. But she said, "No, no! you slut, you have no clothes and cannot dance, you shall not go." And when Ashputtel begged very hard to go, she said, "If you can in one hour's time pick two of those dishes of peas out of the ashes, you shall go too." And thus she thought she should at last get rid of her. So she shook two dishes of peas into the ashes; but the little maiden went out into the garden at the back of the house, and cried out as before –

> "Hither, hither, through the sky,
> Turtle-doves and linnets fly.
> Blackbird, thrush, and chaffinch gay,
> Hither, hither, haste away!
> One and all, come help me quick,
> Haste ye, haste ye, – pick, pick, pick!"

Then first came two white doves in at the kitchen window; and next came the turtle-doves; and after them all the little birds under heaven came chirping and hopping about, and flew down about the ashes: and the little doves put their heads down and set to work, pick, pick, pick; and then the others began pick, pick, pick; and they put all the good grain into the dishes, and left all the ashes. Before half an hour's time all was done, and out they flew again. And then Ashputtel took the dishes to her mother, rejoicing to think that she should now go to the ball. But her mother said, "It is all of no use, you cannot go, you have no clothes, and cannot dance, and you would only put us to shame:" and off she went with her two daughters to the feast.

Now when all were gone, and nobody left at home, Ashputtel went sorrowfully and sat down under the hazel-tree, and cried out –

> "Shake, shake, hazel tree,
> Gold and silver over me!"

Then her friend the bird flew out of the tree and brought a gold and silver dress for her, and slippers of spangled silk; and she put them on, and followed her sisters to the feast. But they did not know her, and thought it must be some strange princess, she looked so fine and beautiful in her rich clothes: and they never once thought of Ashputtel, but took for granted that she was safe at home in the dirt.

The king's son soon came up to her, and took her by the hand and danced with her and no one else: and he never left her hand; but when any one else came to ask her to dance, he said, "This lady is dancing with me." Thus they danced till a late hour of the night; and then she wanted to go home; and the king's son said, "I shall go and take care of you to your home;" for he wanted to see where the beautiful maid lived. But she slipped away from him unawares, and ran off towards home, and the prince followed her; but she jumped up into the pigeon-house and shut the door. Then he waited till her father came home, and told him that the unknown maiden who had been at the feast had hid herself in the pigeon-house. But when they had broken open the door they found no one within; and as they came back into the house, Ashputtel lay, as she always did, in her dirty frock by the ashes, and her dim little lamp burnt in the chimney: for she had run as quickly as she could through the pigeon-house and on to the hazel-tree, and had there taken off her beautiful clothes, and laid them beneath the tree, that the bird might carry them away, and had seated herself amid the ashes again in her little gray frock.

The next day when the feast was again held, and her father, mother, and sisters were gone, Ashputtel went to the hazel-tree, and said –

"Shake, shake, hazel-tree,
Gold and silver over me!"

And the bird came and brought a still finer dress than the one she had worn the day before. And when she came in it to the ball, every one wondered at her beauty: but the king's son, who was waiting for her, took her by the hand, and danced with her; and when any one asked her to dance, he said as before, "This lady is dancing with me." When night came she wanted to go home; and the king's son followed her as before, that he might see into what house she went: but she sprung away from him all at once into the garden behind her father's house. In this garden stood a fine large pear-tree full of ripe fruit; and Ashputtel not knowing where to hide herself jumped up into it without being seen. Then the king's son could not find out where she was gone, but waited till her father came home, and said to him, "The unknown lady who danced with me has slipt away, and I think she must have sprung into the pear-tree." The father thought to himself, "Can it be Ashputtel?" So he ordered an axe to be brought; and they cut down the tree, but found no one upon it. And when they came back into the kitchen, there lay Ashputtel in the ashes as usual; for she had slipped down on the other side of the tree, and carried her beautiful clothes back to the bird at the hazel-tree, and then put on her little gray frock.

The third day, when her father and mother and sisters were gone, she went again into the garden, and said –

> "Shake, shake, hazel-tree,
> Gold and silver over me"

Then her kind friend the bird brought a dress still finer than the former one, and slippers which were all of gold: so that when she came to the feast no one knew what to say for wonder at her beauty: and the king's son danced with her alone, and when any one else asked her to dance, he said, "This lady is my partner." Now when night came she wanted to go home; and the king's son would go with her, and said to himself, "I will not lose her this time;" but however she managed to slip away from him, though in such a hurry that she dropped her left golden slipper upon the stairs.

So the prince took the shoe, and went the next day to the king his father, and said, "I will take for my wife the lady that this golden slipper fits." Then both the sisters were overjoyed to hear this; for they had beautiful feet, and had no doubt that they could wear the golden slipper. The eldest went first into the room where the slipper was and wanted to try it on, and the mother stood by. But her great toe could not go into it, and the shoe was altogether much too small for her. Then the mother gave her a knife, and said, "Never mind, cut it off; when you are queen you will not care about toes, you will not want to go on foot." So the silly girl cut her great toe off, and squeezed the shoe on, and went to the king's son. Then he took her for his bride, and set her beside him on his horse and rode away with her.

But in their way home they had to pass by the hazel-tree that Ashputtel had planted, and there sat a little dove on the branch, singing –

> "Back again! back again! look to the shoe!
> The shoe is too small, and not made for you!
> Prince! prince! look again for thy bride,
> For she's not the true one that sits by thy side."

Then the prince got down and looked at her foot, and saw by the blood that streamed from it what a trick she had played him. So he turned his horse round and brought the false bride back to her home, and said, "This is not the right bride: let the other sister try and put on the slipper." Then she went into the room and got her foot into the shoe, all but the heel, which was too large. But her mother squeezed it in till the blood came, and took her to the king's son; and he set her as his bride by his side on his horse, and rode away with her.

But when they came to the hazel-tree the little dove sat there still, and sang –

> "Back again! back again! look to the shoe!
> The shoe is too small, and not made for you!
> Prince! prince! look again for thy bride,
> For she's not the true one that sits by thy side."

Then he looked down and saw that the blood streamed so from the shoe that her white stockings were quite red. So he turned his horse and brought her back again also. "This is not the true bride," said he to the father; "have you no other daughters?" "No," said he; "there is only a little dirty Ashputtel here, the child of my first wife; I am sure she cannot be the bride." However, the prince told him to send her. But the mother said "No, no, she is much too dirty, she will not dare to show herself:" however, the prince would have her come. And she first washed her face and hands, and then went in and curtsied to him, and he reached her the golden slipper. Then she took her clumsy shoe off her left foot, and put on the golden slipper; and it fitted her as if it had been made for her. And when he drew near and looked at her face he knew her, and said, "This is the right bride." But the mother and both the sisters were frightened and turned pale with anger as he took Ashputtel on his horse, and rode away with her. And when they came to the hazel-tree, the white dove sang –

> "Home! home! look at the shoe!
> Princess! the shoe was made for you!
> Prince! prince! take home thy bride,
> For she is the true one that sits by thy side!"

And when the dove had done its song, it came flying and perched upon her right shoulder, and so went home with her.

The Young Giant and the Tailor

A HUSBANDMAN had once a son, who was born no bigger than my thumb, and for many years did not grow a hair's breadth taller. One day as the father was going to plough in the field, the little fellow said, "Father, let me go too." "No," said his father; "stay where you are, you can do no good out of doors, and if you go perhaps I may lose you." Then little Thumbling fell a-crying: and his father, to quiet him, at last said he might go. So he put him in his pocket, and when he was in the field pulled him out and set him upon a newly made furrow, that he might look about. While he was sitting there, a great giant came striding over the hill. "Do you see that tall steeple-man?" said the father: "he will run away with you." (Now he only said this to frighten the little boy if he should be naughty.) But the giant had long legs, and with two or three strides he really came close to the furrow, and picked up little Thumbling to look at him; and taking a liking to the little chap went off with him. The father stood by all the time, but could not say a word for fright; for he thought his child was really lost, and that he should never see him again.

But the giant took care of him at his house in the woods, and laid him in his bosom and fed him with the same food that he lived on himself. So Thumbling, instead of being a little dwarf, became like the giant – tall and stout and strong; so that at the end of two years when the old giant took him into the wood to try him, and said, "Pull up that birch-tree for yourself to walk with," the lad was so strong that he tore it up by the root. The giant thought he should make him a still stronger man than this: so after taking care of him two years more, he took him into the wood to try his strength again. This time he took hold of one of the thickest oaks, and pulled it up as if it were mere sport to him.

Then the old giant said, "Well done, my man, you will do now." So he carried him back to the field where he first found him.

His father happened to be just then ploughing as the young giant went up to him, saying, "Look here, father, see who I am; – don't you see I am your son?" But the husbandman was frightened, and cried out, "No, no, you are not my son; begone about your business." "Indeed, I am your son; let me plough a little, I can plough as well as you." "No, go your ways," said the father; but as he was afraid of the tall man, he at last let go the plough and sat down on the ground beside it. Then the youth laid hold of the ploughshare, and though he only pushed with one hand, he drove it deep into the earth. The ploughman cried out, "If you must plough, pray do not push so hard; you are doing more harm than good;" but he took off the horses, and said, "Father, go home and tell my mother to get ready a good dinner; I'll go round the field meanwhile." So he went on driving the plough without any horses, till he had done two mornings' work by himself; then he harrowed it, and when all was over, took up plough, harrow, horses and all, and carried them home like a bundle of straw.

When he reached the house he sat himself down on the bench, saying, "Now, mother, is dinner ready?" "Yes," said she, for she dared not deny him; so she brought two large dishes full, enough to have lasted herself and her husband eight days; however, he soon ate it all up, and said that was but a taste. "I see very well, father, that I shan't get enough to eat at your house; so if you will give me an iron walking-stick, so strong that I cannot break it against my knees, I will go away again." The husbandman very gladly put his two horses to the cart and drove them to the forge, and brought back a bar of iron as long and as thick as his two horses could draw; but the lad laid it against his knee; and snap! it went like a broken beanstalk. "I see, father," said he, "you can get no stick that will do for me, so I'll go and try my luck by myself."

Then away he went, and turned blacksmith, and travelled till he came to a village where lived a miserly smith, who earned a good deal of money, but kept all he got to himself, and gave nothing away to anybody. The first thing he did was to step into the smithy, and ask if the smith did not want a journeyman. "Aye," said the cunning fellow (as he looked at him and thought what a stout chap he was, and how lustily he would work and

earn his bread), "what wages do you ask?" "I want no pay," said he; "but every fortnight when the other workmen are paid, you shall let me give you two strokes over the shoulders to amuse myself." The old smith thought to himself he could bear this very well, and reckoned on saving a great deal of money; so the bargain was soon struck.

The next morning the new workman was about to begin to work; but at the first stroke that he hit, when his master brought him the iron red hot, he shivered it in pieces, and the anvil sunk so deep into the earth, that he could not get it out again. This made the old fellow very angry; "Halloo!" cried he, "I can't have you for a workman, you are too clumsy; we must put an end to our bargain." "Very well," said the other, "but you must pay for what I have done, so let me give you only one little stroke, and then the bargain is all over." So saying, he gave him a thump that tossed him over a load of hay that stood near. Then he took the thickest bar of iron on the forge for a walking-stick, and went on his way.

When he had journeyed some way, he came to a farm-house, and asked the farmer if he wanted a foreman. The farmer said, "Yes," and the same wages were agreed for as before with the blacksmith. The next morning the workmen were all to go into the wood; but the giant was found to be fast asleep in his bed when the rest were all up and ready to start. "Come, get up," said one of them to him, "it is high time to be stirring; you must go with us." "Go your way," muttered he sulkily, "I shall have done my work and get home long before you." So he lay in bed two hours longer, and at last got up and cooked and ate his breakfast, and then at his leisure harnessed his horses to go to the wood. Just before the wood was a hollow, through which all must pass; so he drove the cart on first, and built up behind him such a mound of faggots and briars that no horse could pass. This done, he drove on, and as he was going into the wood met the others coming out on their road home; "Drive away," said he, "I shall be home before you still." However, he only went a very little way into the wood and tore up one of the largest timber trees, put it into his cart, and turned about homewards. When he came to the pile of faggots, he found all the others standing there, not being able to pass by. "So," said he, "you see if you had stayed with me, you would have been home just as soon, and might have slept an hour or two longer." Then he took his tree on one shoulder, and his cart on the other, and pushed through as easily as though he were laden with feathers, and when he reached the yard showed the tree to the farmer, and asked if it was not a famous walking-stick. "Wife," said the farmer, "this man is worth something; if he sleeps longer, still he works better than the rest."

Time rolled on, and he had served the farmer his whole year; so when his fellow-labourers were paid, he said he also had a right to take his wages. But great dread came upon the farmer, at the thought of the blows he was to have, so he begged him to give up the old bargain, and take his whole farm and stock instead. "Not I," said he, "I will be no farmer; I am foreman, and so I mean to keep, and be paid as we agreed." Finding he could do nothing with him, the farmer only begged one fortnight's respite, and called together all his friends, to ask their advice in the matter. They bethought themselves for a long time, and at last agreed that the shortest way was to kill this troublesome foreman. The next thing was to settle how it was to be done; and it was agreed that he should be ordered to carry into the yard some great mill-stones, and to put them on the edge of a well; that then he should be sent down to clean it out, and when he was at the bottom, the millstones should be pushed down upon his head. Every thing went right, and when the foreman was safe in the well, the stones were rolled in. As they struck the bottom, the water splashed to the very top. Of course they thought his head must be crashed to pieces; but he only cried out, "Drive away the chickens from the well; they are peeking about in the sand above me, and throwing it into my eyes, so that I cannot see." When his job was done, up he sprung from the well, saying, "Look here! see what a fine neck-cloth I have!" as he pointed to one of the mill-stones, that had fallen over his head, and hung about his neck.

The farmer was again overcome with fear, and begged another fortnight to think of it. So his friends were called together again, and at last gave this advice; that the foreman should be sent and made to grind corn by night at the haunted mill, whence no man had ever yet come out in the morning alive. That very evening he was told to carry eight bushels of corn to the mill, and grind them in the night. Away he went to the loft, put two bushels in his right pocket, two in his left, and four in a long sack slung over his shoulders, and then set off to the mill. The miller told him he might grind there in the day time, but not by night,

for the mill was bewitched, and whoever went in at night had been found dead in the morning: "Never mind, miller, I shall come out safe," said he; "only make haste and get out of the way, and look out for me in the morning."

So he went into the mill and put the corn into the hopper, and about twelve o'clock sat himself down on the bench in the miller's room. After a little time the door all at once opened of itself, and in came a large table. On the table stood wine and meat, and many good things besides: all seemed placed there by themselves; at any rate there was no one to be seen. The chairs next moved themselves round it, but still neither guests nor servants came; till all at once he saw fingers handling the knives and forks and putting food on the plates, but still nothing else was to be seen. Now our friend felt somewhat hungry as he looked at the dishes, so he sat himself down at the table and ate whatever he liked best; and when he had had enough, and the plates were empty, on a sudden he heard something blow out the lights. When it was pitch dark he felt a tremendous blow upon his head; "If I get such another box on the ear," said he, "I shall just give it back again;" and this he really did, when the next blow came. Thus the game went on all night; and he never let fear get the better of him, but kept dealing his blows round, till at day-break all was still. "Well, miller," said he in the morning, "I have had some little slaps on the face, but I've given as good, I'll warrant you; and meantime I have eaten as much as I liked." The miller was glad to find the charm was broken, and would have given him a great deal of money; "I want no money, I have quite enough," said he, as he took the meal on his back, and went home to his master to claim his wages.

But the farmer was in a rage, knowing there was no help for him, and paced the room up and down till the drops of sweat ran down his forehead. Then he opened the window for a little fresh air, and before he was aware, his foreman gave him the first blow, and kicked him out of the window over the hills and far away, and next sent his wife after him; and there, for aught I know, they may be flying in the air still: but the young giant took up his iron walking-stick and walked off.

Perhaps this was the same giant that the Bold little Tailor met, when he set out on his travels, as I will tell you next.

———

It was a fine summer morning when this little man bound his girdle round his body, and looked about his house to see if there was any thing good to take with him on his journey into the wide world. He could only find an old cheese; but that was better than nothing; so he took it up; and, as he was going out, the old hen met him at the door, and he packed her too into his wallet with the cheese. Then off he set, and when he had climbed a high hill, he found the giant sitting on the top. "Good day, comrade," said he, "there you sit at your ease, and look the wide world over: I have a mind to go and try my luck in that same world; what do you say to going with me?" Then the giant looked at him, and said, "You are a poor trumpery little knave." "That may be," said the tailor; "but we shall see who is the best man of the two." The giant, finding the little man so bold, began to be a little more respectful, and said they would soon see who was master. So he took a large stone in his hand and squeezed it till water dropped from it; "Do that," said he, "if you have a mind to be thought a strong man." "Is that all?" said the tailor; "I will soon do as much;" so he put his hand in his wallet, pulled out the cheese (which was quite new), and squeezed it till the whey ran out. "What do you say now, Mr. Giant? my squeeze was a better one than yours." Then the giant, not seeing that it was only a cheese, did not know what to say for himself, though he could hardly believe his eyes; at last he took up a stone, and threw it up so high that it went almost out of sight; "Now then, little pygmy, do that if you can." "Very good," said the other; "your throw was not a bad one, but after all your stone fell to the ground; I will throw something that shall not fall at all." "That you can't do," said the giant: but the tailor took his old hen out of the wallet, and threw her up in the air, and she, pleased enough to be set free, flew away out of sight. "Now, Comrade," said he, "what do you say to that?" "I say you are a clever hand," said the giant, "but we will now try how you can work."

Then he led him into the wood, where a fine oak tree lay felled. "Now let us drag it out of the wood together." "Very well; do you take the thick end, and I will carry all the top and branches, which are much the largest and heaviest." So the giant took the trunk and laid it on his shoulder; but the cunning little rogue, instead of carrying any thing, sat himself at his ease among the branches, and let the giant carry stem, branches, and tailor into the bargain. All the way they went he made merry, and whistled and sang his song as if carrying the tree were mere sport; while the giant after he had borne it a good way could carry it no longer, and said, "I must let it fall." Then the tailor sprung down and held the tree as if he were carrying it, saying, "What a shame that such a big lout as you cannot carry a tree like this!" Then on they went together till they came to a tall cherry-tree; and the giant took hold of the top stem, and bent it down to pluck the ripest fruit, and when he had done, gave it over to his friend that he too might eat; but the little man was so weak that he could not hold the tree down, and up he went with it swinging in the air. "Halloo!" said the giant, "what now? can't you hold that twig?" "To be sure I could," said the other; "but don't you see there's a huntsman who is going to shoot into the bush where we stood? so I took a jump over the tree to be out of his way; do you do the same." The giant tried to follow, but the tree was far too high to jump over, and he only stuck fast in the branches, for the tailor to laugh at him. "Well! you are a fine fellow after all," said the giant; "so come home and sleep with me and a friend of mine in the mountains to-night."

The tailor had no business upon his hands, so he did as he was bid, and the giant gave him a good supper, and a bed to sleep upon; but the tailor was too cunning to lie down upon it, and crept slyly into a corner, and slept there soundly. When midnight came, the giant came softly in with his iron walking-stick, and gave such a stroke upon the bed where he thought his guest was lying, that he said to himself, "It's all up now with that grasshopper; I shall have no more of his tricks." In the morning the giants went off into the woods, and quite forgot him, till all on a sudden they met him trudging along, whistling a merry tune; and so frightened were they at the sight, that they both ran away as fast as they could.

Then on went the little tailor following his spuddy nose, till at last he reached the king's court, and began to brag very loud of his mighty deeds, saying he was come to serve the king. To try him, they told him that the two giants who lived in a part of the kingdom a long way off, were become the dread of the whole land; for they had begun to rob, plunder, and ravage all about them, and that if he was so great a man as he said, he should have a hundred soldiers and should set out to fight these giants, and if he beat them he should have half the kingdom. "With all my heart!" said he; "but as for your hundred soldiers, I believe I shall do as well without them." However, they set off together till they came to a wood: "Wait here, my friends," said he to the soldiers, "I will soon give a good account of these giants:" and on he went casting his sharp little eye here, there, and everywhere around him. After a while he spied them both lying under a tree, and snoring away till the very boughs whistled with the breeze. "The game's won, for a penny," said the little man, as he filled his wallet with stones, and climbed the tree under which they lay.

As soon as he was safely up, he threw one stone after another at the nearest giant, till at last he woke up in a rage, and shook his companion, crying out, "What did you strike me for?" "Nonsense! you are dreaming," said the other, "I did not strike you." Then both lay down to sleep again, and the tailor threw stones at the second giant, till he sprung up and cried, "What are you about? you struck me." "I did not," said the other; and on they wrangled for a while, till as both were tired they made up the matter, and fell asleep again. But then the tailor began his game once more, and flung the largest stone he had in his wallet with all his force and hit the first giant on the nose. "That is too bad," cried he, as if he was mad, "I will not bear it." So he struck the other a mighty blow; he of course was not pleased at this, and gave him just such another box on the ear; and at last a bloody battle began; up flew the trees by the roots, the rocks and stones went bang at one another's heads, and in the end both lay dead upon the spot. "It is a good thing," said the tailor, "that they let my tree stand, or I must have made a fine jump." Then down he ran, and took his sword and gave each of them a very fine wound or two on the breast and set off to look for the soldiers. "There lie the giants," said he; "I have killed them, but it has been no small job, for they even tore trees up in their struggle." "Have you any wounds?" asked they. "That is a likely matter, truly," said he; "they have not touched a hair of my head." But the soldiers would not believe him till they rode into the wood and found the giants weltering in their blood, and the trees lying around torn up by the roots.

The king, after he had got rid of his enemies, was not much

pleased at the thoughts of giving up half his kingdom to a tailor; so he said, "You have not yet done; in the palace court lies a bear with whom you must pass the night, and if when I rise in the morning I find you still living, you shall then have your reward." Now he thought he had got rid of him, for the bear had never yet let any one go away alive who had come within reach of his claws. "Very well," said the tailor, "I am willing."

So when evening came our little tailor was led out and shut up in the court with the bear, who rose at once to give him a friendly welcome with his paw. "Softly, softly, my friend," said he; "I know a way to please you;" then at his ease and as if he cared nothing about the matter, he pulled out of his pocket some fine walnuts, cracked them, and ate the kernels. When the bear saw this, he took a great fancy to having some nuts too; so the tailor felt in his pocket and gave him a handful, not of walnuts, but nice round pebbles. The bear snapt them up, but could not crack one of them, do what he would. "What a clumsy thick head thou art!" thought the beast to itself; "thou canst not crack a nut to-day." Then said he to the tailor, "Friend, pray crack me the nuts." "Why, what a lout you are," said the tailor, "to have such a jaw as that, and not to be able to crack a little nut! Well! engage to be friends with me and I'll help you." So he took the stones, and slyly changed them for nuts, put them in his mouth, and crack! they went. "I must try for myself, however," said the bear; "now I see how you do it, I am sure I can do it myself." Then the tailor gave him the cobble stones again, and the bear lay down and worked away as hard as he could, and bit and bit with all his force till he broke all his teeth, and lay down quite tired.

But the tailor began to think this would not last long, and that the bear might find him out and break the bargain; so he pulled a fiddle out from under his coat and played him a tune. As soon as the bear heard it, he could not help jumping up and beginning to dance; and when he had jigged away for a while, the thing pleased him so much that he said, "Hark ye, friend! is the fiddle hard to play upon?" "No! not at all!" said the other, "look ye, I lay my left hand here, and then I take the bow with my right hand thus, and scrape it over the strings there, and away it goes merrily, hop, sa, sa! fal, lal, la!" "Will you teach me to fiddle," said the bear, "so that I may have music whenever I want to dance?" "With all my heart; but let me look at your claws, they are so very long that I must first clip your nails a little bit."

Then the bear lifted up his paws one after another, and the tailor screwed them down tight, and said, "Now wait till I come with my scissors." So he left the bear to growl as loud as he liked, and laid himself down on a heap of straw in the corner and slept soundly. In the morning when the king came, he found the tailor sitting merrily eating his breakfast, and could no longer help keeping in a word; and thus the little man became a great one.

The Crows and the Soldier

A WORTHY soldier had saved a good deal of money out of his pay; for he worked hard, and did not spend all he earned in eating and drinking, as many others do. Now he had two comrades who were great rogues, and wanted to rob him of his money, but behaved outwardly towards him in a friendly way. "Comrade," said they to him one day, "why should we stay here shut up in this town like prisoners, when you at any rate have earned enough to live upon for the rest of your days in peace and plenty at home by your own fireside?" They talked so often to him in this manner, that he at last said he would go and try his luck with them; but they all the time thought of nothing but how they should manage to steal his money from him.

When they had gone a little way, the two rogues said, "We must go by the right-hand road, for that will take us quickest into another country where we shall be safe." Now they knew all the while that what they were saying was untrue; and as soon as the soldier said, "No, that will take us straight back into the town we came from; we must keep on the left hand;" they picked a quarrel with him, and said, "What do you give yourself airs for? you know nothing about it:" and then they fell upon him and knocked him down, and beat him over the head till he was blind. Then they took all the money out of his pockets and dragged him to a gallows-tree that stood hard by, bound him fast down at the foot of it, and went back into the town with the money; but the poor blind man did not know where he was; and he felt all around him, and finding that he was bound to a large beam of wood, thought it was a cross, and said, "After all, they have done kindly in leaving me under a cross; now Heaven will guard me;" so he raised himself up and began to pray.

When night came on, he heard something fluttering over his head. It turned out to be three crows, who flew round and round, and at last perched upon the tree. By and by they began to talk together, and he heard one of them say, "Sister, what is the best news with you to-day?" "O, if men knew what we know!" said the other; "the princess is ill, and the king has vowed to marry her to any one who will cure her; but this none can do, for she will not be well until yonder flower is burnt to ashes and swallowed by her." "Oh, indeed," said the other crow, "if men did but know what we know! to-night will fall from heaven a dew of such healing power, that even the blind man who washes his eyes with it will see again;" and the third spoke, and said, "O if men knew what we know! the flower is wanted but for one, the dew is wanted but for few; but there is a great dearth of water in the town; all the wells are dried up; and no one knows that they must take away the large square stone out of the market-place, and dig underneath it, and that then the finest water will spring up."

When the three crows had done talking, he heard them fluttering round again, and at last away they flew. Greatly wondering at what he had heard, and overjoyed at the thoughts of getting his sight, he tried with all his strength to break loose from his bonds; at last he found himself free, and plucked some of the grass that grew beneath him and washed his eyes with the dew that had fallen upon it. At once his eye-sight came to him again, and he saw by the light of the moon and the stars that he was beneath the gallows-tree, and not the cross, as he had thought. Then he gathered together in a bottle as much of the dew as he could to take away with him, and looked around till he saw the flower that grew close by; and when he had burned it he gathered up the ashes, and set out on his way towards the king's court.

When he reached the palace, he told the king he was come to cure the princess; and when she had taken of the ashes and been made well, he claimed her for his wife, as the reward that was to be given; but the king looking upon him and seeing that his clothes were so shabby, would not keep his word, and thought to get rid of him by saying, "Whoever wants to have the princess for his wife, must find enough water for the use of the town, where there is this summer a great dearth." Then the soldier went out and told the people to take up the square stone in the market-place and dig for water underneath; and when they had done so there came up a fine spring, that gave enough water for the whole town. So the king could no longer get off giving him his daughter, and they were married and lived happily together.

Some time after, as he was walking one day through a field, he met his two wicked comrades who had treated him so basely. Though they did not know him, he knew them at once, and went up to them and said, "Look upon me, I am your old comrade whom you beat and robbed and left blind; Heaven has defeated your wicked wishes, and turned all the mischief which you brought upon me into good luck." When they heard this they fell at his feet and begged for pardon, and he had a kind and good heart, so he forgave them, and took them to his palace and gave them food and clothes. And he told them all that had happened to him, and how he had reached these honours. After they had heard the whole story they said to themselves, "Why should not we go and sit some night under the gallows? we may hear something that will bring us good luck too."

Next night they stole away; and when they had sat under the tree a little while, they heard a fluttering noise over their heads; and the three crows came and perched upon it. "Sisters," said one of them, "someone must have overheard us, for all the world is talking of the wonderful things that have happened: the princess is well; the flower has been plucked and burnt; a blind man's sight has been given him again; and they have dug a fresh well that gives water to the whole town: let us look about, perhaps we may find someone near; if we do he shall rue the day." Then they began to flutter about, and soon found out the two men below, and flew at them in a rage, beating and pecking them in the face with their wings and beaks till they were quite blind, and lay nearly dead upon the ground under the gallows. The next day passed over and they did not return to the palace; and their old comrade began to wonder where they had been, and went out the following morning in search of them, and at last found them where they lay, dreadfully repaid for all their folly and baseness.

Pee-wit

A POOR countryman whose name was Pee-wit lived with his wife in a very quiet way in the parish where he was born. One day, as he was ploughing with his two oxen in the field, he heard all on a sudden someone calling out his name. Turning round, he saw nothing but a bird that kept crying Peewit! Pee-wit! Now this poor bird is called a Pee-wit, and like the cuckoo always keeps crying out its own name. But the countryman thought it was mocking him, so he took up a huge stone and threw at it; the bird flew off safe and sound, but the stone fell upon the head of one of the oxen, and killed him on the spot. "What is to be done with the odd one;" thought Peewit to himself as he looked at the ox that was left; so without more ado he killed him too, skinned them both, and set out for the neighbouring town, to sell the hides to the tanner for as much as he could get. He soon found out where the tanner lived, and knocked at the door. Before, however, the door was opened, he saw through the window that the mistress of the house was hiding in an old chest a friend of hers, whom she seemed to wish no one should see. By and by the door was opened, "What do you want?" said the woman. Then he told her that he wanted to sell his hides; and it came out that the tanner was not at home, and that no one there ever made bargains but himself. The countryman said he would sell cheap, and did not mind giving his hides for the old chest in the corner; meaning the one he had seen the good woman's friend get into. Of course the wife would not agree to this; and they went on talking the matter over so long, that at last in came the tanner and asked what it was all about. Pee-wit told him the whole story, and asked him whether he would give the old chest for the hides. "To be sure I will," said he; and scolded his wife for saying nay to such a bargain, which she ought to have been glad to make if the countryman was willing. Then up he took the chest on his shoulders, and all the good woman could say mattered nothing; away it went into the countryman's cart, and off he drove. But when they had gone some way, the young man within began to make himself heard, and to beg and pray to be let out. Pee-wit, however, was not to be brought over; till at last after a long parley a thousand dollars were bid and taken; the money was paid, and at that price the poor fellow was set free, and went about his business.

Then Pee-wit went home very happy, and built a new house and seemed so rich that his neighbours wondered, and said, "Pee-wit must have been where the golden snow falls." So they took him before the next justice of the peace, to give an account of himself, and show that he came honestly by his wealth; and then he told them that he had sold his hides for one thousand dollars. When they heard it they all killed their oxen and would sell the hides to the same tanner; but the justice said, "My maid shall have the first chance;" so off she went, and when she came to the tanner, he laughed at them all, and said he had given their neighbour nothing but an old chest.

At this they were all very angry, and laid their heads together to work him some mischief, which they thought they could do while he was digging in his garden. All this, however, came to the ears of the countryman, who was plagued with a sad scold for his wife; and he thought to himself, "If any one is to come into trouble, I don't see why it should not be my wife, rather than me;" so he said to her that he wished she would humour him in a whim he had taken into his head, and would put on his clothes, and dig the garden in his stead. The wife did what was asked, and next morning began digging; but soon came some of the neighbours, and, thinking it was Pee-wit, threw a stone at her (harder perhaps than they meant), and killed her at once. Poor Pee-wit was rather sorry at this, but still thought that he had had a lucky escape for himself, and that perhaps he might after all turn the death of his wife to some account: so he dressed her in her own clothes, put a basket with fine fruit (which was now scarce, it being winter) into her hand, and sat her by the roadside on a broad bench.

After a while came by a fine coach with six horses, servants, and outriders, and within sat a noble lord who lived not far off.

G.C.K fecit

When his lordship saw the beautiful fruit, he sent one of the servants to the woman to ask what was the price of her goods. The man went and asked "What is the price of this fruit?" No answer. He asked again. No answer: and when this had happened three times, he became angry; and, thinking she was asleep, gave her a blow, and down she fell backwards into the pond that was behind the seat. Then up ran Pee-wit, and cried and sorrowed because they had drowned his poor wife and threatened to have the lord and his servants tried for what they had done. His lordship begged him to be easy, and offered to give him the coach and horses, servants and all; so the countryman after a long time let himself be appeased a little, took what they gave, got into the coach and set off towards his own home again.

As he came near, the neighbours wondered much at the beautiful coach and horses, and still more when they stopped, and Pee-wit got out at his own door. Then he told them the whole story, which only vexed them still more; so they took him and fastened him up in a tub and were going to throw him into the lake that was hard by. Whilst, they were rolling the tub on before them towards the water, they passed by an alehouse and stopped to refresh themselves a little before they put an end to Pee-wit; meantime they tied the tub to a tree and there left it while they were enjoying themselves within doors; Pee-wit no sooner found himself alone than he began, to turn over in his mind how he could get free. He listened, and soon heard Ba, ba! from a flock of sheep and lambs that were coming by. Then he lifted up his voice, and shouted out, "I will not be burgomaster, I say; I will not be made burgomaster." The shepherd hearing this went up, and said; "What is all this noise about?" "O!" said Pee-wit, "my neighbours will make me burgomaster against my will; and when I told them I would not agree, they put me into the cask and are going to throw me into the lake." "I should like very well to be burgomaster if I were you," said the shepherd. "Open the cask then," said the other, "and let me out, and get in yourself, and they will make you burgomaster instead of me." No sooner said than done, the shepherd was in, Pee-wit was out; and as there was nobody to take care of the shepherd's flock, he drove it off merrily towards his own house.

When the neighbours came out of the alehouse, they rolled the cask on, and the shepherd began to cry out, "I *will* be burgomaster now; I *will* be burgomaster now." "I dare say you will, but you shall take a swim first," said a neighbour, as he gave the cask the last push over into the lake. This done, away they went home merrily, leaving the shepherd to get out as well as he could.

But as they came in at one side of the village, who should they meet coming in the other way but Pee-wit driving a fine flock of sheep and lambs before him. "How came you here?" cried all with one voice. "O! the lake is enchanted," said he; "when you threw me in, I sunk deep and deep into the water, till at last I came to the bottom; there I knocked out the bottom of the cask and found myself in a beautiful meadow with fine flocks grazing upon it, so I chose a few for myself, and here I am." "Cannot we have some too?" said they. "Why not? there are hundreds and thousands left; you have nothing to do but jump in and fetch them out."

So all agreed they would dive for sheep; the justice first, then the clerk, then the constables, and then the rest of the parish, one after the other. When they came to the side of the lake, the blue sky was covered with little white clouds like flocks of sheep, and all were reflected in the clear water: so they called out, "There they are, there they are already;" and fearing lest the justice should get everything, they jumped in all at once; and Pee-wit jogged home, and made himself happy with what he had got, leaving them to find their flocks by themselves as well as they could.

Hans and His Wife Grettel

I. Showing who Grettel was.

THERE was once a little maid named Grettel: she wore shoes with red heels, and when she went abroad she turned out her toes, and was very merry, and thought to herself," "What a pretty girl I am!" And when she came home, to put herself in good spirits, she would tipple down a drop or two of wine; and as wine gives a relish for eating, she would take a taste of every thing when she was cooking, saying, "A cook ought to know whether a thing tastes well." It happened one day that her master said, "Grettel, this evening I have a friend coming to sup with me; get two fine fowls ready." "Very well, sir," said Grettel. Then she killed the fowls, plucked, and trussed them, put them on the spit, and when evening came put them to the fire to roast. The fowls turned round and round, and soon began to look nice and brown, but the guest did not come. Then Grettel cried out, "Master, if the guest does not come I must take up the fowls, but it will be a shame and a pity if they are not eaten while they are hot and good." "Well," said her master, "I'll run and tell him to come." As soon as he had turned his back, Grettel stopped the spit, and laid it with the fowls upon it on one side, and thought to herself, "Standing by the fire makes one very tired and thirsty; who knows how long they will be? meanwhile I will just step into the cellar and take a drop." So off she ran, put down her pitcher, and said "Your health, Grettel," and took a good draught. "This wine is a good friend," said she to herself, "it breaks one's heart to leave it." Then up she trotted, put the fowls down to the fire, spread some butter over them, and turned the spit merrily round again.

The fowls soon smelt so good, that she thought to herself, "They are very good, but they may want something still; I had better taste them and see." So she licked her fingers, and said, "O! how good! what a shame and a pity that they are not eaten!" Away she ran to the window to see if her master and his friend were coming; but nobody was in sight: so she turned to the fowls again, and thought it would be better for her to eat a wing than that it should be burnt. So she cut one wing off, and ate it, and it tasted very well; and as the other was quite done enough, she thought it had better be cut off too, or else her master would see one was wanting. When the two wings were gone, she went again to look out for her master, but could not see him. "Ah!" thought she to herself, "who knows whether they will come at all? very likely they have turned into some tavern: O Grettel! Grettel! make yourself happy, take another draught, and eat the rest of the fowl; it looks so oddly as it is; when you have eaten all, you will be easy: why should such good things be wasted?" So she ran once more to the cellar, took another drink, and ate up the rest of the fowl with the greatest glee.

Still her master did not come, and she cast a lingering eye upon the other fowl, and said, "Where the other went, this had better go too; they belong to each other; they who have a right to one must have a right to the other; but if I were to take another draught first, it would not hurt me." So she tippled down another drop of wine, and sent the second fowl to look after the first. While she was making an end of this famous meal, her master came home and called out, "Now quick, Grettel, my friend is just at hand!" "Yes, master, I will dish up this minute," said she. In the meantime he looked to see if the cloth was laid, and took up the carving-knife to sharpen it. Whilst this was going on, the guest came and knocked softly and gently at the house door; then Grettel ran to see who was there, and when she saw him she put her finger upon her lips, and said, "Hush! hush! run away as fast as you can, for if my master catches you, it will be worse for you; he owes you a grudge, and asked you to supper only that he might cut off your ears; only listen how he is sharpening his knife." The guest listened, and when he heard the knife, he made as much haste as he could down the steps and ran off. Grettel was not idle in the meantime, but ran screaming, "Master! master! what a fine guest you have asked to supper!" "Why, Grettel, what's the matter?" "Oh!" said she, "he has taken both the fowls that I was going to bring up, and has run away with them." "That is a rascally trick to play," said the master, sorry to lose the fine chickens; "at least he might have left me one, that I might have had something to eat; call out to him to stay." But the guest would not hear; so he ran after him with his knife in his hand, crying out, "Only one, only one, I want only one;" meaning that the guest should leave him one of the fowls, and not take both: but he thought that his host meant nothing less than that he would cut off at least one of his ears; so he ran away to save them both, as if he had hot coals under his feet.

———

II. Hans in love.

Hans's mother says to him "Whither so fast?" "To see Grettel," says Hans. "Behave well." "Very well: Good-bye, mother!" Hans comes to Grettel; "Good day, Grettel!" "Good day, Hans! do you bring me any thing good?" "Nothing at all: have you any thing for me?" Grettel gives Hans a needle. Hans says, "Good-bye, Grettel!" "Good-bye, Hans!" Hans takes the needle, sticks it in a truss of hay, and takes both off home. "Good evening, mother!" "Good evening Hans! where have you been?" "To see Grettel." "What did you take her?" "Nothing at all." "What did she give you?" "She gave me a needle." "Where is it, Hans?" "Stuck in the truss." "How silly you are! you should have stuck it in your sleeve." "Let me alone! I'll do better next time."

"Where now, Hans?" "To see Grettel, mother." "Behave yourself well." "Very well: Good-bye, mother!" Hans comes to Grettel; "Good day, Grettel!" "Good day, Hans! what have you brought me?" "Nothing at all: have you any thing for me?" Grettel gives Hans a knife. "Goodbye, Grettel!" "Good-bye, Hans!" Hans takes the knife, sticks it in his sleeve, and goes home. "Good evening, mother!" "Good evening, Hans! where have you been?" "To see Grettel." "What did you carry her?" "Nothing at all." "What has she given you?" "A knife." "Where is the knife, Hans?" "Stuck in my sleeve, mother." "You silly goose! you should have put it in your pocket." "Let me alone! I'll do better next time."

"Where now, Hans?" "To see Grettel." "Behave your self well." "Very well: Good-bye, mother!" Hans comes to Grettel; "Good day, Grettel!" "Good day, Hans! have you any thing good?" "So: have you any thing for me?" Grettel gives Hans a kid. "Good-bye, Grettel!" "Goodbye, Hans!" Hans takes the kid, ties it up with a cord, stuffs it into his pocket, and chokes it to death. "Good evening, mother!" "Good evening, Hans! where have you been?" "To see Grettel, mother!" "What did you take her?" "Nothing at all." "What did she give you?" "She gave me a kid." "Where is the kid, Hans?" "Safe in my pocket." "You silly goose! you should have led it with a string." "Never mind, mother, I'll do better next time."

"Where now, Hans?" "To Grettel's, mother." "Behave well." "Quite well, mother; Good-bye!" Hans comes to Grettel; "Good day, Grettel!" "Good day, Hans! what have you brought me?" "Nothing at all; have you any thing for me?" Grettel gives Hans a piece of bacon; Hans ties the bacon to a string and drags it behind him, the dog comes after and eats it all up as he walks home. "Good evening, mother!" "Good evening, Hans! where have you been?" "To Grettel's." "What did you take her?" "Nothing at all." "What did she give you?" "A piece of bacon." "Where is the bacon, Hans?" "Tied to the string, and dragged home, but somehow or other all gone." "What a silly trick, Hans! you should have brought it on your head." "Never mind, mother, I'll do better another time."

"Where now, Hans?" "Going to Grettel." "Take care of yourself." "Very well, mother: Good-bye." Hans comes to Grettel; – "Good day, Grettel!" "Good day, Hans! what have you brought me?" "Nothing: have you any thing for me?" Grettel gives Hans a calf. Hans sets it upon his head, and it kicks him in the face. "Good evening, mother!" "Good evening, Hans! where have you been?" "To see Grettel." "What did you take her?" "Nothing." "What did she give you?" "She gave me a calf." "Where is the calf, Hans?" "I put it on my head, and it scratched my face." "You silly goose! you should have led it home and put it in the stall." "Very well; I'll do better another time."

"Where now, Hans?" "To see Grettel." "Mind and behave well." "Good-bye, mother!" Hans comes to Grettel; "Good day, Grettel!" "Good day, Hans! what have you brought?" "Nothing at all: have you any thing for me?" "I'll go home with you." Hans ties a string round her neck, leads her along, and ties her up in the stall. "Good evening, mother!" "Good evening, Hans! where have you been?" "At Grettel's." "What has she given you?" "She has come herself." "Where have you put her?" "Fast in the stall with plenty of hay." "How silly you are! you should have taken good care of her, and brought her home." Then Hans went back to the stall; but Grettel was in a great rage, and had got loose and run away: yet, after all, she was Hans's bride.

———

III. Hans married.

Hans and Grettel lived in the village together, but Grettel did as she pleased, and was so lazy that she never would work and when her husband gave her any yarn to spin she did it in a slovenly way; and when it was spun she did not wind it on the reel, but left it to lie all tangled about. Hans sometimes scolded, but she was always before-hand with her tongue, and said, "Why how should I wind it when I have no reel? go into the wood and make one." "If that's all," said he, "I will go into the wood and cut reel-sticks." Then Grettel was frightened lest when he had cut the sticks he should make a reel, and thus she would be forced to wind the yarn and spin again. So she pondered a while, till at last a bright thought came into her head, and she ran slyly after her husband into the wood. As soon as he had got into a tree and began to bend down a bough to cut it, she crept into the bush below, where he could not see her, and sung:

> "Bend not the bough;
> He who bends it shall die!
> Reel not the reel;
> He who reels it shall die."

Hans listened a while, laid down his axe, and thought to himself, "What can that be?" "What indeed can it be?" said he at last; "it is only a singing in your ears, Hans! pluck up your heart, man!" So he raised up his axe again, and took hold of the bough, but once more the voice sung:

> "Bend not the bough;
> He who bends it shall die!
> Reel not the reel;
> He who reels it shall die."

Once more he stopped his hand; fear came over him, and he began pondering what it could mean. After a while, however, he plucked up his courage again, and took up his axe and began for the third time to cut the wood; again the third time began the song –

> "Bend not the bough;
> He who bends it shall die!
> Reel not the reel;
> He who reels it shall die."

At this he could hold no longer, down he dropped from the tree and set off homewards as fast as he could. Away too ran Grettel by a shorter cut, so as to reach home first, and when he opened the door met him quite innocently, as if nothing had happened, and said, "Well! have you brought a good piece of wood for the reel?" "No," said he, "I see plainly that no luck comes of that reel," and then he told her all that had happened, and left her for that time in peace.

But soon afterwards Hans began again to reproach her with the untidiness of her house. "Wife," said he; "is it not a sin and a shame that the spun yarn should lie all about in that way?" "It may be so," said she; "but you know very well that we have no reel; if it must be done, lie down there and hold up your hands and legs, and so I'll make a reel of you, and wind off the yarn into skeins." "Very well," said Hans (who did not much like the job, but saw no help for it if his wife was to be set to work); so he did as she said, and when all was wound, "The yarn is all in skeins," said he; "now take care and get up early and heat the water and boil it well, so that it may be ready for sale." Grettel disliked this part of the work very much, but said to him, "Very well, I'll be sure to do it very early to-morrow morning." But all the time she was thinking to herself what plan she should take for getting off such work for the future.

Betimes in the morning she got up, made the fire and put on the boiler; but instead of the yarn she laid a large ball of tow in it and let it boil. Then she went up to her husband, who was still in bed, and said to him, "I must go out, pray look meantime to the yarn in the boiler over the fire; but do it soon and take good care, for if the cock crows and you are not looking to it, they say it will turn to tow." Hans soon after got up that he might run no risk, and went (but not perhaps as quickly as he might have done) into the kitchen, and when he lifted up the boiler lid and looked in, to his great terror nothing was there but a ball of tow. Then off he slunk as dumb as a mouse, for he thought to himself that he was to blame for his laziness; and left Grettel to get on with her yarn and her spinning as fast as she pleased and no faster.

One day, however, he said to her, "Wife, I must go a little way this morning; do you go into the field and cut the corn." "Yes, to be sure, dear Hans!" said she; so when he was gone she cooked herself a fine mess and took it with her into the field. When she came into the field, she sat down for a while and said to herself, "What shall I do? shall I sleep first or eat first? Heigho! I'll first eat a bit." Then she ate her dinner heartily, and when she had had enough she said again to herself, "What shall I do? shall I reap first or sleep first? Heigho! I'll first sleep a bit." So she laid herself down among the corn and went fast asleep. By and by Hans came home, but no Grettel was to be seen, and he said to himself, "What a clever wife I have! she works so hard that she does not even come home to her dinner!" Evening came and still she did not come; then Hans set off to see how much of the corn was reaped, but there it all stood untouched, and Grettel lay fast asleep in the middle. So he ran home and got a string of little bells and tied them quietly round her waist, and went back and set himself down on his stool and locked the house door.

At last Grettel woke when it was quite dark, and as she rose up the bells jingled around her every step she took. At this she was greatly frightened, and puzzled to tell whether she was really Grettel or not. "Is it I, or is it not?" said she as she stood doubting what she ought to think. At last, after she had pondered a while, she thought to herself, "I will go home and ask if it is I or not; Hans will know." So she ran to the house door, and when she found it locked she knocked at the window and cried out, "Hans! is Grettel within?" "She is where she ought to be, to be sure," said Hans; "O dear then!" said she frightened, "this is not I." Then away she went and knocked at the neighbours' doors; but when they heard her bells rattling no one would let her in, and so at last off she ran back to the field again.

Cherry, or the Frog-Bride

THERE was once a king who had three sons. Not far from his kingdom lived an old woman who had an only daughter called Cherry. The king sent his sons out to see the world, that they might learn the ways of foreign lands, and get wisdom and skill in ruling the kingdom that they were one day to have for their own. But the old woman lived at peace at home with her daughter, who was called Cherry, because she liked cherries better than any other kind of food, and would eat scarcely anything else. Now her poor old mother had no garden, and no money to buy cherries every day for her daughter; and at last there was no other plan left but to go to a neighbouring nunnery-garden and beg the finest she could get of the nuns; for she dared not let her daughter go out by herself, as she was very pretty, and she feared some mischance might befall her. Cherry's taste was, however, very well known; and as it happened that the abbess was as fond of cherries as she was, it was soon found out where all the best fruit went; and the holy mother was not a little angry at missing some of her stock and finding whither it had gone.

The princes while wandering on came one day to the town where Cherry and her mother lived; and as they passed along the street saw the fair maiden standing at the window, combing her long and beautiful locks of hair. Then each of the three fell deeply in love with her, and began to say how much he longed to have her for his wife! Scarcely had the wish been spoken, when all drew their swords, and a dreadful battle began; the fight lasted long, and their rage grew hotter and hotter, when at last the abbess hearing the uproar came to the gate. Finding that her neighbour was the cause, her old spite against her broke forth at once, and in her rage she wished Cherry turned into an ugly frog, and sitting in the water under the bridge at the world's end. No sooner said than done; and poor Cherry became a frog, and vanished out of their sight. The princes had now nothing to fight for; so sheathing their swords again, they shook hands as brothers, and went on towards their father's home.

The old king meanwhile found that he grew weak and ill fitted for the business of reigning: so he thought of giving up his kingdom; but to whom should it be? This was a point that his fatherly heart could not settle; for he loved all his sons alike. "My dear children," said he, "I grow old and weak, and should like to give up my kingdom; but I cannot make up my mind which of you to choose for my heir, for I love you all three; and besides, I should wish to give my people the cleverest and best of you for their king. However, I will give you three trials, and the one who wins the prize shall have the kingdom. The first is to seek me out one hundred ells of cloth, so fine that I can draw it through my golden ring." The sons said they would do their best, and set out on the search.

The two eldest brothers took with them many followers, and coaches and horses of all sorts, to bring home all the beautiful cloths which they could find; but the youngest went alone by himself. They soon came to where the roads branched off into several ways; two ran through smiling meadows, with smooth paths and shady groves, but the third looked dreary and dirty, and went over barren wastes. The two eldest chose the pleasant ways; and the youngest took his leave and whistled along over the dreary road. Whenever fine linen was to be seen, the two elder brothers bought it, and bought so much that their coaches and horses bent under their burthen. The youngest, on the other hand, journeyed on many a weary day, and found not a place where he could buy even one piece of cloth that was at all fine and good. His heart sunk beneath him, and every mile he grew more and more heavy and sorrowful. At last he came to a bridge over a stream, and there he sat himself down to rest and sigh over his bad luck, when an ugly-looking frog popped its head out of the water, and asked, with a voice that had not at all a harsh sound to his ears, what was the matter. The prince said in a pet, "Silly frog!, thou canst not help me." "Who told you so?" said the frog; "tell me what ails you." After a while the prince opened the whole story, and told why his father had sent him out. "I will help you," said the frog; so it jumped back into the stream and soon came back dragging a small piece of linen not bigger than one's hand, and by no means the cleanest in the world in its look. However, there it was, and the prince was told to take it away with him. He had no great liking for such a dirty rag; but still there was something in the frog's speech that pleased him much, and he thought to himself, "It can do no harm, it is better than nothing;" so he picked it up, put it in his pocket, and thanked the frog, who dived down again, panting and quite tired, as it seemed, with its work. The further he went the heavier he found to his great joy the pocket grow, and so he turned himself homewards, trusting greatly in his good luck.

He reached home nearly about the same time that his brothers came up, with their horses and coaches all heavily laden. Then the old king was very glad to see his children again, and pulled the ring off his finger to try who had done the best; but in all the stock which the two eldest had brought there was not one piece a tenth part of which would go through the ring. At this they were greatly abashed; for they had made a laugh of their brother, who came home, as they thought, empty-handed. But how great was their anger, when they saw him pull from his pocket a piece that for softness, beauty, and whiteness, was a thousand times better than anything that was ever before seen! It was so fine that it passed with ease through the ring; indeed, two such pieces would readily have gone in together. The father embraced the lucky youth, told his servants to throw the coarse linen into the sea, and said to his children, "Now you must set about the second task which I am to set you; – bring me home a little dog, so small that it will lie in a nut-shell."

His sons were not a little frightened at such a task; but they all longed for the crown, and made up their minds to go and try their hands, and so after a few days they set out once more on their travels. At the cross-ways they parted as before, and the youngest chose his old dreary rugged road with all the bright hopes that his former good luck gave him. Scarcely had he sat himself down again at the bridge foot, when his old friend the frog jumped out, set itself beside him, and as before opened its big wide mouth, and croaked out, "What is the matter?" The prince had this time no doubt of the frog's power, and therefore told what he wanted. "It shall be done for you," said the frog; and springing into the stream it soon brought up a hazel-nut, laid it at his feet, and told him to take it home to his father, and crack it gently; and then see what would happen. The prince went his way very well pleased, and the frog, tired with its task, jumped back into the water.

His brothers had reached home first, and brought with them a great many very pretty little dogs. The old king willing to help them all he could, sent for a large walnut-shell and tried it with every one of the little dogs; but one stuck fast with the hind-foot out, and another with the head, and a third with the fore-foot, and a fourth with its tail, – in short, some one way and some another; but none were at all likely to sit easily in this new kind of kennel. When all had been tried the youngest made his father a dutiful bow, and gave him the hazel-nut, begging him to crack it very carefully: the moment this was done out ran a beautiful little white dog upon the king's hand, wagged its tail, fondled his new master, and soon turned about and barked at the other little beasts in the most graceful manner, to the delight of the whole court. The joy of every one was great; the old king again embraced his lucky son, told his people to drown all the other dogs in the sea and said to his children, "Dear sons! your weightiest tasks are now over; listen to my last wish; whoever brings home the fairest lady shall be at once the heir to my crown."

The prize was so tempting and the chance so fair for all, that none made any doubts about setting to work, each in his own way, to try and be the winner. The youngest was not in such good spirits as he was the last time; he thought to himself, "The old frog has been able to do a great deal for me but all its power must be nothing to me now, for where should it find me a fair maiden, still less a fairer maiden than was ever seen at my father's court? The swamps where it lives have no living things in them, but toads, snakes, and such vermin." Meantime he went on, and sighed as he sat down again with a heavy heart by the bridge. "Ah frog!" said he, "this time thou canst do me no good." "Never mind," croaked the frog; "only tell me what is the matter now." Then the prince told his old friend what trouble had now come upon him. "Go thy ways home," said the frog; "the fair maiden will follow hard after; but take care and do not laugh at whatever may happen!" This said, it sprang as before into the water and was soon out of sight. The prince still sighed on, for he trusted very little this time to the frog's word; but he had not set

G. Cruikshank

many steps towards home before he heard a noise behind him, and looking round saw six large water rats dragging along a large pumpkin like a coach, full trot. On the box sat an old fat toad as coachman, and behind stood two little frogs as footmen, and two fine mice with stately whiskers ran before as outriders; within sat his old friend the frog, rather misshapen and unseemly to be sure, but still with somewhat of a graceful air as it bowed to him in passing. Much too deeply wrapt in thought as to his chance of finding the fair lady whom he was seeking, to take any heed of the strange scene before him, the prince scarcely looked at it, and had still less mind to laugh. The coach passed on a little way, and soon turned a corner that hid it from his sight; but how astonished was he, on turning the corner himself, to find a handsome coach and six black horses standing there, with a coachman in gay livery, and within, the most beautiful lady he had ever seen, whom he soon knew to be the fair Cherry, for whom his heart had so long ago panted! As he came up, the servants opened the coach door, and he was allowed to seat himself by the beautiful lady.

They soon came to his father's city, where his brothers also came, with trains of fair ladies; but as soon as Cherry was seen, all the court gave her with one voice the crown of beauty. The delighted father embraced his son, and named him the heir to his crown, and ordered all the other ladies to be thrown like the little dogs into the sea and drowned. Then the prince married Cherry, and lived long and happily with her, and indeed lives with her still – if he be not dead.

Mother Holle

A WIDOW had two daughters; one of them was very pretty and thrifty, but the other was ugly and idle. Odd as you may think it, she loved the ugly and idle one much the best, and the other was made to do all the work, and was in short quite the drudge of the whole house. Every day she had to sit on a bench by a well on the side of the high-road before the house, and spin so much that her fingers were quite sore, and at length the blood would come. Now it happened that once when her fingers had bled and the spindle was all bloody, she dipt it into the well, and meant to wash it, but unluckily it fell from her hand and dropt in. Then she ran crying to her mother, and told her what had happened; but she scolded her sharply, and said, "If you have been so silly as to let the spindle fall in, you must get it out again as well as you can." So the poor little girl went back to the well, and knew not how to begin, but in her sorrow threw herself into the water and sank down to the bottom senseless. In a short time, she seemed to wake as from a trance, and came to herself again; and when she opened her eyes and looked around, she saw she was in a beautiful meadow, where the sun shone brightly, the birds sang sweetly on the boughs, and thousands of flowers sprang beneath her feet.

Then she rose up, and walked along this delightful meadow, and came to a pretty cottage by the side of a wood; and when she went in she saw an oven full of new bread baking, and the bread said, "Pull me out! pull me out! or I shall be burnt, for I am quite done enough." So she stepped up quickly and took it all out. Then she went on further, and came to a tree that was full of fine rosy-cheeked apples, and it said to her, "Shake me! shake me! we are all quite ripe!" So she shook the tree, and the apples fell down like a shower, until there were no more upon the tree. Then she went on again, and at length came to a small cottage where an old woman was sitting at the door: the little girl would have run away, but the old woman called out after her, "Don't be frightened my dear child! stay with me, I should like to have you for my little maid, and if you do all the work in the house neatly you shall fare well; but take care to make my bed nicely, and shake it every morning out at the door, so that the feathers may fly, for then the good people below say it snows. – I am Mother Holle."

As the old woman spoke so kindly to her, the girl was willing to do as she said; so she went into her employ, and took care to do everything to please her, and always shook the bed well, so that she led a very quiet life with her, and every day had good meat both boiled and roast to eat for her dinner.

But when she had been some time with the old lady, she became sorrowful, and although she was much better off here than at home, still she had a longing towards it, and at length said to her mistress, "I used to grieve at my troubles at home, but if they were all to come again, and I were sure of faring ever so well here, I could not stay any longer." "You are right," said her mistress; "you shall do as you like; and as you have worked for me so faithfully, I will myself show you the way back again." Then she took her by the hand and led her behind her cottage, and opened a door, and as the girl stood underneath there fell a heavy shower of gold, so that she held out her apron and caught a great deal of it. And the fairy put a shining golden dress over her, and said, "All this you shall have because you have behaved so well;" and she gave her back the spindle too which had fallen into the well, and led her out by another door. When it shut behind her, she found herself not far from her mother's house; and as she went into the court-yard the cock sat upon the well-head and clapt his wings and cried out,

"Cook a-doodle-doo!
Our golden lady's come home again."

Then she went into the house, and as she was so rich she was welcomed home. When her mother heard how she got these riches, she wanted to have the same luck for her ugly and idle daughter, so she too was told to sit by the well and spin. That her spindle might be bloody, she pricked her fingers with it, and when that would not do she thrust her hand into a thorn-bush. Then she threw it into the well and sprang in herself after it. Like her sister, she came to a beautiful meadow, and followed the same path. When she came to the oven in the cottage, the bread called out as before, "Take me out! take me out! or I shall burn, I am quite done enough." But the lazy girl said, "A pretty story, indeed! just as if I should dirty myself for you!" and went on her way. She soon came to the apple-tree that cried, "Shake me! shake me! for my apples are quite ripe!" but she answered, "I will take care how I do that, for one of you might fall upon my head;" so she went on. At length she came to Mother Holle's house, and readily agreed to be her maid. The first day she behaved herself very well, and did what her mistress told her; for she thought of the gold she would give her; but the second day she began to be lazy, and the third still more so, for she would not get up in the morning early enough, and when she did she made the bed very badly, and did not shake it so that the feathers would fly out. Mother Holle was soon tired of her, and turned her off; but the lazy girl was quite pleased at that, and thought to herself, "Now the golden rain will come." Then the fairy took her to the same door; but when she stood under it, instead of gold a great kettle full of dirty pitch came showering upon her. "That is your wages," said Mother Holle as she shut the door upon her. So she went home quite black with the pitch, and as she came near her mother's house the cock sat upon the well, and clapt his wings, and cried out –

"Cock a-doodle-doo!
Our dirty slut's come home again!"

The Water of Life

LONG before you and I were born there reigned, in a country a great way off, a king who had three sons. This king once fell very ill, so ill that nobody thought he could live. His sons were very much grieved at their father's sickness; and as they walked weeping in the garden of the palace, an old man met them and asked what they ailed. They told him their father was so ill that they were afraid nothing could save him. "I know what would," said the old man; "it is the Water of Life. If he could have a draught of it he would be well again, but it is very hard to get." Then the eldest son said, "I will soon find it," and went to the sick king, and begged that he might go in search of the Water of Life, as it was the only thing that could save him. "No," said the king; "I had rather die than place you in such great danger as you must meet with in your journey." But he begged so hard that the king let him go; and the prince thought to himself, "If I bring my father this water, I shall be his dearest son, and he will make me heir to his kingdom."

Then he set out, and when he had gone on his way some time he came to a deep valley overhung with rocks and woods; and as he looked around there stood above him on one of the rocks a little dwarf, who called out to him and said, "Prince, whither hastest thou so fast?" "What is that to you, little ugly one?" said the prince sneeringly, and rode on his way. But the little dwarf fell into a great rage at his behaviour, and laid a spell of ill luck upon him, so that, as he rode on, the mountain pass seemed to become narrower and narrower, and at last the way was so straightened that he could not go a step forward, and when he thought to have turned his horse round and gone back the way he came, the passage he found had closed behind also, and shut him quite up; he next tried to get off his horse and make his way on foot, but this he was unable to do, and so there he was forced to abide spell-bound.

Meantime the king his father was lingering on in daily hope of his return, till at last the second son said, "Father, I will go in search of this Water;" for he thought to himself, "My brother is surely dead, and the kingdom will fall to me if I have good luck in my journey." The king was at first very unwilling to let him go, but at last yielded to his wish. So he set out and followed the same road which his brother had taken, and met the same dwarf, who stopped him at the same spot, and said as before, "Prince, whither hastest thou so fast?" "Mind your own affairs, busybody!" answered the prince scornfully, and rode off. But the dwarf put the same enchantment upon him, and when he came like the other to the narrow pass in the mountains he could neither move forward nor backward. Thus it is with proud silly people, who think themselves too wise to take advice.

When the second prince had thus stayed away a long while, the youngest said he would go and search for the Water of Life, and trusted he should soon be able to make his father well again. The dwarf met him too at the same spot, and said, "Prince, whither hastest thou so fast?" and the prince said, "I go in search of the Water of Life, because my father is ill and like to die: – can you help me?" "Do you know where it is to be found?" asked the dwarf. "No," said the prince. "Then as you have spoken to me kindly and sought for advice, I will tell you how and where to go. The Water you seek springs from a well in an enchanted castle, and that you may be able to go in safety I will give you an iron wand and two little loaves of bread; strike the iron door of the castle three times with the wand, and it will open: two hungry lions will be lying down inside gaping for their prey; but if you throw them the bread they will let you pass; then hasten on to the well and take some of the Water of Life before the clock strikes twelve, for if you tarry longer the door will shut upon you for ever."

Then the prince thanked the dwarf for his friendly aid, and took the wand and the bread and went travelling on and on over sea and land till he came to his journey's end, and found everything to be as the dwarf had told him. The door flew open at the third stroke of the wand, and when the lions were quieted he went on through the castle, and came at length to a beautiful hall;

around it he saw several knights sitting in a trance; then he pulled off their rings and put them on his own fingers. In another room he saw on a table a sword and a loaf of bread, which he also took. Further on he came to a room where a beautiful young lady sat upon a couch, who welcomed him joyfully, and said, if he would set her free from the spell that bound her, the kingdom should be his if he would come back in a year and marry her; then she told him that the well that held the Water of Life was in the palace gardens, and bade him make haste and draw what he wanted before the clock struck twelve. Then he went on, and as he walked through beautiful gardens he came to a delightful shady spot in which stood a couch; and he thought to himself, as he felt tired, that he would rest himself for a while and gaze on the lovely scenes around him. So he laid himself down, and sleep fell upon him unawares and he did not wake up till the clock was striking a quarter to twelve; then he sprung from the couch dreadfully frightened, ran to the well, filled a cup that was standing by him full of Water, and hastened to get away in time. Just as he was going out of the iron door it struck twelve, and the door fell so quickly upon him that it tore away a piece of his heel.

When he found himself safe he was overjoyed to think that he had got the Water of Life; and as he was going on his way homewards, he passed by the little dwarf, who when he saw the sword and the loaf said, "You have made a noble prize; with the sword you can at a blow slay whole armies, and the bread will never fail." Then the prince thought to himself, "I cannot go home to my father without my brothers," so he said, "Dear dwarf, cannot you tell me where my two brothers are, who set out in search of the Water of Life before me and never came back?" "I have shut them up by a charm between two mountains," said the dwarf, "because they were proud and ill-behaved, and scorned to ask advice." The prince begged so hard for his brothers that the dwarf at last set them free, though unwillingly, saying, "Beware of them, for they have bad hearts." Their brother, however, was greatly rejoiced to see them, and told them all that had happened to him, how he had found the Water of Life, and had taken a cup full of it, and how he had set a beautiful princess free from a spell that bound her; and how she had engaged to wait a whole year, and then to marry him and give him the kingdom. Then they all three rode on together, and on their way home came to a country that was laid waste by war and a dreadful famine, so that it was feared all must die for want. But the prince gave the king of the land the bread, and all his kingdom ate of it. And he slew the enemy's army with the wonderful sword, and left the kingdom in peace and plenty. In the same manner he befriended two other countries that they passed through on their way.

When they came to the sea, they got into a ship, and during their voyage the two eldest said to themselves, "Our brother has got the Water which we could not find, therefore our father will forsake us, and give him the kingdom which is our right," so they were full of envy and revenge, and agreed together how they could ruin him. They waited till he was fast asleep, and then poured the Water of Life out of the cup and took it for themselves, giving him bitter sea-water instead. And when they came to their journey's end, the youngest son brought his cup to the sick king, that he might drink and be healed. Scarcely, however, had he tasted the bitter sea-water when he became worse even than he was before, and then both the elder sons came in and blamed the youngest for what he had done, and said that he wanted to poison their father, but that they had found the Water of Life and had brought it with them. He no sooner began to drink of what they brought him, than he felt his sickness leave him, and was as strong and well as in his young days; then they went to their brother and laughed at him, and said, "Well, brother, you found the Water of Life, did you? you have had the trouble and we shall have the reward; pray, with all your cleverness why did not you manage to keep your eyes open? Next year one of us will take away your beautiful princess, if you do not take care; you had better say nothing about this to our father, for he does not believe a word you say, and if you tell tales, you shall lose your life into the bargain, but be quiet and we will let you off."

The old king was still very angry with his youngest son, and thought that he really meant to have taken away his life; so he called his court together and asked what should be done; and it was settled that he should be put to death. The prince knew nothing of what was going on, till one day when the king's chief huntsman went a-hunting with him, and they were alone in the wood together, the huntsman looked so sorrowful that the prince said, "My friend, what is the matter with you?" "I cannot and dare not tell you," said he. But the prince begged hard and said, "Only say what it is, and do not think I shall be angry, for I will forgive you." "Alas!" said the huntsman, "the king has ordered me to shoot you." The prince started at this, and said, "Let me live, and I will change dresses with you; you shall take my royal coat to show to my father, and do you give me your shabby one." "With all my heart," said the huntsman; "I am sure I shall be glad to save you, for I could not have shot you." Then he took the prince's coat, and gave him the shabby one, and went away through the wood.

Some time after, three grand embassies came to the old king's court, with rich gifts of gold and precious stones for his youngest son, which were sent from the three kings to whom he had lent his sword and loaf of bread, to rid them of their enemy, and feed their people. This touched the old king's heart, and he thought his son might still be guiltless, and said to his court, "Oh! that my son were still alive! how it grieves me that I had him killed!" "He still lives," said the huntsman; "and I rejoice that I had pity on him, and saved him, for when the time came, I could not shoot him, but let him go in peace and brought home his royal coat." At this the king was overwhelmed with joy, and made it known throughout all his kingdom, that if his son would come back to his court, he would forgive him.

Meanwhile the princess was eagerly waiting the return of her deliverer, and had a road made leading up to her palace all of shining gold; and told her courtiers that whoever came on horseback and rode straight up to the gate upon it, was her true lover, and that they must let him in; but whoever rode on one side of it, they must be sure was not the right one, and must send him away at once.

The time soon came, when the eldest thought he would make haste to go to the princess, and say that he was the one who had set her free, and that he should have her for his wife, and the kingdom with her. As he came before the palace and saw the golden road, he stopt to look at it, and thought to himself, "It is a pity to ride upon this beautiful road;" so he turned aside and rode on the right of it. But when he came to the gate the guards said to him, he was not what he said he was, and must go about his business. The second prince set out soon afterwards on the same errand; and when he came to the golden road, and his horse had set one foot upon it, he stopt to look at it, and thought it very beautiful, and said to himself, "What a pity it is that anything should tread here!" then he too turned aside and rode on the left of it. But when he came to the gate the guards said he was not the true prince, and that he too must go away.

Now when the full year was come, the third brother left the wood, where he had laid for fear of his father's anger, and set out in search of his betrothed bride. So he journeyed on, thinking of her all the way, and rode so quickly that he did not even see the golden road, but went with his horse straight over it; and as he came to the gate, it flew open, and the princess welcomed him with joy, and said he was her deliverer and should now be her husband and lord of the kingdom, and the marriage was soon kept with great feasting. When it was over, the princess told him she had heard of his father having forgiven him, and of his wish to have him home again: so he went to visit him, and told him everything, how his brothers had cheated and robbed him, and yet that he had borne all these wrongs for the love of his father. Then the old king was very angry, and wanted to punish his wicked sons; but they made their escape, and got into a ship and sailed away over the wide sea, and were never heard of any more.

Peter the Goatherd

IN the wilds of the Hartz Forest there is a high mountain, where the fairies and goblins dance by night, and where they say the great Emperor Frederic Barbarossa still holds his court among the caverns. Now and then he shows himself and punishes those whom he dislikes, or gives some rich gift to the lucky wight whom he takes it into his head to befriend. He sits on a throne of marble with his red beard sweeping on the ground, and once or twice in a long course of years rouses himself for a while from the trance in which he is buried, but soon falls again into his former forgetfulness. Strange chances have befallen many who have strayed within the range of his court: – you shall hear one of them.

A great many years ago there lived in the village at the foot of the mountain, one Peter, a goatherd. Every morning he drove his flock to feed upon the green spots that are here and there found on the mountain's side, and in the evening he sometimes thought it too far to drive his charge home, so he used in such cases to shut it up in a spot amongst the woods, where an old ruined wall was left standing, high enough to form a fold, in which he could count his goats and rest in peace for the night. One evening he found that the prettiest goat of his flock had vanished soon after they were driven into this fold, but was there again in the morning. Again and again he watched, and the same strange thing happened. He thought he would look still more narrowly, and soon found a cleft in the old wall, through which it seemed that his favourite made her way. Peter followed, scrambling as well as he could down the side of the rook, and wondered not a little, on overtaking his goat, to find it employing itself very much at its ease in a cavern, eating corn, which kept dropping from some place above. He went into the cavern and looked about him to see where all this corn, that rattled about his ears like a hail-storm, could come from: but all was dark, and he could find no clue to this strange business. At last, as he stood listening, he thought he heard the neighing and stamping of horses. He listened again; it was plainly so; and after a while he was sure that horses were feeding above him, and that the corn fell from their mangers. What could these horses be, which were thus kept in a mountain where none but the goat's foot ever trod? Peter pondered a while; but his wonder only grew greater and greater, when on a sudden a little page came forth and beckoned him to follow; he did so, and came at last to a courtyard surrounded by an old wall. The spot seemed the bosom of the valley; above rose on every hand high masses of rock; wide branching trees threw their arms over head, so that nothing but a glimmering twilight made its way through; and here, on the cool smooth shaven turf, were twelve old knights, who looked very grave and sober, but were amusing themselves with a game of nine-pins.

Not a word fell from their lips; but they ordered Peter by dumb signs to busy himself in setting up the pins, as they knocked them down. At first his knees trembled, as he dared to snatch a stolen sidelong glance at the long beards and old-fashioned dresses of the worthy knights. Little by little, however, he grew bolder; and at last he plucked up his heart so far as to take his turn in the draught at the can, which stood beside him and sent up the smell of the richest old wine. This gave him new strength for his work; and as often as he flagged at all, he turned to the same kind friend for help in his need.

Sleep at last overpowered him; and when he awoke he found himself stretched out upon the old spot where he had folded his flock. The same green turf was spread beneath, and the same tottering walls surrounded him: he rubbed his eyes, but neither dog nor goat was to be seen, and when he had looked about him again the grass seemed to be longer under his feet, and trees hung over his head, which he had either never seen before or had forgotten. Shaking his head, and hardly knowing whether he were in his right mind, he wound his way among the mountain steeps, through paths where his flocks were wont to wander; but still not a goat was to be seen. Below him in the plain lay the village where his home was, and at length he took the downward path, and set out with a heavy heart in search of his flock. The people who met him as he drew near to the village were all unknown to him; they were not even dressed as his neighbours were, and they seemed as if they hardly spoke the same tongue; and when he eagerly asked after his goats, they only stared at him and stroked their chins. At last he did the same too, and what was his wonder to find that his beard was grown at least a foot long! The world, thought he now to himself, is turned over, or at any rate bewitched, and yet he knew the mountain (as he turned round to gaze upon its woody heights); and he knew the houses and cottages also, with their little gardens, all of which were in the same places as he had always known them; he heard some children, too, call the village by its old name, as a traveller that passed by was asking his way.

Again he shook his head and went straight through the village to his own cottage. Alas! it looked sadly out of repair; and in the court-yard lay an unknown child, in a ragged dress, by the side of a rough, toothless dog, whom he thought he ought to know, but who snarled and barked in his face when he called him to him. He went in at an opening in the wall where a door had once stood, but found all so dreary and empty that he staggered out again like a drunken man, and called his wife and children loudly by their names; but no one heard, at least no one answered him.

A crowd of women and children soon flocked around the long gray bearded man, and all broke upon him at once with the questions, "Who are you?" "Whom do you want?" It seemed to him so odd to ask other people at his own door after his wife and children, that in order to get rid of the crowd he named the first man that came into his head; – "Hans, the blacksmith!" said he. Most held their tongues and stared, but at last an old woman said, "He went these seven years ago to a place that you will not reach to-day." "Frank the tailor, then!" "Heaven rest his soul!" said an old beldame upon crutches; "he has laid these ten years in a house that he'll never leave."

Peter looked at the old woman, and shuddered as he saw her to be one of his old friends, only with a strangely altered face. All wish to ask further questions was gone; but at last a young woman made her way through the gaping throng with a baby in her arms, and a little girl about three years old clinging to her other hand; all three looked the very image of his wife. "What is thy name?" asked he wildly. "Mary." "And your father's?" "Heaven bless him! Peter! It is now twenty years since we sought him day and night on the mountain; his flock came back, but he never was heard of any more. I was then seven years old." The goatherd could hold no longer. "I am Peter," cried he; "I am Peter, and no other;" as he took the child from his daughter's arms and kissed it. All stood gaping, and not knowing what to say or think, till at length one voice was heard, "Why it is Peter!" and then several others cried, "Yes, it is, it is Peter! "Welcome neighbour, welcome home, after twenty long years."

The Four Clever Brothers

"DEAR children," said a poor man to his four sons, "I have nothing to give you; you must go out into the world and try your luck. Begin by learning some trade, and see how you can get on." So the four brothers took their walking-sticks in their hands, and their little bundles on their shoulders, and, after bidding their father good-bye, went all out at the gate together. When they had got on some way they came to four cross-ways, each leading to a different country. Then the eldest said, "Here we must part; but this day four years we will come back to this spot; and in the mean time each must try what he can do for himself." So each brother went his way; and as the oldest was hastening on, a man met him, and asked him where he was going and what he wanted. "I am going to try my luck in the world, and should like to begin by learning some trade," answered he. "Then," said the man, "go with me, and I will teach you how to become the cunningest thief that ever was." "So," said the other, "that is not an honest calling, and what can one look to earn by it in the end but the gallows?" "Oh!" said the man, "you need not fear the gallows; for I will only teach you to steal what will be fair game; I meddle with nothing but what no one else can get or care anything about, and where no one can find you out." So the young man agreed to follow his trade, and he soon showed himself so clever that nothing could escape him that he had once set his mind upon.

The second brother also met a man, who, when he found out what he was setting out upon, asked him what trade he meant to learn. "I do not know yet," said he. "Then come with me, and be a star-gazer. It is a noble trade, for nothing can be hidden from you when you understand the stars." The plan pleased him much, and he soon became such a skilful star-gazer, that when he had served out his time, and wanted to leave his master, he gave him a glass, and said, "With this you can see all that is passing in the sky and on earth, and nothing can be hidden from you."

The third brother met a huntsman, who took him with him, and taught him so well all that belonged to hunting, that he became very clever in that trade; and when he left his master he gave him a bow, and said, "Whatever you shoot at with this bow you will be sure to hit."

The youngest brother likewise met a man who asked him what he wished to do. "Would not you like," said he, "to be a tailor?" "Oh no!" said the young man; "sitting cross-legged from morning to night, working backwards and forwards with a needle and goose, will never suit me." "Oh!" answered the man, "that is not my sort of tailoring; come with me, and you will learn quite another kind of trade from that." Not knowing what better to do, he came into the plan, and learnt the trade from the beginning; and when he left his master, he gave him a needle, and said, "You can sew anything with this, be it as soft as an egg, or as hard as steel, and the joint will be so fine that no seam will be seen."

After the space of four years, at the time agreed upon, the four brothers met at the four cross-roads, and having welcomed each other, set off towards their father's home, where they told him all that had happened to them, and how each had learned some trade. Then one day, as they were sitting before the house under a very high tree, the father said, "I should like to try what each of you can do in his trade." So he looked up, and said to the second son, "At the top of this tree there is a chaffinch's nest; tell me how many eggs there are in it." The star-gazer took his glass, looked up, and said, "Five." "Now," said the father to the eldest son, "take away the eggs without the bird that is sitting upon them and hatching them knowing anything of what you are doing." So the cunning thief climbed up the tree, and brought away to his father the five eggs from under the bird, who never saw or felt what he was doing, but kept sitting on at her ease. Then the father took the eggs, and put one on each corner of the table and the fifth in the middle, and said to the huntsman, "Cut all the eggs in two pieces at one shot." The huntsman took up his bow, and at one shot struck all the five eggs as his father wished. "Now comes your turn," said he to the young tailor; "sew the eggs and the young birds in them together again, so neatly that the shot shall have done them no harm." Then the tailor took his needle and sewed the eggs as he was told; and when he had done, the thief was sent to take them back to the nest, and put them under the bird, without its knowing it. Then she went on sitting, and hatched them; and in a few days they crawled out, and had only a little red streak across their necks where the tailor had sewed them together.

"Well done, sons!" said the old man, "you have made good use of your time, and learnt something worth the knowing; but I am sure I do not know which ought to have the prize. Oh! that the time might soon come for you to turn your skill to some account!"

Not long after this there was a great bustle in the country; for the king's daughter had been carried off by a mighty dragon, and the king mourned over his loss day and night, and made it known that whoever brought her back to him should have her for a wife. Then the four brothers said to each other, "Here is a chance for us; let us try what we can do." And they agreed to see whether they could not set the princess free. "I will soon find out where she is, however," said the star-gazer as he looked through his glass, and soon cried out, "I see her afar off, sitting upon a rock in the sea, and I can spy the dragon close by, guarding her." Then he went to the king, and asked for a ship for himself and his brothers, and went with them upon the sea till they came to the right place. There they found the princess sitting, as the star-gazer had said, on the rock, and the dragon was lying asleep with his head upon her lap. "I dare not shoot at him," said the huntsman, "for I should kill the beautiful young lady also." "Then I will try my skill," said the thief; and went and stole her away from under the dragon so quickly and gently that the beast did not know it, but went on snoring.

Then away they hastened with her full of joy in their boat towards the ship; but soon came the dragon roaring behind them through the air, for he awoke and missed the princess; but when he got over the boat, and wanted to pounce upon them and carry off the princess, the huntsman took up his bow and shot him straight at the heart, so that he fell down dead. They were still not safe; for he was such a great beast, that in his fall he overset the boat, and they had to swim in the open sea upon a few planks. So the tailor took his needle, and with a few large stitches put some of the planks together, and set down upon them, and sailed about and gathered up all the pieces of the boat, and tacked them together so quickly that the boat was soon ready, and they then reached the ship and got home safe.

When they had brought home the princess to her father, there was great rejoicing; and he said to the four brothers, "One of you shall marry her, but you must settle amongst yourselves which it is to be." Then there arose a quarrel between them; and the star-gazer said, "If I had not found the princess out, all your skill would have been of no use; therefore she ought to be mine." "Your seeing her would have been of no use," said the thief, "if I had not taken her away from the dragon; therefore she ought to be mine." "No, she is mine," said the huntsman; "for if I had not killed the dragon, he would after all have torn you and the princess into pieces." "And if I had not sewed the boat together again," said the tailor, "you would all have been drowned; therefore she is mine." Then the king put in a word, and said, "Each of you is right; and as all cannot have the young lady, the best way is for neither of you to have her; and to make up for the loss, I will give each, as a reward for his skill, half a kingdom." So the brothers agreed that would be much better than quarrelling; and the king then gave each half a kingdom, as he had said; and they lived very happily the rest of their days, and took good care of their father.

The Elfin-Grove

"I HOPE," said a woodman one day to his wife, "that the children will not run into that fir-grove by the side of the river; who they are that have come to live there I cannot tell, but I am sure it looks more dark and gloomy than ever, and some queer-looking beings are to be seen lurking about it every night, as I am told." The woodman could not say that they brought any ill luck as yet, whatever they were; for all the village had thriven more than ever since they came; the fields looked gayer and greener, and even the sky was a deeper blue. Not knowing what to say of them, the farmer very wisely let his new friends alone, and in truth troubled his head very little about them.

That very evening little Mary and her playfellow Martin were playing at hide and seek in the valley. "Where can he be hid?" said she; "he must have gone into the fir-grove," and down she ran to look. Just then she spied a little dog that jumped round her and wagged his tail, and led her on towards the wood. Then he ran into it, and she soon jumped up the bank to look after him, but was overjoyed to see, instead of a gloomy grove of firs, a delightful garden, where flowers and shrubs of every kind grew upon turf of the softest green; gay butterflies flew about her, the birds sang sweetly, and, what was strangest, the prettiest little children sported about on all sides, some twining the flowers, and others dancing in rings upon the shady spots beneath the trees. In the midst, instead of the hovels of which Mary had heard, there was a palace that dazzled her eyes with its brightness. For a while she gazed on the fairy scene around her, till at last one of the little dancers ran up to her, and said, "And you are come at last to see us? we have often seen you play about, and wished to have you with us." Then she plucked some of the fruit that grew near; and

Mary at the first taste forgot her home, and wished only to see and know more of her fairy friends.

Then they led her about with them and showed her all their sports. One while they danced by moonlight on the primrose banks; at another time they skipped from bough to bough among the trees that hung over the cooling streams; for they moved as lightly and easily through the air as on the ground: and Mary went with them everywhere, for they bore her in their arms wherever they wished to go. Sometimes they would throw seeds on the turf, and directly little trees sprung up; and then they would set their feet upon the branches, while the trees grew under them, till they danced, upon the boughs in the air, wherever the breezes carried them; and again the trees would sink down into the earth and land them safely at their bidding. At other times they would go and visit the palace of their queen; and there the richest food was spread before them, and the softest music was heard; and there all around grew flowers which were always changing their hues, from scarlet to purple and yellow and emerald. Sometimes they went to look at the heaps of treasure which were piled up in the royal stores; for little dwarfs were always employed in searching the earth for gold. Small as this fairy land looked from without, it seemed within to have no end; a mist hung around it to shield it from the eyes of men; and some of the little elves sat perched upon the outermost trees, to keep watch lest the step of man should break in and spoil the charm.

"And who are you?" said Mary one day. "We are what are called elves in your world," said one whose name was Gossamer, and who had become her dearest friend: "we are told you talk a great deal about us; some of our tribes like to work you mischief, but we who live here seek only to be happy: we meddle little with mankind; but when we do come among them, it is to do them good." "And where is your queen?" said little Mary. "Hush! hush! you cannot see or know her: you must leave us before she comes back, which will be now very soon, for mortal step cannot come where she is. But you will know that she is here when you see the meadows gayer, the rivers more sparkling, and the sun brighter."

Soon afterwards Gossamer told Mary the time was come to bid her farewell, and gave her a ring in token of their friendship, and led her to the edge of the grove. "Think of me," said she;

Geo Cruikshank fc.

"but beware how you tell what you have seen, or try to visit any of us again, for if you do, we shall quit this grove and come back no more." Turning back, Mary saw nothing but the gloomy fir-grove she had known before. "How frightened my father and mother will be!" thought she as she looked at the sun, which had risen some time, "They will wonder where I have been all night, and yet I must not tell them what I have seen." She hastened homewards, wondering however, as she went, to see that the leaves, which were yesterday so fresh and green, were now falling dry and yellow around her. The cottage too seemed changed, and, when she went in, there sat her father looking some years older than when she saw him last; and her mother whom she hardly knew, was by his side. Close by was a young man; "father," said Mary, "who is this?" "Who are you that call me father?" said he; "are you – no you cannot be – our long-lost Mary?" But they soon saw that it was their Mary; and the young man, who was her old friend and playfellow Martin, said, "No wonder you had forgotten me in seven years; do not you remember how we parted seven years ago while playing in the field? We thought you were quite lost; but we are glad to see that someone has taken care of you and brought you home at last." Mary said nothing, for she could not tell all; but she wondered at the strange tale, and felt gloomy at the change from fairy land to her father's cottage.

Little by little she came to herself, thought of her story as a mere dream, and soon became Martin's bride. Everything seemed to thrive around them; and Mary called her first little girl Elfie, in memory of her friends. The little thing was loved by every one. It was pretty and very good-tempered; Mary thought that it was very like a little elf; and all, without knowing why, called it the fairy child.

One day, while Mary was dressing her little Elfie, she found a piece of gold hanging round her neck by a silken thread, and knew it to be of the same sort as she had seen in the hands of the fairy dwarfs. Elfie seemed sorry at its being seen, and said that she had found it in the garden. But Mary watched her and soon found that she went every afternoon to sit by herself in a shady place behind the house: so one day she hid herself to see what the child did there; and to her great wonder Gossamer was sitting by her side. "Dear Elfie," she was saying, "your mother and I used to sit thus when she was young and lived among us.

Oh! if you could but come and do so too! but since our queen came to us it cannot be; yet I will come and see you and talk to you, whilst you are a child; when you grow up we must part for ever." Then she plucked one of the roses that grew around them and breathed gently upon it, and said, "Take this for my sake. It will keep its freshness a whole year."

Then Mary loved her little Elfie more than ever; and when she found that she spent some hours of almost every day with the elf, she used to hide herself and watch them without being seen, till one day when Gossamer was bearing her little friend through the air from tree to tree, her mother was so frightened lest her child should fall that she could not help screaming out, and Gossamer set her gently on the ground and seemed angry, and flew away. But still she used sometimes to come and play with her little friend, and would soon have done so perhaps the game as before, had not Mary one day told her husband the whole story, for she could not bear to hear him always wondering and laughing at their little child's odd ways, and saying he was sure there was something in the fir-grove that brought them no good. So to show him that all she said was true, she took him to see Elfie and the fairy; but no sooner did Gossamer know that he was there (which she did in an instant), than she changed herself into a raven and flew off into the fir-grove.

Mary burst into tears, and so did Elfie, for she knew she should see her dear friend no more: but Martin was restless and bent upon following up his search after the fairies; so when night came he stole away towards the grove. When he came to it nothing was to be seen but the gloomy firs and the old hovels; and the thunder rolled, and the wind groaned and whistled through the trees. It seemed that all about him was angry; so he turned homewards frightened at what he had done.

In the morning all the neighbours flocked around, asking one another what the noise and bustle of the last night could mean; and when they looked about them, their trees looked blighted, and the meadows parched, the streams were dried up and everything seemed troubled and sorrowful; but they all thought that some how or other the fir-grove had not near so forbidding a look as it used to have. Strange stories were told, how one had heard flutterings in the air, another had seen the fir-grove as it were alive with little beings that flew away from it. Each neighbour told his tale, and all wondered what could have happened; but Mary and her husband knew what was the matter, and bewailed their folly; for they foresaw that their kind neighbours, to whom they owed all their luck, were gone for ever. Among the bystanders none told a wilder story than the old ferryman who plied across the river at the foot of the grove; he told how at midnight his boat was carried away, and how hundreds of little beings seemed to load it with treasures; how a strange piece of gold was left for him in the boat, as his fare; how the air seemed full of fairy forms fluttering around; and how at last a great train passed over that seemed to be guarding their leader to the meadows on the other side; and how he heard soft music floating around as they flew; and how sweet voices sang as they hovered over his head.

Fairy Queen!
Fairy Queen!
Mortal steps are on the green;
Come away!
Haste away!
Fairies, guard your Queen
Hither, hither, fairy Queen!
Lest thy silvery wing be seen;
O'er the sky
Fly, fly, fly!
Fairies, guard your lady Queen!
O'er the sky
Fly, fly, fly!
Fairies, guard your Queen!

Fairy Queen!
Fairy Queen!
Thou hast pass'd the treach'rous scene;
Now we may
Down and play
O'er the daisied green.
Lightly, lightly, fairy Queen!
Trip it gently o'er the green:
Fairies gay,
Trip away
Bound about your lady Queen!
Fairies gay,
Trip away
Bound about your Queen!

Poor Elfie mourned their loss the most, and would spend whole hours in looking upon the rose that her playfellow had given her, and singing over it the pretty airs she had taught her;

till at length when the year's charm had passed away and it began to fade, she planted the stalk in her garden, and there it grew and grew till she could sit under the shade of it and think of her friend Gossamer.

The Salad

AS a merry young huntsman was once going briskly along through a wood, there came up a little old woman, and said to him "Good day, good day; you seem merry enough, but I am hungry and thirsty; do pray give me something to eat." The huntsman took pity on her and put his hand in his pocket and gave her what he had. Then he wanted to go his way; but she took hold of him, and said, "Listen, my friend, to what I am going to tell you; I will reward you for your kindness; go your way, and after a little time you will come to a tree where you will see nine birds sitting on a cloak. Shoot into the midst of them, and one will fall down dead: the cloak will fall too; take it, it is a wishing-cloak, and when you wear it you will find yourself at any place where you may wish to be. Cut open the dead bird, take out its heart and keep it, and you will find a piece of gold under your pillow every morning when you rise. It is the bird's heart that will bring you this good luck."

The huntsman thanked her, and thought to himself, "If all this does happen, it will be a fine thing for me." When he had gone a hundred steps or so, he heard a screaming and chirping in the branches over him, and looked up and saw a flock of birds pulling a cloak with their bills and feet; screaming, fighting, and tugging at each other as if each wished to have it himself. "Well," said the huntsman, "this is wonderful; this happens just as the old woman said;" then he shot into the midst of them so that their feathers flew all about. Off went the flock chattering away; but one fell down dead, and the cloak with it. Then the huntsman did as the old woman told him, cut open the bird, took out the heart, and carried the cloak home with him.

The next morning when he awoke he lifted up his pillow,

and there lay the piece of gold glittering underneath; the same happened next day, and indeed every day when he arose. He heaped up a great deal of gold, and at last thought to himself, "Of what use is this gold to me whilst I am at home? I will go out into the world and look about me."

Then he took leave of his friends, and hung his bag and bow about his neck, and went his way. It so happened that his road one day led through a thick wood, at the end of which was a large castle in a green meadow, and at one of the windows stood on old woman with a very beautiful young lady by her side looking about them. Now the old woman was a fairy and said to the young lady, "There is a young man coming out of the wood who carries a wonderful prize; we must get it away from him, my dear child, for it is more fit for us than for him. He has a bird's heart that brings a piece of gold under his pillow every morning." Meantime the huntsman came nearer and looked at the lady, and said to himself, "I have been travelling so long that I should like to go into this castle and rest myself, for I have money enough to pay for anything I want;" but the real reason was that he wanted to see more of the beautiful lady. Then he went into the house, and was welcomed kindly; and it was not long before he was so much in love that he thought of nothing else but looking at the lady's eyes, and doing everything that she wished. Then the old woman said, "Now is the time for getting the bird's heart." So the lady stole it away, and he never found any more gold under his pillow, for it lay now under the young lady's, and the old woman took it away every morning, but he was so much in love that he never missed his prize.

"Well," said the old fairy, "We have got the bird's heart, but not the wishing-cloak yet, and that we must also get." "Let us leave him that," said the young lady; "he has already lost his wealth." Then the fairy was very angry, and said, "Such a cloak is a very rare and wonderful thing, and I must and will have it." So she did as the old woman told her, and set herself at the window, and looked about the country and seemed very sorrowful; then the huntsman said, "What makes you so sad?" "Alas! dear sir," said she, "yonder lies the granite rock where all the costly diamonds grow, and I want so much to go there, that whenever I think of it I cannot help being sorrowful, for who can reach it? only the birds and the flies, – man cannot." "If that's all your grief," said the huntsman, "I'll take you there with all my heart;" so he drew her under his cloak, and the moment he wished to be on the granite mountain they were both there. The diamonds glittered so on all sides that they were delighted with the sight and picked up the finest. But the old fairy made a deep sleep come upon him, and he said to the young lady, "Let us sit down and rest ourselves a little, I am so tired that I cannot stand any longer." So they sat down, and he laid his head in her lap and fell asleep; and whilst he was sleeping on she took the cloak from his shoulders, hung it on her own, picked up the diamonds, and wished herself home again.

When he awoke and found that his lady had tricked him, and left him alone on the wild rock, he said, "Alas! what roguery there is in the world!" and there he sat in great grief and fear, not knowing what to do. Now this rock belonged to fierce giants who lived upon it; and as he saw three of them striding about, he thought to himself, "I can only save myself by feigning to be asleep;" so he laid himself down as if he were in a sound sleep. When the giants came up to him, the first pushed him with his foot, and said, "What worm is this that lies here curled up?" "Tread upon him and kill him," said the second. "It's not worth the trouble," said the third; "let him live, he'll go climbing higher up the mountain, and some cloud will come rolling and carry him away." And they passed on. But the huntsman had heard all they said; and as soon as they were gone, he climbed to the top of the mountain, and when he had sat there a short time a cloud came rolling around him, and caught him in a whirlwind and bore him along for some time, till it settled in a garden, and he fell quite gently to the ground amongst the greens and cabbages.

Then he looked around him, and said, "I wish I had something to eat, if not I shall be worse off than before; for here I see neither apples nor pears, nor any kind of fruits, nothing but vegetables." At last he thought to himself, "I can eat salad, it will refresh and strengthen me." So he picked out a fine head and ate of it; but scarcely had he swallowed two bites when he felt himself quite changed, and saw with horror that he was turned into an ass. However, he still felt very hungry, and the salad tasted very nice; so he ate on till he came to another kind of salad, and scarcely had he tasted it when he felt another change come over him, and soon saw that he was lucky enough to have found his old shape again.

Then he laid himself down and slept off a little of his weariness; and when he awoke the next morning he broke off a head both of the good and the bad salad, and thought to himself, "This will help me to my fortune again, and enable me to pay off some folks for their treachery." So he went away to try and find the castle of his old friends; and after wandering about a few days he luckily found it. Then he stained his face all over brown, so that even his mother would not have known him, and went into the castle and asked for a lodging; "I am so tired," said he, "that I can go no further." "Countryman," said the fairy, "who are you? and what is your business?" "I am," said he, "a messenger sent by the king to find the finest salad that grows under the sun. I have been lucky enough to find it, and have brought it with me; but the heat of the sun scorches so that it begins to wither, and I don't know that I can carry it farther."

When the fairy and the young lady heard of this beautiful salad, they longed to taste it and said, "Dear countryman, let us just taste it." "To be sure," answered he; "I have two heads of it with me, and will give you one;" so he opened his bag and gave them the bad. Then the fairy herself took it into the kitchen to be dressed; and when it was ready she could not wait till it was carried up, but took a few leaves immediately and put them in her mouth, and scarcely were they swallowed when she lost her own form and ran braying down into the court in the form of an ass. Now the servant-maid came into the kitchen, and seeing the salad ready was going to carry it up; but in the way she too felt a wish to taste it as the old woman had done, and ate some leaves; so she also was turned into an ass and ran after the other, letting the dish with the salad fall on the ground. The messenger sat all this time with the beautiful young lady, and as nobody came with the salad and she longed to taste it, she said," I don't know where the salad can be." Then he thought something must have happened, and said, "I will go into the kitchen and see." And as he went he saw two asses in the court running about, and the salad lying on the ground. "All right!" said he; "those two have had their share." Then he took up the rest of the leaves, laid them on the dish and brought them to the young lady, saying, "I bring you the dish myself that you may not wait any longer." So she ate of it, and like the others ran off into the court, braying away.

Then the huntsman washed his face and went into the court that they might know him. "Now you shall be paid for your roguery," said he; and tied them all three to a rope and took them along with him till he came to a mill and knocked at the window. "What's the matter?" said the miller." I have three tiresome beasts here," said the other; "if you will take them, give them food and room, and treat them as I tell you, I will pay you whatever you ask." "With all my heart," said the miller; "but how shall I treat them?" Then the huntsman said, "Give the old one stripes three times a day and hay once; give the next (who was the servant-maid) stripes once a day and hay three times; and give the youngest (who was the beautiful lady) hay three times a day and no stripes:" for he could not find it in his heart to have her beaten. After this he went back to the castle, where he found everything he wanted.

Some days after the miller came to him and told him that the old ass was dead; "the other two," said he, "are alive and eat, but are so sorrowful that they cannot last long." Then the huntsman pitied them, and told the miller to drive them back to him, and when they came, he gave them some of the good salad to eat. And the beautiful young lady fell upon her knees before him, and said, "O dearest huntsman! forgive me all the ill I have done you; my mother forced me to it, it was against my will, for I always loved you very much. Your wishing-cloak hangs up in the closet, and as for the bird's heart, I will give it you too." But he said, "Keep it, it will be just the same thing, for I mean to make you my wife." So they were married, and lived together very happily till they died.

The Nose

DID you ever hear the story of the three poor soldiers, who, after having fought hard in the wars, set out on their road home begging their way as they went?

They had journeyed on a long way, sick at heart with their bad luck at thus being turned loose on the world in their old days, when one evening they reached a deep gloomy wood through which they must pass; night came fast upon them, and they found that they must, however unwillingly, sleep in the wood; so to make all as safe as they could, it was agreed that two should lie down and sleep, while a third sat up and watched lest wild beasts should break in and tear them to pieces; when he was tired he was to wake one of the others and sleep in his turn, and so on with the third, so as to share the work fairly among them.

The two who were to rest first soon lay down and fell fast asleep, and the other made himself a good fire under the trees and sat down by the side to keep watch. He had not sat long before all on a sudden up came a little man in a red jacket. "Who's there?" said he. "A friend," said the soldier. "What sort of a friend?" "An old broken soldier," said the other, "with his two comrades who have nothing left to live on; come, sit down and warm yourself." "Well, my worthy fellow," said the little man, "I will do what I can for you; take this and show it to your comrades in the morning." So he took out an old cloak and gave it to the soldier, telling him that whenever he put it over his shoulders anything that he wished for would be fulfilled; then the little man made him a bow and walked away.

The second soldier's turn to watch soon came, and the first laid himself down to sleep; but the second man had not sat by himself long before up came the little man in the red jacket again. The soldier treated him in a friendly way as his comrade had done, and the little man gave him a purse, which he told him was always full of gold, let him draw as much as he would.

Then the third soldier's turn to watch came, and he also had the little man for his guest, who gave him a wonderful horn that drew crowds around it whenever it was played; and made every one forget his business to come and dance to its beautiful music.

In the morning each told his story and showed his treasure; and as they all liked each other very much and were old friends, they agreed to travel together to see the world, and for a while only to make use of the wonderful purse. And thus they spent their time very joyously, till at last they began to be tired of this roving life, and thought they should like to have a home of their own. So the first soldier put his old cloak on, and wished for a fine castle. In a moment it stood before their eyes; fine gardens and green lawns spread round it, and flocks of sheep and goats and herds of oxen were grazing about, and out of the gate came a fine coach with three dapple gray horses to meet them and bring them home.

All this was very well for a time; but it would not do to stay at home always, so they got together all their rich clothes and houses and servants, and ordered their coach with three horses, and set out on a journey to see a neighbouring king. Now this king had an only daughter, and as he took the three soldiers for king's sons, he gave them a kind welcome. One day, as the second soldier was walking with the princess, she saw him with the wonderful purse in his hand; and having asked him what it was, he was foolish enough to tell her; – though indeed it did not much signify, for she was a witch and knew all the wonderful things that the three soldiers brought. Now this princess was very cunning and artful; so she set to work and made a purse so like the soldier's that no one would know one from the other, and then asked him to come and see her, and made him drink some wine that she had got ready for him, till he fell fast asleep. Then she felt in his pocket, and took away the wonderful purse and left the one she had made in its place.

The next morning the soldiers set out home, and soon after they reached their castle, happening to want some money, they went to their purse for it, and found something indeed in it, but to their great sorrow when they had emptied it, none came in the place of what they took. Then the cheat was soon found out; for the second soldier knew where he had been, and how he had told the story to the princess, and he guessed that she had betrayed him. "Alas!" cried he, "poor wretches that we are, what shall we do?" "Oh!" said the first soldier, "let no gray hairs grow for this mishap; I will soon get the purse back." So he threw his cloak across his shoulders and wished himself in the princess's chamber. There he found her sitting alone, telling her gold that fell around her in a shower from the purse. But the soldier stood looking at her too long, for the moment she saw him she started up and cried out with all her force, "Thieves! Thieves!" so that the whole court came running in and tried to seize him. The poor soldier now began to be dreadfully frightened in his turn, and thought it was high time to make the best of his way off; so without thinking of the ready way of travelling that his cloak gave him, he ran to the window, opened it, and jumped out; and unluckily in his haste his cloak caught and was left hanging, to the great joy of the princess, who knew its worth.

The poor soldier made the best of his way home to his comrades, on foot and in a very downcast mood; but the third soldier told him to keep up his heart, and took his horn and blew a merry tune. At the first blast a countless troop of foot and horse came rushing to their aid, and they set out to make war against their enemy. Then the king's palace was besieged, and he was told that he must give up the purse and cloak, or that not one stone should be left upon another. And the king went into his daughter's chamber and talked with her; but she said, "Let me try first if I cannot beat them some other way." So she thought of a cunning scheme to overreach them, and dressed herself out as a poor girl with a basket on her arm; and set out by night with her maid, and went into the enemy's camp as if she wanted to sell trinkets.

In the morning she began to ramble about, singing ballads so beautifully, that all the tents were left empty, and the soldiers ran round in crowds and thought of nothing but hearing her sing. Amongst the rest came the soldier to whom the horn belonged, and as soon as she saw him she winked to her maid, who slipped slily through the crowd and went into his tent where it hung, and stole it away. This done, they both got safely back to the palace; the besieging army went away, the three wonderful gifts were all left in the hands of the princess, and the three soldiers were as pennyless and forlorn as when the little man with the red jacket found them in the wood.

Poor fellows! they began to think what was now to be done. "Comrades," at last said the second soldier, who had had the purse, "we had better part, we cannot live together, let each seek his bread as well as he can." So he turned to the right, and the other two to the left; for they said they would rather travel together. Then on he strayed till he came to a wood (now this was the same wood where they had met with so much good luck before); and he walked on a long time till evening began to fall, when he sat down tired beneath a tree, and soon fell asleep.

Morning dawned, and he was greatly delighted, at opening his eyes, to see that the tree was laden with the most beautiful apples. He was hungry enough, so he soon plucked and ate first one, then a second, then a third apple. A strange feeling came over his nose: when he put the apple to his mouth something was in the way; he felt it; it was his nose, that grew and grew till it hung down to his breast. It did not stop there, still it grew and grew; "Heavens!" thought he, "when will it have done growing?" And well might he ask, for by this time it reached the ground as he sat on the grass, and thus it kept creeping on till he could not bear its weight, or raise himself up; and it seemed as if it would never end, for already it stretched its enormous length all through the wood.

Meantime his comrades were journeying on, till on a sudden one of them stumbled against something." What can that be?" said the other. They looked, and could think of nothing that it was like but a nose. "We will follow it and find its owner, however," said they; so they traced it up till at last they found their poor comrade lying stretched along under the apple-tree. What was to be done? They tried to carry him, but in vain. They caught an ass that was passing by, and raised him upon its back; but it was soon tired of carrying such a load. So they sat down in despair, when up came the little man in the red jacket. "Why, how now, friend?" said he, laughing; "well, I must find a cure for you, I see." So he told them to gather a pear from a tree that grew close by, and the nose would come right again, No time was lost, and the nose was soon brought to its proper size, to the poor soldier's joy.

"I will do something more for you yet," said the little man; "take some of those pears and apples with you; whoever eats one of the apples will have his nose grow like yours just now; but if you give him a pear, all will come right again. Go to the princess

G Cruikshank fe??

and get her to eat some of your apples; her nose will grow twenty times as long as yours did; then look sharp, and you will get what you want of her."

Then they thanked their old friend very heartily for all his kindliness, and it was agreed that the poor soldier who had already tried the power of the apple should undertake the task. So he dressed himself up as a gardener's boy, and went to the king's palace, and said he had apples to sell, such as were never seen there before. Every one that saw them was delighted and wanted to taste, but he said they were only for the princess; and she soon sent her maid to buy his stock. They were so ripe and rosy that she soon began eating, and had already eaten three when she too began to wonder what ailed her nose, for it grew and grew, down to the ground, out at the window, and over the garden, nobody knows where.

Then the king made known to all his kingdom, that whoever would heal her of this dreadful disease should be richly rewarded. Many tried, but the princess got no relief. And now the old soldier dressed himself up very sprucely as a doctor, who said he could cure her; so he chopped up some of the apple, and to punish her a little more gave her a dose, saying he would call to-morrow and see her again. The morrow came, and of course, instead of being better, the nose had been growing fast all night, and the poor princess was in a dreadful fright. So the doctor chopped up a very little of the pear and gave her, and said he was sure that would do good, and he would call again the nest day. Next day came, and the nose was to be sure a little smaller, but yet it was bigger than it was when the doctor first began to meddle with it.

Then he thought to himself, "I must frighten this cunning princess a little more before I shall get what I want of her;" so he gave her another dose of the apple, and said he would call on the morrow. The morrow came, and the nose was ten times as bad as before. "My good lady," said the doctor, "something works against my medicine, and is too strong for it; but I know by the force of my art what it is; you have stolen goods about you, I am sure, and if you do not give them back, I can do nothing for you." But the princess denied very stoutly that she had anything of the kind. "Very well," said the doctor, "you may do as you please, but I am sure I am right, and you will die if you do not own it." Then he went to the king, and told him how the matter stood.

"Daughter," said he, "send back the cloak, the ring, and the horn, that you stole from the right owners."

Then she ordered her maid to fetch all three, and gave them to the doctor, and begged him to give them back to the soldiers; and the moment he had them safe he gave her a whole pear to eat, and the nose came right. And as for the doctor, he put on the cloak, wished the king and all his court a good day, and was soon with his two brothers, who lived from that time happily at home in their palace, except when they took airings in their coach with the three dapple gray horses.

The Five Servants

SOME time ago there reigned in a country many thousands of miles off an old queen who was very spiteful and delighted in nothing so much as mischief. She had one daughter, who was thought to be the most beautiful princess in the world; but her mother only made use of her as a trap for the unwary; and whenever any suitor who had heard of her beauty came to seek her in marriage, the only answer the old lady gave to each was, that he must undertake some very hard task and forfeit his life if he failed. Many, led by the report of the princess's charms, undertook these tasks, but failed in doing what the queen set them to do. No mercy was ever shown them; but the word was given at once, and off their heads were cut.

Now it happened that a prince who lived in a country far off, heard of the great beauty of this young lady, and said to his father, "Dear father, let me go and try my luck." "No," said the king; "if you go you will surely lose your life." The prince, however, had set his heart so much upon the scheme, that when he found his father was against it he fell very ill, and took to his bed for seven years, and no art could cure him, or recover his lost spirits: so when his father saw that if he went on thus he would die, he said to him with a heart full of grief, "If it must he so, go and try your luck." At this he rose from his bed, recovered his health and spirits, and went forward on his way light of heart and full of joy.

Then on he journeyed over hill and dale, through fair weather and foul, till one day, as he was riding through a wood, be thought he saw afar off some large animal upon the ground, and as he drew near he found that it was a man lying along upon the grass under the trees; but he looked more like a mountain than a man, he was so fat and jolly. When this big fellow saw the traveller, he arose, and said, "If you want any one to wait upon you, you will do well to take me into your service." "What should I do with such a fat fellow as you?" said the prince. "It would be nothing to you if I were three thousand times as fat," said the man, "so that I do but behave myself well." "That's true," answered the prince, "so come with me, I can put you to some use or another I dare say." Then the fat man rose up and followed the prince, and by and by they saw another man lying on the ground with his ear close to the turf. The prince said "What are you doing there?" "I am listening," answered the man. "To what?" "To all that is going on in the world, for I can hear everything, I can even hear the grass grow." "Tell me," said the prince, "what you hear is going on at the court of the old queen, who has the beautiful daughter." "I hear," said the listener, "the noise of the sword that is cutting off the head of one of her suitors." "Well!" said the prince, "I see I shall be able to make you of use; – come along with me!" They had not gone far before they saw a pair of feet, and then part of the legs of a man stretched out; but they were so long that they could not see the rest of the body, till they had passed on a good deal further, and at last they came to the body, and, after going on a while further, to the head; "Bless me!" said the prince, "what a long rope you are!" "Oh!" answered the tall man, "this is nothing; when I choose to stretch myself to my full length, I am three times as high as any mountain you have seen on your travels, I warrant you; I will willingly do what I can to serve you if you will let me." "Come along then," said the prince, "I can turn you to account in some way."

The prince and his train went on further into the wood, and next saw a man lying by the roadside basking in the heat of the sun, yet shaking and shivering all over, so that not a limb lay still. "What makes you shiver," said the king, "while the sun is shining so warm?" "Alas!" answered the man, "the warmer it is, the colder I am; the sun only seems to me like a sharp frost that thrills through all my bones; and on the other hand, when others are what you call cold I begin to be warm, so that I can neither bear the ice for its heat nor the fire for its cold." "You are a queer fellow," said the prince; "but if you have nothing else to do, come along with me." The next thing they saw was a man standing, stretching his neck and looking around him from hill to hill. "What are you looking for so eagerly?" said the prince. "I have such sharp eyes," said the man, "that I can see over woods and fields and hills and dales; – in short, all over the world." "Well," said the prince, "come with me if you will, for I want one more to make up my train."

Then they all journeyed on, and met with no one else till they came to the city where the beautiful princess lived. The prince went straight to the old queen, and said, "Here I am, ready to do any task you set me, if you will give me your daughter as a reward when I have done." "I will set you three tasks," said the queen; "and if you get through all, you shall be the husband of my daughter. First, you must bring me a ring which I dropped in the red sea." The prince went home to his friends and said, "The first task is not an easy one; it is to fetch a ring out of the red sea, so lay your heads together and say what is to be done." Then the sharp-sighted one said, "I will see where it lies," and looked down into the sea, and cried out, "There it lies upon a rock at the bottom." "I would fetch it out," said the tall man, "if I could but see it." "Well!" cried out the fat one, "I will help you to do that," and laid himself down and held his mouth to the water, and drank up the waves till the bottom of the sea was as dry as a meadow. Then the tall man stooped a little and pulled out the ring with his hand, and the prince took it to the old queen, who looked at it, and wondering said, "It is indeed the right ring; you have gone through this task well: but now comes the second; look yonder at the meadow before my palace; see! there are a hundred fat oxen feeding there; you must eat them all up before noon: and underneath in my cellar there are a hundred casks of wine, which you must drink all up." "May I not invite some guests to share the feast with me?" said the prince. "Why, yes!" said the old woman with a spiteful laugh; "you may ask one of your friends to breakfast with you, but no more."

Then the prince went home and said to the fat man, "You must be my guest to-day, and for once you shall eat your fill." So the fat man set to work and ate the hundred oxen without leaving a bit, and asked if that was to be all he should have for his breakfast? and he drank the wine out of the casks without leaving a drop, licking even his fingers when he had done. When the meal was ended, the prince went to the old woman and told her the second task was done. "Your work is not all over, however," muttered the old hag to herself; "I will catch you yet, you shall not keep your head upon your shoulders if I can help it." "This evening," said she, "I will bring my daughter into your house and leave her with you; you shall sit together there, but take care that you do not fall asleep; for I shall come when the clock strikes twelve, and if she is not then with you, you are undone." "O!" thought the prince, "it is an easy task to keep such a watch as that; I will take care to keep my eyes open." So he called his servants and told them all that the old woman had said. "Who knows though," said he, "but there may be some trick at the bottom of this? it is as well to be upon our guard and keep watch that the young lady does not get away." When it was night the old woman brought her daughter to the prince's house; then the tall man twisted himself round about it, the listener put his ear to the ground, the fat man placed himself before the door so that no living soul could enter, and the sharp-eyed one looked out afar and watched. Within sat the princess without saying a word, but the moon shone bright through the window upon her face, and the prince gazed upon her wonderful beauty. And while he looked upon her with a heart full of joy and love, his eyelids did not droop; but at eleven o'clock the old woman cast a charm over them so that they all fell asleep, and the princess vanished in a moment.

And thus they slept till a quarter to twelve, when the charm had no longer any power over them, and they all awoke. "Alas! alas! woe is me," cried the prince; "now I am lost for ever." And his faithful servants began to weep over their unhappy lot; but the listener said, "Be still and I will listen;" so he listened a while, and cried out, "I hear her bewailing her fate;" and the sharp-sighted man looked, and said, "I see her sitting on a rock three hundred miles hence; now help us, my tall friend; if you stand up, you will reach her in two steps." "Very well," answered the tall man; and in an instant, before one could turn one's head round, he was at the foot of the enchanted rock. Then the tall man took the young lady in his arms and carried her back to the prince a moment before it struck twelve; and they all sat down again and made merry. And when the clock struck twelve the old queen came sneaking by with a spiteful look, as if she was going to say "Now he is mine," nor could she think otherwise, for she knew that her daughter was but the moment before on the rock three hundred miles off; but when she came and saw her daughter in the prince's room, she started, and said "There is somebody here who can do more than I can." However, she now saw that she could no longer avoid giving the prince her daughter for a wife, but said to her in a whisper, "It is a shame that you should be won by servants, and not have a husband of your own choice."

Now the young lady was of a very proud haughty temper, and her anger was raised to such a pitch, that the next morning she ordered three hundred loads of wood to be brought and piled up; and told the prince it was true he had by the help of his servants done the three tasks, but that before she would marry him someone must sit upon that pile of wood when it was set on fire and bear the heat. She thought to herself that though his servants had done everything else for him, none of them would go so far as to burn themselves for him, and that then she should put his love to the test by seeing whether he would sit upon it himself. But she was mistaken; for when the servants heard this, they said, "We have all done something but the frosty man; now his turn is come;" and they took him and put him on the wood and set it on fire. Then the fire rose and burned for three long days, till all the wood was gone; and when it was out, the frosty man stood in the midst of the ashes trembling like an aspen-leaf, and said, "I never shivered so much in my life; if it had lasted much longer, I should have lost the use of my limbs."

When the princess had no longer any plea for delay, she saw that she was bound to marry the prince; but when they were going to church, the old woman said, "I will never consent;" and sent secret orders out to her horsemen to kill and slay all before them and bring back her daughter before she could be married. However, the listener had pricked up his ears and heard all that the old woman said, and told it to the prince. So they made haste and got to the church first, and were married; and then the five servants took their leave and went away saying, "We will go and try our luck in the world on our own account."

The prince set out with his wife, and at the end of the first day's journey came to a village, where a swineherd was feeding his swine; and as they came near he said to his wife, "Do you know who I am? I am not a prince, but a poor swineherd; he whom you see yonder with the swine is my father, and our business will be to help him to tend them." Then he went into the swineherd's hut with her, and ordered her royal clothes to be taken away in the night; so that when she awoke in the morning, she had nothing to put on, till the woman who lived there made a great favour of giving her an old gown and a pair of worsted stockings. "If it were not for your husband's sake," said she, "I would not have given you anything." Then the poor princess gave herself up for lost, and believed that her husband must indeed be a swineherd; but she thought she would make the best of it, and began to help him to feed them, and said, "It is a just reward for my pride." When this had lasted eight days she could bear it no longer, for her feet were all over wounds, and as she sat down and wept by the wayside, some people came up to her and pitied her, and asked if she knew what her husband really was. "Yes," said she; "a swineherd; he is just gone out to market with some of his stock." But they said, "Come along and we will take you to him;" and they took her over the hill to the palace of the prince's father; and when they came into the hall, there stood her husband so richly drest in his royal clothes that she did not know him till he fell upon her neck and kissed her, and said, "I have borne much for your sake, and you too have also borne a great deal for me." Then the guests were sent for, and the marriage feast was given, and all made merry and danced and sung, and the best wish that I can wish is, that you and I had been there too.

Cat-Skin

THERE was once a king, whose queen had hair of the purest gold, and was so beautiful that her match was not to be met with on the whole face of the earth. But this beautiful queen fell ill, and when she felt that her end drew near, she called the king to her and said, "Vow to me that you will never marry again, unless you meet with a wife who is as beautiful as I am, and who has golden hair like mine." Then when the king in his grief had vowed all she asked, she shut her eyes and died. But the king was not to be comforted, and for a long time never thought of taking another wife. At last, however, his counsellors said, "This will not do; the king must marry again, that we may have a queen." So messengers were sent far and wide, to seek for a bride who was as beautiful as the late queen. But there was no princess in the world so beautiful; and if there had been, still there was not one to be found who had such golden hair. So the messengers came home and had done all their work for nothing.

Now the king had a daughter who was just as beautiful as her mother, and had the same golden hair. And when she was grown up, the king looked at her and saw that she was just like his late queen: then he said to his courtiers, "May I not marry my daughter? she is the very image of my dead wife; unless I have her, I shall not find any bride upon the whole earth, and you say there must be a queen." When the courtiers heard this, they were shocked, and said, "Heaven forbid that a father should marry his daughter! out of so great a sin no good can come." And his daughter was also shocked, but hoped the king would soon give up such thoughts; so she said to him, "Before I marry any one I must have three dresses; one must be of gold like the sun, another must be of shining silver like the moon, and a third must be dazzling as the stars: besides this, I want a mantle of a thousand different kinds of fur put together, to which every beast in the kingdom must give a part of his skin." And thus she thought he would think of the matter no more. But the king made the most skilful workmen in his kingdom weave the three dresses, one as golden as the sun, another as silvery as the moon, and a third shining like the stars; and his hunters were told to hunt out all the beasts in his kingdom and take the finest fur out of their skins; and so a mantle of a thousand furs was made.

When all was ready, the king sent them to her; but she got up in the night when all were asleep, and took three of her trinkets, a golden ring, a golden necklace, and a golden broach; and packed the three dresses of the sun, moon, and stars, up in a nutshell, and wrapped herself up in the mantle of all sorts of fur and besmeared her face and hands with soot. Then she threw herself upon heaven for help in her need, and went away and journeyed on the whole night, till at last she came to a large wood. As she was very tired, she sat herself down in the hollow of a tree and soon fell asleep: and there she slept on till it was mid-day: and it happened, that as the king to whom the wood belonged was hunting in it, his dogs came to the tree, and began to snuff about and run round and round, and then to bark. "Look sharp," said the king to the huntsmen, "and see what sort of game lies there." And the huntsmen went up to the tree, and when they came back again said, "In the hollow tree there lies a most wonderful beast, such as we never saw before; its skin seems of a thousand kinds of fur, but there it lies, fast asleep." "See," said the king, "if you can catch it alive, and we will take it with us." So the huntsmen took it up, and the maiden awoke and was greatly frightened, and said, "I am a poor child that has neither father nor mother left; have pity on me and take me with you." Then they said, "Yes, Miss Cat-skin, you will do for the kitchen; you can sweep up the ashes and do things of that sort." So they put her in the coach and took her home to the king's palace. Then they showed her a little corner under the staircase where no light of day ever peeped in, and said, "Cat-skin, you may lie and sleep there." And she was sent into the kitchen, and made to fetch wood and water, to blow the fire, pluck the poultry, pick the herbs, sift the ashes, and do all the dirty work.

Thus Cat-skin lived for a long time very sorrowfully. "Ah! pretty princess!" thought she, "what will now become of thee?"

But it happened one day that a feast was to be held in the king's castle; so she said to the cook, "May I go up a little while and see what is going on? I will take care and stand behind the door." And the cook said, "Yes, you may go, but be back again in half an hour's time to rake out the ashes." Then she took her little lamp, and went into her cabin, and took off the fur skin, and washed the soot from off her face and hands, so that her beauty shone forth like the sun from behind the clouds. She next opened her nutshell, and brought out of it the dress that shone like the sun, and so went to the feast. Every one made way for her, for nobody knew her, and they thought she could be no less than a king's daughter. But the king came up to her and held out his hand and danced with her, and he thought in his heart, "I never saw any one half so beautiful."

When the dance was at an end, she curtsied and when the king looked round for her, she was gone, no one knew whither. The guards who stood at the castle gate were called in; but they had seen no one. The truth was that she had run into her little cabin, pulled off her dress, blacked her face and hands, put on the fur-skin cloak, and was Cat-skin again. When she went into the kitchen to her work, and began to rake the ashes, the cook said, "Let that alone till the morning, and heat the king's soup; I should like to run up now and give a peep; but take care you don't let a hair fall into it, or you will run a chance of never eating again."

As soon as the cook went away, Cat-skin heated the king's soup and toasted up a slice of bread as nicely as ever she could; and when it was ready, she went and looked in the cabin for her little golden ring, and put it into the dish in which the soup was. When the dance was over, the the king ordered his soup to be brought in, and it pleased him so well, that he thought he had never tasted any so good before. At the bottom he saw a gold ring lying, and as he could not make out how it had got there, he ordered the cook to be sent for. The cook was frightened when he heard the order, and said to Cat-skin, "You must have let a hair fall into the soup; if it be so, you will have a good beating." Then he went before the king, and he asked him who had cooked the soup. "I did," answered he. But the king said, "That is not true; it was better done than you could do it." Then he answered, "To tell the truth, I did not cook it, but Cat-skin did." "Then let Cat-skin come up," said the king: and when she came, he said to her,

"Who are you?" "I am a poor child," said she, "who has lost both father and mother." "How came you in my palace?" asked he. "I am good for nothing," said she, "but to be scullion girl, and to have boots and shoes thrown at my head." "But how did you get the ring that was in the soup?" asked the king. But she would not own that she knew anything about the ring; so the king sent her away again about her business.

After a time there was another feast, and Cat-skin asked the cook to let her go up and see it as before. "Yes," said he, "but come back again in half an hour, and cook the king the soup that he likes so much." Then she ran to her little cabin, washed herself quickly, and took the dress out which was silvery as the moon, and put it on; and when she went in looking like a king's daughter, the king went up to her and rejoiced at seeing her again, and when the dance began, he danced with her. After the dance was at an end, she managed to slip out so slily that the king did not see where she was gone; but she sprang into her little cabin and made herself into Cat-skin again, and went into the kitchen to cook the soup. Whilst the cook was above, she got the golden necklace, and dropped it into the soup; then it was brought to the king, who ate it, and it pleased him as well as before; so he sent for the cook, who was again forced to tell him that Cat-skin had cooked it. Cat-skin was brought again before the king; but she still told him that she was only fit to have the boots and shoes thrown at her head.

But when the king had ordered a feast to be got ready for the third time, it happened just the same as before. "You must be a witch, Cat-skin," said the cook; "for you always put something into the soup, so that it pleases the king better than mine." However, he let her go up as before. Then she put on the dress which sparkled like the stars, and went into the ball-room in it; and the king danced with her again, and thought she had never looked so beautiful as she did then: whilst he was dancing with her, he put a gold ring on her finger without her seeing it, and ordered that the dance should be kept up a long time. When it was at an end, he would have held her fast by the hand; but she slipt away and sprang so quickly through the crowd that he lost sight of her; and she ran as fast as she could into her little cabin under the stairs. But this time she kept away too long, and stayed beyond the half-hour; so she had not time to take off her fine dress, but threw her fur mantle over it, and in her haste did not soot herself all over, but left one finger white.

Then she ran into the kitchen, and cooked the king's soup; and as soon as the cook was gone, she put the golden broach into the dish. When the king got to the bottom, he ordered Cat-skin to be called once more, and soon saw the white finger and the ring that he had put on it whilst they went dancing; so he seized her hand, and kept fast hold of it, and when she wanted to loose herself and spring away, the fur cloak fell off a little on one side, and the starry dress sparkled underneath it. Then he got hold of the fur and tore it off, and her golden hair and beautiful form were seen, and she could no longer hide herself: so she washed the soot and ashes from off her face, and showed herself to be the most beautiful princess upon the face of the earth. But the king said, "You are my beloved bride, and we will never more be parted from each other." And the wedding feast was held, and a merry day it was.

The Robber-Bridegroom

THERE was once a miller who had a pretty daughter; and when she was grown up, he thought to himself, "If a seemly man should come to ask her for his wife, I will give her to him that she may be taken care of." Now it so happened, that one did come, who seemed to be very rich, and behaved very well; and as the miller saw no reason to find fault with him, he said he should have his daughter. Yet the maiden did not love him quite so well as a bride ought to love her bridegroom, but, on the other hand, soon began to feel a kind of inward shuddering whenever she saw or thought of him.

One day he said to her, "Why do you not come and see my home, since you are to be my bride?" "I do not know where your house is," said the girl. "'Tis out there," said her bridegroom, "yonder in the dark greenwood." Then she began to try and avoid going, and said, "But I cannot find the way thither." "Well, but you must come and see me next Sunday," said the bridegroom; "I have asked some guests to meet you, and that you may find your way through the wood, I will strew ashes for you along the path."

When Sunday came and the maiden was to go out, she felt very much troubled, and took care to put on two pockets, and filled them with peas and beans. She soon came to the wood, and found her path strewed with ashes; so she followed the track, and at every step threw a pea on the right and a bean on the left side of the road; and thus she journeyed on the whole day till she came to a house which stood in the middle of the dark wood. She saw no one within, and all was quite still, till on a sudden, she heard a voice cry,

> "Turn again, bonny bride!
>   Turn again home!
> Haste from the robber's den,
>   Haste away home!"

She looked around, and saw a little bird sitting in a cage that hung over the door; and he flapped his wings, and again she heard him cry,

> "Turn again, bonny bride!
>   Turn again home!
> Haste from the robber's den,
>   Haste away home!"

However, the bride went in, and roamed along from one room to another, and so over all the house; but it was quite empty, and not a soul could she see. At last she came to a room where a very very old woman was sitting. "Pray, can you tell me, my good woman," said she, "if my bridegroom lives here?" "Ah! my dear child!" said the old woman, "you are come to fall into the trap laid for you: your wedding can only be with Death, for the robber will surely take away your life! if I do not save you, you are lost!" so she hid the bride behind a large cask, and then said to her, "Do not stir or move yourself at all lest some harm should befall you; and when the robbers are asleep we will run off, I have long wished to get away."

She had hardly done this when the robbers came in, and brought another young maiden with them that had been en- snared like the bride. Then they began to feast and drink, and were deaf to her shrieks and groans: and they gave her some wine to drink, three glasses, one of white, one of red, and one of yellow; upon which she fainted and fell down dead. Now the bride began to grow very uneasy behind the cask, and thought that she too must die in her turn. Then the one that was to be her bridegroom, saw that there was a gold ring on the little finger of the maiden they had murdered; and as he tried to snatch it off, it flew up in the air and fell down again behind the cask just in the bride's lap. So he took a light, and searched about all round the room for it, but could not find anything; and another of the robbers said, "Have you looked behind the large cask yet?" "Pshaw!" said the old woman, "Come, sit still and eat your supper now, and leave the ring alone till to-morrow; it won't run away, I'll warrant."

So the robbers gave up the search, and went on with their eating and drinking; but the old woman dropped a sleeping-draught into their wine, and they laid themselves down and slept, and snored roundly. And when the bride heard this, she stepped out from behind the cask; and as she was forced to walk over the sleepers, who were lying about on the floor, she trembled lest she should awaken some of them. But heaven aided her, so that she soon got through her danger; and the old woman went up stairs with her, and they both ran away from this murderous den. The ashes that had been strewed were now all blown away, but the peas and beans had taken root and were springing up, and showed her the way by the light of the moon. So they walked the whole night, and in the morning reached the mill; when the bride told her father all that had happened to her.

As soon as the day arrived when the wedding was to take place; the bridegroom came; and the miller gave orders that all his friends and relations should be asked to the feast. And as they were all sitting at table, one of them proposed that each of the guests should tell some tale. Then the bridegroom said to the bride, when it came to her turn, "Well, my dear, do you know nothing? come tell us some story." "Yes," answered she, "I can tell you a dream that I dreamt. I once thought I was going through a wood, and went on and to till I came to a house where there was not a soul to be seen, but a bird in a cage, that cried out twice,

"Turn again, bonny bride!
   Turn again home!
Haste from the robber's den,
   Haste away home!"

– I only dreamt that, my love. Then I went through all the rooms, which were quite empty, until I came to a room where there sat a very old woman; and I said to her, 'Does my bride-groom live here?' but she answered, 'Ah! my dear child! you hare fallen into a murderer's snare; your bridegroom will surely kill you;' – I only dreamt that, my love. But she hid me behind a large cask; and hardly had she done this, when the robbers came in dragging a young woman along with them; then they gave her three kinds of wine to drink, white, red, and yellow, till she fell dead upon the ground; – I only dreamt that, my love. After they had done this, one of the robbers saw that there was a gold ring on her little finger, and snatched at it; but it flew up to the ceiling, and then fell behind the great cask just where I was, and into my lap; and here is the ring!" At these words she brought out the ring and showed it to the guests.

When the robber saw all this, and heard what she said, he grew as pale as ashes with fright, and wanted to run off; but the guests held him fast and gave him up to justice, so that he and all his gang met with the due reward of their wickedness.

The Three Sluggards

THE king of a country a long way off had three sons. He liked one as well as another, and did not know which to leave his kingdom to after his death: so when he was dying he called them all to him, and said, "Dear children, the laziest sluggard of the three shall be king after me." "Then," said the eldest, "the kingdom is mine; for I am so lazy that when I lie down to sleep, if anything were to fall into my eyes so that I could not shut them, I should still go on sleeping." The second said, "Father, the kingdom belongs to me; for I am so lazy that when I sit by the fire to warm myself, I would sooner have my toes burnt than take the trouble to draw my legs back." The third said, "Father, the kingdom is mine; for I am so lazy that if I were going to be hanged, with the rope round my neck, and somebody were to put a sharp knife into my hands to cut it, I had rather be hanged than raise my hand to do it." When the father heard this, he said, "You shall be the king; for you are the fittest man."

The Seven Ravens

THERE was once a man who had seven sons, and last of all one daughter. Although the little girl was very pretty, she was so weak and small that they thought she could not live; but they said she should at once be christened.

So the father sent one of his sons in haste to the spring to get some water, but the other six ran with him. Each wanted to be first at drawing the water, and so they were in such a hurry that all let their pitchers fall into the well, and they stood very foolishly looking at one another, and did not know what to do, for none dared go home. In the meantime the father was uneasy, and could not tell what made the young men stay so long. "Surely," said he, "the whole seven must have forgotten themselves over some game of play;" and when he had waited still longer and they yet did not come, he flew into a rage and wished them all turned into ravens. Scarcely had he spoken these words when he heard a croaking over his head, and looked up and saw seven ravens as black as coals flying round and round. Sorry as he was to see his wish so fulfilled, he did not know how what was done could be undone, and comforted himself as well as he could for the loss of his seven sons with his dear little daughter, who soon became stronger and every day more beautiful.

For a long time she did not know that she had ever had any brothers; for her father and mother took care not to speak of them before her: but one day by chance she heard the people about her speak of them. "Yes," said they, "she is beautiful indeed, but still 'tis a pity that her brothers should have been lost for her sake." Then she was much grieved, and went to her father and mother, and asked if she had any brothers, and what had become of them. So they dared no longer hide the truth from her, but said it was the will of heaven, and that her birth was only the innocent cause of it; but the little girl mourned sadly about it every day, and thought herself bound to do all she could to bring her brothers back; and she had neither rest nor ease, till at length one day she stole away, and set out into the wide world to find her brothers, wherever they might be, and free them, whatever it might cost her.

She took nothing with her but a little ring which her father and mother had given her, a loaf of bread in case she should be hungry, a little pitcher of water in case she should be thirsty, and a little stool to rest upon when she should be weary. Thus she went on and on, and journeyed till she came to the world's end; then she came to the sun, but the sun looked much too hot and fiery; so she ran away quickly to the moon, but the moon was cold and chilly, and said, "I smell flesh and blood this way!" so she took herself away in a hurry and came to the stars, and the stars were friendly and kind to her, and each star sat upon his own little stool; but the morning star rose up and gave her a little piece of wood, and said, "If you have not this little piece of wood, you cannot unlock the castle that stands on the glass-mountain, and there your brothers live." The little girl took the piece of wood, rolled it up in a little cloth, and went on again until she came to the glass-mountain, and found the door shut. Then she felt for the little piece of wood; but when she unwrapped the cloth it was not there, and she saw she had lost the gift of the good stars. What was to be done? she wanted to save her brothers, and had no key of the castle of the glass-mountain; so this faithful little sister took a knife out of her pocket and cut off her little finger, that was just the size of the piece of wood she had lost, and put it in the door and opened it.

As she went in, a little dwarf came up to her, and said, "What are you seeking for?" "I seek for my brothers, the seven ravens," answered she. Then the dwarf said, "My masters are not at home; but if you will wait till they come, pray step in." Now the little dwarf was getting their dinner ready, and he brought their food upon seven little plates, and their drink in seven little glasses, and set them upon the table, and out of each little plate their sister ate a small piece, and out of each little glass she drank a small drop; but she let the ring that she had brought with her fall into the last glass.

On a sudden she heard a fluttering and croaking in the air,

and the dwarf said, "Here come my masters." When they came in, they wanted to eat and drink, and looked for their little plates and glasses. Then said one after the other, "Who has eaten from my little plate? and who has been drinking out of my little glass?

"Caw! Caw! well I ween
Mortal lips have this way been."

When the seventh came to the bottom of his glass, and found there the ring, he looked at it, and knew that it was his father's and mother's, and said, "O that our little sister would but come! then we should be free." When the little girl heard this (for she stood behind the door all the time and listened), she ran forward, and in an instant all the ravens took their right form again; and all hugged and kissed each other, and went merrily home.

Roland and the May-Bird

THERE was once a poor man who went every day to cut wood in the forest. One day as he went along he heard a cry like a little child's; so he followed the sound till at last he looked up a high tree, and on one of the branches sat a very little girl. Its mother had fallen asleep, and a vulture had taken it out of her lap and flown away with it and left it on the tree. Then the wood-cutter climbed up, took the little child down, and said to himself, "I will take this poor child home and bring it up with my own son Roland." So he brought it to his cottage, and both grew up together; and he called the little girl May-bird, because he had found her on a tree in May; and May-bird and Roland were so very fond of each other that they were never happy but when they were together.

But the wood-cutter became very poor, and had nothing in the world he could call his own, and indeed he had scarcely bread enough for his wife and the two children to eat. At last the time came when even that was all gone, and he knew not where to seek for help in his need. Then at night, as he lay on his bed and turned himself here and there, restless and full of care, his wife said to him, "Husband, listen to me, and take the two children out early tomorrow morning; give each of them a piece of bread, and then lead them into the midst of the wood where it is thickest, make a fire for them, and go away and leave them alone to shift for themselves, for we can no longer keep them here." "No, wife," said the husband, "I cannot find it in my heart to leave the children to the wild beasts of the forest, who would soon tear them to pieces." "Well, if you will not do as I say," answered the wife, "we must all starve together:" and she let him have no peace until he came into her plan.

Meantime the poor children too were awake restless, and

weak from hunger, so that they heard all that their mother said to her husband. "Now," thought May-bird to herself, "it is all up with us:" and she began to weep. But Roland crept to her bed-side, and said, "Do not be afraid, May-bird, I will find out some help for us." Then he got up, put on his jacket, and opened the door and went out.

The moon shone bright upon the little court before the cottage, and the white pebbles glittered like daisies on the green meadows. So he stooped down, and put as many as he could into his pocket, and then went back to the house. "Now, May-bird," said he, "rest in peace," and he went to bed and fell fast asleep.

Early in the morning, before the sun had risen, the wood-man's wife came and awoke them. "Get up, children," said she, "we are going into the wood; there is a piece of bread for each of you, but take care of it and keep some for the afternoon." May-bird took the bread and carried it in her apron, because Roland had his pocket full of stones, and they made their way into the wood.

After they had walked on for a time, Roland stood still and looked towards home, and after a while turned again, and so on several times. Then his father said, "Roland, why do you keep turning and lagging about so? move your legs on a little faster." "Ah! father," answered Roland, "I am stopping to look at my white cat that sits on the roof, and wants to say good bye to me." "You little fool!" said his mother, "that is not your cat; 'tis the morning sun shining on the chimney top." Now Roland had not been looking at the cat, but had all the while been staying behind to drop from his pocket one white pebble after another along the road.

When they came into the midst of the wood, the woodman said, "Run about, children, and pick up some wood, and I will make a fire to keep us all warm." So they piled up a little heap of brush-wood, and set it a-fire; and as the flame burnt bright, the mother said, "Now set yourselves by the fire and go to sleep, while we go and cut wood in the forest; be sure you wait till we come again and fetch you." Roland and May-bird sat by the fire-side till the afternoon, and then each of them ate their piece of bread. They fancied the woodman was still in the wood, because they thought they heard the blows of his axe; but it was a bough which he had cunningly hung upon a tree, so that the wind blew it backwards and forwards, and it sounded like the axe as it hit the other boughs. Thus they waited till evening; but the wood-man and his wife kept away, and no one came to fetch them.

When it was quite dark May-bird began to cry; but Roland said, "Wait awhile till the moon rises." And when the moon rose, he took her by the hand, and there lay the pebbles along the ground, glittering like new pieces of money, and marked the way out. Towards morning they came again to the woodman's house, and he was glad in his heart when he saw the children again; for he had grieved at leaving them alone. His wife also seemed to be glad; but in her heart she was angry at it.

Not long after there was again no bread in the house, and May-bird and Roland heard the wife say to her husband, "The children found their way back once, and I took it in good part; but there is only half a loaf of bread left for them in the house; tomorrow you must take them deeper into the wood, that they may not find their way out, or we shall all be starved." It grieved the husband in his heart to do as his wife wished, and he thought it would be better to share their last morsel with the children; but as he had done as she said once, he did not dare to say no. When the children had heard all their plan, Roland got up and wanted to pick up pebbles as before; but when he came to the door he found his mother had locked it. Still he comforted May-bird, and said "Sleep in peace, dear May-bird; God is very kind and will help us." Early in the morning a piece of bread was given to each of them, but still smaller than the one they had before. Upon the road Roland crumbled his in his pocket, and often stood still, and threw a crumb upon the ground. "Why do you lag so behind, Roland?" said the woodman; "go your ways on before." "I am looking at my little dove that is sitting upon the roof and wants to say good bye to me." "You silly boy!" said the wife, "that is not your little dove, it is the morning sun that shines on the chimney top." But Roland went on crumbling his bread, and throwing it on the ground. And thus they went on still further into the wood, where they had never been before in all their life. There they were again told to sit down by a large fire, and sleep; and the woodman and his wife said they would come in the evening and fetch them away. In the afternoon Roland shared May-bird's bread, because he had strewed all his upon the road; but the day passed away, and evening passed away too, and no one came to the poor children. Still Roland comforted May-bird, and said, "Wait till the moon rises; then I shall see the crumbs of bread which I have strewed, and they will show us the way home."

The moon rose; but when Roland looked for the crumbs, they were gone; for thousands of little birds in the wood had found them and picked them up. Roland, however, set out to try and find his way home; but they soon lost themselves in the wilderness, and went on through the night and all the next day, till at last they lay down and fell asleep for weariness: and another day they went on as before, but still did not reach the end of the wood, and were as hungry as could be, for they had nothing to eat.

In the afternoon of the third day they came to a strange little hut, made of bread, with a roof of cake, and windows of sparkling sugar. "Now we will sit down and eat till we have had enough," said Roland, "I will eat off the roof for my share; do you eat the windows, May-bird, they will be nice and sweet for you." Whilst May-bird, however, was picking at the sugar, a sweet pretty voice called from within;

"Tip, tap! who goes there?"

But the children answered;

"The wind, the wind,
That blows through the air;"

and went on eating; and May-bird broke out a round pane of the window for herself, and Roland tore off a large piece of cake from the roof, when the door opened, and a little old fairy came gliding out. At this May-bird and Roland were so frightened, that they let fall what they had in their hands. But the old lady shook her head, and said, "Dear children, where have you been wandering about? come in with me; you shall have something good." So she took them both by the hand, and led them into her little hut, and brought out plenty to eat, – milk and pancakes, with sugar, apples, and nuts; and then two beautiful little beds were got ready, and May-bird and Roland laid themselves down, and thought they were in heaven: but the fairy was a spiteful one, and had made her pretty sweetmeat house to entrap little children. Early in the morning, before they were awake, she went to their little bed, and when she saw the two sleeping and looking so sweetly, she had no pity on them, but was glad they were in her power. Then she took up Roland, and put him in a little coop by himself; and when he awoke, he found himself behind a grating, shut up as little chickens are: but she shook May-bird, and called out, "Get up you lazy little thing, and fetch some water; and go into the kitchen and cook something good to eat: your brother is shut up yonder; I shall first fatten him, and when he is fat, I think I shall eat him."

When the fairy was gone, the little girl watched her time and got up and ran to Roland, and told him what she had heard, and said, "We must run away quickly, for the old woman is a bad fairy, and will kill us." But Roland said, "You must first steal away her fairy wand, that we may save ourselves, if she should follow." Then the little maiden ran back and fetched the magic wand, and away they went together; so when the old fairy came back, she could see no one at home, and sprang in a great rage to the window, and looked out into the wide world (which she could do far and near), and a long way off she spied May-bird running away with her dear Roland; "You are already a great way off," said she; "but you will still fall into my hands." Then she put on her boots, which walked several miles at a step, and scarcely made two steps with them, before she overtook the children: but May-bird saw that the fairy was coming after them, and by the help of the wand turned her dear Roland into a lake, and herself into a swan which swam about in the middle of it. So the fairy set herself down on the shore, and took a great deal of trouble to decoy the swan, and threw crumbs of bread to it; but it would not come near her, and she was forced to go home in the evening, without taking her revenge. And May-bird changed herself and her dear Roland back into their own forms once more, and they went journeying on the whole night until the dawn of day; and then the maiden turned herself into a beautiful rose, which grew in the midst of a quickset hedge, and Roland sat by the side and played upon his flute.

The fairy soon came striding along. "Good piper," said she, "may I pluck the beautiful rose for myself?" "O yes," answered he; "and I will play to you meantime." So when she had crept into the hedge in a great hurry to gather the flower (for she well knew what it was), he began to play upon his flute; and, whether she liked it or not, such was the wonderful power of the music that she was forced to dance a merry jig, on and on without any rest. And as he did not cease playing a moment, the thorns at length tore the clothes from off her body, and pricked her sorely, and there she stuck quite fast.

Then May-bird was free once more; but she was very tired, and Roland said, "Now I will hasten home for help, and by and by we will be married." And May-bird said, "I will stay here in the mean time and wait for you; and, that no one may know me, I will turn myself into a stone and lie in the corner of yonder field." Then Rolaud went away, and May-bird was to wait for him. But Roland met with another maiden, who pleased him so much that he stopped where she lived, and forgot his former friend; and when May-bird had stayed in the field a long time, and found he did not come back, she became quite sorrowful, and turned herself into a little daisy, and thought to herself, "Some one will come and tread me under foot, and so my sorrows will end." But it so happened that as a shepherd was keeping watch in the field he found the flower, and thinking it very pretty, took it home, placed it in a box in his room, and said, "I have never found so pretty a flower before." From that time everything throve wonderfully at the shepherd's house: when he got up in the morning, all the household work was ready done; the room was swept and cleaned; the fire made, and the water fetched; and in the afternoon, when he came home, the table-cloth was laid and a good dinner ready set for him. He could not make out how all this happened; for he saw no one in his house: and although it pleased him well enough, he was at length troubled to think how it could be, and went to a cunning woman who lived hard by, and asked her what he should do. She said, "There must be witchcraft in it; look out tomorrow morning early, and see if anything stirs about in the room; if it does, throw a white cloth at once over it, and then the witchcraft will be stopped." The shepherd did as she said, and the next morning saw the box open and the daisy come out: then he sprang up quickly and threw a white cloth over it: in an instant the spell was broken, and May-bird stood before him; for it was she who had taken care of his house for him; and as she was so beautiful he asked her if she would marry him. She said, "No," because she wished to be faithful to her dear Roland; but she agreed to stay and keep house for him.

Time passed on, and Roland was to be married to the maiden that he had found; and according to an old custom in that land, all the maidens were to come and sing songs in praise of the bride and bridegroom. But May-bird was so grieved when she heard that her dearest Roland had forgotten her, and was to be married to another, that her heart seemed as if it would burst within her, and she would not go for a long time. At length she was forced to go with the rest; but she kept hiding herself behind the others until she was left to last. Then she could not any longer help coming forward; and the moment she began to sing, Roland sprang up, and cried out, "That is the true bride; I will have no other but her;" for he knew her by the sound of her voice; and all that he had forgotten came back into his mind, and his heart was opened towards her. So faithful May-bird was married to her dear Roland, and there was an end of her sorrows; and from that time forward she lived happily till she died.

The Mouse, the Bird,
and the Sausage

ONCE upon a time a mouse, a bird, and a sausage took it into their heads to keep house together: and to be sure they managed to live for a long time very comfortably and happily; and beside that added a great deal to their store, so as to become very rich. It was the bird's business to fly every day into the forest and bring wood; the mouse had to carry the water, to make the fire, and lay the cloth for dinner; but the sausage was cook to the household.

He who is too well off often begins to be lazy and to long for something fresh. Now it happened one day that our bird met with one of his friends, to whom he boasted greatly of his good plight. But the other bird laughed at him for a poor fool, who worked hard, whilst the two at home had an easy job of it: for when the mouse had made her fire and fetched the water, she went and laid down in her own little room till she was called to lay the cloth; and the sausage sat by the pot, and had nothing to do but to see that the food was well cooked; and when it was meal time, had only to butter, salt, and get it ready to eat, which it could do in a minute. The bird flew home, and having laid his burden on the ground, they all sat down to table, and after they had made their meal slept soundly until the next morning. Could any life be more glorious than this?

The next day the bird, who had been told what to do by his friend, would not go into the forest, saying, he had waited on them, and been made a fool of long enough; they should change about, and take their turns at the work. Although the mouse and the sausage begged hard that things might go on as they were, the bird carried the day. So they cast lots, and the lot fell upon the sausage to fetch wood, while the mouse was to be cook, and the bird was to bring the water.

What happened by thus taking people from their proper work? The sausage set out towards the wood, the little bird made a fire, the mouse set on the pot, and only waited for the sausage to come home and bring wood for the next day. But the sausage kept away so long that they both thought something must have happened to him, and the bird flew out a little way to look out for him; but not far off he found a dog on the road, who said he had met with a poor little sausage, and taking him for fair prey, had laid hold of him and knocked him down. The bird made a charge against the dog of open robbery and murder; but words were of no use, for the dog said he found the sausage out of its proper work, and under false colours; and so he was taken for a spy and lost his life. The little bird took up the wood very sorrowfully, and went home and told what he had seen and heard. The mouse and he were very much grieved, but agreed to do their best and keep together.

The little bird undertook to spread the table, and the mouse got ready the dinner; but when she went to dish it up, she fell into the pot and was drowned. When the bird came into the kitchen and wanted the dinner to put upon the table; no cook was to be seen; so he threw the wood about here, there, and every where, and called and sought on all sides, but still could not find the cook. Meantime the fire fell upon the wood and set it on fire; the bird hastened away to get water, but his bucket fell into the well, and he after it, and so ends the story of this clever family.

The Juniper Tree

A LONG while ago, perhaps as much as two thousand years, there was a rich man who had a wife of whom he was very fond; but they had no children. Now in the garden before the house where they lived, there stood a juniper tree; and one winter's day as the lady was standing under the juniper tree, paring an apple, she cut her finger, and the drops of blood trickled down upon the snow. "Ah!" said she, sighing deeply and looking down upon the blood, "how happy should I be if I had a little child as white as snow and as red as blood!" And as she was saying this, she grew quite cheerful, and was sure her wish would be fulfilled. And after a little time the snow went away, and soon afterwards the fields began to look green. Next the spring came, and the meadows were dressed with flowers; the trees put forth their green leaves; the young branches shed their blossoms upon the ground; and the little birds sung through the groves. And then came summer, and the sweet smelling flowers of the juniper tree began to unfold; and the lady's heart leaped within her, and she fell on her knees for joy. But when autumn drew near, the fruit was thick upon the trees. Then the lady plucked the red berries from the juniper tree, and looked sad and sorrowful; and she called her husband to her, and said, "If I die, bury me under the juniper tree." Not long after this a pretty little child was born; it was, as the lady wished, as red as blood, and as white as snow; and as soon as she had looked upon it, her joy overcame her, and she fainted away and died.

Then her husband buried her under the juniper tree, and wept and mourned over her; but after a little while he grew better, and at length dried up his tears, and married another wife.

Time passed on and he had a daughter born; but the child

of his first wife, that was as red as blood, and as white as snow, was a little boy. The mother loved her daughter very much, but hated the little boy, and bethought herself how she might get all her husband's money for her own child; so she used the poor fellow very harshly, and was always pushing him about from one corner of the house to another, and thumping him one while and pinching him another, so that he was for ever in fear of her, and when he came home from school, could never find a place in the house to play in.

Now it happened that once when the mother was going into her store-room, the little girl came up to her, and said, "Mother, may I have an apple?" "Yes, my dear," said she, and gave her a nice rosy apple out of the chest. Now you must know that this chest had a very thick heavy lid, with a great sharp iron lock upon it. "Mother," said the little girl, "pray give me one for my little brother too." Her mother did not much like this; however, she said, "Yes, my child; when he comes from school, he shall have one too." As she was speaking, she looked out of the window and saw the little boy coming; so she took the apple from her daughter, and threw it back into the chest and shut the lid, telling her that she should have it again when her brother came home. When the little boy came to the door, this wicked woman said to him with a kind voice, "Come in, my dear, and I will give you an apple." "How kind you are, mother!" said the little boy; "I should like to have an apple very much." "Well, come with me then," said she. So she took him into the store-room and lifted up the cover of the chest, and said, "There, take one out yourself," and then, as the little boy stooped down to reach one of the apples out of the chest, bang! she let the lid fall, so hard that his head fell off amongst the apples. When she found what she had done, she was very much frightened, and did not know how she should get the blame off her shoulders. However, she went into her bedroom, and took a white handkerchief out of a drawer, and then fitted the little boy's head upon his neck, and tied the handkerchief round it, so that no one could see what had happened, and seated him on a stool before the door with the apple in his hand.

Soon afterwards Margery came into the kitchen to her mother, who was standing by the fire, and stirring about some hot water in a pot. "Mother," said Margery, "my brother is sitting before the door with an apple in his hand; I asked him to give it me, but he did not say a word, and looked so pale that I was quite frightened." "Nonsense!" said her mother; "go back again, and if he won't answer you, give him a good box on the ear." Margery went back, and said, "Brother, give me that apple." But he answered not a word; so she gave him a box on the ear; and immediately his head fell off. At this, you may be sure she was sadly frightened, and ran screaming out to her mother that she had knocked off her brother's head, and cried as if her heart would break. "O Margery!" said her mother, "what have you been doing? However, what is done cannot be undone; so we had better put him out of the way, and say nothing to any one about it."

When the father came home to dinner, he said," "Where is my little boy?" And his wife said nothing, but put a large dish of black soup upon the table; and Margery wept bitterly all the time, and could not hold up her head. And the father asked after his little boy again. "Oh!" said his wife, "I should think he is gone to his uncle's." "What business could he have to go away without bidding me good-bye?" said his father. "I know he wished very much to go," said the woman; "and begged me to let him stay there some time; he will be well taken care of there." "Ah!" said the father, "I don't like that; he ought not to have gone away without wishing me goodbye." And with that he began to eat; but he seemed still sorrowful about his son, and said, "Margery, what do you cry so for? your brother will come back again, I hope." But Margery by and by slipped out of the room and went to her drawers and took her best silk handkerchief out of them, and tying it round her little brother's bones, carried them out of the house weeping bitterly all the while, and laid them under the jumper tree; and as soon as she had done this, her heart felt lighter, and she left off crying. Then the juniper tree began to move itself backwards and forwards, and to stretch its branches out, one from another, and then bringing them together again, just like a person clapping hands for joy: and after this, a kind of cloud came from the tree, and in the middle of the cloud was a burning fire, and out of the fire came a pretty bird, that flew away into the air, singing merrily. And as soon as the bird was gone, the handkerchief and the little boy were gone too, and the tree looked just as it had done before; but Margery felt quite happy and joyful within herself, just as if she had known that her brother had been alive again, and went into the house and ate her dinner.

But the bird flew away, and perched upon the roof of a goldsmith's house, and sang,

> "My mother slew her little son;
> My father thought me lost and gone:
> But pretty Margery pitied me,
> And laid me under the juniper tree;
> And now I rove so merrily,
> As over the hills and dales I fly:
>   O what a fine bird am I!"

The goldsmith was sitting in his shop finishing a gold chain; and when he heard the bird singing on the house-top, he started up so suddenly that one of his shoes slipped off; however, without stopping to put it on again, he ran out into the street with his apron on, holding his pincers in one hand, and the gold chain in the other. And when he saw the bird sitting on the roof with the sun shining on its bright feathers, he said, "How sweetly you sing, my pretty bird! pray sing that song again." "No," said the bird, "I can't sing twice for nothing; if you will give me that gold chain, I'll try what I can do." "There," said the goldsmith, "take the chain, only pray sing that song again." So the bird flew down, and taking the chain, in its right claw, perched a little nearer to the goldsmith, and sang:

> "My mother slew her little son;
> My father thought me lost and gone:
> But pretty Margery pitied me,
> And laid me under the juniper tree;
> And now I rove so merrily,
> As over the hills and dales I fly:
>   O what a fine bird am I!"

After that the bird flew away to a shoemaker's, and sitting upon the roof of the house, sang the same song as it had done before.

When the shoemaker heard the song, he ran to the door without his coat, and looked up to the top of the house; but he was obliged to hold his hand before his eyes, because the sun shone so brightly. "Bird," said he, "how sweetly you sing!" Then he called into the house, "Wife! wife! come out here, and see what a pretty bird is singing on the top of our house!" And he called out his children and workmen; and they all ran out and stood gazing at the bird, with its beautiful red and green feathers, and the bright golden ring about its neck, and eyes which glittered like the stars. "O bird!" said the shoemaker," pray sing that song again." "No," said the bird, "I cannot sing twice for nothing; you must give me something if I do." "Wife," said the shoemaker, "run up stairs into the workshop, and bring me down the best pair of new red shoes you can find." So his wife ran and fetched them. "Here, my pretty bird," said the shoemaker, "take these shoes; but pray sing that song again." The bird came down, and taking the shoes in his left claw, flew up again to the house-top, and sang:

> "My mother slew her little son;
> My father thought me lost and gone:
> But pretty Margery pitied me,
> And laid me under the jumper tree;
> And now I rove so merrily,
> As over the bills and dales I fly:
>   O what a fine bird am I!"

And when he had done singing, he flew away, holding the shoes in one claw and the chain in the other. And he flew a long, long way off, till at last he came to a mill. The mill was going clipper! clapper! clipper! clapper! and in the mill were twenty millers, who were all hard at work hewing a millstone, and the millers hewed, hick! hack! hick! hack! and the mill went on, clipper! clapper! clipper! clapper!

So the bird perched upon a linden tree close by the mill, and began its song:

> "My mother slew her little son;
> My father thought me lost and gone:"

here two of the millers left off their work and listened:

> "But pretty Margery pitied me,
> And laid me under the juniper tree;"

now all the millers but one looked up and left their work;

> "And now I rove so merrily;
> As over the hills and dales I fly:
>   O what a fine bird am I!"

Just as the song was ended, the last miller heard it, and

started up, and said, "O bird! how sweetly you sing! do let me hear the whole of that song, pray, sing it again!" "No," said the bird, "I cannot sing twice for nothing; give me that millstone, and I'll sing again." "Why," said the man, "the millstone does not belong to me; if it was all mine, you should have it and welcome." "Come," said the other millers, "if he will only sing that song again, he shall have the millstone." Then the bird came down from the tree: and the twenty millers fetched long poles and worked and worked, heave, ho! heave, ho! till at last they raised the millstone on its side; and then the bird put its head through the hole in the middle of it, and flew away to the linden tree, and sang the same song as it had done before.

And when he had done, he spread his wings, and with the chain in one claw, and the shoes in the other, and the millstone about his neck, he flew away to his father's house.

Now it happened that his father and mother and Margery were sitting together at dinner. His father was saying, "How light and cheerful I am!" But his mother said, "Oh I am so heavy and so sad, I feel just as if a great storm was coming on." And Margery said nothing, but sat and cried. Just then the bird came flying along, and perched upon the top of the house; "Bless me!" said the father, "how cheerful I am; I feel as if I was about to see an old friend again." "Alas!" said the mother, "I am so sad, and my teeth chatter so, and yet it seems as if my blood was all on fire in my veins!" and she tore open her gown to cool herself. And Margery sat by herself in a corner, with her plate on her lap before her, and wept so bitterly that she cried her plate quite full of tears.

And the bird flew to the top of the juniper tree and sang:

"My mother slew her little son; –"

Then the mother held her ears with her hands, and shut her eyes close, that she might neither see nor hear; but there was a sound in her ears like a frightful storm, and her eyes burned and glared like lightning.

"My father thought me lost and gone: –"

"O wife!" said the father, "what a beautiful bird that is, and how finely he sings; and his feathers glitter in the sun like so many spangles!"

> "But pretty Margery pitied me,
> And laid me under the juniper tree; –"

At this Margery lifted up her head and sobbed sadly, and her father said, "I must go out, and look at that bird a little nearer." "Oh! don't leave me alone," said his wife; "I feel just as if the house was burning." However, he would go out to look at the bird; and it went on singing:

> "But now I rove so merrily,
> As over the hills and dales I fly:
>   O what a fine bird am I!"

As soon as the bird had done singing, he let fall the gold chain upon his father's neck, and it fitted so nicely that he went back into the house and said, "Look here, what a beautiful chain the bird has given me; only see how grand it is!" But his wife was so frightened that she fell all along on the floor, so that her cap flew off, and she lay as if she were dead. And when the bird began singing again, Margery said, "I must go out and see whether the bird has not something to give me." And just as she was going out of the door, the bird let fall the red shoes before her; and when she had put on the shoes, she all at once became quite light and happy, and jumped into the house and said, "I was so heavy and sad when I went out, and now I am so happy! see what fine shoes the bird has given me!" Then the mother said, "Well, if the world should fall to pieces, I must go out and try whether I shall not be better in the air." And as she was going out, the bird let fall the mill-stone upon her head and crushed her to pieces.

The father and Margery hearing the noise ran out, and saw nothing but smoke and fire and flame rising up from the place; and when this was passed and gone, there stood the little boy beside them; and he took his father and Margery by the hand, and they went into the house, and ate their dinner together very happily.

Notes

We have another popular song to the lady-bird under a different name,

> "Bless you, bless you, Burnie-bee
>   Tell me where your wedding be;
> If it be to-morrow day,
>   Take your wings and fly away."

Hans In Luck.

The "Hans im Gluck" of MM. Grimm; a story of popular currency communicated by Aug. Wernicke to the *Wünschelruthe*, a periodical publication, 1818, no. 33.

The Travelling Musicians.

The "Bremer Stadtmusikanten" of Grimm; current in Pader-born. Rollenhagen, who in the 16th century wrote his poem called *Froschmäuseler* (a collection of popular satirical dramatic scenes, in which animals are the acting characters), has admirably versified the leading incidents of this story. The occupant parties who are ejected by the travellers are, with him, wild beasts, not robbers. The Germans are eminently successful in their beast stories. The origin of them it is not easy to trace: as early as the age of the Minnesingers (in the beginning of the 13th century) a collection of fables, told with great spirit and humour by Boner, was current; but they are more Æsopian, and have not the dramatic and instructive character of the tales before us, which bear the features of the oldest Oriental fables. In later times *Reineke de Voss* seems to be the matured result of this taste, and whether originating in Germany or elsewhere, it had there its chief popularity. To that cycle belong many of the tales collected by MM. Grimm; and accordingly the Fox is constantly present, and displays everywhere the same characteristics. The moral tendency of these delightful fables is almost invariably exemplary; they always give their rewards to virtue and humanity, and afford protection to the weaker but more amiable animals, against their wily or violent aggressors. Man is sometimes introduced, but generally, as in "The Dog and the Sparrow," to his disadvantage, and for the purpose of reproof and correction.

The Golden Bird.

"Der Goldene Vogel;" a Hessian story; told also with slight variations in Paderborn. The substance of this tale, in which the Golden Bird is generally called the Phoenix, is of great antiquity. Perinskiold in the catalogue to Hickes mentions the *Saga af Artus Fagro*, and describes the contents thus: "Hist. de tribus fratribus, Carolo, Vilhialmo, atque Arturo, cogn. Fagra, regis Angliæ filiis, qui ad inquirendum Phœnicem, ut eâ curaretur morbus immedicabilis patris illorum, in ultimas usque Indiæ oras missi sunt." It appears that the same subject forms a Danish popular tale. The youngest and successful son is a character of perpetual recurrence in the German tales. He is generally despised for diminutive stature, or supposed inferiority of intellect, and passes by the contemptuous appellation of the "Dummling," of whom we shall have occasion to say more hereafter.

The Fisherman and his Wife.

"De Fischer un siine Fru," a story in the Pomeranian Low German dialect, admirably adapted to this species of narrative, and particularly pleasing to an English ear, as bearing a remarkable affinity to his own language, or rather that of the Lowland Scotch. Take the second sentence as a specimen: "Daar satt he eens an de see, bi de angel, un sach in dat blanke water, un he sach immer (ever) na de angel," & c. During the fervour of popular feeling on the downfall of the power of the late Emperor of France, this tale became a great favourite. In the original the last object of the wife's desires is to be as "de lewe Gott" (der liebe Gott, le bon Dieu). We have softened the boldness of the lady's ambition.

The Tomtit and the Bear.

"Der Zaunkönig und der Bär;" from Zwehrn. We have Reynard here in his proper character, and the smaller animals triumphing by superior wit over the larger, in the same manner as in many of the Northern traditions the dwarfs obtain a constant superiority over their opponents the giants. In *Tuhti Nameh's* eighth fable [Calcutta and London, 1801], an elephant is punished for an attack upon the sparrow's nest, by an alliance which she forms with another bird, a frog, and a bee.

The Twelve Dancing Princesses.

"Die zertanzten Schuhe;" a Munster tale; known also with variations in other parts, and even in Poland, according to the report made by Dobrowsky to MM. Grimm. The story is throughout of a very Oriental cast, except that the soldier has the benefit of the truly Northern Nebel, or Tarn-kappe, which makes the wearer invisible. It should be observed, however, that in the Calmuck *Relations of Ssidi Kur* we have the cap, the wearer of which is "seen neither by the gods nor men, nor Tchadkurrs," and also the swiftly moving boots or shoes.

Rose-Bud.

"Dornröschen;" a Hessian story. We have perhaps in our alteration of the heroine's name lost one of the links of connexion, which MM. Grimm observe between this fable and that of the ancient tradition of the restoration of Brynhilda, by Sigurd, as narrated in the *Edda* of Sæmund, in *Volsunga Saga*. Sigurd pierces the enchanted fortifications, and rouses the heroine. "Who is it," said she, "of might sufficient to rend my armour and to break my sleep?" She afterwards tells the cause of her trance: "Two kings contended; one high Hialmgunnar, and he was old but of mickle might, and Odin had promised him the victory. I felled him in fight; but Odin struck my head with the sleepy-thorn [the Thorn-rose or Dog-rose, see *Altdeutsche Wälder*, I, 135.], and said I should never be again victorious, and should be hereafter wedded." Herbert's *Miscell. Poetry*, vol. ii. p. 23. Though the allusion to the sleep-rose is preserved in our heroine's name, she suffers from the wound of a spindle, as in the *Pentamerone* of G. B. Basile, V. 5. The further progress of Sigurd's, or Siegfried's, adventures will be seen in "The King of the Golden Mountain."

Tom Thumb.

The "Daumesdick" of Grimm, from Mühlheim, on the Rhine. In this tale the hero appears in his humblest domestic capacity; but there are others in which he plays a most important and heroic character, as the outwitter and vanquisher of giants and other powerful enemies, the favourite of fortune, and the winner of the hands of kings' daughters. We should have been glad, if it had been consistent with the immediate design of this publication, to have given two or three other stories from different parts of Germany, illustrative of the worth and ancient descent of the personage who appears with the same general characteristics, under the various names in England of Tom Thumb, Tom-a-lyn, Tamlane, & c.; in Germany of Daumesdick, Däumling, Daumerling, and Dummling (for though the latter word bears a different and independent meaning, we incline to think it originally the same); in Austria of Daumenlang; in Denmark of Svend Tomling, or Swain Tomling; and further north, as the Thaumlin, or dwarfish hero of Scandinavia.

We must refer to the *Quarterly Review*, No. xli., for a speculation as to the connexion of Tom's adventures, particularly that with the cow, with some of the mysteries of Indian mythology. It must suffice here briefly to notice the affinities which some of the present stories bear to the earliest Northern traditions, leaving the reader to determine whether, as Hearne concludes, our hero was King Edgar's page, or, as tradition says, ended his course and found his last home at Lincoln.

In one of the German stories, "Des Schneiders Daumerling Wanderschaft" (the Travels of the Tailor's Thumbling), his first wandering is through the recesses of a glove, to escape his mother's anger. So Thor, in the 23rd fable of the *Edda*, reposes in the giant's glove. In another story, "Der junge Riese" (the young Giant), the hero is in his youth a thumb long; but, being nurtured by a giant, acquires wonderful power, and passes through a variety of adventures, resembling at various times those of Siegfried, or Sigurd (the doughty champion, who, according to the Heldenbuch, "caught the lions in the woods and hung them over the walls by their tails"), of Thor, and of Grettir (the hero who kept geese on the common), and corresponding with the achievements ascribed in England to his namesake, to Jack the Giant-killer, and Tom Hycophric (whose sphere of action Hearne would limit to the contracted boundaries of Tylney in Norfolli), and in the Serbian tale, quoted by MM. Grimm from Schottky, given to "the son of the bear," Medvedovitsh.

He serves the smith, whose history as the Velint (or Weyland) of Northern fable is well known; outwits, like Eulenspiegel (Owl-glass), those who are by nature his betters; wields a weapon as powerful as Thor's hammer; and, like his companion, is somewhat impregnable to tolerably rude attacks. He is equally voracious, too, with Loke, whose "art consisted in eating more than any other man in the world," and with the son of Odin, when "buks'd as a bride so fair," in the *Song of Thrym*,

> "Betimes at evening he approached,
> And the mantling ale the giants broached;
> The spouse of Sifia ate alone
> Eight salmons and an ox full grown,
> And all the cates on which women feed,
> And drank three firkins of sparkling mead."
>   Herbert's *Icelandic Poetry*, i. p. 6.

In one of the tales before us, a mill-stone is treacherously thrown upon him while employed in digging at the bottom of a well. "Drive away the hens," said he, "they scratch the sand about till it flies into my eyes." So in the *Edda*, the Giant Skrymmer only notices the dreadful blows of Thor's hammer as the falling of a leaf, or some other trifling matter. In the English story of *Jack the Giant-Killer*, Jack under similar circumstances says, that a rat had given him three or four slaps with his tail.

In the story of "The King of the Golden Mountain," it will be seen how the giants are outwitted and deprived of the great Northern treasures, the tarn-kap, the shoes, and the sword, which are equally renowned in the records of the *Niebelungen Lied* and *Niflunga Saga*, and in our own *Jack the Giant-killer*. The other Thumb tales are full of such adventures. They are all exceedingly curious, and deserve to be brought together in one view as forming a singular group. At present we can only refer to the pages of MM. Grimm, and particularly to the observations in their notes.

The Grateful Beasts.

"Die treuen Thiere;" from the Schwalm-gegend, in Hesse. It is singular that nearly the same story is to be found in the *Relations of Ssidi Kur,* a collection of tales current among the

Calmuck Tartars. A benevolent Bramin there receives the grateful assistance of a mouse, a bear, and a monkey, whom he has severally rescued from the hands of their tormentors; *Quarterly Review*, No. xli. p. 99. There is a very similar story, "Lo Scarafone, lo Sorece, e lo Grillo," in the *Pentamerone*, iii. 5. Another in the same work, iv. 1. "La Preta de lo Gallo," embraces the incidents of the latter part of our tale. The *Gesta Romanorum* also contains a fable somewhat similar in plot, though widely different in details. The cunning device of the mouse reminds MM. Grimm of Loke, in the form of a fly, stinging the sleeping Freya till she throws off her necklace.

Jorinda and Jorindel.

"Jorinde und Joringel". This is taken from *Heinrich Stillings Leben*, i. 104-108; but a story of precisely the same nature is popular in the Schwalmgegend.

The Wonderful Musician.

"Der wunderliche Spielmann (the wayward musician);" from Lorsch, by Worms. The story seems imperfect, as no reason appears for the spite of the musician towards the animals who follow his Orphean strains.

The Queen Bee.

"Die Bienen-Königin;" from Hesse, where another story of similar plot is current. The resemblance to that of "The Grateful Beasts" will of course be obvious. We have here the favourite incident of the despised and neglected member of the family, who bears the name of "Dummling," setting out on his adventures, and overcoming all disadvantages by talent and virtue. (See note on "The Golden Goose," in which story we have left the hero his name, as perhaps we ought to have done here.) MM. Grimm mention a Jewish tale of Rabbi Chanina, who befriends a raven, a hound, and a fish, and receives similar tokens of gratitude. In the Hungarian stories, collected from popular narration by Georg von Gaal (Vienna, 1822), there is one (No. 8) to the same effect. The incident of picking up the pearls will remind the reader of the task of Psyche, in *Apuleius*, lib. vi., in which she is assisted by the ants.

The Dog and the Sparrow.

"Der Hund und der Sperling;" told with variations in Zwehrn, Hesse, and Göttingen.

Frederick and Catherine.

"Der Frieder und das Catherlieschen;" from Zwehrn and Hesse. Some of the incidents in this story are to be found in that of Bardiello, in the *Pentamerone,* i. 4. We have frequently heard it told in our younger days as a popular story in England.

The Three Children of Fortune.

"Die drei Glückskinder;" from Paderborn. It is not necessary to point out the coincidence of one of the adventures of this story with that of Whittngton, once Lord Mayor of London.

But it is not merely in Germany that the same tale is traced. "We learn from Mr. Morier's entertaining narrative that Whittington's cat realized its price in India." In Italy, the merry priest Arlotto told the story in his *Facezie,* before the Lord Mayor was born or thought of; he describes the adventure as happening to a Geneway merchant, and adds that another upon hearing of the profitable adventure made a voyage to Rat Island with a precious cargo, for which the king repaid him with one of the cats. – *Quarterly Review,* xli. p. 100.

King Grisly-beard.

"König Drosselbart;" from Hesse, the Main, and Paderborn. The story of "La Soperbia castecata," *Pentamerone,* iv. 10, has a similar turn. There are of course many other tales in different countries, having for their burthen "The Taming of the Shrew." It hardly need be observed that our title is not meant as a translation of the German name.

Chanticleer and Partlet.

This comprises three stories, "Das Lumpengesindel," "Herr Korbes," and "Von dem Tod des Hühnchens," from Paderborn, the Main, and Hess, placed together as naturally forming one continuous piece of biography. We shall perhaps be told that the whole is tolerably childish; but we wished to give a specimen of each variety of these tales, and at the same time an instance of the mode in which inanimate objects are pressed into the service. The death of Hühnchen forms a balladized story published in

Wunderhorn, vol. iii., among the Kinderlieder. Who "Herr Korbes" is, or what his name imports, we know not; and we should therefore observe that we have of our own authority alone turned him into an enemy, and named him "the fox," in order to give some sort of reason for the outrage committed on his hospitality by uninvited guests.

Snow-drop.

"Schneewitchen;" told with several minor variations in Hesse; also at Vienna with more important alterations. In one version, Spiegel (the glass) is the name of a dog, who performs the part of the queen's monitor. The wish of the queen, which opens this story, has been illustrated in the *Altdeutsche Wälder*, vol. i. p. 1, in a dissertation on a curious passage in Wolfram von Eschenbach's romance of *Parcifal*, where the hero bursts forth into a pathetic allusion to his lady's charms on seeing drops of blood fallen on snow,

> "Trois gotes de fres sanc
> Qui enluminoient le blanc,"

as Chrétien de Troyes expresses it in the French romance on the same subject:

> " – panse tant, qu'il s'oblie;
> Ausins estoit en son avis
> Li vermauz sor le blanc asis,
> Come les gotes de sanc furent,
> Qui desor le blanc aparurent;
> Au l'esgarder, que il faisoit,
> Li est avis, tant li pleisoit,
> Qu'il veist la color novelle
> De la face s'amie belle."

Several parallel wishes are selected from the ancient traditionary stories of different countries, from the Irish legend of Deirda and Navis, the son of Visneach, in Keating's *History of Ireland*, to the Neapolitan stories in *Pentamerone*, iv. 9, and v. 8.

"O cielo!" says the hero in the latter, "e non porria havere un mogliere acossi janco, e rossa, comme e chella preta, e che havesse li capello e le ciglia acossi negro, comme fo le penne di chisto cuervo," & c. The unfading corpse placed in the glass coffin is to be found also in the *Pentamerone*, ii. 8 (la Schiavottella): and in *Haralds Saga,* Snäfridr his beauteous wife dies, but her countenance changes not, its bloom continuing; and the king sits by the body watching it three years.

The dwarfs who appear in this story are of genuine Northern descent. They are Metallarii, live in mountains, and are of the benevolent class; for it must be particularly observed that this, and the mischievous race, are clearly distinguishable. The *Heldenbuch* says, "God produced the dwarfs because the mountains lay waste and useless, and valuable stores of silver and gold with gems and pearls were concealed in them. Therefore he made them right wise, and crafty, that they could distinguish good and bad, and to what use all things should be applied. They knew the use of gems; that some of them gave strength to the wearer, others made him invisible, which were called fog-caps; therefore God gave art and wisdom to them, that they built them hollow hills," & c. (*Illustrations of Northern Antiquities,* p. 41.) The most beautiful example of the ancient Teutonic romance is that which contains the adventures, and the description of the abode in the mountains, of Laurin the King of the Dwarfs. Those who wish to obtain full and accurate information on the various species, habits and manners of these sons of the mountains, may consult Olaus Magnus, or, at far greater length, the *Anthropodemus Plutonicus* of Prætorius.

We ought to observe that this story has been somewhat shortened by us, the style of telling it in the original being rather diffuse; and we have not entered into the particulars of the queen's death, which in the German is occasioned by the truly Northern punishment of being obliged to dance in red-hot slippers or shoes.

The Elves and the Shoemaker.

"Die Wichtelmänner – von einem Schuster dem sie die Arbeit gemacht," a Hessian tale. We have no nomenclature sufficiently accurate for the classification of the goblin tribes of the North. The personages now before us are of the benevolent and working class; they partake of the general character given of such personages by Olaus Magnus, and of the particular qualities of the Housemen (Hausmänner), for whose history we must refer to *Prætorius,* cap. viii. These sprites were of a very domestic turn, attaching themselves to particular households, very pleasant inmates when favourably disposed, very troublesome when of a mischievous temperament, and generally expecting some share of the good things of the family as a reward for services which they were not accustomed to give gratuitously. "The drudging goblin" works, but does so

> "To earn his cream-bowl duly set,
> When in one night, e'er glimpse of morn,
> His shadowy flail had threshed the corn,
> That ten day labourers could not end."
>
> Milton, *L'Allegro*.

The Turnip.

"Die Rübe." The first part of this story is well known. The latter part is the subject of an old Latin poem of the 14th century, entitled "Raparius" (who was probably the versifier), existing in MS. at Strasburg, and also at Vienna. MM. Grimm think they see, through the comic dress of this story, various allusions to ancient Northern traditions, and they particularly refer to the wise man (*Runa capituli*), who imbibes knowledge in his airy suspension.

> Veit ek, at ek hiek vindga meidi a
> Nuatur allar niu.
> Tha nam ek frevaz ok frodr vera.

"I know that I hung on the wind-agitated tree nine full nights; there began I to become – wise."

Old Sultan.

"Der alte Sultan;" from Hesse and Paderborn; in four versions, each varying in some slight particulars.

The Lady and the Lion.

"Das singende, springende Löweneckerchen;" from Hesse. Another version with variations comes from the Schwalmgegend, and from this latter we have taken the opening incident of the summer and winter garden, in preference to the parallel adventure in the story which MM. Grimm have adopted in their text. We have made two or three other alterations in the way of curtailment of portions of the story. The common tale of "Beauty and the Beast" has always some affinity to the legend of Cupid and Psyche. In the present version of the same fable the resemblance is striking throughout. The poor heroine pays the price of her imprudence in being compelled to wander over the world in search of her husband; she goes to heavenly powers for assistance in her misfortunes, and at last, when within reach of the object of her hopes, is near being defeated by the allurements of pleasure. Mrs. Tighe's beautiful poem would seem purposely to describe some of the immediate incidents of our tale, particularly that of the dove.

The incidents in which the misfortune originates are to be found in *Pentamerone*, ii. 9 (Lo Catennaccio), and still further in v. 4: (Lo Turzo d'Oro). The scene in the bridegroom's chamber is in *Pemamerone* v. 3 (Pintosmauto). Prætorius, ii. p. 266, gives a Beauty and the Beast story from Sweden.

The Jew in the Bush.

"Der Jude im Dorn." The dance-inspiring instrument will be recognized, in its most romantic and dignified form, as Oberon's Horn in *Huon de Bordeaux*. The dance in the bush forms the subject of two Old German dramatic pieces of the 16th century. A disorderly monk occupies the place of the Jew; the waggish musician is called Dulla, whom MM. Grimm connect with Tyll or Dyll Eulenspiegel (Owl-glass), and the Swedish and Scandinavian word, Thulr (facetus, nugator), the clown and minstrel of the populace. In *Herrauds ok Bosa Saga*, the table, chairs, & c. join the dance. Merlin in the old romance is entrapped into a bush by a charm given him by his mistress Viviane.

In England we have *A mery Geste of the Frere and the Boye*, first "emprynted at London in Flete-streete, at the sygne of the Sonne, by Wynkyn de Worde," and edited by Ritson in his *Pieces of ancient popular Poetry*. The boy receives

> – "a bowe
> Byrdes for to shete,"

and a pipe of marvellous power:

> "All that may the pype here
> Shall not themselfe stere,
> But laugh and lepe aboute."

The third gift is a most special one for the annoyance of his stepdame. The dancing trick is first played on a "Frere," who loses

> "His cope and his scapelary
> And all his other wede."

And the urchin's ultimate triumph is over the "offycyall" before whom he is brought.

The King of the Golden Mountain.

"Der König vom goldenen Berg;" from Zwehrn and other quarters. There are many remarkable features in this story, more especially its striking resemblance to the story of Sigurd or Siegfried, as it is to be collected from the *Edda*, the *Volsunga Saga*, *Wilkina Saga*, the *Niebelungen Lied*, and the popular tale of *The Horny Siegfried*. It is neatly abridged in Herbert's *Misc. Poetry*, vol. ii. part ii. p. 14. The placing upon the waters; the arrival at the castle of the dragon or snake; the treasures there; the disenchantment of Brynhylda (see our tale of Rose-Bud); the wishing ring; the gift of the ring or girdle; the separation from which jealousy and mischief are to flow; the disguise of the old cloak, which we can easily believe to have been a genuine tarn-cap; the encountering of the discordant guardians of the treasures, as in the *Niebelungen Lied*; the wonderful sword Balmung or Mimung;

> "(Thro' hauberk as thro harpelon
> The smith's son swerd shall hew;[1])"

the boots "once worn by Loke when he escaped from Valhalla;" and the ultimate revenge; are all points more or less coincident with adventures well known to those who have made the old fables of the North the objects of their researches. It should be recollected, however, that both the cap of invisibility and the boots of swiftness are to be found in the *Relations of Ssidi Kur*. The Hungarian tales published by Georg von Gaal, Vienna, 1822, contain one very similar to this in many particulars. Three dwarfs are there the inheritors of the wonderful treasures, which consist of a cloak, mile-shoes, and a purse which is always full.

The Golden Goose.

"Die Goldene Gans;" from Hesse and Paderborn. "The manner in which Loke, in the *Edda*, hangs to the eagle is," MM. Grimm observe, "better understood after the perusal of the story

---

1 "Ettin Langshanks," translated from the *Kämpe Visir* in the *Illustrations of Northern Antiquities*.

of the Golden Goose, to which the lads and lasses who touch it adhere." – *Quarterly Review*, xli. They add that the Golden Goose, buried at the root of an oak, and fated to be the reward of virtue, and to bring blessing on its owner, seems only one of the various types by which, in these tales, happiness, wealth and power, are conferred on the favourites of fortune. The prize is here poetically described, as so attractive that whatever approaches clings to it as to a magnet.

The Dummling is drawn with his usual characteristics; he is sometimes inferior in stature, sometimes in intellect, and at other times in both; his resemblance to the Däumling or Thumbling is obvious; and though his name has now an independent meaning, perhaps we should suspect it to have been originally the same; unless the appearance of the character in the *Pentamerone*, iii. 8, by the unambiguous name of "Lo Gnorante," be against our theory. We leave this singular personage in the hands of MM. Grimm, referring also to the *Altdeutsche Wälder*, where our hero is pointed out as appearing under the appellation of "Dummeklare" in the romance of *Parcifal*.

Mrs. Fox.

"Von der Frau Füchsin." A popular fable in several places, clearly belonging to the class of which Reynard the Fox is the chief.

Hansel and Grettel.

The first part of "Brüderchen und Schwesterchen;" the remainder we omitted as branching into a new series of distinct adventures. The story is very common in Germany, and is also known in Sweden. Prætorius, vol. ii. p. 255, will give the curious the whole art, mystery, and history of transformation of men into animals. This story is one of a most numerous class, in which a stepmother unsuccessfully exerts a malicious influence over her charge.

The Giant With the Three Golden Hairs.

"Der Teufel mit den drei Goldnen Haaren," from Zwehrn, the Main and Hesse. We have taken the appellation "Giant" to avoid offence, and felt less reluctance in the alteration when we found that some other versions of the same story (as the Popanz in *Büschings Volkssagen*) omit the diabolic agency. For similar reasons we have not called, the cave by its proper name of "Holle," the Scandinavian Hell. The old lady called in the German the "Eller-mutter," we suspect has some connexion with the Scandinavian deity "Hela," or "Hella," whom Odin (when he "saddled, straight his coal-black steed."), Hermod Huat, and Brynhylda, after crossing the water as here, severally found in the same position, at the entrance of the infernal regions.

The child is described in our translation as owing its reput-ation to being born under a lucky star. In the original it is born with a Glückshaut (caul). The tradition in Iceland is that a good genius dwells in this envelope, who accompanies and blesses the child, through life. The giant's powers of scent will of course remind the curious reader of the

> "Snouk but, Snouk ben,
> I find the smell of earthly men,"

in *Jack and the Bean-stalk*.
So in Mad Tom's ballad in Shakespeare,

> "Child Rowland to the dark tower came –
> His word was still – Fie, Foe, Fum,
> I smell the blood of a British man," & c.

Is Child Rowland the "liebste Roland" of the German popular story, No. 56 of MM. Grimm's collection? The similarity of the "Child's" adventures with those of Danish ballads in the *Kämpe Viser* has been pointed out by Jamieson in his *Popular Ballads*, and in the *Illustrations of Northern Antiquities*, p. 397.

The Frog-Prince.

"Der Froschkönig, oder der Eiserne Heinrich." This story is from Hesse, but is also told in other parts with variations. It is one of the oldest German tales, as well as of extensive currency elsewhere. Dr. Leyden gives a story of the "Frog-lover" as popular in Scotland. A lady is sent by her step-mother to draw water from the Well of the World's End. She arrives at the well after encountering many dangers, but soon perceives that her adventures have not reached a conclusion; a frog emerges from the well, and before it suffers her to draw water obliges her to betroth herself to him under penalty of being torn to pieces. The lady returns safe; but at midnight the frog-lover appears at the door and demands entrance, according to promise, to the great consternation of the lady and her nurse.

> "Open the door my hinny, my heart,
> Open the door, mine ain wee thing;
> And mind the words that you and I spak
> Down in the meadow by the well-spring."

The frog is admitted, and addresses her,

> "Take me upon your knee, my dearie,
> Take me upon your knee, my dearie,
> And mind the words that you and I spak
> At the cauld well sae weary."

The frog is finally disenchanted, and appears as a prince in his original form. (See *Complaint of Scotland*, Edinburgh, 1801.) "These enchanted frogs," says the Quarterly Reviewer, "have migrated from afar, and we suspect that they were originally crocodiles: we trace them in *The Relations of Ssidi Kur.*" The name "Iron Henry" in the German title alludes to an incident which we have omitted, though it is one of considerable antiquity. The story proceeds to tell how Henry, from grief at his master's misfortune, had bound his heart with iron bands to prevent its bursting; and a doggrel is added in which the prince on his journey, hearing the cracking of the bands which his servant is now rending asunder as useless, inquires if the carriage is breaking, and receives an explanation of the cause of the disturbance.

> "Heinrich, der Wagen bricht!"
> "Nein, Herr, der Wagen nicht:
> Es ist ein Band von meinem Herzen,
> Das da lag in grossen Schmerzen.
> Als ihr in dem Brunnen sast
> Als ihr eine Fretsche (Frosch) wast."

In several of the poets of the age of the Minnesingers the suffering heart is described as confined in bands; "stahelhart," according to Heinrich von Sax. (See Sir Walter Scott's letter, p. 357.)

The Fox and the Horse.
"Der Fuchs und das Pferd," from Munster. See the story of "Old Sultan."

Rumpel-stilts-kin.

"Rumpelstilzchen." A story of considerable currency, told with several variations. We remember to have heard a similar story from Ireland in which the song ran,

> "Little does my Lady wot
> That my name is Trit-a-Trot."

In the "Tour tenebreuse et les jours lumineux, Contes Anglois tirez d'une ancienne chronique composée par Richard surnommé Cœur de Lion, Roy d'Angleterre, Amst 1708," the story of "Ricdin-Ricdon" contains the same incident. The song of the dwarf is as follows:

> "Si jeune et tendre femelle
> N'aimant qu'enfantins ebats,
> Avoit mis dans sa cervelle
> Que Ricdin-Ricdon, je m'appelle
> Point ne viendroit dans mes laqs:
> Mais sera pour moi la belle
> Car un tel nom ne sçait pas."

There is a good deal of learned and mythologic speculation in MM. Grimm, as to the spinning of gold, for which we must refer the reader to their work. The dwarf has here, as usual, his abode in the almost inaccessible part of the mountains. In the original he rends himself asunder in his efforts to extricate the foot which in his rage he had struck into the ground.

The Goose-Girl.

"Die Gänse-magd" of MM. Grimm; a story from Zwehrn. In the *Pentamerone*, iv. 7, there is a story which remarkably agrees with the present in some of its circumstances. The intended bride is thrown overboard while sailing to her betrothed husband, and the false one takes her place. The king is dissatisfied with the latter, and in his passion sends the brother of the lost lady (who had recommended his sister) to keep his geese. The true bride, who has been saved by a beautiful mermaid, or sea-nymph, rises from the water, and feeds the geese with princely food and rose-water. The king watches, observes the fair lady combing her beautiful locks, from which pearls and diamonds fall; and the fraud is discovered. The story of the Goose-Girl is certainly a very remarkable one, and has several traits of very original and highly traditional character. Tacitus mentions the divination of the ancient Germans by horses. Saxo Grammaticus also tells how the heads of horses offered in sacrifices were cut off: and the same practice among the Wendi is mentioned by Prætorius. The horse without a head is mentioned by the Quarterly Reviewer as appearing in a Spanish story, and he vouches for its having also migrated into this country. "A friend," he adds, "has pointed out a passage in *Plato de Legibus*, lib. vi., in which the sage alludes to a similar superstition among the Greeks." Where the horse got his name of Falada MM. Grimm profess not to know, though the coincidence of the first syllable inclines them to assign to it some consanguinity with Roland's steed. The golden and silvery hair is often met with in these tales, and the speaking charm given by the mother (which is in the original a drop of blood, not a lock of hair) is also not uncommon.

In the original, an oath is extorted by force from the true bride, and it is that which prevents her disclosure of the story to the king, who finds out a plan for her evading the oath, by telling the tale into the oven's month, whence of course it reaches him, though in a sufficiently second-hand way to save the fair lady's conscience.

Faithful John.

"Der getreue Johannes;" from Zwehrn. Another somewhat similar story is current in Paderborn. The tale is a singular one, and contains so much of Orientalism that the reader would almost suppose himself in the *Arabian Nights' Entertainments*.

In the *Pentamerone*, iv. 9, is a story very much resembling this: the birds who foretell and forewarn against the disasters are two doves; and the whole happens by the contrivance, and is finally remedied by the power of an enchanter, the lady's father, who had sent the perils that menace the prince, in revenge for the carrying away of his daughter.

It should be added, that in the original, the father really cuts off the heads of his two children, who are restored to life in reward for his faith.

The reader will observe the coincidence of one portion of the story with the Greek fable of the Garment of Dejanira.

The Blue Light.

"Das blaue Licht;" a Mecklenburgh story. In the collection

of Hungarian Tales of Georg von Gaal, it appears that there is one like this, called "The Wonderful Tobacco Pipe."

Ashputtel.

"Aschen-puttel." Several versions of this story are current in Hesse and Zwehrn, and it is one of the most universal currency. We understand that it is popular among the Welsh, as it is also among the Poles; and Schottky found it among the Serbian fables. Rollenhagen in his *Froschmäuseler* (a Satire of the sixteenth century) speaks of the tale of the despised Aschen-pössel; and Luther illustrates from it the subjection of Abel to his brother Cain. MM. Grimm trace out several other proverbial allusions even in the Scandinavian traditions. And lastly, the story is in the Neapolitan *Pentamerone*, under the title of "Cennerentola." An ancient Danish ballad has the incident of the mother hearing from her grave the sorrows of her child ill-used by the step-mother, and ministering thence to its relief. "The Slipper of Cinderella finds a parallel, though somewhat sobered, in the history of the celebrated Rhodope," – so says the Editor of the new edition of Warton, vol. i. (86).

The Young Giant and the Tailor.

This is compounded of two of MM. Grimm's tales, "Der junge Riese" and "Das tapfere Schneiderlein," with some curtailments, particularly in the latter. The whole has an intimate connexion with the oldest Northern traditions, and will be recognized as concurring in many of its incidents with the tales of *Owlglass, Hickathrift,* & c. so well known, and on which a good deal was said in the notes to the earlier portion of the volume. The service to the smith is a remarkable coincidence with Siegfried's adventures; and the mill-stone that falls harmless, reminds us of Thor's adventure with Skrimnir. The giant, moreover, is in true keeping with the Northern personages of that description, for whom the shrewd dwarf is generally more than a match; and the pranks played belong to the same class of performances as those of the hero Grettir when he kept geese upon the common. MM. Grimm quote a Serbian tale given by Schottky, which resembles closely the conflict of the wits between, the giant and the young man.

See further on the subject of the smith, the remarks of the Editor of the new edition of Warton's *History of English Poetry*, in his Preface (p. 89).

The Crows and the Soldier.

"Die Krähen;" a Mecklenburgh story. MM. Grimm mention a similar tale by the Persian poet Nisami, recently noticed by Hammer; and they also notice coincidences in Bohemian and Hungarian tales.

Peewit.

Is a translation of a story called Kibitz, from the *Volks-Sagen, Märchen, und Legenden,* of J.G. Büsching; but the tale in almost all its incidents coincides in substance with "Das Bürle" of MM. Grimm, who give two versions of it. It resembles in some instances the "Scarpafico" of Straparola, i. 3; and also *Pentamerone,* ii. 10; as well as an adventure in the English *History of Friar Bacon and his Man.*

Hans and his Wife.

This comprises the three stories of Grimm, "Die kluge Grethel," "Der gescheidte Hans," and "Die faule Spinnerin," which we have taken the liberty of ascribing to one couple. The first is taken immediately by MM. Grimm (though a story also of popular currency), from what they describe to be a rare book, *Ovum Paschale,* Salzburg, 1700. It is also the subject of a Meister-gesang in a MS. in the possession of Arnim, and of one of Hans Sachs' tales, "Die vernaschte Köchin." The second resembles two different stories given in books printed in Germany in 1557 and 1565. "Bardiello," in the *Pentamerone,* i. 4, resembles the story in several particulars. The third is from Zwehrn, and resembles *Pentamerone,* iv. 4, as well as an old German tale printed in the *Altdeutsche Wälder.*

Cherry, or the Frog-Bride.

This is a translation of "Das Märchen von der Padde," from Büching's *Volks-Sagen;* changing the heroine from Petersilie" (Parsley) into Cherry.

Mother Holle.

The "Frau Holle" of MM. Grimm: from Hesse and West-phalia, and several other places, but with variations. It is a common saying in Hesse, when it snows, "Mother Holle is making her bed." Mother Holle, or Hulda, is a potent personage of some repute, exercising her power for the public good, in rewarding the industrious and well-disposed, and punishing the slovenly and mischievous. MM. Grimm have collected some of her traditions in vol. i. of their *Deutsche Sagen*; and the same will be found in Prætorius. She seems to be of heathen origin.

The Water of Life.

"Das Wasser des Lebens," from Hesse, Paderborn, and (with variations) other places. The story has in many particulars a very Oriental cast. It resembles one of the *Arabian Nights*; but it is also connected with one of the tales of Straparola, iv. 3. Another of MM. Grimm's stories, "De drei Vügelkens," with which it coincides in several respects, has still more of the Oriental character. The "Water of Life" is a very ancient tradition, even in Rabbinical lore. In Conrad of Wurtzburg's *Trojan War* (written in the 13th century), Medea gets the water from Paradise to renew the youth of Jason's father.

Peter the Goatherd.

Is the "Ziegenhirt" of Otmar's Collection of the Ancient Tales and Traditions current in the Hartz. The name of Frederic Barbarossa is associated with the earliest cultivation of the muses in Germany. During the Swabian dynasty (at the head of which he is to be placed), arose and flourished the Minnesingers, or poets of love, cotemporary with the Troubadours, whom they rival in the quantity, and far excel in the quality of their compositions. Frederic was a patron of the minstrel arts; and it is remarkable that the Hartz traditions still make him attached to similar pursuits, and tell how musicians, who have sought the caverns where he sits entranced, have been richly rewarded by his bounty.

The author of *The Sketch Book* has made use of this tale as the plot of his "Rip van Winkle." There are several German traditions and ballads which turn on the unsuspected lapse of time under enchantment; and we may remember in connexion with it, the ancient story of the "Seven Sleepers" of the fifth century (*Gibbon*, vi. 32). That tradition was adopted by Mahomet, and has, as Gibbon observes, been also adopted and adorned by the nations from Bengal to Africa, who profess the Mahometan religion. It was translated into Latin before the end of the sixth century, by the care of Gregory of Tours; and Paulus Diaconus (*de gestis Longobardorum*), in the eighth century, places seven sleepers in the North under a rock by the sea-shore. The incident has considerable capability of interest and effect; and it is not wonderful that it should become popular, and form the basis of various traditions. The next step is to animate the period dropt from real life – the parenthesis of existence – with characteristic adventures, as in the succeeding story of "The Elfin Grove;" and as in "The Dean of Santiago," a Spanish tale from the Conde Lucanor, translated in the *New Monthly Magazine for August 1824*, where several similar stories are referred to.

The Four Clever Brothers.

"Die vier kunstreichen Brüder;" from Paderborn. There is a story exceedingly like this in the *Pentamerone*, v. 7, "Li cinco Figlie," and in Straparola, vii. 5. In another old German story, a smith arrives at such perfection, as to shoe a fly with a golden shoe and twenty-four nails to each foot. In the Persian *Tuhti Nameh*, there is also a story closely resembling the one before us. In a fabliau (to which we cannot refer at the moment), we recollect the thief is so dexterous as to steal off his companion's breeches without his observation.

The Elfin Grove.

This is an abridgement of a story in Tieck's *Phantasus*, founded on an old and well-known tradition, but considerably amplified by him. We have reduced it nearer to its primitive elements; but it is, of course, to a great extent, a fancy piece, and does not pretend to that authenticity of popular currency which is claimed for the other stories. The principal incident resembles that in "Peter the Goatherd;" and more closely, that which has been turned to so much account by Mr. Hogg, in the *Queen's Wake*. The song is written by a friend, and has been adapted to a German popular air.

The Salad.

The "Krautesel" of MM. Grimm. The transformation will of course remind the reader of *Apuleius*. See also Prætorius, ii. 452, "where the lily has the restorative power. But the whole is only another version of the story of Fortunatus, the origin of which is not known, though the common version of it was probably got up in Spain, if we may judge by the names Andalusia, Marsepia, and Ampedo. One version of it is in the *Gesta Romanorum*.

See some observations on the nature of the precious gifts, on which the plot of this and the following story turns, in the preface to the new edition of Warton's *History of English Poetry* (p. 66).

The Nose.

This story comes from Zwehrn, and has been given by MM. Grimm only in an abridged form in their notes; but we wished to preserve the adventures substantially, as connected with the last story, and as illustrating the antiquity and general diffusion of the leading incidents of both. The usual excrescence is a horn or horns; not as here, "nasus, qualem noluerit ferre rogatus Atlas."

The Five Servants.

In MM. Grimm there are six, but we have omitted one for delicacy's sake. The story was heard by them in Paderborn. In several other places they found a story agreeing with it in general character, as do also "Lo Gnarante" (Dummling), in the *Pentamerone*, iii. 8, an Arabian story translated in the Cabinet des Fées, tom. xxxix. p. 421; and another in the *Gesta Romanorum*.

Cat-Skin.

The "Allerlei-rauh" of MM. Grimm; a Hessian and Pader-born tale. It is known as Perrault's "Peau d'Anne," and "Ll'orza," of the *Pentamerone*, ii. 6. – See also Straparola, i. 4.

The Robber-bridegroom.

"Der Raüberbraütigam" of MM. Grimm. This tale has a general affinity to that of *Bluebeard*, most of the incidents of which story are found in others of the German collection. It should, perhaps, be observed, that in the original, the *finger* is chopped off, and is carried away by the bride, as well as the ring upon it.

The Three Sluggards.

The "Drei Faulen," of MM. Grimm, who quote a similar story from the *Gesta Romanorum*.

The Seven Ravens.

"Die sieben Raben," of MM. Grimm. This story, wild and incoherent as it is, will perhaps be considered curious, as peculiarly Northern and original in its character and incidents. The "Glasberg," or Glass Mountain at the World's End, receives from MM. Grimm some interesting illustrations.

Roland and May-bird.

We must apologize to the reader of the original, for the way in which three stories, viz. "Fundevogel," "Der Liebste Roland," and "Hansel and Grethel," have been here combined in one. Several of the incidents will be familiar to the English reader: indeed, they are common to almost every country, and are found as well in the Neapolitan *Pentamerone* as in the Hungarian Collection of Georg von Gaal. We apprehend that the concluding part of the story is not quite correctly preserved; and that, for the credit of the hero, the maiden who seduces him from his old attachment, ought to be, as in "The Lady and the Lion," an enchantress, whose spell is broken by the sound of the true mistress's voice. Those who wish to trace the dance-inspiring instrument of music, through all its forms of tradition, must be referred to "The Editor's preface" to the new edition of Warton (p. 64.)

The Mouse, the Bird, and The Sausage.

This is translated here only as a specimen of the whimsical assortments of *dramatis personæ* which the German story-tellers have sometimes made.

The Juniper Tree.

"Van den Machandel-Boom" of MM. Grimm. We must acquaint the reader that in the original the black broth which the father eats, is formed by the step-mother from the limbs of the murdered child. This incident we thought right to omit, though it must be noted here as one of the curious circumstances of coincidence with other traditions. The bones buried by Margery are those which the father unconsciously picks and throws under the table. The song in the original is as follows; –

> "Min Moder de mi slacht't,
> Min Vader de mi att,
> Min Swester de Marleeniken
> Söcht alle mine Beeniken,
> Un bindt se in een syden Dook,
> Legts unner den Machandel-boom.

Kywitt! Kywitt! ach watt een schön Vagel bin ick!"

A literal translation of which would be,

"My mother me slew;
My father me ate;
My sister Margery
Gather'd all my bones,
And bound them up in a silken shroud,
And laid them under the jumper tree.
Kywit! Kywit! ah, what a fine bird am I!"

On this story we meant to have added some observations of our own; but as the Editor of Warton has renewed us by a sort of anticipation, we will with pleasure content ourselves with a quotation of his remarks (Preface, 87). "The most interesting tale in the whole collection, whether we speak with reference to its contents, or the admirable style of the narrative, the 'Machandel-Boom,' is but a popular view of the same mythos upon which the Platonists have expended so much commentary – the history of the Cretan Bacchus, or Zagreus. This extraordinary tale will be found at p. 301 of the present volume. The points of coincidence may be thus briefly stated. In the Cretan fable, the destruction of Zagreus is attributed to the jealousy of his step-mother Juno; and the Titans (those telluric powers who were created to avenge their mother's connubial wrongs) are the instruments of her cruelty. The infant god is allured to an inner chamber, by a present of toys and fruit (among these an apple), and is forthwith murdered. The dismembered body is now placed in a kettle, for the repast of his destroyers; but the vapour ascending to heaven, the deed is detected, and the perpetrators struck dead by the lightning of Jove. Apollo collects the bones of his deceased brother, and buries them at Delphi, where the palingenesy of Bacchus was celebrated periodically by the Hosii and Thyades. (Compare *Clemens Alex. Protrept.* p. 15. ed. Potter; *Nonnus Dionys.* vi. 174, & c., and *Plutarch, de Isid. et Osirid.* c. 35. et *De Esu Carnium,* i. c. vii.) But this again is only another version of the Egyptian mythos relative to Osiris, which will supply us with the chest, the tree, the sisterly affection, and perhaps the bird (though the last may be explained on other grounds). (*Plut. de Isid,* & c. c. 13. et seqq.) Mr. Grimm wishes to consider the Machandel-Boom the juniper tree, and not the Mandel, or almond-tree. It will be remembered, that the latter was believed by the ancient world to possess very important properties. The fruit of one species, the Amydala, impregnated the daughter of the river Sangarius with the Phrygean Attys (*Paus.* vii. 17); and another, the Persea, was the sacred plant of Isis, so conspicuous on Egyptian monuments. (For this interpretation of the Persea, see S. de Saey's *Abd-allatif, Relation de l'Egypte,* p. 47-72, and the Christian and Mahommedan fictions there cited.) This story of dressing and eating a child is historically related of Atreus, Tantalus, Procne, Harpalice [*Hyginus.* ed. Staveren, 206), and Astyages (*Herod,* i. 119); and is obviously a piece of traditional scandal borrowed from ancient mythology. The Platonistic exposition of it will be found in Mr. Taylor's tract upon the Bacchic Mysteries (*Pamphleteer*, No. 15)."

The Translator cannot close his work, without congratulating those who have a taste for these subjects, on the publication of the volume which has lately appeared under the title of "Fairy Legends and Traditions of the South of Ireland." – It may be referred to throughout, for the curious illustrations which it affords of mutual affinities between the traditionary tales of widely separated nations; and it will, it is trusted, give rise to similar endeavours to preserve, while it can yet be done, the popular stories of other parts of the British Empire. Cornwall, Wales, the North of England, and Scotland might each afford an interesting addition to the common stock.

Introduction[1]

By JOHN RUSKIN, M.A.

Long since, longer ago perhaps than the opening of some fairy tales, I was asked by the publisher who has been rash enough, at my request, to reprint these my favourite old stories in their earliest English form, to set down for him my reasons for preferring them to the more polished legends, moral and satiric, which are now, with rich adornment of every page by very admirable art, presented to the acceptance of the Nursery.

But it seemed to me to matter so little to the majestic independence of the child-public, who, beside themselves, liked, or who disliked, what they pronounced entertaining, that it is only on strict claims of a promise unwarily given that I venture on the impertinence of eulogy; and my reluctance is the greater, because there is in fact nothing very notable in these tales, unless it be their freedom from faults which for some time have been held to be quite the reverse of faults, by the majority of readers.

In the best stories recently written for the young, there is a taint which is not easy to define, but which inevitably follows on the author's addressing himself to children bred in school-rooms and drawing-rooms, instead of fields and woods – children whose favourite amusements are premature imitations of the vanities of elder people, and whose conception of beauty are dependent partly on costliness of dress. The fairies who interfere in the fortunes of these little ones are apt to be resplendent chiefly in milllinery and satin slippers, and appalling more by their airs than their enchantments.

The fine satire which gleaming through every playful word,

---

1 Introduction by John Ruskin to the 1868 Edition of *German Popular Stories*.

renders some of these recent stories as attractive to the old as to the young, seems to me no less to unfit them for their proper function. Children should laugh, but not mock; and when they laugh, it should not be at the weaknesses or faults of others. They should be taught, as far as they are permitted to concern themselves with the characters of those around them, to seek faithfully for good, not to lie in wait maliciously to make themselves merry with evil: they should be too painfully sensitive to wrong, to smile at it; and too modest to constitute themselves its judges.

With these minor errors a far graver one is involved. As the simplicity of the sense of beauty has been lost in recent tales for children, so also the simplicity of their conception of love. That word which, in the heart of a child, should represent the most constant and vital part of its being; which ought to be the sign of the most solemn thoughts that inform its awakening soul and, in one wide mystery of pure sunrise, should flood the zenith of its heaven, and gleam on the dew at its feet; this word, which should be consecrated on its lips, together with the Name which it may not take in vain, and whose meaning should soften and animate every emotion through which the inferior things and the feeble creatures, set beneath it in its narrow world, are revealed to its curiosity or companionship; – this word, in modern child-story, is too often restrained and darkened into the hieroglyph of an evil mystery, troubling the sweet peace of youth with premature gleams of uncomprehended passion, and flitting shadows of unrecognized sin.

These grave faults in the spirit of recent child-fiction are connected with a parallel folly of purpose. Parents who are too indolent and self-indulgent to form their children's characters by wholesome discipline, or in their own habits and principles of life are conscious of setting before them no faultless example, vainly endeavour to substitute the persuasive influence of moral precept, intruded in the guise of amusement, for the strength of moral habit compelled by righteous authority: – vainly think to inform the heart of infancy with deliberative wisdom, while they abdicate the guardianship of its unquestioning innocence; and warp into the agonies of an immature philosophy or conscience the once fearless strength of its unsullied and unhesitating virtue.

A child should not need to choose between right and wrong. It should not be capable of wrong; it should not conceive of wrong. Obedient; as bark to helm, not by sudden strain or effort, but in the freedom of its bright course of constant life; true, with an undistinguished, painless, unboastful truth, in a crystalline household world of truth; gentle, through daily entreatings of gentleness, and honourable trusts, and pretty prides of child-fellowship in offices of good; strong, not in bitter and doubtful contest with temptation, but in peace of heart, and armour of habitual right, from which temptation falls like thawing hail; self-commanding, not in sick restraint of mean appetites and covetous thoughts, but in vital joy of unluxurious life, and contentment in narrow possession, wisely esteemed.

Children so trained have no need of moral fairy tales; but they will find in the apparently vain and fitful courses of any tradition of old time, honestly delivered to them, a teaching for which no other can be substituted, and of which the power cannot be measured; animating for them the material world with inextinguishable life, fortifying them against the glacial cold of selfish science, and preparing them submissively, and with no bitterness of astonishment, to behold, in later years, the mystery – divinely appointed to remain such to all human thought – of the fates that happen alike to the evil and the good.

And the effect of the endeavour to make stories moral upon the literary merit of the work itself, is as harmful as the motive of the effort is false. For every fairy tale worth recording at all is the remnant of a tradition possessing true historical value; – historical, at least in so far as it has naturally arisen out of the mind of a people under special circumstances, and risen not without meaning, nor removed altogether from their sphere of religious faith. It sustains afterwards natural changes from the sincere action of the fear or fancy of successive generations; it takes new colour from their manner of life, and new form from their changing moral tempers. As long as these changes are natural and effortless, accidental and inevitable, the story remains essentially true, altering its form, indeed, like a flying cloud, but remaining a sign of the sky; a shadowy image, as truly a part of the great firmament of the human mind as the light of reason which it seems to interrupt. But the fair deceit and innocent error of it cannot be interpreted nor restrained by a wilful purpose, and all additions to it by art do but defile, as the shepherd disturbs the flakes of morning mist with smoke from his fire of dead leaves.

There is also a deeper collateral mischief in this indulgence of licentious change and retouching of stories to suit particular tastes, or inculcate favourite doctrines. It directly destroys the child's power of rendering any such belief as it would otherwise have been in his nature to give to an imaginative vision. How far it is expedient to occupy his mind with ideal forms at all may be questionable to many, though not to me; but it is quite beyond question that if we do allow of the fictitious representation, that representation should be calm and complete, possessed to the full, and read down its utmost depth. The little reader's attention should never be confused or disturbed, whether he is possessing himself of fairy tale or history. Let him know his fairy tale accurately, and have perfect joy or awe in the conception of it as if it were real; thus he will always be exercising his power of grasping realities: but a confused, careless, and discrediting tenure of the fiction will lead to as confused and careless reading of fact. Let the circumstances of both be strictly perceived, and long dwelt upon, and let the child's own mind develop fruit of thought from both. It is of the greatest importance early to secure this habit of contemplation, and therefore it is a grave error, either to multiply unnecessarily, or to illustrate with extravagant richness, the incidents presented to the imagination. It should multiply and illustrate them for itself; and, if the intellect is of any real value, there will be a mystery and wonderfulness in its own dreams which would only be thwarted by external illustration. Yet I do not bring forward the text or the etchings in this volume as examples of what either ought to be in works of the kind: they are in many respects common, imperfect, vulgar; but their vulgarity is of a wholesome and harmless kind. It is not, for instance, graceful English, to say that a thought "popped into Catherine's head;" but it nevertheless is far better, as an initiation into literary style, that a child should be told this than that "a subject attracted Catherine's attention!" And in genuine forms of minor tradition, a rude and more or less illiterate tone will always be discernible; for all the best fairy tales have owed their birth, and the greater part of their power, to narrowness of social circumstances; they belong properly to districts in which walled cities are surrounded by bright and unblemished country, and in which a healthy and bustling town life, not highly refined, is relieved by, and contrasted with, the calm enchantment of pastoral and woodland scenery, either under humble cultivation by peasant masters, or left in its natural solitude. Under conditions of this kind the imagination is enough excited to invent instinctively, (and rejoice in the invention of) spiritual forms of wildness and beauty, while yet it is restrained and made cheerful by the familiar accidents and relations of town life, mingling always in its fancy humorous and vulgar circumstances with pathetic ones, and never so much impressed with its supernatural phantasies as to be in danger of retaining them as any part of its religious faith. The good spirit descends gradually from an angel into a fairy, and the demon shrinks into a playful grotesque of diminutive malevolence, while yet both keep an accredited and vital influence upon the character and mind. But the language in which such ideas will be usually clothed must necessarily partake of their narrowness; and art is systematically incognizant of them, having only strength under the conditions which awake them to express itself in an irregular and gross grotesque, fit only for external architectural decoration.

The illustrations of this volume are almost the only exceptions I know to the general rule. They are of quite sterling and admirable art, in a class precisely parallel in elevation to the character of the tales which they illustrate; and the original etchings, as I have before said in the Appendix to my 'Elements of Drawing,' were unrivalled in masterfulness of touch since Rembrandt; (in some qualities of delineation unrivalled even by him). These copies have been so carefully executed that at first I was deceived by them, and supposed them to be late impressions from the plates (and what is more, I believe the master himself was deceived by them, and supposed them to be his own); and although, on careful comparison with the first proofs, they will be found no exception to the terrible law that literal repetition of entirely fine work shall be, even to the hand that produced it, – much more to any other, – forever impossible, they still represent, with sufficient fidelity to be in the highest degree instructive, the harmonious light and shade, the manly simplicity of execution, and the easy, unencumbered fancy, of designs which belonged to the best period of Cruikshank's genius. To make somewhat enlarged copies of them, looking at them through a magnifying-glass, and never putting two lines where Cruikshank has put only one, would be an exercise in decision and severe drawing which would leave afterwards little to be learnt in schools. I would gladly also say much in their praise as imaginative designs; but the power of genuine imaginative work, and its difference from that which is compounded and patched together from borrowed sources, is of all qualities of art the most difficult to explain; and I must be content with the simple assertion of it.

And so I trust the good old book, and the honest work that adorns it, to such favour as they may find with children of open hearts and lowly lives.

Denmark Hill, Easter, 1868.

Sir Walter Scott's Letter
to Edgar Taylor

Edinbg 16 January 1823.

Sir.

I have to return my best thanks for the very acceptable present your goodness has made me in your interesting volume of German tales and traditions. I have often wished to see such a work undertaken by a gentleman of taste sufficient to adapt the simplicity of the German narrative to our own, which you have done so successfully. When my family were at the happy age of being auditors of fairy tales I have very often endeavoured to translate to them in such an ex tempore manner as I could and I was always gratified by the pleasure which the German fictions seemed to convey. In memory which our old family cat still bears the foreign name of Hinze which so often occurs in these little narratives. In a great number of them tales I can perfectly remember the nursery stories of my childhood, some of them distinctly and others like the memory of a dream. Should you ever think of enlargening your very interesting notes I would with pleasure forward to you such of the tales as I remember. The Prince Paddock was for instance a legend well known to me where a princess is sent to fetch water in a sieve from the Well of the World's End succeeds by the advice of the frog who aids her (on promise to become his bride).

Stop with moss and dugg with clay
And that will weize the water away

The frog comes to claim his bride (and to tell the tale with effect the sort of plash which he makes in leaping on the floor ought to be imitated), singing this nuptial ditty.

> "Open the door my hinny my heart
>   Open the door my ain wee thing
> And mind the words that you and me spoke
>   Down in the meadow the well-spring."

In the same strain as the song of the little bird:

> My mother me killed
> My father me ate & c & c

Independently of the curious circumstance that such tales should be found existing in very different countries and languages which augurs a greater poverty of human invention than we would have expected there is also a sort of wild fairy interest in them which makes me think them fully better adapted to awaken the imagination and soften the heart of childhood than the good-boy stories which have been in later years composed for them. In the latter case their minds are as it were put into the stocks like their feet at the dancing school and the moral always consists in good moral conduct... being crowned with temporal success. Truth is I would not give one tear shed over Little Red Ridinghood for all the benefit to be derived from a hundred histories of Tommy Goodchild. Miss Edgeworth who has with great genius trod the more modern path is to be sure an exception from my utter dislike of these moral narrations but it [is] because they are really fitter for grown people than for children. I must say however that I think the story of Simple Susan in particular quite inimitable. But Waste not, Want not, though a most ingenious tale is I fear – more apt to make a curmudgeon of a boy who has from nature a close cautious temper than to correct a careless idle destroyer of whip-cord. In a word I think the selfish tendencies will be soon enough acquired in this arithmetical age and that to make the higher class of character our old wild fictions like our own simple music will have more effect in awakening the fancy and elevating the disposition than the colder and more elevated compositions of more clever authors and composers.

I am not acquainted with Basile's collection but I have both editions of Straparola which I observe differ considerably – I could add a good deal but there is enough here to show that it is with sincere interest that I subscribe myself

Your Obliged Servant

Walter Scott.

Correspondence between Edgar Taylor and the Brothers Grimm

M.M. Grimm.

Gentlemen

Not knowing the precise address of either of you I trust the accompanying packet to a friendly hand hoping it may reach you in safety.

It contains a copy of a little work consisting of translations (made by my friend Mr. Jardine lately a student at Göttingen and myself) from your volumes of Kinder und Hausmärchen, and we beg your acceptance of it as a small tribute of gratitude for the information and amusement afforded us by your entertaining work as well as by your other valuable productions.

In compiling our little volume we had the amusement of some young friends principally in view, and were therefore compelled sometimes to conciliate local feelings and deviate a little from strict translation; but we believe that all these variations are recorded in the Notes which were hastily drawn with a view to show that our book had some little pretensions to literary consideration though deep research was out of plan.

In forming these notes you will see that we are eminently indebted to yourselves and to the article in the Quarterly Review by our friend and neighbour Mr. T. Cohen. –

I take the opportunity of adding to the parcel a little collection of our Nursery songs some of them of great antiquity and extensive currency. – And though the collection is done with no care it may perhaps have some interest in your eyes.

I have a great desire to publish here (with the assistance of our engraver and designer Mr. Cruickshank to whose talents such a work would be very suitable) a translation of Reineke Vos, of which the English have no metrical version. – I am told that Dr. W. Soltan who translated our Hudibras into German, translated Reineke into English verse. – Now though as a foreigner his translation would require considerable revision, it might still save much labor and it would be a great favor to me if you could either from personal knowledge or through any channel inform me where Soltan's version is. – I do not even know whether he is alive, but I know that the version was offered to a London Bookseller who declined publishing it. – If it is in existence and could be obtained I should be glad to negotiate for it.

I am Gentlemen
with the highest respect
Your obedt serv.

Edgar Taylor.
Inner Temple
London 26th June 1823

Rem: who is Herr Korbes? – he has puzzled us greatly –

M. Edgar Taylor. to the care of David Jardine. Esq.
London
88 Guildford Street
Russell Square.

Hochgeehrter Herr,

Für die Uebersetzung der Kinder und Hausmaerchen, die uns richtig zugekommen ist, sagen wir Ihnen den verbindlichsten Dank. Das Unternehmen an sich muss uns schon schmeichelhaft seyn, allein wir hoffen auch, dass es für die Sache selbst, das heisst für die Erforschung der lebendigen Sage von Nutzen seyn wird. Wenn naemlich Ihre Landsleute an dieser Art Poesie Geschmack finden, so regt das Buch wahrscheinlich irgend jemand auf, in aehnlicher Weise eine Sammlung dort zu veranstalten. Hoffentlich findet sich sich im Lande noch ein und der andere Erzaehler, aus dessen Munde man die Ueberlieferung aufschreiben und ohne Zuthat ordnen kan. Waren nur erst die Mabinogion gedruckt und in einer engl. Uebersetzung zugaenglich gemacht! wie sehr ist der Verlust der Handschrift von William Owen zu bedauern! Sollte denn kein anderer im Stande seyn, diese Lücke auszufüllen? Für die altgaelische Ueberlieferung wäre dann gesorgt und so reichhaltig diese seyn mag, uns liegt die Angelsaechsische naeher und für diese ist noch nichts geschehen. Beide Quellen, die sich auch wohl vermischt haben, müssten wohl gefasst werden. Ihre Übersetzung ist treu und liest sich gut. Sie haben hier und da etwas abgeschnitten, oder eine Kleinigkeit geaendert, das ist bei dem Zweck, den Sie im Auge haben, natürlich und kann auch, da der Stoff einmal gesichert ist, weiter keinen Nachtheil haben. Bei dem Auffassen der Sage selbst, ist aber jede kritische Berührung schaedlich und verletzt irgend einen kleinen Zweig oder ein noch lebendiges Auge der Pflanze; auch sollte es nicht schwer fallen, die Lesearten des Originals zu vertheidigen. Die zugegebenen Kupfer sind ein eigener Vorzug Ihres Buches. Sie sind leicht und geistreich gearbeitet und dem Gegenstand angemessen. Bei uns wüssten wir in diesem Augenblick keinen Künstler, der ein aehnliches Geschick besaesse, dagegen hatte es der verstorbene Chodowiecki in Berlin in hohem Grade. Nur hatten wir gewünscht, dass Sie auch das Bild der Frau Viehmaennin, vor dem zweiten Bande, das an sich einen angenehmen Eindruck macht, Ihren Lesern mitgetheilt haetten. Sie haetten wohl gerne das Gesicht einer so klugen deutschen Baeurin einmal angesehen.

Vielleicht ist Ihnen auch unsere Sammlung von „Deutschen Sagen" zu Gesicht gekommen, von welcher zwei Baende in Berlin erschienen sind, welchen noch ein dritter folgen sollte. In Daenemark hat Herr Thiele etwas aehnliches mit Erfolg unternommen: sollte nicht auch in England etwas der Art können zu Stande gebracht werden? Haetten Sie nicht Lust dabei thaetig zu seyn und würde nicht unsere Sammlung anregend wirken, wenn Sie eine Probe daraus durch Überssetzung bekannt machten?

Für die beigelegte Sammlung von Kinderliedern sind wir Ihnen sehr verbunden; durch Ihre Zusaetze und Verbesserungen hat sie einen doppelten Werth erhalten. Sie war uns unbekannt und wir haben manches darin gefunden, was auch bei uns üblich ist, aber auch manches eigenthümliche und hübsche Stück.

Von einer Übersetzung des plattd. Reinecke Voss ins Englische durch Hn. Soltan haben wir nichts gehört, auch in keinem litterarischen Blatte etwas gelesen. Vermüthlich beruht die Angabe auf einem Irrthum, indem Soltan den plattdeutschen Reinecke (nicht Göthes Bearbeitung) ins hochdeutsche übersetzt hat; aber schon vor längerer Zeit. (1802)

Sie fragen noch in der Nachschrift was Herr Korbes in den Maerchen bedeute? Es heisst nichts mehr, als etwa Knecht Ruprecht, oder der Butzemann, worunter man sich einen wilden oder strengen und harten Mann denkt, der bei seinem Erscheinen die Kinder in Angst jagt.

Mit vollkommener Hochachtung
Ew. Wohlgebornen
ergebenste D. D.

Cassel 25t Juni, Jacob und Wilhelm Grimm.
1823.

M. M. Grimm.

Sirs,

It is so long since I was favored with your observations on the subject of the volume of German Popular Stories which I had a share in translating, that I am almost afraid I come too late, though in truth I had hoped long e'er this to have been enabled to revive the subject in the manner I wished, namely in presenting you with the second volume, which I have prepared by myself and which I at length inclose. – I am afraid you will still think me sacrificing too much to the public taste, but in truth I began the work as an antiquarian Man as one who meant to amuse, and the literary taste for the subject came upon me only when I had got upon a plan which I could not well abandon in consistency. – You will see that I have been obliged to take two or three stories from other collections to make up my volume of the character I wished.

Has my vol. "Lays of the Minnesingers" reached you – If it has I must bespeak a charitable judgment for that too. – It aims at nothing more than an introduction of the English reader to a subject, which would amply repay the labor of a more able hand. – But Germany should not complain of other countries when she is herself still deficient of a complete history of the literature etc. of the Swabian Area.

I have some inclination to publish a volume or two of the popular stories of the middle ages in various countries of Europe, selecting those which are best known and most worth preserving in each – of course all translated and to a certain extent therefore a little retold. – I mean in this collection to take what we called here "Chapbooks", and what you call Folks-books; many of which are as you are aware the romances of older times abridged – of course they would generally be longer than what come within the class of child's stories.

For instance I should give – Fortunatus Magelone – Faustus – Valentine and Orin (?) – Guy of Warwick – Owlglafs etc. –

Now these of an early date are not very easily to be got in a genuine state – Ours in England are rarely to be met with and it has struck me that probably those of them which either belong properly to Germany or have been translated into and current in its language would probably be most correctly and most easily found in that language. – Can you tell me whether many of these are easily to be had and how a little collection of them (including perhaps 2 or 3 in a metrical form) could be got from Germany – Such for instance as Görres has given an account of in his little volume. –

I should be very thankful for being put in the way of getting what I want, and probably if these things be still current, they are to be got for a mere trifle so far as regards the cost.

I do not know whether you are in any habits of intercourse with M. Benecke – I should like to know whether a packet I sent him some little time ago with my "Minnesingers" reached him. I had the curiosity when at Paris to take tracings or outlines of all the remarkable Illuminations of what is called the Maness M.S. – They form a curious vo'ume.

I ought to apologize for intruding upon you at so much length and am Your very obed. serv.

Temple, Edgar Taylor.
London 24 Jan. 1826.

Cassel in Hessen. 4' Aug. 1826.

Ich benutze die Gelegenheit die sich darbietet, Ihnen, hochgeehrtester Herr, unsern aufrichtigen Dank für die Übersetzung des zweiten Bandes der Märchen zu sagen, welche wir im Frühjahr richtig empfangen haben. Er schliesst sich ganz dem ersten an und der Ausdruck scheint mir, wie dort, natürlich und angemessen. Die Auswahl ist Ihrem Plane gemäß, und die radierten Blätter sind leicht und geistreich behandelt. Während der Zeit ist auch von uns eine Auswahl der Märchen, als kleine, nur 50 Stück enthaltende Ausgabe bei Reimer in Berlin erschienen; sieben Bilder dabei nach Zeichnungen meines jüngern Bruders, sind zwar in einer andern weniger humoristischen Manier, aber doch wie mir däucht, ganz artig. Ich nenne Ihnen diese Ausgabe bloß weil darin von einigen Märchen ein neuer und besserer Text ist geliefert worden.

Mit Vergnügen habe ich die Theilnahme gesehen, mit welcher der Herausgeber von. Wartons Geschichte der englischen Poesie unsere Sammlung in seine Untersuchungen gezogen hat und wir sind im (sic) für manche erläuternde Bemerkung und Nachweisung Dank schuldig: neue Belege, wie solche Traditionen auch wissenschaftliche Betrachtungen fördern können.

Wir haben seitdem Hn. Crokers Fairy legends unter dem Titel: Irische Elfenmärchen übersetzt und eine eigene Abhandlung über das Wesen der Elfen überhaupt hinzugefügt, die, wie ich hoffe den Gegenstand von einer neuen Seite betrachtet und zu nicht unmerkwürdigen Resultaten leitet. Ich bedauere sehr, keine Gelegenheit zu finden, mit welcher ich Ihnen das Buch zusenden kan, weil es vielleicht von einigem Interesse für Sie wäre.

Ihre Minnelieder habe ich noch nicht erhalten. Hr. Prof. Benecke hat mir indessen versprochen, sein Exemplar mitzutheilen. Sie besitzen die Bilder aus dem Pariser Codex, wollen Sie diese Schätze nicht bekannt machen? Sie würden einen schönen Beitrag zu der Bildungsgeschichte des Mittelalters liefern und ich besonders würde ihn sehr willkommen heißen.

Indem ich Ihren literarischen Arbeiten den besten Fortgang wünsche, empfehle ich mich und meinen Bruder Ihrem Andenken und bin mit aufrichtiger Hochachtung

Ew. Wohlgebornen
ergebenster Dr
Dr. Wilhelm Grimm
Secretär der Kurfürstlichen Bibliothec.

Gammer Grethel
Who She Was and What She Did[2]

Gammer Grethel was an honest good-humoured farmer's wife, who, a while ago, lived far off in Germany.

She knew all the good stories that were told in that country; and every evening about Christmas time, the boys and girls of the neighbourhood gathered around her, to hear her tell them some of her budget of strange stories

One Christmas, being in that part of the world, I joined the party; and begged her to let me write down what I heard, for the benefit of my young friends in England. And so, for twelve merry evenings, beginning with Christmas eve, we met and listened to her budget.

Many a time have my acquaintances, of both sexes, called for a chapter out of my Tale-book: and as I have reason to think that there may be a great many more – not only of boys and girls, but of men and women too – than I know or should like the trouble of reading to, who would be glad to have been of Gammer Grethel's party, or at least would like to know how it was that she so much amused her friends, I at last resolved to print the collection, for the benefit of all those who may wish to read it,

"And so, Gentle Reader," as a worthy old writer has said with regard to some similar matter of amusement, "craving thy kind acceptance, I wish thee as much willingness to the reading, as I have been forward in the printing; and so I end, –

---

2 From Edgar Taylor's *Gammer Grethel* (1839). The Frontispiece, Title Page and opening page are overleaf.

From *Gammer Grethel* (this page and following pages)

GAMMER GRETHEL;

OR

GERMAN FAIRY TALES,

AND

POPULAR STORIES,

FROM THE COLLECTION OF MM. GRIMM,

AND OTHER SOURCES; WITH

ILLUSTRATIVE NOTES.

LONDON:

JOHN GREEN, 121, NEWGATE STREET.

MDCCCXXXIX.

GAMMER GRETHEL.

WHO SHE WAS AND WHAT SHE DID.

GAMMER GRETHEL was an honest good-humoured farmer's wife, who, a while ago, lived far off in Germany.

She knew all the good stories that were told in that country: and every evening about Christmas time, the boys and girls of the neighbourhood gathered round her, to hear her tell them some of her budget of strange stories.

Preface[1]

Nearly fifteen years ago the English public had its first regular introduction to the curious and amusing popular Tales circulating among the Germans, as collected, and so admirably edited, by the learned and excellent MM. Grimm, brethren not only in kindred but in literary taste and industry.

Another race of that class of readers for whose entertainment such stories are more peculiarly adapted has since arisen, and the Translators been induced once again to resort to the sources from whence they drew their former supply, for the purpose of re-arranging, revising, and adding to their budget, so as to produce it in a new form, and with the omission of those parts for which it is probable least interest will be felt

Such as it is, they present their compilation to their young friends, and will add, in substance, a few of the observations which they before prefixed in explanation of them.

They admit, as they did then, that they were first induced to compile this little work by the eager relish with which a few of the tales were received by the young friends to whom they were narrated. In this feeling the Translators did not hesitate to avow their own participation; added years have left them pretty much in the same position; and Sir Walter Scott, in his letter to one of the translators (which will be found at the end of this volume), has given to their feelings the sanction of his weighty authority. Popular fictions and traditions are somewhat gone out of fashion; yet most will own them to be associated with the brightest recoll-ections of their youth. They are, like the Christmas Pantomime, ostensibly brought forth to tickle the palate of the young, but are often received with as keen an appetite by those of graver years.

---

1 Edgar Taylor's Preface to *Gammer Grethel*.

There is, moreover, a debt of gratitude due to these ancient friends and comforters. "They have been the revivers of drowsy age at midnight; old and young have with such tales chimed mattins till the cock crew in the morning; batchelors and maides have compassed the Christmas fire-block till the curfew bell rang candle out; the old shepheard and the young plow-boy, after their daye's labor, have carold out the same to make them merrye with; and who but they have made long nightes seem short, and heavy toyles easie?"

Much might be urged against that too rigid and philosophic (we may rather say, unphilosophic) exclusion of works of fancy and fiction from the libraries of children, which is advocated by some. Our imagination is surely as susceptible of improvement by exercise as our judgment or our memory; and so long as such fictions only are presented to the young mind as do not interfere with the important department of moral education, there can surely be no objection to the pleasurable employment of a faculty in which so much of our happiness in every period of life consists.

But the amusement of the hour was not the Translators' only object. The rich collection from which the following tales are selected is very interesting in a literary point of view, as affording a new proof of the wide and early diffusion of these gay creations of the imagination; apparently flowing from some great and mysterious fountain-head, whence Calmuck, Russian, Celt, Scandinavian, and German, in their various ramifications, have imbibed their earliest lessons of moral instruction.

It is probably owing principally to accidental causes that some countries have carefully preserved their ancient stores of fiction, while they have been suffered, in England, to pass to oblivion or corruption, notwithstanding the patriotic example of a few such names as Hearne, Spelman, and Le Neve; who did not disdain to turn towards them the light of their carefully-trimmed lamp, scanty and ill-furnished as it often was. A very interesting and ingenious article in the *Quarterly Review* (No. XII) to which the Translators readily acknowledge their particular obligations, first revived attention to the subject, and showed how wide a field lay open, interesting to the antiquarian as well as to the reader who only seeks amusement.

Since that period, and especially since the appearance of the Translators' first publication, the subject has been actively enough investigated. Mr. Keightley, in his *"Fairy Mythology"* and his

"*Tales and Popular Fictions,*" has pretty well exhausted the subject, and has elevated it into a branch of literary science, from which probably the public will be glad to turn to the practical and more amusing form in which the stories themselves elucidate their own nature and history.

The collection from which the following Tales are mainly taken is one of great extent, obtained for the most part by MM. Grimm from the mouths of German peasants. The result of their labours ought to be peculiarly interesting to English readers, inasmuch as many of their national tales are proved to be of the highest northern antiquity, and common to the parallel classes of society in countries whose populations have been long and widely disjoined. Strange to say, "Jack, commonly called the Giant-killer, and Thomas Thumb," as the Quarterly Reviewer observes, "landed in England from the very same hulls and warships which conveyed Hengist and Horse, and Ebba the Saxon." The Cat, whose identity and London citizenship, in the story of Whittington, appeared so certain; Tom Thumb, whose parentage Hearne had traced; and the Giant-destroyer of Tylney, are equally renowned among the humblest inhabitants of Munster and Paderborn.

The connexion between the popular tales of remote and unconnected regions is very remarkable, in the richest collection of this sort of narrative which any country can boast – disguised as it is under a bombastic and almost unreadable style – we mean the "*Pentamerone, overo Trottonemiento de li Piccerille,*" – "Fun for the Little Ones," by Giov. Battista Basile, early in the 17th century, as compiled from the stories current among the Neapolitans. It is singular that the German and the Neapolitan tales (though the latter were till lately quite unknown to foreigners, and never, we believe, translated), bear the strongest and most minute resemblances. The elements of some of "*The Nights [Notti piacevoli] of Straparola*" were published first in 1550; but in the latter collection this class of fictions occupies apparently only an accidental station, the bulk of his tales being of the Italian School of Novelle. The *Pentamerone* seems drawn from original sources, and was probably compiled without any knowledge of *Straparola,* although the latter is earlier in date. The two works have only four pieces in common. The French "*Contes des Fées*" have many points in common with the *Pentamerone* and the German Stories.

The nature and immediate design of the present publication exclude the introduction of some of those stories which would, in a literary point of view, be most curious. With a view to variety, the Translators have rather avoided than selected those, the leading incidents of which are already familiar to the English reader; and have therefore often deprived themselves of the interest which comparison would afford. There were also many stories of great merit, and tending highly to the elucidation of ancient mythology, customs, and opinions, which the fastidiousness of modern taste, especially in works likely to attract the attention of youth, warned them to pass by. In those tales which they have selected they have occasionally made variations which divers considerations dictated. They have, however, generally noticed these variations, when they are substantial, in the Notes; but, in most cases, the alteration consists merely in the curtailment of adventures or details, not affecting the main plot or character of the story; or amounts to little more than the license necessarily taken in recounting a popular story, according to the humour of the reciter.

A few Notes are added, but the Translators trust it will always be borne in mind that their little work makes no literary pretensions; that its immediate design precludes several of the subjects which would be most attractive to many as matters of research; that professedly critical dissertations would therefore be out of place; and that such subjects have, as before observed, been abundantly elucidated in works professedly directed to that object.

With regard to style, the Translators have been anxious to adopt that which they have ever found, by experience, most suitable to the class of readers whose tastes and capacities they had mainly in view; and, indeed, that which appears in every respect best adapted to the subject – namely, the purely English elements of our language. From these they have very rarely, and only under the pressure of almost absolute necessity, departed.

Our GAMMER GRETHEL, the supposed narrator of the stories, in fact lived, though under a different name. She was the Frau Viehmännin, the wife of a peasant in the neighbourhood of Hesse-Cassel, and from her mouth a great portion of the stories were written down by MM. Grimm. She died not long after MM. Grimm's first publication, her family having suffered much in the latter part of the last French war. M. Ludwig Grimm himself sketched her intelligent and characteristic features for the frontispiece to a later edition of his brother's collection; and we, with great satisfaction, place a copy of it at the head of this volume. His designs, also, form the bases of our illustrations of ROSE-BUD, THE GOOSE-GIRL (tailpiece), SNOWDROP, and HANSEL AND GRETHEL. Most of the others are from the old designs of Geo. Cruikshank; the whole being now engraved on wood by Byfield.

An Introduction

To the Present Edition
of "Grimms' Goblins"[2]

An implicit belief, and unwavering faith, in beings endowed with supernatural gifts, and possessing unlimited powers, are ever prevailing traits in a child's credulity. This belief is long before it vanishes away under the disenchantments of prosaic realities, or melts into thin air under the stern actualities of after life.

Thank Heaven, we have a vast opulence of Fairy lore, admirably adapted to gratify this intuition, and amply sufficient to satisfy every small believer in the kingdom of Fairyland. Drawing from this abundant source many a delightful theme, children can refresh and charm their minds to the full as much as they can invigorate their bodies by copious drafts of fresh air; so pure is it of its kind. To them, with their first yearnings after food for the mind, no purer literature exists than the literature of Fairy Tales. Ever presenting in an alluring style, fictitious forms and quaint strange figures, such literature opens to them flights of fancy perfectly adapted to their infantine tastes, which they eagerly seize upon and enjoy. Here is a pure seminary of learning wherein fresh hearts, receiving their first impressions, are trained to appease the hunger of their earliest longings with wholesome food, that will satisfy them until they grow old enough to seek other and richer pabulum. Such a collective body of writings will never be other than a great power, fascinating by its weird influences the instincts of childish nature, and fostering in them an education of mind, rich in after harvests.

2 R. Meek's Introduction to the 1876 Edition of *Grimm's Goblins*. *Grimm's Household Stories*.

How welcome then are the Authors who weave these spells of grotesque fancies, and weird witchcrafts. They flood upon us a boundless wealth of golden sunlight and silver moonlight, fairy bowers and marble palaces, flowery balconies and orange groves, beauteous princesses and handsome princes, enchanters and magicians, giants and dwarfs, elves and sprites, *et hoc genus omne*. They encircle us with an unfading aureola of rich humorous fantasy.

Have any one of our readers ever watched the countenance of a child listening to his first Fairy Tale, noticed the starting tear, the ecstasy of delight, or the tremble of distress playing o'er the mobile face? No astute physiognomist is needed there to tell us what is passing in the tiny mind. The child is in a world of actual living reality. He hears not merely – he sees it all; with parted lip, with flashing eye and heaving breast, he devours every word with an implicit faith that is well-nigh inspired. It is no Fairy world to him now. Every character lives and breathes before him with a startling embodiment one would not dare dispel the illusion. What more beautiful picture? Painter, where is thy pencil? Canst thou paint me a better picture than this? That little child, emblem of all purity and innocence, with hushed awe and rapt attention, spellbound under the fascinations of a magician like an Andersen or a Grimm, is receiving in its spotless mind its first enthralling lesson; whilst, full of wonderment and reverence, it lives in an atmosphere of Fairy entrancement. Look at the attitude of that lovely girl laughing with delight, every feature lighted up in a bath of sunshine; look at her dimpled rounded arms as she clasps her hands in ecstasy, eager to catch every syllable, and fearing lest a word should escape – every pose, every gesture full of grace and beauty! Surely this is a picture more beautiful than ever met the gaze of Praxiteles, or arrested the eye of Phidias? And this is what we have seen when a mother has been reading out the exquisite tales of Grimm or Andersen to a delighted group of lovely children. Would we could paint such a picture! And then, when the spell is loosed and the little tongues set free, how they prattle for hours together over every incident with a pure faith in what they have heard that nought can upset, shouting forth their various heroes' praises with eager boundless joy. Fairy lore is rich with the magic names of these championed heroes and heroines, who dwell in that vast land, discovered by our authors, that lies between truth and fiction; and these all touch the heart and imagination with a nameless indescribable spell – a spell enhanced to infant minds by the, to them, absolute and literal reality of the romance. It is the normal phenomena of these tales that the tiny listener actually sees – these spirits and beings of a brighter world. One has only to teach some little urchin to read "Grimm's Goblins," feed his mind upon it, excite and stimulate his hunger by it; and, fed upon such nutriment, his tastes will expand, his soul will grow larger; and you have in embryo already made a man of him. Would that we could live again in those halcyon days when we too revelled in Fairyland! Lavater says, "Keep him at least three paces distant who hates music and the laugh of a child." Keep him out of sight altogether, say we, who hates the sound of a Fairy Tale.

We have already alluded to the purity of this class of literature. All literature ministers to some form of taste – some specially to one taste, another to other tastes; but all supply a demand and represent respectively the intellectual status of particular bias in mind. Fairy Tales are the earliest cultivators of the purest bias in the youngest and freshest of soils: they are the especial prerogative and boon of children's libraries. Their world-wide popularity, their boundless influence, form a striking contrast to that immense flood of writing distinguished by bad taste and low aims, which, if not positively pernicious, is at best vulgar trash. With no higher standard than the reading of Fairy Stories, children would ever, from these sources, learn how good and holy is virtue and benevolence – how bad and wicked is craft and cunning. Nay, moral lessons may be learned from these sources, not only by the little world of wondering, believing minds, but by many minds that have long since passed the age of wondering.

The Brothers Grimm, with an imagination as rich and fanciful as any writers of Fairy Tales, leave most kindred writers far behind in the especial adaptability of their tales to the tastes of children. In many, animals represent the leading characters, and with inimitable drollery retain their animal traits with a fidelity that teaches as much Natural History as a study of Buffon would to some minds. In the finer ideal embodiments of men and things, birds and butterflies, beasts and fishes; they rival Hans Andersen, that prince of fairy writers: wonderful word pictures have they revealed to the fresh pure minds of millions of little ones, in the magic mirror of Fairyland – creations in words, that all artists in colour fall short of. Their intrinsic merit to be called the princes of Fairy Tale writers, is pre-eminent in the bewitchery of the style and the grace of these stories. "Blessed is the man who invented sleep!" said honest old Sancho Panza. "Thrice blessed is the man," say we, "who invented Fairy Tales!" And if not the inventors, at any rate the Brothers Grimm, are entitled to the augmented blessings of every fresh reader, who, we trust, will be added to the innumerable company that have gone before the publication of this Edition. May this present Edition increase their number by fresh thousands; and may every reader (big or little) swell the pæan of praise and blessing we now raise to the immortal Brothers Grimm for this work of theirs, which is the paradise of our nurseries and the heaven of our infancy.

R. M.

Bibliography

Texts

Jacob and Wilhelm Grimm Editions

Ölenberg Manuscript

—. *Die älteste Märchensammlung der Brüder Grimm. Synopse der hand-schriftlichen Urfassung von 1810 und der Erstdrucke von 1812.* Ed. Heinz Rölleke. Cologny-Geneva: Fondation Martin Bodmer, 1975.
—. *Die ursprünglichen Märchen der Brüder Grimm: Handschriften, Urfassung und Texte zur Kulturgeschichte.* Ed. Kurt Derungs. Bern: Edition Amalia, 1999.

Large Edition

—. *Kinder- und Hausmärchen gesammelt durch die Brüder Grimm* [1812/1815, Erstausgabe]. Ed. Ulrike Marquardt and Heinz Rölleke. 2 vols. Göttingen: Vandenhoeck & Ruprecht, 1986.
—. *Kinder- und Hausmärchen der Gebrüder Grimm: Erstdruckfassung 1812-1815.* Frankfurt am Main: Dietmar Klotz, 1997.
—. *Kinder- und Hausmärchen gesammelt durch die Brüder Grimm* [1819, zweite Ausgabe]. Ed. Heinz Rölleke. 2 vols. Cologne: Diederichs, 1982.
—. *Kinder- und Hausmärchen gesammelt durch die Brüder Grimm* [1837, dritte Aufgabe]. Ed. Heinz Rölleke. Frankfurt am Main: Deutscher Klassiker Verlag, 1985.
—. *Kinder- und Hausmärchen gesammelt durch die Brüder Grimm* [vierte Ausgabe]. 2 vols. Göttingen: Verlag der Dieterichschen Buch-handlung, 1840.
—. *Kinder- und Hausmärchen gesammelt durch die Brüder Grimm.* [fünfte Ausgabe]. 2 vols. Göttingen: Verlag der Dieterichschen Buch-

handlung, 1843.

—. *Kinder- und Hausmärchen gesammelt durch die Brüder Grimm.* [fünfte Ausgabe]. 2 vols. Göttingen: Verlag der Dieterichschen Buchhandlung, 1850.

—. *Kinder- und Hausmärchen gesammelt durch die Brüder Grimm letzter Hand mit Originalenanmerkungen* [1857, siebte Ausgabe] Ed. Heinz Rölleke. 3 vols. Stuttgart: Reclam, 1980.

—. *Kinder- und Hausmärchen. Nach der Großen Ausgabe von 1857, textkritisch revidiert, kommentiert und durch Register erschlossen.* Ed. Hans-Jörg Uther. 7th ed. Darmstadt: Wissenschaftliche Buchgesellschaft, 1996.

Small Edition

—. *Grimms Märchen: Die kleine Ausgabe aus dem Jahr 1825.* Ed. Hermann Gerstner. Dortmund: Harenberg, 1982.

—. *Kinder- und Hausmärchen gesammelt durch die Brüder Grimm* [Kleine Ausgabe, 1825]. Ed. Peter Rühmkorf. Zurich: Haffmans Verlag bei Zweitausendeins, 2007.

—. *Kinder- und Hausmärchen gesammelt durch die Brüder Grimm: Kleine Ausgabe von 1858.* Ed. Heinz Rölleke. Illustr. Ludwig Pietsch. Frankfurt am Main: Insel, 1985.

Edgar Taylor Editions

German Popular Stories

German Popular Stories. Translated from the Kinder und Haus Marchen, collected by M.M. Grimm, from Oral Tradition. London: C. Baldwyn, 1823. (Reissued 1823)

German Popular Stories. Translated from the Kinder und Haus Marchen, collected by M.M. Grimm, from Oral Tradition. London: James Robins & Co., 1825.

German Popular Stories. Translated from the Kinder und Hausmarchen, collected by M. M. Grimm, from Oral Tradition, vol. 2. London: James Robins & Co., and Dublin, Joseph Robins & Co., 1826. (reissued 1827).

German Popular Stories. Translated from the Kinder und Haus Marchen, collected by M. M. Grimm, from Oral Tradition. London: J. Robins & Sherwood Gilbert & Piper, 1834.

German Popular Tales and Household Stories. 2 vols., New York: Francis, 1853.

German Popular Tales and Household Stories. Newly translated. 2 vols. Boston: Crosby, Nichols, Lee & Co., 1861.

German Popular Stories. With Illustrations, after the original designs of

George Cruikshank. Edited by Edgar Taylor. A New Edition, with Introduction by John Ruskin, M.A. London: John Camden Hotten, 1869.

German Popular Stories. Translated from the Kinder und Hans Marchen of Jacob and Wilhelm Grimm. New York and Boston: Charles S. Francis and Munroe & Francis, n.d.

Grimm's Fairy Tales and Other Popular Stories with Numerous Illustrations. London: Ward, Lock, & Co., 1881. (Reissued 1884).

Grimms' Fairy Tales. With an introduction by John Ruskin. Illustrated by Charles Folkard.London: A. & C. Black, 1911.

Grimms' Fairy Tales. Ed. Henry Newbolt. London: Thomas Nelson, 1923.

Grimms' Fairy Tales. Illustrated by Ruth Morwood and H. Rountree. London: Thomas Nelson, 1932.

Grimms' Fairy Tales. With Twenty-one Illustrations by George Cruikshank, London: Puffin Books, 1948. (Reissued 1971).

Gammer Grethel

Gammer Grethel or German Fairy Tales, and Popular Stories. From the collection of MM. Grimm, and other sources; with illustrative notes, London: John Green, 1839.

Gammer Grethel; or, German Fairy Tales and Popular Stories. From the collection of MM. Grimm, and other sources. Edited by Mrs Follen. Boston: J. Munroe & Co. 1840.

German Fairy Tales and Popular Stories as Told by Gammer Grethel. 1846. Translated from the Collection of M.M. Grimm, by Edgar Taylor. With Illustrations from Designs by George Cruikshank & Ludwig Grimm, London: Joseph Cundall, 1846.

German Fairy Tales and Popular Stories as Told by Gammer Grethel. Translated from the Collection of MM. Grimm by Edgar Taylor. With Illustrations and Designs by George Cruikshank & Ludwig Grimm. London: H. G. Bohn, 1848. (Reissued 1849, 1851, 1856, 1862, 1863 and 1864)

German Popular Stories and Fairy Tales as Told by Gammer Grethel. From the Collection of MM. Grimm. Revised Translation by Edgar Taylor, with Illustrations from Designs by George Cruikshank and Ludwig Grimm, London: Bell & Daldy, 1869. (Reissued by George Bell of London in 1878, 1888, and 1908).

Gammer Grethel's Fairy Tales. Illustrated by George Cruikshank and Others with an Introduction by Laurence Housman. London: Alexander Moring, 1905.

Grimm's Goblins

Grimms' Goblins. London: George Vickers, 1861.
Grimm's Goblins. Selected from the Household Stories of the Brothers Grimm, with Illustrations in Colors, from Cruikshank's Designs, Boston: Ticknor & Fields, 1867.
Grimm's Goblins: Grimm's Household Stories. London: R. Meek, 1876.
Grimm's Goblins and Wonder Tales. London: F. Warne, 1890.

John Edward Taylor Editions

The Fairy Ring: A New Collection of Popular Tales. Translated from the German of Jacob and Wilhelm Grimm with twelve illustrations by Richard Doyle. London: John Murray, 1846.
The Fairy Ring: A New Collection of Popular Tales. Translated from the German of Jacob and Wilhelm Grimm with twelve illustrations by Richard Doyle. 2nd rev. and enlarged edition. London: John Murray, 1847.
The Fairy Ring: A New Collection of Popular Tales. Translated from the German of Jacob and Wilhelm Grimm with twelve illustrations by Napoleon Saroney. 3rd ed. Philadelphia A. Hart. 1854.
Stray Leaves from Fairy Land, for Boys and Girls. New Translation from the German of Jacob & Wilhelm Grimm, by J. Edward Taylor. 5th ed. Philadelphia: G. Collins, 1855. (Reissued 1856)
The Fairy Ring: A New Collection of Popular Tales. Translated from the German of Jacob and Wilhelm Grimm. Illustrated by Richard Doyle. New Edition. London: John Murray, 1857.
Stray Leaves from Fairy Land, for Boys and Girls. New Translation from the German of Jacob & Wilhelm Grimm, by J. Edward Taylor. 7th ed. Philadelphia: Peck & Bliss, 1858.

Other Editions of Complete Tales of the Brothers Grimm (in chronological order)

Paull, Mrs. H. B. *Grimms' Fairy Tales*. Illustr. W. J. Weigand. London: Frederick Warne, and New York: Scribner, Welford and Armstrong, 1872.
Crane, Lucy, trans. *Household Stories from the Collection of the Bros. Grimm*. Illustr. Walter Crane. London: Macmillan, 1882.
Hunt, Margaret, ed. and trans. *Grimm's Household Tales*. Intro. Andrew Lang. 2 vols. London: George Bell and Sons, 1884.
Magoun, Francis, and Alexander Krappe, eds. and trans. *The Grimms' German Folk Tales*. Carbondale, IL: Southern Illinois University Press, 1960.
Manheim, Ralph, trs. *Grimms Tales for Young and Old. The Complete*

Stories. London: Victor Gollancz, 1978.

Zipes, Jack, ed. and trans. *The Complete Fairy Tales of the Brothers Grimm* [1988]. 3rd rev. and enlarged ed. New York: Bantam, 2003.

Primary Literature

Carryl, Guy Wettmore. *Grimm Tales Made Gay*. Illustr. Albert Levering. Boston: Houghton, Mifflin & Co., 1902.

Fairy Tales from Grimm (Christmas Stocking Seires). Intro. L. Frank Baum. Chicago: Reilly & Britton, 1905.

Hunt, Margaret, trans. *Grimm's Fairy Tales*. Illustr. John B. Gruelle. New York: Cupples & Leon, 1914.

Gross, Milt. *Nize Baby*. New York: George Doran, 1926.

Wells, Joel. *Grim Fairy Tales for Adults*. Illustr. Marilyn Fitschen. New York: Macmillan, 1967.

Reference

Alderson, Brian. "The Spoken and the Read: *German Popular Stories* and English Popular Diction." In Donald Haase, ed. *The Reception of Grimms' Fairy Tales: Reponses, Reactions, Revisions*. Detroit: Wayne State University Press, 1993. 59-77.

Blamires, David. "The Early Reception of the Grimms' Kinder- und Hausmärchen in England." *Bulletin of the John Rylands University Library of Manchester*. 71.3 (1989): 63-77.

—. "From Madame d'Aulnoy to Mother Bunch: Popularity and the Fairy Tale." In Julia Briggs, Dennis Butts, and M. O. Grenby, eds. *Popular Children's Literature in Britain*. Aldershot, Hampshire: Ashgate, 2008. 69-86.

Bluhm, Lothar. "Sir Francis Cohen/Palgrave. Zur frühen Rezeption der Kinder- und Hausmärchen in England." In *Brüder Grimm Gedenken*. Ed. Ludwig Denecke. Vol. 7, Marburg: N.G. Elwert, 1987. 224-42.

Bluhm, Lothar and Achim Hölter, eds. *"daß gepflegt werde der feste Buchstab": Festschrift für Heinz Rölleke zum 65. Geburtstag am 6. November 2001*. Trier: Wissenschaftlicher Verlag Trier, 2001.

Bottigheimer, Ruth. "The Publishing History of Grimms' Tales: Reception at the Cash Register." In Donald Haase, ed. *The Reception of the Grimms' Fairy Tales: Responses, Reactions, Revisions*. Detroit: Wayne State University Press, 1993: 78-101.

Briggs, Katharine. "The Influence of the Brothers Grimm in England." In *Brüder Grimm Gedenken*. Ed. Ludwig Denecke and Ina-Maria Greverus. Vol. 1, Marburg: N.G. Elwert, 1963. 511-24.

Brill, Edward. "The Correspondence between Jacob Grimm and Walter Scott." *Brüder Grimm Gedenken*. Ed. Ludwig Denecke and Ina-Maria Greverus. Vol. 1, Marburg: N.G. Elwert, 1963. 489-510.

Bronner, Simon. "The Americanization of the Brothers Grimm." In *Following Tradition: Folklore in the Discourse of American Culture*.

Logan, UT: Utah State University Press, 1998. 184-236.

Brown, Nicola. *Fairies in Nineteenth-century Art and Literature*. Cambridge: Cambridge University Press, 2001.

Büsching, Johann Gustav, ed. *Volksagen, Märchen und Legenden* [1813]. Hildesheim: Georg Olms, 1969.

Cohen, Francis. "Antiquities of Nursery Literature: Review of Fairy Tales, or the Lilliputian Cabinet, Containing Twenty-four Choice Pieces of Fancy and Fiction, collected by Benjamin Tabart." *Quarterly Review* 21.41 (January 1819): 91-112.

Darton, F. J. Harvey. *Children's Books in England: Five Centuries of Social Life*. 3rd Rev. Ed. by Brian Alderson. Cambridge: Cambridge University Press, 1982.

Dollerup, Cay. "Translation as a Creative Force in Literature: The Birth of the Bourgeois Fairy Tale." *The Modern Language Review*, 90.1 (1995): 94-102.

—. *The Grimm Tales from Pan-Germanic Narratives to Shared International Fairy Tales*. Amsterdam: John Benjamins, 1999.

Grenby, Matthew. "Tame Fairies Make Good Teachers: The Popularity of Early British Fairy Tales." *The Lion and the Unicorn*, 30 (2006): 1-24.

Grierson, Herbert. *The Letters of Sir Walter Scott*. 12 vols. London: Constable, 1932-37.

Grimm, Jacob. *Über den Ursprung der Sprache* [1851]. Frankfurt am Main: Insel, 1958.

—. *Reden und Aufsätze: Eine Auswahl*. Ed. Wilhelm Schoof. Munich: Winkler, 1966.

Haase, Donald, ed. *The Reception of Grimms' Fairy Tales: Reponses, Reactions, Revisions*. Detroit: Wayne State University Press, 1993.

Hand, Wayland. "Die Märchen der Brüder Grimm in den Vereinigten Staaten." In *Brüder Grimm Gedenken*. Ed. Ludwig Denecke and Ina-Maria Greverus. Vol. 1, Marburg: N.G. Elwert, 1963. 525-44.

Harris, Jason. *Folklore and the Fantastic in Nineteenth-Century British Fiction*. Aldershot, Hampshire: Ashgate, 2008.

Hartwig, Otto. "Zur ersten englischen Übersetzung der Kinder- und Hausmärchen der Brüder Grimm." *Centralblatt der Bibliothekswesen*, 15.1/2 (January-February, 1898): 1-16.

Heidenreich, Bernd and Ewald Grothe, eds. *Die Grimms – Kultur und Politik*. 2nd rev. Ed. Frankfurt am Main: Societäts-Verlag, 2008.

Heyer, Siegfried. "Der Briefwechsel Thomas Crofton Crokers und Thomas Keightleys mit Wilhelm Grimm über die 'Fairy Legends.'" In *Brüder Grimm Gedenken*. Ed. Ludwig Denecke. Vol. 7, Marburg: N.G. Elwert, 1987. 110-39.

Kamenetsky, Christa. *The Brothers Grimm and Their Critics: Folktales and the Quest for Meaning*. Athens, OH: Ohio University Press, 1992.

Kosok, Heinz. "Thomas Croker, die Brüder Grimm und die irische Erzählliteratur." In *"daß gepflegt werde der feste Buchstab": Festschrift für Heinz Rölleke zum 65. Geburtstag am 6. November 2001*. Ed. Lothar Bluhm and Achim Hölter. Trier: Wissenschaftlicher Verlag Trier, 2001. 288-302.

Kyritsi, Maria-Venetia. "The Untranslated Grimms' *Kinder- und Hausmärchen*. Tales of Violence and Terror." *New Review of Children's Literature and Librarianship* 10/1 (2004): 27-40.

Lathey, Gillian. *The Role of Translators in Children's Literature: Invisible*

Storytellers. New York: Routledge, 2010.

Leitzmann, Albert, ed. *Briefwechsel der Brüder Jacob und Wilhelm Grimm mit Karl Lachmann*. Vol. 1. Jena: Verlag der Frommannschen Buchhandlung, 1927.

Martus, Steffen. *Die Brüder Grimm: Eine Biografie*. Berlin: Rowohlt, 2009.

Michaelis-Jena, Ruth. "Edgar and John Edward Taylor, die ersten englischen Übersetzer der Kinder- und Hausmärchen." In *Brüder Grimm Gedenken*. Ed. Ludwig Denecke. Vol. 2, Marburg: N.G. Elwert, 1975. 183-202.

Patten, Robert. "George Cruikshank's Grimm Humor." In Joachim Müller, ed. *Imagination on a Long Rein: English Literature Illustrated*. Marburg: Jonas, 1988. 13-28.

—. *George Cruikshank: Life, Times, and Art*. 2 vols. New Brunswick, NJ: Rutgers University Press, 1992.

Rölleke, Heinz. *Die Märchen der Brüder Grimm: Eine Einfürhung*. Stuttgart: Philipp Reclam, 2004.

Schacker, Jennifer. *National Dreams: The Remaking of Fairy Tales in Nineteenth Century England*. Philadelphia: University of Penn-sylvania Press, 2003.

Schede, Hans-Gorg. *Die Brüder Grimm*. Rev. Ed. Hanau: CoCon-Verlag, 2009.

Sennewald, Jens. *Das Buch, das Wir Sind: Zur Poetik der "Kinder- und Hausmärchen, gesammelt durch die Brüder Grimm."* Würzbrug: Königshausen & Neumann, 2004.

Steig, Reinhold and Herman Grimm, eds. *Achim von Arnim und die ihm nahe standen*. Vol. 3, Stuttgart: J. G. Cotta'schen Buchhandlung, 1904.

Sumpter, Caroline. "Fairy Tale and Folklore in the Nineteenth Century." *Literature Compass*, 6/3 (2009): 785-98.

Sutton, Martin. *The Sin-Complex: A Critical Study of English Versions of the Grimms' Kinder- und Hausmärchen in the Nineteenth Century*. Kassel: Schriften der Brüder Grimm-Gesellschaft, 1996.

Tatar, Maria. *The Hard Facts of the Grimms' Fairy Tales*. Princeton: Princeton University Press, 1987.

Taylor, Edgar. "German Popular and Traditionary Literature." *New Monthly Magazine and Literary Journal,* 2 (1821): 146-52, 329-36, 537-44, and 4 (1822): 289-96.

Uther, Hans-Jörg. *Handbuch zu den "Kinder- und Hausmärchen der Brüder Grimm: Entstehung – Wirkung – Interpretation*. Berlin: Walter de Gruyter, 2008.

—. "Die Brüder Grimm als Sammler von Märchen und Sagen." In *Die Grimms – Kultur und Politik*. Ed. Bernd Heidenreich and Ewald Grothe. 2nd rev. Ed. Frankfurt am Main: Societäts-Verlag, 2008. 81-137.

Zirnbauer, Heinz. "Grimms Märchen mit englischen Augen. Eine Studie zur Entwicklung der Illustration von Grimms Märchen in englischer Übersetzung von 1823 bis 1970." In *Brüder Grimm Gedenken*. Ed. Ludwig Denecke. Vol. 2, Marburg: N.G. Elwert, 1975. 203-41.

Zipes, Jack. *The Brothers Grimm: From Enchanted Forests to the Modern World* [1988]. rev. and expanded 2nd ed. New York: Palgrave, 2002.

Jack Zipes

Jack Zipes is professor emeritus of German and comparative literature at the University of Minnesota. In addition to his scholarly work, he is an active storyteller in public schools and has worked with children's theaters in Europe and the United States. Some of his major publications include *Breaking the Magic Spell: Radical Theories of Folk and Fairy Tales* (1979), *Fairy Tales and the Art of Subversion* (1983, rev. ed. 2006), *Don't Bet on the Prince: Contemporary Feminist Fairy Tales in North America and England* (1986), *The Brothers Grimm: From Enchanted Forests to the Modern World* (1988), *Sticks and Stones: The Troublesome Success of Children's Literature from Slovenly Peter to Harry Potter* (2000), *Speaking Out: Storytelling and Creative Drama for Children* (2004), *Hans Christian Andersen: The Misunderstood Storyteller* (2005), *Why Fairy Tales Stick: The Evolution and Relevance of a Genre* (2006) and *The Enchanted Screen: The Unknown History of Fairy Tale Films* (2011). He has also translated *The Complete Fairy Tales of the Brothers Grimm* (1987) and edited *The Oxford Companion to Fairy Tales* (2000), and *The Great Fairy Tale Tradition* (2001). Most recently he has translated and edited *The Folk and Fairy Tales of Giuseppe Pitrè* (2008) and *Lucky Hans and other Merz Fairy Tales* (2008) by Kurt Schwitters.

CRESCENT MOON PUBLISHING

web: www.crmoon.com e-mail: cresmopub@yahoo.co.uk

ARTS, PAINTING, SCULPTURE

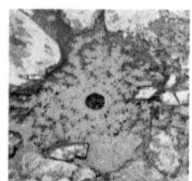

The Art of Andy Goldsworthy
Andy Goldsworthy: Touching Nature
Andy Goldsworthy in Close-Up
Andy Goldsworthy: Pocket Guide
Andy Goldsworthy In America
Land Art: A Complete Guide
The Art of Richard Long
Richard Long: Pocket Guide
Land Art In the UK
Land Art in Close-Up
Land Art In the U.S.A.
Land Art: Pocket Guide
Installation Art in Close-Up
Minimal Art and Artists In the 1960s and After
Colourfield Painting
Land Art DVD, TV documentary
Andy Goldsworthy DVD, TV documentary
The Erotic Object: Sexuality in Sculpture From Prehistory to the Present Day
Sex in Art: Pornography and Pleasure in Painting and Sculpture
Postwar Art
Sacred Gardens: The Garden in Myth, Religion and Art
Glorification: Religious Abstraction in Renaissance and 20th Century Art
Early Netherlandish Painting
Leonardo da Vinci
Piero della Francesca
Giovanni Bellini
Fra Angelico: Art and Religion in the Renaissance
Mark Rothko: The Art of Transcendence
Frank Stella: American Abstract Artist
Jasper Johns
Brice Marden
Alison Wilding: The Embrace of Sculpture
Vincent van Gogh: Visionary Landscapes
Eric Gill: Nuptials of God
Constantin Brancusi: Sculpting the Essence of Things
Max Beckmann
Caravaggio
Gustave Moreau
Egon Schiele: Sex and Death In Purple Stockings
Delizioso Fotografico Fervore: Works In Process 1
Sacro Cuore: Works In Process 2
The Light Eternal: J.M.W. Turner
The Madonna Glorified: Karen Arthurs

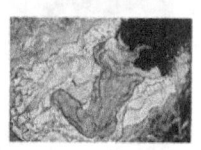

LITERATURE

J.R.R. Tolkien: The Books, The Films, The Whole Cultural Phenomenon
J.R.R. Tolkien: Pocket Guide
Tolkien's Heroic Quest
The *Earthsea* Books of Ursula Le Guin
Beauties, Beasts and Enchantment: Classic French Fairy Tales
German Popular Stories by the Brothers Grimm
Philip Pullman and *His Dark Materials*
Sexing Hardy: Thomas Hardy and Feminism
Thomas Hardy's *Tess of the d'Urbervilles*
Thomas Hardy's *Jude the Obscure*
Thomas Hardy: The Tragic Novels
Love and Tragedy: Thomas Hardy
The Poetry of Landscape in Hardy
Wessex Revisited: Thomas Hardy and John Cowper Powys
Wolfgang Iser: Essays and Interviews
Petrarch, Dante and the Troubadours
Maurice Sendak and the Art of Children's Book Illustration
Andrea Dworkin
Cixous, Irigaray, Kristeva: The *Jouissance* of French Feminism
Julia Kristeva: Art, Love, Melancholy, Philosophy, Semiotics and Psychoanalysis
Hélène Cixous I Love You: The *Jouissance* of Writing
Luce Irigaray: Lips, Kissing, and the Politics of Sexual Difference
Peter Redgrove: Here Comes the Flood
Peter Redgrove: Sex-Magic-Poetry-Cornwall
Lawrence Durrell: Between Love and Death, East and West
Love, Culture & Poetry: Lawrence Durrell
Cavafy: Anatomy of a Soul
German Romantic Poetry: Goethe, Novalis, Heine, Hölderlin
Feminism and Shakespeare
Shakespeare: Love, Poetry & Magic
The Passion of D.H. Lawrence
D.H. Lawrence: Symbolic Landscapes
D.H. Lawrence: Infinite Sensual Violence
Rimbaud: Arthur Rimbaud and the Magic of Poetry
The Ecstasies of John Cowper Powys
Sensualism and Mythology: The Wessex Novels of John Cowper Powys
Amorous Life: John Cowper Powys and the Manifestation of Affectivity (H.W. Fawkner)
Postmodern Powys: New Essays on John Cowper Powys (Joe Boulter)
Rethinking Powys: Critical Essays on John Cowper Powys
Paul Bowles & Bernardo Bertolucci
Rainer Maria Rilke
Joseph Conrad: *Heart of Darkness*
In the Dim Void: Samuel Beckett
Samuel Beckett Goes into the Silence
André Gide: Fiction and Fervour
Jackie Collins and the Blockbuster Novel
Blinded By Her Light: The Love-Poetry of Robert Graves
The Passion of Colours: Travels In Mediterranean Lands
Poetic Forms

POETRY

Ursula Le Guin: Walking In Cornwall
Peter Redgrove: Here Comes The Flood
Peter Redgrove: Sex-Magic-Poetry-Cornwall
Dante: Selections From the Vita Nuova
Petrarch, Dante and the Troubadours
William Shakespeare: Sonnets
William Shakespeare: Complete Poems
Blinded By Her Light: The Love-Poetry of Robert Graves
Emily Dickinson: Selected Poems
Emily Brontë: Poems
Thomas Hardy: Selected Poems
Percy Bysshe Shelley: Poems
John Keats: Selected Poems
Joh n Keats: Poems of 1820
D.H. Lawrence: Selected Poems
Edmund Spenser: Poems
Edmund Spenser: Amoretti
John Donne: Poems
Henry Vaughan: Poems
Sir Thomas Wyatt: Poems
Robert Herrick: Selected Poems
Rilke: Space, Essence and Angels in the Poetry of Rainer Maria Rilke
Rainer Maria Rilke: Selected Poems
Friedrich Hölderlin: Selected Poems
Arseny Tarkovsky: Selected Poems
Arthur Rimbaud: Selected Poems
Arthur Rimbaud: A Season in Hell
Arthur Rimbaud and the Magic of Poetry
Novalis: Hymns To the Night
German Romantic Poetry
Paul Verlaine: Selected Poems
Elizaethan Sonnet Cycles
D.J. Enright: By-Blows
Jeremy Reed: Brigitte's Blue Heart
Jeremy Reed: Claudia Schiffer's Red Shoes
Gorgeous Little Orpheus
Radiance: New Poems
Crescent Moon Book of Nature Poetry
Crescent Moon Book of Love Poetry
Crescent Moon Book of Mystical Poetry
Crescent Moon Book of Elizabethan Love Poetry
Crescent Moon Book of Metaphysical Poetry
Crescent Moon Book of Romantic Poetry
Pagan America: New American Poetry

MEDIA, CINEMA, FEMINISM and CULTURAL STUDIES

J.R.R. Tolkien: The Books, The Films, The Whole Cultural Phenomenon
J.R.R. Tolkien: Pocket Guide
The *Lord of the Rings* Movies: Pocket Guide
The Cinema of Hayao Miyazaki
Hayao Miyazaki: *Princess Mononoke*: Pocket Movie Guide
Hayao Miyazaki: *Spirited Away*: Pocket Movie Guide
Tim Burton : Hallowe'en For Hollywood
Ken Russell
Ken Russell: *Tommy*: Pocket Movie Guide
The Ghost Dance: The Origins of Religion
The Peyote Cult
Cixous, Irigaray, Kristeva: The *Jouissance* of French Feminism
Julia Kristeva: Art, Love, Melancholy, Philosophy, Semiotics and Psychoanalysis
Luce Irigaray: Lips, Kissing, and the Politics of Sexual Difference
Hélène Cixous I Love You: The *Jouissance* of Writing
Andrea Dworkin
'Cosmo Woman': The World of Women's Magazines
Women in Pop Music
HomeGround: The Kate Bush Anthology
Discovering the Goddess (Geoffrey Ashe)
The Poetry of Cinema
The Sacred Cinema of Andrei Tarkovsky
Andrei Tarkovsky: Pocket Guide
Andrei Tarkovsky: *Mirror*: Pocket Movie Guide
Andrei Tarkovsky: *The Sacrifice*: Pocket Movie Guide
Walerian Borowczyk: Cinema of Erotic Dreams
Jean-Luc Godard: The Passion of Cinema
Jean-Luc Godard: *Hail Mary*: Pocket Movie Guide
Jean-Luc Godard: *Contempt*: Pocket Movie Guide
Jean-Luc Godard: *Pierrot le Fou*: Pocket Movie Guide
John Hughes and Eighties Cinema
Ferris Bueller's Day Off: Pocket Movie Guide
Jean-Luc Godard: Pocket Guide
The Cinema of Richard Linklater
Liv Tyler: Star In Ascendance
Blade Runner and the Films of Philip K. Dick
Paul Bowles and Bernardo Bertolucci
Media Hell: Radio, TV and the Press
An Open Letter to the BBC
Detonation Britain: Nuclear War in the UK
Feminism and Shakespeare
Wild Zones: Pornography, Art and Feminism
Sex in Art: Pornography and Pleasure in Painting and Sculpture
Sexing Hardy: Thomas Hardy and Feminism

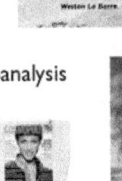

The Light Eternal is a model monograph, an exemplary job. The subject matter of the book is beautifully
organised and dead on beam. (Lawrence Durrell)
It is amazing for me to see my work treated with such passion and respect. (Andrea Dworkin)

CRESCENT MOON PUBLISHING
P.O. Box 1312, Maidstone, Kent, ME14 5XU, Great Britain. www.crmoon.com

cresmopub@yahoo.co.uk   www.crescentmoon.org.uk